Holding Fire

Holding Fire

a love story

Elissa Wald

context books   new york

Published in the United States of America
Context Books, New York.
Distributed by Publishers Group West

www.contextbooks.com

Designer: Cassandra J. Pappas
Jacket design: Charles Kreloff
Typeface: Monotype Sabon

Context Books
368 Broadway
Suite 314
New York, NY 10013

Library of Congress Cataloging-in-Publication Data
Wald, Elissa.
  Holding fire : a love story / Elissa Wald.
    p. cm.
  ISBN 1-893956-14-8
  1. Married people—Fiction.   2. Women authors—Fiction.
  3. Fire fighters—Fiction. 4. Stripteasers—Fiction. I. Title.
PS3573.A42115 H65 2001
813'.54—dc21

                                          2001002860

9   8   7   6   5   4   3   2

Manufactured in the United States of America

This book is dedicated to the FDNY:
The beautiful Bravest;
The last American heroes

And especially to Chief Mike

Holding Fire is a work of fiction. Certain events and rescues depicted within the novel were directly inspired by events and rescues in the history of the FDNY, which were a matter of public knowledge and record and extensively documented in medal books, news articles, television segments, ect. While the author drew on these events and rescues in the creation of the novel, there is no character in Holding Fire that represents any actual person, living or dead. Every character in the novel is a composition drawn from countless different interviews and testimonies, as well as the author's imagination.

He spoke to fire as to an old and respected adversary, but one he had beaten consistently and had come to beat again. *Fire,* he said, *this child is mine. This bed is mine. This room is mine. Ain't nothing here that's yours. There's a lot that is, but nothing here that is.*

—HARRY CREWS

Contents

Prologue

The three firemen were burned alive in the hallway of a Brooklyn tenement. They went down fighting a door that would not open. That door was their access to oxygen and life, and it almost yielded to the body of Captain Seamus O'Day, a big man with broad shoulders who was used to tackling things. It was dented and battered, but it stayed closed, and the three men burned in 2000 degrees of heat for a little over five minutes. On the other side of the door, there was a goldfish in a bowl, swimming in water that wasn't even warm.

The fire company that lost its three men took the goldfish back with them to their firehouse. No one challenged their claim. And they keep it there even now and take care of it. They dote on it, as much as it's possible for a group of men to dote on a fish; they change its room-temperature water and they feed it every day.

Brooklyn, 1995

L ate August.
The filmy sun fading between buildings.

Six o'clock in the evening, and Alicia was waiting for Jake. She had, in fact, spent most of the summer waiting for him, something she hated to admit even to herself. At least he would never know it. Her waiting was a near-miracle of camouflage and self-possession. She didn't sit by the phone, didn't even stay home. It was something invisible: an inner ear cocked, an ache.

Jake had become her lover in early June. Now he was going back to Caryn, his fiancée, whom he was trying to convince himself to marry. Leaving Alicia with the dregs of summer, like backwash at the bottom of a glass.

She stood at the window and watched the street. He was coming over after work to return her keys. And then it would really be over, whatever "it" might have been. For her own part, it had required too much discipline to be called a fling.

Alicia first met Jake on her way to The Catwalk, where she worked the last shift, dancing topless from eight at night until four in the morning.

He was standing, on that evening, in front of his firehouse. And like any other firehouse, it made her turn in her tracks, drew her across the street to its open garage.

Once, firemen had saved her life.

It seemed to be her earliest memory, or perhaps it had just obliterated all that had come before. She still dreamed about it sometimes, the blazing visitation that had come to her bedside, spread its cloak, and tried to take her away. Its invasion marked the end of one kind of innocence, the beginning of another. Within that hour, she stopped belonging to her mother and father and began to belong to a stranger.

She was five years old, living in another part of Brooklyn, when she woke one night to find her bedroom burning. Fire was filling the space, making its rampant way across the floor. Embers lay scattered like seeds in its wake, seeds that flourished into life on the spot, blood-orange blossoms flowering from roots of blue. She sat transfixed as it climbed the walls, erased the drapes and spread like a stain across the ceiling.

And the smoke. The words she found years later for the smoke—*suffocating, noxious, acrid*—weren't yet available to her. Only: her eyes hurt, her throat too; and breathing in, she tasted cinders and ash.

She didn't attempt to make sense of the scene before her; she accepted it as she would a landscape in a dream, and somehow waking in its midst had not even come as a real surprise. Hadn't she always known, lying in bed at night, that the darkness was like an empty stage, waiting . . . ? That some terror beyond her imagination was just biding its time?

Here it was, then. Here for her.

When the headboard caught, a scream took her last breath and dissolved into the roar. The crackling swelter was nearly upon her, searing even at the distance of a few feet, and somehow in a primal place beyond words or terror or bewilderment, she understood that she was done for. And then *he* materialized, stepped out of the smoke like a magician's trick. He wore a coat with bright yellow stripes and a strange black hat. He walked through the fire and lifted her into his arms. For a moment she floated above the flames, hovered like an angel over the remains of her room.

"Come on, honey," he said, though she was unresisting. "Let's go, I've got you, we're gettin' out of here." He shifted her to one side, onto his hip, and pulled his coat around her. She wrapped her legs around him and clung to his shirt. His heart thudded, through the fabric, against her ear.

Within seconds they were out of the smoke and in a stairwell and she was able to see. His neck was covered with stubble and soot, and a shiny scar snaked along his throat. He looked down at her and though his eyes were frightening in their intensity—a bright, crazy blue—he spoke to her again in a reassuring way.

"You all right, honey? Are you awake? Don't be scared, everything's fine. Everyone's outside waiting for you—"

In another moment they were on the floor below, which was also hazy with smoke but not as bad, and then they were at the window and he was handing her to another man in the same kind of coat and hat.

"Let Pete take you down the ladder, okay? Don't be afraid, he'll take you down to your mother."

He started to lift her from his hip. She clung to him a moment. He had blue eyes in a blackened face. And a mustache . . .

"C'mon, honey, Pete's gonna take you now. I have to stay here and help put out the fire."

Pete reached out with both hands. "Any others?" he asked.

"Last one," said the man.

And then they were moving down the ladder, she in the crook of Pete's strong arm, and there was her mother in her nightgown, crying Alicia's name. And they never learned the name of the man who'd gotten her out of bed; her mother took her from Pete, clutching her and sobbing, thanking him over and over, and they went to Aunt Ginny's to sleep that night and Alicia never saw that first fireman again. Her father was in the army and they left Brooklyn soon afterward, moving on to Houston and Meridian and Baltimore and Greenbelt and Cincinnati and Cleveland and Allentown and Erie. But six years ago—at twenty-one—Alicia had come back to New York to be a writer, and she stopped by every firehouse she saw, to look into every face.

In front of this firehouse was a makeshift shrine, of flowers, candles, and other token gifts. A placard above read: *In Memory of Seamus*

O'Day, Daniel Flanagan, and Joseph Moore: Three Who Made the Supreme Sacrifice. (Dead. For all she knew he was dead.)

She was distracted from these offerings by the sight of a tall, light-haired fireman walking out to his car. Handsome, yes: hard biceps and hewed shoulders, a neatly tapering back.

"He's single!"

She turned. The caller was another fireman, this one shorter and more powerfully built.

"Hard to believe," she tossed back, with a sidelong smile at the blond.

"It's a fact," the caller said. "Timmy's the most eligible bachelor in the company."

"Oh yeah?" she countered. "And what about you?"

This was her pride: to flirt like a man. With aggression and assurance. Why did men get to make all the overtures? They were allowed to be appreciative: to flatter, appraise, and fantasize aloud. While women were supposed to just walk on, averting their eyes and pretending not to hear.

"I'm single too," he told her.

"Impossible," Alicia said. Smiling. Sardonic. "This must be my lucky day."

He was wearing dark glasses, which he removed. His skin was rutted, as if streams of water had cut shallow paths down his face. His eyes too—something was wrong with them—the irises were incomplete, eroded in places. He was tattered, weathered, no longer young though probably not yet forty. He grinned at her, wolfishly, she thought. There was something in his bearing that menaced the air.

Alicia stared at him. She was allowed to do this as a stripper: shamelessly check someone out. There was a lot she was allowed to do: touch men anywhere, rub up against them, talk all kinds of sweet trash. She wasn't at work yet, but she found she never quite relinquished this license. So she looked him over, taking her time.

His light brown hair was slivered with gray, cut short at the sides but curling over his brow. And dry, as if sun and salt water had taken their due. She took in each of his features in turn: the bloodshot eyes; a flattened, broken nose; pale, chapped lips.

He was not—by any stretch—a pretty boy. But his body was layered with muscle and his tan looked years in the making. His uniform left only his arms uncovered, but she could see how well he filled out his blue work pants. And his arms were something to see: sculpted, bulging, veins standing out in sharp relief.

"So what are you up to?" he asked.

"Just going to work," Alicia said. She knew the next question and waited for it.

"What do you do?"

"Well, I'm a writer. I write during the day," she said.

"Oh yeah? What do you write?"

She never knew how to answer this one. *Stories* sounded lame; *poetry* was even worse.

"I'm working on a novel," she lied. And then with a certain practiced and not quite genuine reluctance, she added, "But to pay the bills I'm also a dancer at The Catwalk."

"Oh, *really.*" One corner of his mouth quirked up.

"Yeah . . . but listen, please don't ever come in there."

This request, at least, was sincere. She didn't want him coming in, catching her off guard. Something came over her when people she knew dropped in. It put pressure on her: to not be rejected by customers in front of them, to be tipped onstage . . . to look good, even, in whatever slight costume she might be wearing.

"No, no, don't worry, I never go into those places," he said, and she understood his implication: that he didn't have to.

Now other firemen were appearing in the garage, and she turned away from Jake to look at them. All of them were young men. None were old enough to be *him.* But in the meantime, their uniform good looks were startling. They might have been posing for a group shot in some pin-up calendar, all of them chiseled and square-jawed and strong.

"My God, you're *all* beautiful!" she announced. "How is this possible?"

And with this declaration, she was suddenly Jezebel—her stripper persona—forty-five minutes early. She was delighted with herself at this moment, and delighted with the way the firemen grinned, blushed, scuffed their boots on the floor. She watched her words penetrate them like an electric current, saw the pleased ripple come over each of them in turn, and felt the same rush that came to her in the Catwalk cage.

"I guess you like firemen," remarked the one who'd called out to her.

"I love firemen," she said, and for the first time she didn't smile.

"Well, listen, we'll give you the number here at the firehouse and— do you live around here?"

"Right around the corner, on Bedford. Just moved in," she said.

"Well, good, so the next time you're around you can come over and hang out, get a tour, whatever. It can get real slow around here between jobs." He was scribbling a number on a scrap of paper. "I'm Jake," he said. "And you are . . . ?" She wavered a moment, wondering whether to give her stage name or her real one. "Alicia," she said finally, and watched the corner of Jake's mouth quirk up again.

"Forget your name, little girl?"

She glanced once again at the tall blond, Timmy, but he seemed far away, and bland in his perfection. Then she turned back to the tattered Jake, with his strange eyes and his scars. He was someone who would have his luck with certain women but wouldn't, probably wouldn't, be *spoiled*.

"So do we get your number too?" he was asking and though he said *we* she knew he meant only himself. She hesitated once again, because after all she didn't know him.

But then what the hell, it was only a phone number, and she said, "Okay," and wrote it down on the same scrap of paper before tearing it in half. Why not? It wasn't like she met men like this at work. The Catwalk was a "Gentlemen's Club," catering to white-collar clientele. They wore suits and ties, carried briefcases and cellular phones. They were accountants and consultants, traders and lawyers, bankers and brokers. They were swollen with self-importance, with their wealth and what they imagined was their power.

In her notebook at home, right now, was the beginning of a poem. *The men I dance for work in boxes/ And pay too many unspoken taxes/ All joined at the neck by an unseen yoke . . . .*

She put his number in her pocket and held out her own.

Down the street, then, past chalk drawings on the sidewalk, past barbed wire curling at the top of fences, and graffiti on walls, and smokestacks in rows. In the distance were the tracks for the elevated train, which flanked the walkway across the Williamsburg Bridge. The bridge was the best part of the walk to work: the sun-stained water beneath her as she made her way toward Manhattan, the Domino Sugar factory lit up beside the East River, the jewel box of the city sparkling at the other side.

Once on the ground again, it was west on Delancey all the way to Soho, where couples sat at posh outdoor bistros, wreathed in cigarette smoke and ashing into oyster shells. Even the pavement glittered in this part of town. She was learning not to mind it. Her own share of glamour was waiting.

She had an idea of what The Catwalk was supposed to be, underneath its pedestrian trappings. Never mind the illuminated stock tickers above the stage that announced up-to-the-minute news from Wall Street. Never mind the men in corporate attire. Wasn't the club, at its essence, a tavern where hunters came fresh from the kill, to raise a raucous toast and pound the table for attention? A place of hospitality, where slender, fawn-eyed girls were always within reach? And didn't it border on medieval fantasy to be one of these girls, slated to dance for the crowd's entertainment? There should have been private chambers on the premises, with flickering lanterns and furs strewn on the floor, where a man could take the girl of his choice and put her on her back.

Instead, there was just the Champagne Lounge, where nothing much happened. There were thin white-collar men looking ill at ease. Still, she brought her own fantasy to work with her every evening, where it pervaded her every interaction, and though she was not—by far—the best or most beautiful dancer, she knew it was what made her a house favorite night after night. The Catwalk ran on fantasy.

It was twenty to eight when she arrived at the club, a little later than she would have liked. The transformation from Alicia to Jezebel required about thirty minutes; twenty was cutting it close. As always, two bouncers flanked the entrance—imposing, closemouthed men who nodded as she passed between them.

The dressing room was on the second floor of the club. Eighteen girls were crowded into a space meant for twelve, and the fluorescent tube lighting was not kind. Still, when Alicia found a small space in the corner to open her duffel bag, some of the evening's promise glinted up at her. One of the best aspects of the job was the chance to wear the kind of clothing it would be hard to carry off elsewhere: elbow-length gloves, thigh-high boots, boas and garter belts and velvet gowns that laced up the front. The shelves were cluttered with makeup and more trappings of the masquerade: feathers and sequins, fishnets and glitter.

By two minutes to eight, she was Jezebel, a persona that changed with every man: maybe wicked and wisecracking and sly; or maybe wide-eyed and candy-colored and smiling.

She thought of Jake all night as she danced for the other kind of men, and when she got home at four in the morning, he had left a message on her machine.

"**W**hat's happening, Jake?"

The question came from Jonah Malone, who was standing in the doorway of the housewatch office. At the sight of him, Jake—who could barely be bothered to stand when greeting anyone—sprang to his feet. Malone was the captain of Rescue 2 in Brooklyn and probably the most decorated fireman in New York. At least he had more medals than anyone else Jake could think of. He was a legend, not only for the dozens of rescues to his name, but for the insane chances he took all the time. Sometimes after reading the accounts in the medal books, it was hard to believe Malone was alive and walking around.

Besides that, he had been with Captain O'Day in the hospital all those weeks, at his bedside up to the end. He had suffered over O'Day as much as anyone in Ladder 104. Now he often dropped by to see how everyone here was holding up. He was Jake's hero, as much for that as for the rest of it.

Jake himself was thirty-five and had been a fireman for seventeen years. But he wasn't even a lieutenant and never would be. Achieving rank required a diligence that he couldn't bring to the job. He was a good fireman but his heart didn't completely belong to it, any more than it belonged to anyone or anything. He was a—what had Alicia called him? A maverick. He liked the words she used when she talked about him. *Elemental. Elusive.* That girl could talk some talk. The point was, he was a lone wolf. If he didn't need the money, he would be a full-time outdoorsman, maybe. Firefighting was a good job because it left him a lot of time to do just that. He could put in his two twenty-four-hour tours every week and spend the other five days pursuing his many extracurricular passions.

"What's happening with Caryn? You figure anything out yet?" Malone was asking. He was referring to Jake's engagement, on-again-off-again for going on six months now. Jake was glad he asked, grateful for the opportunity to tell him about Alicia.

Of course, the one he really wished he could talk to about her was gone. Captain O'Day used to get the lowdown whenever Jake was making it with someone new. Used to be there was nothing you couldn't tell that guy, even if he was the captain. He never judged anyone, maybe because in his younger years he'd done some misbehaving of his own. Jake had heard, a few times, that the reason O'Day had transferred into Ladder 104 in the first place was because of some trouble with a woman on the side. Whatever the case, O'Day never acted like he was better than the next guy. Talking to Malone wasn't the same, but it was better than nothing.

"No, man, it gets worse every day. I can't make a fuckin' decision; it's pathetic, it's fucked up, and it's causing so much havoc. But wait! It gets worse. I had to go and throw another monkey wrench into the whole thing."

Malone's eyebrows went up. "How's that?" he asked.

"I've been cheating on Caryn with this other girl. It started in June and it's been going on all summer."

"Yeah?" Malone looked mildly amused. "Oh boy. Anyone I know?"

"Nah, she just moved in nearby, I met her right here, in front of the firehouse. This topless dancer, she's hotter 'n hell, what could I do, man? You got to see her to believe her."

He stole a sidelong glance at Malone, to see how he was taking this news. There was no denying he wanted to impress Malone, but the captain wasn't the type to join in locker room talk; he was a quiet, private kind of guy. Sometimes Jake wondered if he was even into women; he never seemed to have any in the picture.

"So what're you going to do?" Malone asked.

"Fuck me if I know, man. But I promised Caryn I'd give the whole thing one more shot, so I've got to break it off with this other one. In fact, I'm going to do that tonight before the benefit."

Jake was talking about tonight's party at the Brooklyn Brewery, which the firehouse was holding in memory of O'Day, Danny and Joe. There would be a ten-dollar cover; the money was for The Widows and Orphans Fund.

"Well, good luck," said Malone. "Do the right thing."

Jake watched Malone walk away. *Do the right thing*. Malone hadn't said what the right thing was, but Jake knew it was to marry Caryn. He'd done enough work to get his ring on her finger, so what was his problem?

Caryn had been Jake's hardest conquest ever. They'd been together— what? four months?—before she broke it off to get engaged to some Wall Street asshole. Her family was giving her hell for dating a fireman. When she left, it laid him out; he was broken up about it for weeks. It was his first and only time for something like that. No girl had ever just dropped him before.

There was only one time in his life that he'd ever felt worse, and that was when O'Day, Joe and Danny had died. That was as bad as it got. There was nothing to compare that to.

But losing Caryn—that was fucked up too, and he didn't know how to roll with it. Once he even saw her on the street with the other guy, a little pinstriped pussy-whipped tie-wearing fairy with gold-rimmed glasses and a soft jaw. It was beyond belief, that this mincing little prick had come along and taken his woman.

In fact, it was the sight of them together that settled it for him; a campaign began that very day. A campaign to take back what was his, no matter what he had to do. And one by one, he pulled out every stop. He did his drinking in her neighborhood and called her morning, noon and night. He sent flowers and wrote painstaking letters, looking up the spelling of every third word in the dictionary. Slowly but surely he stripped away her resolve to marry The Asshole, tried to make her see that she could change her mind. And then the impossible happened: *she changed her mind.* She broke off her engagement and came back to him. *Okay,* she said. *You win.*

And just like that, he'd won. Fuckin' A—he'd fuckin' won! Gotten her away from a near-millionaire! It was a score for firemen everywhere; another white collar was in the dust. Caryn was back where she belonged, at his side and in his bed.

The only trouble was, once this was accomplished, there was nothing to burn over. Nothing to fight for. What was left was the most stifling calm, as well as some very unsettling thoughts about the life he was verging on. Like: no other women, ever again. No more calling his own shots. He wouldn't be able to disappear into the wilderness for weeks at a time if he heard the call. Life would be about family insurance and mortgage payments and babies on the way. Caryn with her liberal guilt and bleeding heart had given up a fashion designer's six-figure salary to be a social worker in the Bronx. A social worker's income plus a fireman's didn't stack up to much more than a pillbox in the suburbs, dinners out on Saturdays, a half-decent Christmas and a week at the Jersey shore every summer.

That's what Caryn wanted, he knew. A dependable husband and a bunch of kids jumping up and down on the couch. The little house with the picket fence. She wanted him mowing the goddamn lawn. That would be their foreplay, her watching him sweat from the upstairs window while their baby suckled at her small breasts. He'd finish up just as she put the kid down for a nap and they'd sneak a quickie during this reprieve, her tits still leaking milk. It was kind of sexy if he thought about it for no more than half a minute.

It would be forever sexy if Caryn were the bored housewife next door, watching from the neighboring house while he cut his sister's grass. Shirtless in the heat of July. And Caryn's husband, the broker commuting the two hours to Wall Street each morning, was in Chicago till the end of the week.

Or it could be hot to cut Alicia's grass. As penance for something. Something he'd done to her. It could be sexy to work on her lawn, his back bare under the noon sun, while she lounged on her porch swing and watched in amusement, hollering that he'd missed a spot. If she

would play slave driver—and he knew she could if she wanted to, she'd
know how to do it—she could torment him, lazy in the shade of her
porch, wearing short shorts and a half-unbuttoned halter, drinking
Sangria. Sultry, sucking on ice . . . rubbing the ice all over herself; it was
so easy to see it.

Or he could even get off on cutting Malone's grass, himself a probie
punk paying dues to a senior officer during the hazing process all new
guys went through. Stripped to the waist and glistening under Malone's impassive gaze, Malone whom he would bet had taken his share
of service from younger men. Most probies would perform a task like
this sheepishly, grinning and awkward, game but not fervent. Whereas
he, Jake, would be—in his shirtlessness—deferent and serious, quiet
and diligent. He would show, without making too much of it, that it
meant something to him.

Yes, he could find it exciting—endlessly and in a thousand varieties
arousing—to mow any lawn, cut any grass, but his own.

From her bedroom window now Alicia could see what she thought
of as her scrap of the sky: a thin strip of space between tenements.
And her own faint reflection etched upon it: see-through blue. Framed
like a portrait of loss; transparent after all.

It wasn't that she'd had illusions about a future with Jake. Another
woman was already trying to drag him to the altar and Alicia didn't
envy her. Jake wasn't going to commit to anyone, whether or not he
ever went through with a wedding. For one thing, firemen belonged to
a boys club so tight that even their most beloved women always came
second. Further, she had never met anyone so disinterested in domes-
ticity. Jake was, among other things, a hunter who liked to disappear
into the woods for days on end. He was a fisherman who would never
pass up the chance to spend a solitary week out at sea. And he had
never tried to hide this. Not even at the beginning, which she remembered well: the message on her machine at four a.m., like a light at the
end of the night's tunnel.

*Alicia, hi, it's Jake from the firehouse. Listen . . . they're splitting my
usual 24-hour tour in two. I have to work during the day on Friday and*

then again on Saturday, so I—in that situation, I usually just stay over because I live out in Montauk and it's a two-hour drive each way. So I was thinking you might like to have a drink Friday night. You can call me at the firehouse anytime tomorrow and let me know.

She fell asleep smiling into her pillow. The next day she called late in the afternoon and worked hard to sound offhand. "Jake? Hey, Alicia here, got your message. . . . Listen, if we get together Friday night it'll have to be later on, I've got to go to this party first. Could we maybe hook up around one-thirty or two?"

She loved being able to say this. She liked looking like the kind of girl who was just getting started at two a.m. And he said that was fine, he would be awake. Could she come by the firehouse when she was ready?

When she picked him up that Friday night she stood outside the red garage doors for a moment and looked through the window. Inside was a fire truck with its front cab door open and just below that was a pair of boots. It took a moment for her to realize that no one was standing in those boots. That they were lying in wait, for a fireman springing from sleep. In the dark quiet of the garage, their emptiness was ghostly.

She went to the entrance and found it unlocked. There was an office just off the garage where calls came in. Jake was in there, his back to her. He was busying himself in front of a small aquarium.

"Jake," she said softly so as not to startle him.

He turned. "Hey girl!" he said. "How was the party?"

"It was great," she said, although it had been a drag. "What are you doing?"

"Oh," Jake said. "Just feeding the fish." He stepped away so she could see it.

She studied the tank. "You guys have a whole aquarium for just one goldfish?"

"That's a special fish," Jake said.

She smiled, waiting for the punch line, but he remained serious. "No, really. That fish survived the Bedford Blaze. The fire that took our guys."

"The three guys that were killed in May?"

"Right. It was in the very next room. Never even started to simmer. So we, well, it probably looks a little bizarre. But we kind of adopted it."

He wasn't kidding, Alicia realized. She stared at it. It seemed like the tail end of a complicated magic act: something turned into a goldfish in a bowl. She thought of the one time she'd been given one of her own, as a small child at some roadside, honky-tonk, sawdust-covered carnival in one of her many hometowns. She remembered throwing a ping-pong ball at a grid of glass cups, each of which held a fish. She wasn't tall enough to see her targets without someone holding her up to the railing, and her ball didn't even land on the table. But there was the tattooed carny—sinewy, kindly, twisting a plastic bag at the neck and fastening it with a piece of wire. In the bag was some water and her tiny, animate prize. Her very own goldfish.

By morning it was dead. Her mother flushed it down the toilet. The dead mouse left on their doorstep by the family cat had gotten more of a funeral than that. In the hierarchy of pets, it was hard to imagine something lower than a goldfish.

As Alicia came to know Jake better, the scene she had just witnessed would seem even more incredible. He would describe his deep-sea expeditions in enthusiastic detail, show her photographs of himself with his catches. Often they were massive, shining, as tall as he was or taller. And these magnificent fish he hauled into the deadly air and casually slit throat to tail while bantering with his buddies.

Once, looking at these pictures, she asked if he would ever want to scuba dive.

"Only with a spear gun," he answered. "I don't think I could stand it otherwise, to be surrounded by all those moving targets with no way to nab 'em."

"Oh for Christ's sake. Can't you imagine enjoying an animal without having to destroy it?"

"Hey," he said. "They can have their chance at me too. Remember, I cordially invited them."

By this she knew he was referring to the message he'd painted on the underside of his surfboard: EAT ME.

Yet here he was, the same man who had tossed dozens of bass, tuna, and shark into a tortured pile, leaving them to their death spasms. The same man who strung up razor-toothed bluefish by passing the rope through their eye sockets while they were still alive. This very man was hovering over a goldfish in a bowl, dispensing a measured amount of flakes as if performing a sacred rite.

Jake set the canister of fish food on a shelf.

"Well," he said. "Makes me think about drinking."

There was a bar around the corner with intricately carved wooden booths and windows of stained glass. It had a small seating area inside and another one in the backyard. Jake seemed to be a regular there. The bouncers greeted him by name and so did the bartenders.

"Come here often?" Alicia cracked.

"It's a firehouse joint," Jake told her. "The guys behind the bar are from my company, and so are the ones at the door."

Above the bar hung a picture of a fireman in full regalia—turnout coat and helmet—a photograph with the dignity and finality of a portrait. The heavy gilt frame encasing it was several feet high and almost as wide, as if to emphasize the might of the man within its borders. And the man presiding there was an awe-inspiring sight—towering and powerful, with the brow of a thunder god and the brawn of a linebacker. Standing by the bar, gazing up into that resolute face, Alicia was transfixed.

"Who is that man?" she heard herself ask.

A moment went by before Jake answered. "That man," he said, "was Captain Seamus O'Day. The captain of Ladder 104." Then: "*My* captain."

"Oh," Alicia said. "So was he one of the three who—"

"Yeah. He was killed in the Bedford Blaze. Took him a long time to die though."

"And the other two?"

"Joe and Danny died right away. It was a fuckin' meltdown, and they were all trapped in it for about five minutes. But Captain O'Day, he hung on. He hung in there almost six whole weeks."

"My God," Alicia murmured, turning to Jake. "He must have been near indestructible."

"He was one tough bastard. Best captain I'll ever have."

"I'm so sorry."

"Everyone loved him," Jake went on. "He was everyone's father. You want to see how the guys feel about him?" He turned to the juke-box against the near wall. "Watch this."

And sliding a dollar into the slot, he pressed a series of numbers he apparently knew by heart. "Fiddler's Green," he said. "It was his favorite song. He used to sing it in the firehouse all the time."

A low Irish brogue filled the room.

> As I roved by the dockside one evening so rare,
> To view the still water and take the salt air,
> I heard an old fisherman singing this song:
> "Oh take me away boys, me time is not long.
>
> "Wrap me up in me oilskins and jumper.
> No more on the docks I'll be seen.
> Just tell me ol' shipmates I'm taking a trip, mates,
> And I'll see them in Fiddler's Green."

Jake nudged her. "Look at them," he said, nodding toward the bar.

Both bartenders had stopped serving customers. They were holding their own mugs of beer, swilling and singing with the record.

> "Now Fiddler's Green is a place I hear tell
> Where fishermen go when they don't go to hell
> The weather is fair and the dolphins do play,
> And the cold coast of Greenland is far, far away."

"He sang this in the firehouse all the time," Jake said again, speaking close to her ear to be heard above the music. "I used to think he was singing it for me, because I'm a fisherman. But now I think he just liked it."

> "I don't want a harp, nor a halo, not me —
> Just give me a breeze and the smooth rolling sea.
> I'll play me ol' squeezebox, as we sail along,
> With a wind in the riggin' to sing me this song."

It was as if the men behind the bar were no longer aware of the crowd waiting for drinks. She watched from across the room as they swayed and sang and cried. Beside her she could sense that even Jake was fighting tears. Wordlessly, without looking at him, she took his hand.

"Come on," he said after a minute, his voice gone hoarse. "There are tables out back in the yard."

"I should probably tell you now," he said during their second round. Alicia had switched from Coors Lite to red wine. Jake was drinking Guinness and seemed recovered from his earlier emotion. "I'm not looking for any long-term thing. And look, I don't mean to sound presumptuous—I'm not saying that's what *you* want—but I'll feel better once that's on the table. I'm not into lying, and I don't want to waste your time."

"That's fine," Alicia said. Ignoring the sting. The wine had gone to her skin already; she was flushed and warm. Jake's arm was on the tabletop, just inside her peripheral vision: dark bronze, powerful, the blue work shirt rolled to just above the elbow.

She lifted her gaze to his. "I'm not looking for a boyfriend," she said. It was true, as far as she knew. She was looking for a feeling. It had been a long time since she'd been with someone. She'd been stripping for more than a year and the men she danced for were so far from her tavern fantasy that they left her cold even outside the club. Jake was like a flame held to that place inside her; he kindled a heat she was glad to feel again.

"I like being alone," she went on. "I want my freedom too."

What was going on here? What was she trying to prove? She struck this pose that first night and held it—held it for all she was worth through the weeks and months that followed, till she ached from the contortion, the rigidity. But for the moment it got her what she wanted, which was to be lying beneath him, and soon.

"Dance for me," Jake said when they were back at her apartment. "Like you dance for the men at your club."

She loved this idea, of giving it away for once.

"Okay," she said. "But! If you want the real experience, you have to follow the rules." She positioned him on her loveseat. "Remember, you can't touch me. There are bouncers a few feet away waiting to kick your ass. Now I'm going to change. Stay right there."

In the bathroom, she put on one of her bikinis and peered anxiously in the mirror. Would it work outside The Catwalk? Would she look all right without the neon? Better snap off the overhead, light a candle for atmosphere. And play some Marvin Gaye.

"Ba-a-a-by, I'm hot just like an oven . . . I need some lovin' . . . "

And then as she crossed the room and started to dance, she felt Jake being pulled into her territory, felt the power shift at last. Few men remained immune to the fantasy created by the lowered lights, the revealing costume, the scented oil and sultry music. It was just like at work. There came a moment when you knew you had them: a turning point where they would empty their wallets, open a tab on their credit cards, whine and plead, make preposterous promises.

"Ba-a-a-by, I think I'm capsizin' . . . the waves are risin' . . . and risin' . . . "

Jake wasn't a customer, but he was under the spell—wide-eyed, mouth slightly open, sweating. Hard as a rock beneath his jeans. When the song ended, she stepped back, smiling, to admire her handiwork.

"Okay," she said, adjusting her top. "Now show me what *you* can do."

" . . . hmmm," Jake said after a moment, recovering himself with some effort. "I guess I could show you the fireman's carry."

"What's that?" she asked, and he leaned forward.

One hard-muscled arm locked tight around her legs. He stood abruptly, tossing her over his shoulder. She dangled upside down, her gaze sweeping along the floorboards as he crossed the room. But everything righted itself once again as he flung her down onto the bed.

J ake turned slowly under the firehouse shower, letting the water carry the scent of smoke from his skin. He loved this ritual, showering after a hard shift, stripping off boots and turnout coat and bunker gear and finally his uniform to stand naked under the jet. With or without the other guys around. After this he would get dressed and go to Alicia's; she wanted her keys back. They had said they would stay friends, but he knew this might be his last time in her apartment.

Her apartment. It was where she had danced for him that first night. This was after he had stated his position and she invited him up anyway. It was confirmation that they wanted the same thing, that they had an understanding. So what was coming was inevitable, but he wanted her to make him crazy first.

"You want a private show?" she smiled. "Let me get dressed then ... give me a few minutes ... "

She disappeared into the bathroom with a gym bag. He took a seat on the sofa and leaned back. This girl was all right. In fact she was probably going to be a lot of fun.

When she emerged in her costume—all in hot pink, from string bikini and spike heels to rhinestone earrings and feather boa—he was struck a little breathless. For the first time she seemed truly beautiful. The girl was in kick-ass shape; her body was almost as amazing as his.

Her tape deck was playing "Sexual Healing." She moved in to dance, invading the space between his knees. He breathed in her scent: coconut lotion with a touch of something else, mango maybe. The fragrance was summer itself: a cocktail of tropical oil and sweat and heat. Her top came off and her tits swayed in his face. Her smile was wide and genuinely happy and she was grazing his skin with her fingertips, stroking his face and neck and arms. She leaned into him, sighing and intent, sinuous as a snake charmer's snake, an image which could also apply to something else, something that was coming out of hiding, rising ...

How many guys got to experience something like that, outside a strip joint? Couldn't be a lot, or Alicia wouldn't be making all that money. The poor bastards—girls making 'em pay and pay. But then again, fuck 'em; if they were willing to, they deserved it.

Reluctantly he stepped from the shower and put on street clothes, then went outside to see if his replacement was there yet. It was right here that he'd met Alicia. She'd strutted up to the firehouse just like the new kid on the block wandering into a street game, not asking permission. *I can take on the whole lot of you,* she might have said. She'd flirted with all the firemen at once, a challenge implicit in everything she said.

Little girl, I love your fuckin' attitude, he remembered thinking. The other guys were pleased but somewhat bewildered. This girl was not their speed. He was the only one who was really gonna take her on, because she translated into something he could take down—respectfully in a way, and not without some regret—how could he explain it? It had to do with a certain kind of tact, the tact of a great hunter.

Yes, a high-flying, in-your-face girl like that made his blood sing. Something in him rose to answer. She was enough like him to spark competition. She made him want to lay himself down on her, cover her: the silencer on her gun.

It was the only way he knew to merge with her. Your prey became part of you. It clothed you and fed you and furnished your space. You could climb into its skin and let it warm you on the outside even as its flesh filled you from the inside. Communion, fusion. You could string its teeth or claws to encircle your neck; it lent you its menace. Like stripping the weapons from an opponent and carrying them with you.

What did he take from women? Their self-assurance and pride. Their charades and alibis and pretensions. Their lies. When they got to this place it was like he and a trembling doe looking at each other across a clearing—a doe soon beyond trembling, her imminent downfall an understanding between them. His gaze like a finger pressed to a pair of lips, to silence and still; or a hand laid across the strings of an instrument, just before putting it to rest. This moment seemed to make it all worth it, all the energy and effort. Communion again, surrender. Acceptance; even invitation. The deer frozen in the headlights, stunned and still in the path of the oncoming car: *Come,* it might say if it could speak. *Come on and come.*

Jake saw his replacement pull in and was about to leave when the dark red Chevy he still thought of as the Captain's car pulled in right behind it. He was not immune to the sight, and he wasn't past forgetting, moment to moment, that Captain O'Day was gone. It was a split-second kind of thing before the sickening stab of memory.

But there was Matilda O'Day and she was a comforting sight. She and the Captain had been married so long that they had come to look a little alike. She was about half her husband's size, or so it seemed, but she had his warm blue eyes and steel spine.

"Mrs. O'Day," Jake said, rushing to kiss her cheek and take whatever she might be carrying.

"Jake," she said, touching him lightly. "How are you, sweetheart?"

"Getting by." He felt his throat catch and hoped she couldn't tell.

"Is Jonah here?" She didn't look at him as she asked this, but kept her eyes trained on the garage. There was something strange about her tone, too; it seemed to soften around Malone's name. What was that about?

"Sure thing, he's in the backyard," Jake said after a second. "Shooting some hoops with the guys."

"Is he really? Could he possibly be having some fun?"

Jake laughed. "You have to kind of trick him into it, right? Yeah, I know what you're saying. He's intense. And he got a lot older this past spring. But then I guess we all did."

"Oh, Jake. Sweetheart. I know you did. I barely knew Jonah before Seamus got hurt, but he took it so hard. Harder in some ways than even me." She stopped short. "These days I hear myself and I can't believe it. You can't imagine how dreary it is, this poster-widow business. Let's talk about something else. The baseball team. You're going to the playoffs this month, aren't you?"

"That's right." Jake brightened. He was the shortstop on the team. "It's down to us and Ladder 11. Those bozos better eat their Wheaties."

"I'll be there when it comes around. Seamus would have wanted me to see it. That team meant a lot to him." She broke off to scan the parking lot, one hand shielding her eyes. "Now, where's Wes? You know our friend Wes, don't you? He's supposed to meet us here. But I don't see his car."

"Yeah, I know who he is," Jake said. "I don't think he's come yet. At least I haven't seen him."

Wes was an older man, a friend of Malone's, who had put in a lot of time during the whole ordeal—running errands, driving Matilda around, bringing meals into the hospital for the family. He was a homo for sure, but Jake could never tell what was going on between him and Malone. He had to wonder. They didn't seem intimate—not *that* way, anyway. It wouldn't really make sense. If Malone wanted a man, he'd want a *real* man. And probably a younger man. Another fireman, maybe.

"Wes has been like a guardian angel to me," Matilda was saying. "He distracts me from my grief. I think he's taken me to every museum in Manhattan, and I tell you, it's better than having a guided tour. He knows so much."

"That must be nice," Jake said, to be polite. Nothing interested him less than pansy-ass faggots and their art lectures.

"The Impressionists, that's his specialty. Earlier this week he took me to see the original *Water Lilies* painting."

A silver Lexus pulled up to the firehouse curb.

"Oh, here he is now," Matilda said.

Jake felt some indignation that Wes, a civilian without even an FDNY sticker on his car, would presume to park on firehouse property. He had a brief fantasy of hot-wiring the Lexus and taking it for a spin while the three of them were at dinner. It looked like it floated like a cloud, just as easy and smooth . . . and here came Wes himself, his silver hair nearly the same shade as the car.

"Darling," Wes said, approaching Matilda. He kissed her on both cheeks, fussing and clucking like an old hen. "How was your afternoon?"

"Just an average day in the life of a tragic celebrity," Matilda said. "NBC called again. Now they want to do a follow-up segment on me and the kids. Wes, I'm sure you must have met Jake at the hospital. He's with Ladder 104, and he's our shortstop in the play-offs."

Jake forced a smile. "Sir," he said, extending his hand. He could've sworn the other man's palm broke out in a sweat as they shook. He fought the urge to wipe his own on his jeans.

"I see Jonah has already arrived," Wes said, eyeing Malone's battered Pontiac.

"He's in the back, Jake tells me. Actually playing a basketball game."

Wes pretended to be shocked. "Can we interrupt such a rare occurrence for something as mundane as dinner?"

Time to leave. "Take care, Mrs. O'Day," Jake said.

"We'll see you later, right? At the benefit?"

"I'll be there," he promised.

Alicia's apartment was just a few blocks from the firehouse. He would walk, as always. It pained him a little to think he wouldn't be over there anymore. She had continued to flirt with all the guys in the firehouse but so far no one else had ever gotten an invitation to her room. It made him think of that Springsteen riff:

She'll let you in her house, if you come knocking late at night . . .

She'll let you in her mouth, if the words you say are right . . .

She had shown him some of her secret garden and like most women was probably trying to weave him into her web. She had her little mating dance like all the rest, her wiles and strategems. It would be nice if he could be drawn in, if one of them ever had what it took to keep him under her heel. Instead they always fell for him, always wanted more than he could give, probably because he could give so little and made no effort to pretend otherwise. For some reason this always drew them like flies to shit.

This was fine with him, of course. There was nothing better than a slow and hard-won conquest. But as in any hunt, after the kill there was nothing left but the trophy, the ghost.

He was already infamous for his successes. There was the one he was supposed to be marrying and another on the side. A would-be wife and a willing mistress. And there had been others, so many others. For a short, half-ugly guy he'd had more than his fair share and it was like a testimony to something special about him, something they all recognized.

He loved the way Alicia had been drawn deeper and deeper into him in spite of herself. She knew him for what he was and she was trying to carry off the part of hip and happening stripper chick, doing what she liked with whomever she pleased. She brought this image to everything she did, but whenever Jake had a block of free time she took it, and every time he saw her she was wearing something else, another dress, probably a new one just for him . . .

And she looked damn good in every one of them too, he had to admit it. She looked like something he wanted to sink his teeth into, ravish, dismember. The other guys at the firehouse were jumping out of their skin; they were openly jealous, and sometimes during an unguarded moment they looked at Jake with hatred. This flash of malice—sudden, unmistakable—was like scoring all over again.

Yes, he would miss her. A little. She had done him right and then some.

Alicia fought the urge to break something. To put her hand through this very window. She had known what she was getting into when she started up with Jake. No one had to tell her he wasn't going to love her. Or stay with her. But still. She kept thinking about a line from a poem by Maxine Kumin. Something about an elk shedding its antlers.

No matter how hardened, it seems there was pain.
Blood on the snow from rubbing, rubbing, rubbing.

He had been the most exciting part of her summer, and maybe even her year. She thought of the way they always talked for hours before having sex, firing themselves up, exchanging fantasies. Once Jake told her about a guy at the firehouse who used to be a warden in a women's prison. He'd left that job because he didn't trust himself around so many sex-starved women.

"What about you?" Alicia asked. "Could *you* have done that job with integrity?" Who knew what she was hoping for—some sensitivity in the answer, maybe. Some rueful, hard-won restraint.

"No way, man," Jake laughed. "They would've had to've gotten rid of *me!* I'd be like: Turn around, drop those prison pants, come and *get* it! Back right up against the bars."

It wasn't what she'd had in mind. In her fantasy, she had Jake in his guard's uniform, making his rounds with a clipboard, and herself at the far end of a cellblock. He would come by during his count to check her off. She would sink to her knees and reach through the bars, surround his legs with her arms. *Let me have it,* her eyes would plead. *Have mercy.*

His response would be wordless. His hands would go to his belt. His gaze would hold hers as he unbuckled it, opened his fly. She would press herself to the bars, grateful tears falling, lips parting. Panting. She'd take him the way a baby animal would take a teat, sucking for her life, and maybe his hand would rest for a moment at the back of her head.

To his credit, he liked to listen to her version of things.

It was her rape fantasy that made her give him her keys in the first place. A set of keys along with her work schedule for the next several months. He could only use them once, she said. She didn't want to know when.

And in fact it was so many weeks before he did that she had no longer believed he would. She was no longer mounting the stairs with trepidation; her heart wasn't pounding as she unlocked the apartment door. By the time he used them, she would have screamed had his powerful arm not cut off her air, coming around her throat in the dark. She had a moment of unadulterated terror as her hand flew to claw at that arm, and then in that first second of contact—her fingertips touching that muscle—she knew exactly who it was. She knew who it was but even in the wake of relief her heart hammered on. And then he was dragging her, one hand over her mouth, the other like a steel band around her waist. Not to the bed but to the table, where he forced her over it facedown and pulled her head back by the hair.

Not all their encounters were violent, of course. There were gentle ones too. They had taken a bath together one time: scented, candlelit, where she took a sea sponge and polished his whole bronze body: shoulders, chest, rock-hard thighs and calloused feet. A body made newly radiant by the water . . .

And there had even been some romance. An old fire coat he had given her. A present of striped bass, caught that afternoon in Montauk, which he blackened on her stove before his night shift. He brought her other treasures of the sea as well: fresh caviar, a jagged shark's tooth, bits of beach glass: azure, mint-green.

She brought him offerings too. Once she bought a dozen bluepoint oysters at the South Street Seaport and brought them to the firehouse. A brazen gift: a veiled invitation to come by after work.

She also liked to cook, would have cooked elaborately had it not cost so much leverage. As it was, she often painstakingly put something together and then took equal pains to mask the effort—she would cut it into pieces, stash it in the fridge, say it was left over from something and offer to "reheat" it. She would set a place for him at the table as if it were an afterthought, and with a half-ironic smile, she might light a candle.

"I made a pie for Josie's party, there's one piece left, are you hungry?"

And the slice would be taken from the fridge, having been separated from the rest of the pie that afternoon. The rest, wrapped in tin foil, would stay hidden at the back of the freezer. One of several elaborate charades; one of many efforts to be kept under wraps.

She had to do it this way. The truth would not be forgiven. Though it seemed that none of it had made a difference, in the end.

Six-fifteen. Jake was on his way. After Alicia's, he would make a polite appearance at this benefit and then leave for Montauk. By trading tours with his mutuals partner, he had secured five uninterrupted days on the beach.

There was a deserted cove he knew about where he could be alone. Naked all day long, and lulled by the crashing surf through the night. There everything was peaceful. Even the sand beneath his body was strangely soft. The moon in the night sky was like his heart: singular, cold, having its way with the tides. Showing itself a sliver at a time. Sometimes disappearing altogether; sometimes fully present and startlingly tender.

He could set up camp there after a day's expedition, or he could fish there, from the water's edge, if he hadn't been able to get on a boat. When darkness fell, he dug a pit for a fire and cooked whatever the afternoon had yielded. Now August had come, and with it the tuna. Tuna he preferred to eat raw, skinning and cleaning and cutting it into strips. In August, his fires were for reading purposes only.

He was most of the way through *Leaves of Grass*. Alicia had given him the book after he told her he hated poetry. He'd been reading it, slowly and surreptitiously, for weeks now.

Sea of stretch'd ground-swells, sea of the brine of life . . .

Alicia. She'd been a hell of a ride. Good girl. Wild thing. He would never regret a minute with her.

They had acted out a lot of fantasies but Jake had to admit that the "rape" gave him as much pleasure as just about anything he could remember. It was almost like hunting—his stealthy, unannounced arrival at her apartment at quarter to four in the morning. She always worked the last shift at The Catwalk, always from eight at night till four a.m. He could've come earlier, could've read her damn diary or something if he'd had the interest, which he really didn't, and besides, she was the kind of girl who had probably devised some ingenious way to *know* if anyone ever fucked with it.

No, he arrived close to when he knew she'd be getting off work and didn't even bother to snap on the overhead. He'd memorized the apartment already with a fireman's flair for spatial detail; he knew where everything was and he stayed just inside the entrance, positioning himself behind the open door of the hall closet to wait.

It *was* like hunting, crouching patient and knowing in the dark with the intimate apprehension of his prey. He heard her coming up the building stairs, knew it was her beyond a shadow of a doubt, knew her tread as he knew the gait of every animal he'd ever lain in wait for. When her key turned in the lock he felt a stab of predatory joy and no sooner had she bolted the door behind her—the light wasn't even on yet—than he was upon her, with an easy, instinctive knowledge of exactly how to do it. She never had a chance to make a sound and he felt her confusion, her terror, and it aroused him almost to the point of creaming right there, that female panic and ineffectual blind struggle.

Her nails found the arm he had locked across her windpipe and with this he felt her body change. Recognition and understanding trailed her runaway pulse, and then almost immediately excitement—receptivity—*surrender*—set in; without a word spoken, he felt all that in succession. It was like his exchanges with the animals: the giving over, the final abandon, of prey to predator. Didn't the weaker wolf ultimately offer its throat to the stronger one, in battle? He dragged her to the table and flung her over it, for the first time now somewhat inefficient, clumsy in his haste. He could not get his pants unbuckled fast enough, couldn't impale her a second too soon. Sinking himself into her like planting a flag on enemy territory, like staking a claim.

T he sound of the phone pulled Alicia away from the window, and though it no longer held the prospect of gratification, she went toward it with a certain breathlessness.

"Hello . . . ?"

"My relief just got here," Jake told her. "I'll be right over."

Before tonight this five-minute notice had always made her half-crazy with anticipation. But now . . .

"Fine," she said. "See you in a few." Marveling at her ability to sound careless even as tears were building inside like a storm: a sorrow she pictured as gray-green, like a sky before rain. Not to break until after he'd come and gone.

She had done her best for him. Been nothing but a sultry good time. Not one demand had ever made it past her lips. He never even gave her his phone number, and she never asked for it.

When she discussed him with her friends, she didn't say she was in love. Or in pain. Or in despair. She said he was a great lay. This was allowed. These days a girl was allowed to get laid. She was permitted (as long as she insisted on condoms) to take whatever measures were necessary to satisfy, gratify, herself. The only forbidden thing, really, was to *need* a man. And therefore, Alicia was merely enjoying Jake. Toying with him, even. He was, perhaps, her favorite toy.

Working as a stripper made it easier to maintain this image. But when it came to keeping up the act outside the club, she was no match for Jake, who didn't appear to be acting. He seemed to be getting exactly what he wanted. It was clear that he was enjoying her, that he would come over and play whenever he had the impulse, and that his intentions did not extend beyond playing. He was appreciative, kindly, but never fervent or passionate. No declarations would be forthcoming.

Sometimes this was all right. Sometimes the picture pleased her: the stripper with her lovers, one of them a hard-muscled fireman. They came in turn, paying homage, bearing gifts, bringing her pleasure. And she received them each with equanimity, a gracious hostess, a mysterious lady in her tower, a girl who had to have it.

Jake's permanent departure was not in this script, and suddenly Alicia did not see how she could do without him. His calloused palms and cracked nails. His air of absolute competence. He might not be a deep or complex thinker, might not spend a moment of his life pondering unanswerable questions, but he would be competent at whatever he put those strong square hands to: steering wheel, rod and reel, bow and arrow, a woman's body.

More than competent at breaking and entering; better still at escaping.

Jake made his way to Alicia's with a pleasant sense of purpose. Bedford Avenue was dusky and peaceful, dappled with shadows from the trees. Her door keys were heavy in his pocket, a weight he was soon to be rid of. Like in a hotel, he was returning them and checking out.

Out of the frying pan and into the fire, really. Caryn would be waiting for him in Montauk. But hell, even if he did end up getting married, he was glad to have had this thing with Alicia first. Girls like her didn't come along every day. Game for anything. The memories alone would get him off for a long time to come.

He still couldn't believe that she'd gone along with his ultimate fantasy—couldn't believe, even, that she'd gotten it out of him. How had it come up? The only time he got near it was when he asked her if she'd ever had anal sex.

"No," she said, unexpectedly. "I've always wanted to . . . but by now I kind of think about it as a second virginity. I really want to give it to the right person."

"How about you take mine and I'll take yours?" he asked.

She smirked at him. The bitch. "I'll take yours," she said, and at this, her first flicker of one-sided greed, his pulse quickened and his cock got hard. They left it at that. He wasn't going to confess that she could have his cherry on a silver plate if only she'd *take* it as her due.

It didn't come up again for several weeks, until the afternoon she pulled *it* out of some sleeve. A strap-on, and just as important, a black harness to secure it to her body—a tangle of narrow, ominous strips of leather like bondage gear, like sex itself.

"Look what I've got," she said, smiling with something like good-natured ridicule. "I borrowed this just for you." Then she went on with some story about the dyke friend who provided it. Already he was erect, his heart pounding. Watering at the mouth.

"Let me see that," he said, reaching out almost involuntarily. She handed it over. He touched the rubber cock, fingered the harness straps. They put a tremor in his hands and knees. Man, what the hell was that about? He knew one thing for sure: it wasn't about fucking. No ma'am.

It was about getting fucked.

"Listen," he heard himself say. "Would you do me with this?"

Alicia seemed startled. "You mean *now?*" she asked, wide-eyed. "*Today?*"

"Please," he said. He couldn't recall ever being so serious before, with her. "Would you? I mean, this is a—I don't know how to tell you, this is a very heavy fantasy of mine. It would mean a lot to me."

For the first time since he'd met her, she was at a loss for words. "Well," she said finally. "I could *try* . . . I mean, I've never done it before, I don't really know *how* . . ."

"That's okay," he told her. "Try. Just do it, I mean, how could you really go wrong?" He tried to smile. "At least you know you won't have a problem getting it up."

It took some time to convince her to do him on the spot, still longer for her to equip herself. He waited on her sofa, hot with anticipation and unable to sit still. At one point she emerged, a sheepish look on her face.

"I can't figure this out," she said. "The harness. How are the straps supposed to go?"

Jake took it from her, figured it out immediately—it wasn't that different from how you rigged up a rope harness, creating loopholes for the legs. He unbuckled the straps where they were mismatched and refastened them to girdle her. He did this with deference, a slave equipping his mistress to mount him. She took it and disappeared again. The next time the bathroom door opened, she was ready. Clad in black, in a kind of half-catsuit stretching from shoulder to mid-thigh, with a rubber cock jutting out between her legs. She was heeled, as tall as him now or taller. In full armor and coming to conquer.

Jake was ready to burst. "Where and how do you want me?" he asked, his voice gone husky with submission and a rare humility.

"Go bend over my bed," she said, command edging delightfully into her tone. "Take your pants off but leave your underwear on. Pull it down around your thighs where you'll feel it."

He complied—obeyed—in silence, trembling.

"Stay there," she ordered. "I'm going to get some Vaseline."

Bent over, waiting, feeling the breeze from the open window against his ass—this might be the finest moment of his life. And here she came, a five-foot four-inch woman turned Amazon. A woman with a cock.

"They've got a phrase for girls like me," she said, dipping four fingers into the lube. "Chicks with dicks," and then her hand was on him, in the crevice of his ass, such an intimate, hidden, vulnerable spot. That hand was opening him up, priming him for invasion, readying him for her use.

"All right, then," she said, and he felt the tip of her cock enter him. "How's that?"

"Fine, go ahead," he said through gritted teeth.

She pushed part of the way in and ah, the pain—it was the thrill and the pain so close together there was no taking them apart—

"Does it hurt?" she was asking.

"A little, yeah," he gasped, and she withdrew as suddenly as she'd entered. Relief, yes, and loss—

"I'll put some more Vaseline on you, then," she said. "I don't want to hurt you," and of course she didn't, that was maybe her fatal flaw though he never would have admitted as much. The hand again, the slick warmth spreading over that sensitive membrane just before she impaled him all the way. It was amazing, much less painful, a sensation of the deepest, most profound penetration and it was happening to *him,* being done to *him.* He was squirming against her like a woman would, like a bitch in heat, and he felt his climax imploding at the very picture of it—

"Ah yeah," he moaned, "yeah . . . " and she reached around to stroke him but no, she shouldn't, that would bring it on in an instant—

"No, no, it's okay, you don't have to do that," he said, but already it was too late. He came in the next moment, spurted helplessly all over her Indian quilt.

Her laughter stayed with him for days.

W as there, Alicia wondered, a moral to this story? Because maybe someday she would get a story out of it. What other consolation was there? The affair had already, at least, inspired part of a poem. The lines she'd written the afternoon before meeting Jake were becoming a poem for him:

> *The men I dance for work in boxes,*
> *And pay too many unspoken taxes,*
> *All joined at the neck by an unseen yoke;*
>
> *But you're of a tribe that carries axes,*
> *With danger trailing you like a cloak*
> *And irises eaten away by smoke.*
>
> *You came to me always from fire or sun,*
> *Forged in a different furnace each day . . .*

That was all she had so far. There were other stray lines she wanted to work in. Fragments jotted down in her notebook like scraps waiting to be fitted into a quilt. *You gave me a reason to give it away . . .*

The intercom finally sounded. She walked over and pressed the button that would admit Jake for the last time. Within a minute he was at her door.

"Hey, babe. Here are your keys."

His hair was damp and slicked back. He looked fresh and boyish, more handsome than usual.

"Thanks," she said, taking them. Her throat tightened as their fingers touched.

"Listen," he said. "I don't want a sad good-bye. We had such a great thing, nothing can ever take that away, and we're going to stay friends.

Okay? There's a firemen's benefit happening tonight, it's just a few blocks from here, I think it's going on right now. Why don't you come check it out with me?"

She recognized it as an offering. He could have made a cold, clean break but he was choosing not to. And she took it. Now, as before, she would take whatever she could get.

"That sounds nice," she said. "Just give me a few minutes to get ready."

The Brewery was crowded with women, children, and men in blue uniform shirts. Above the clamor was the sound of bagpipes. Jake seemed to know everyone. He pulled her through the throng to the bar.

"What do you want? A lite beer, right? Is Amstel okay?"

But as soon as the glass was in her hand, before he'd even gotten his own beer, Jake was suddenly tugging at her arm. "Hey," he said. "Listen—do you mind saying hello to someone real quick? I see a friend of mine I want you to meet."

"Sure," she said. He was already making his way across the room, pulling her by the wrist. He went up to another man and tapped him on the back.

"Alicia, I want you to meet this guy," he said. "This is my hero. Truly the bravest. Captain Jonah Malone."

The man turned.

Alicia saw his face and waited to be able to breathe. He was clean-shaven now, and about twenty years older, but there was no mistaking him.

Blue eyes still burned in his weathered face. The same scar, somewhat faded over the decades, curved along his throat. A few seconds went by before she could speak.

"It's you," she said.

Wake of the War

On the street in the South Bronx where Jonah grew up, there was a firehouse with a small side door. It opened on steps leading down to the cellar; it was where the milkman brought the milk. Jonah would crawl into that space and descend to the dim room beneath, where he could hear the booted feet of the men overhead. It was a sound that steadied him and made him feel safe.

What would bring him here? It could be anything. Sometimes his own house was cold and dark, with his old lady passed out on the couch and nothing but beer in the icebox. Other times, coming home, he could hear his parents fighting from the street. Then there were the nights he'd sneaked out of the house and knew better than to come back before the next day. Like the night of the high school dance, for instance; that was typical.

It was the last dance before school let out for the summer. St. Xavier—where he was in the ninth grade—had two dances a year: one in the fall and the other in the spring. They were held in the gym, and girls from Sacred Heart were brought over on a bus. There was a girl Jonah remembered from the last one, a girl with honey-colored hair and a light blue sweater. A lot of the Sacred Heart girls looked trashy and hard, but not her. Jonah didn't know her name. He had never talked to her. But he'd thought about her all these months, and the spring dance was the only way to see her again.

He had a ticket, paid for with his own money. Also with his own money, he got the Chinese man around the corner to starch his good shirt. He spent most of the afternoon shining his shoes and trying to comb his hair so it stayed flat in the back. Finally it was six o'clock and he was on his way out the door when his mother screeched at him from the kitchen.

"Jonah!"

If his father hadn't been there too, Jonah could have pretended not to hear. As it was, he was trapped. He stood there with his hand on the doorknob, hoping against hope that she just wanted him to bring her something.

"Yeah, Ma?"

"Get in here."

The kitchen air was heavy with Thunderbird. His mother was at the table, trying to pour the last of it into a glass. Her hands were shaking and half the liquor sloshed over the rim. She fixed him with a watery glare.

"Where do you think you're going?"

"The school's having a dance."

"Oh, and you think you're going to this dance? So every slut in shoe leather can rub her tits up against you? So you can end up in somebody's backseat knocking one of them up?"

"Ma," he said quietly. "It's just a dance."

"You ain't goin'. Not while I have breath in my body. I know those little plaid-skirted whores. You'll thank me one day."

He knew better than to argue. With his gaze trained on the linoleum, he said only, "C'mon, Ma."

His father's hand cracked against the side of his head. "Don't answer your mother back."

He had to wait until his father left for the corner bar to sneak out the back door. The dance was half over by the time he got there and he spent the rest of it standing against the wall. The girl with the honey-colored hair was there; she looked at him a few times and even smiled at him once. But he was too shy to talk to her and he didn't know how to dance anyway.

Afterward it was dangerous to go home. By the next day maybe it would be all right—there was a chance his father never knew he was gone and his mother wouldn't remember any of it. In the meantime, he was better off finding somewhere else to sleep.

There were old cots in the firehouse cellar, of army-green canvas and faulty wood. There were mildewed and moth-eaten blankets, worn-out boots and faded fire coats. He could make use of anything. Wrap an old turnout coat around him like a husk. Breathe in the stale scent of sweat and smoke. Garth would sense his presence sometimes and appear on the stairs. Garth was a lieutenant, a big man with rusty hair and a handlebar mustache.

"Is that you, Malone?"

"It's me."

"Anyone asks, I ain't seen you," Garth would say. He'd come over, sit down on the cot, drop an arm around Jonah's shoulders. "Your old man know where you are?"

Jonah would shrug.

"I never saw you," Garth would repeat. "You gonna be warm enough?" Or: "Have you eaten anything?"

If he had, it was something like a bowl of cold cereal, or Spaghetti-Os straight from the can. Garth would warm whatever was left of the company's dinner and bring it down to him, along with a clean blanket and pillow, before resuming discussion.

"What's going on at home, Malone?"

Jonah would shrug, look away.

Garth never pressed him. "Are you still goin' to school? You ain't dropped out, have you now?"

"I'm still goin'." Though St. Xavier with its yardstick-wielding priests was almost as bad as home.

"Look here, Malone. You can come to dinner at our house tomorrow night. My old lady's making fried chicken. How's your brother and sister?"

"They're all right."

Garth would turn then to other topics. "I just put twenty bucks on the Giants," he might say. "What do you think the point-spread will be?" As long as there was no alarm bell, Garth would sit with him. Talk to him about football or local politics. He'd ask Jonah's opinion seriously, man to man. "What do you think of Mattie McVeigh running for Council? You trust that one, Malone?" Sometimes he smoked his pipe.

Garth could talk a long time. He liked to tell stories, of fires he'd fought and of World War II. He had two medals for valor and a Purple Heart. He showed Jonah where he'd taken a bullet in the shoulder: a dent like a thumbprint aggravating an eagle tattoo. He showed the boy scars from where he'd been burned too, and there were plenty of those.

"It's a dangerous job, son," he liked to say, "but there's none better."

"The captain can't know about this, Malone," he'd say, "or I'm in trouble. You're a good kid, though. I know you a long time already. Your old man's a good guy too. He just gets a little confused. The bottle can turn a good man inside out."

"You stay away from it, Malone," he always concluded. "Don't start drinkin'. It's probably already in the blood with you. That's the way it is, it's in the blood. I seen it time and again. And stay out of the gangs. You listenin' to me? Just stay straight and clean and make it easy on yourself."

Jonah, full of his late dinner, lulled by Garth's nearness, dazed and bone tired, might drop off in the middle of conversation. Fall asleep with the aroma of pipe tobacco and a protective male presence watching over him: gentler than his father or the priests at St. Xavier or any grown man he'd ever known. Garth would arrange the blanket around him, pull it up to his chin. He would take the plates back upstairs, then come back down in the morning to wake Jonah in time for school.

There were others besides Garth. All the firemen were kind to him and always had been. Even when he was a little kid, they had taken him along in the truck, shown him the upstairs quarters and let him slide down the pole. They were different from the cops who were his father's friends, different from his father. Whenever his father touched him, even in affection, it was rough: stinging claps on the back, rabbit jabs to the shoulder. The firehouse was where he liked to be most and the men who worked there were the best men he knew.

Which was why, at age nineteen—even after the Marine's IQ test had revealed that he could be anything he wanted—what he wanted was to be a fireman. And he was willing to wait. The city couldn't take him until he was twenty-one—a hard pill to swallow after Vietnam had seen fit to take him at seventeen. But that was the way it was. In the meantime, there was boxing and men like Wes.

Boxing was a fix. It was way too late to go anywhere with it, but even as a dead end it kept his head together. It was a soul sport, it took everything out of you for a while: the rage, the hate, the killer instinct, even some of the fear.

It was his father who had taught him to box, when he was seven or eight years old. It was about the only thing they did together: put on the gloves and go at it in the backyard. Everything faded when they sparred: the street noise and crickets, the passing cars. His father's hoarse commentary filled up the night.

Get your hands up! You're wide open. Move, move! Come on and hit me.

It was just the two of them. Sometimes they went on until long after dark, and then they were boxing under the stars. After a while, instruction always gave way to reminiscence. His father could feint and cross and hook without missing a beat of his boyhood stories.

When I was a kid, I come fresh off the boat to the Bronx we're standing in right now. I was a little immigrant mick what talked funny and the big boys on the block used to nail me with potatoes. Every damn day they chased me around, wonder I didn't turn into a champion runner. I'm showin' you the ol' one-two so you're better off than your old man. Don't ever run from a fight, you hear? It don't matter if you ain't the biggest guy around. You just gotta have heart. Look at Rinty Monaghan.

He never forgot a word his father said, and he never lost his love of boxing. Even after the war, it still meant something. The ring was a real place. In the midst of civilian life and all its restraints, there was still a corral where men stripped down to almost nothing and tried to beat each other senseless. This was terrain he recognized. It almost got him high—to wrap his hands and slam them into the stiffness of the heavy bag, into the rhythmic resistance of the ceiling weight, into flesh and muscle and bone. He loved the dance, he loved the sweat, he loved the marvelous agreement with the other to climb through the ropes and hammer away at each other. To *take* it, and give it, close enough to see each other's pores, the bands of color within the iris. No matter who the opponent was or where he was coming from, there was something important they shared: the need to grapple and jab, let knuckle speak to bone.

On the street afterward, bruised and purged, he had the closest thing to peace he'd known in years. He had *taken* it again, absorbed his punishment; he had bought his freedom for the evening. The ache in his muscles, the tender places, were like a stamp across a private receipt: PAID.

Now he could have a drink if he wanted, have several—the cold burn in his throat sealing it all like wax on the flap of an envelope. Now he could allow a woman to lay him down, tend to his aches with some temporary balm. Or he could go home with a rich man. Wes, if he was around. Lie back and float.

O n September 10, 1971, Wes Hansen turned forty. It was reasonable to think that half his life was over. There was no one special with whom to celebrate his birthday.

The day had been uneventful by design. He went to Mass that morning to kneel at the altar, take the body of Christ onto his tongue and thrill to the brief invasion of his mouth by the priest's hand.

He could not look at this priest. There was the issue of his own desires, which the priest knew from confession, and though there was never any acknowledgment of these outside the dark booth, it was still impossible to meet the other man's eyes.

After Mass, he put in an ordinary day at the management consulting job that had, over the last decade, afforded him a penthouse apartment on Manhattan's Upper East Side, a second home in Westport, Connecticut, and an enviable collection of art.

Night, and perhaps the angst of such a mundane milestone birthday, had brought him to The Hellfire Club in the eleventh hour. He had been here before, more as voyeur than participant. There were back rooms that he had never set foot in, for all the hours spent at the bar.

He had heard of the glory holes where men serviced each other, and were served, without so much as a glimpse of the other's face. It seemed to him just another kind of confessional booth: a place where you knelt in anonymity, with the admission that you were no better than an animal, and got your due.

Wes wasn't at Hellfire for any of that. He was here to contemplate boys like Jonah.

Jonah in 1971 was still a wild-eyed kid, just out of Vietnam and strung tight enough to snap. He was on the fire department waiting list and marking time: boxing at the Soul Gym by day and hustling subtly at night, haunting the netherworld in his fatigues, still trembling.

Even in a club like Hellfire, Jonah had an unnerving presence. He had a feral gaze and a stealthy way of moving. His eyes were always set in a narrowed stare, as if he were sighting along the barrel of a gun. People tended to stay out of his way.

The club on that night was packed and heated. The cement walls were washed in red fluorescent light. Everyone there was dressed in leather or some semblance of a uniform. The space was crowded with dungeon masters, drill sergeants, cowboys, and cops.

Wes's reputation as a generous tipper had earned him a tacit exemption from the club's dress code. He could sit at the bar in a tailored suit and no one would bother him. Furthermore, experience had shown that even this attire could draw its share of interest here. There were always a few who would condone it, conjure some persona they could work with. Some men looked at him and saw Daddy, the headmaster, or the boss. Necessity had proven the mother of tireless invention.

When Wes saw Jonah at the other end of the bar, he felt the old rush. He saw in a flash that the boy contained all he had yearned to rub up against in his own youth (and hadn't)—hard initiations, back alleys, danger. His face was blank and cold, but Wes could see the boy was scared. Strutting like a rooster to cover up the cringing dog.

"Another Dewar's, Mr. Hansen?" Gregory, the bartender, picked up his empty glass.

"Please, Gregory. Thank you. And Gregory," he motioned the other man closer, "please don't look just yet, but that boy in the corner . . . our little toy soldier . . . ? Might you know something about him?"

"Mr. Hansen, that one is no one's toy. No sir, he's the true blue—an ex-Marine and combat vet to boot. From what I understand, he just did two back-to-back tours over there. I've heard him called G.I. Joe Malone. But never to his face."

Wes took a moment to absorb these thrilling credentials.

"Is he usually with anyone?" he asked at last.

"It's my impression that he's a free agent." These words were accompanied by a wry glance.

"Well, then—from what you've seen, has he a 'type'?"

More cynical still: "He seems to like money."

As if this were bad news! When Wes showed no sign of censure, the barman asked, "Did you want to send him a drink?"

"Please, Gregory. Anything he wants." Wes placed a fifty-dollar bill on the bar.

He watched anxiously as Gregory approached the boy and did not relax until a drink was in the making. A moment later the bartender returned to Wes with a shot of Scotch and his change. In his elation, Wes waved the money away.

"Thank you, Mr. Hansen!" Gregory said, then added: "The kid wanted a Kamikaze."

As soon as the barman moved away, Wes looked over in an attempt to catch the boy's eye. But he was no longer there.

A touch on his shoulder. He turned to meet those flinty blue eyes. The boy was miraculously easing himself onto the empty barstool beside his own. "Thanks for the drink, sir. Can I join you?"

Jonah was nineteen when he came back from overseas. As a platoon sergeant in Vietnam, he'd led dozens of men into situations where their next collective breath hinged on his intuition. There was nothing to go on but instinct; you couldn't even trust the dirt beneath your feet. It was a different jungle he was navigating now, but he hadn't lost his knack for split-second assessments.

At first sight, he could tell that Wes was a flawless prospect. Nothing irked him more than most of the men in this kind of club: dressed up to look tough, strutting in macho costumes. What had they ever faced in their lives, to earn their airs?

Wes, at least, had no shred of pretension. What he did have was class. And Jonah's instant read on him—anxious, mild-mannered, eager to please—would prove right on the money. Wes would be an inexhaustible sugar daddy who wanted almost nothing back. Sexually, he wanted only to put out, not get off. And this was crucial, for although Jonah knew many straight hustlers who would endure penetration for the right price, he himself had suffered it only once—a lifetime ago—and if the blade he carried now had anything to say, it wasn't going to happen again.

This incident had gone down in Central Park—a landscape that, at night, was a country of its own, where the trees seemed a harbor for free-floating souls, the bodies slipping between them so swift and hidden they were gone in the time it took for a double-take. Jonah had left a party and, as usual, didn't want to go home. He was sixteen, getting old for Garth to be taking care of him. He was light-headed with beer and the night was warm. So he decided, with a drunk's nerve, to sleep on a park bench.

It started with a dream of being flattened by a bulldozer. He woke facedown on the cold bench to someone sitting on his back. It was a man's weight, and a man's heavy hand holding the back of his neck so he couldn't raise his head.

He would never know how many of them there were. His bomber jacket was wrapped around his head so he couldn't see, couldn't yell, could barely breathe. Through it all, his worst terror was that he would suffocate before they were through with him.

Torn open. Plowed like so much dirt. Close to passing out from the pain, but finally no such luck. Pounded so hard that he was sure something inside him was broken.

They took turns, spitting in the crack of his ass first. Over and over, his head was picked up and slammed into the seat of the bench, the jacket that hooded him probably saving his skull.

So there was a major service Jonah did not provide to the rich men who took care of him. In fact, there were several. But there were always a few who craved something more than sex—like a good working over with Jonah's belt, for instance, or something even easier. Once a guy had paid seventy-five bucks just to lick his boots.

"Are you here most nights?" this Hansen was asking.

"Nah, just once in a while."

"Where can you be found the rest of the time?"

"Sometimes I'm at Cellblock." Like earlier that night, in fact.

The older man winced before he could stop himself.

"What's the matter?" Jonah asked. "Cellblock too hard-core for you?"

"Well. Let's just say I think it takes fantasy to an unhealthy extreme."

Jonah felt one corner of his mouth jerk up. Since coming back from overseas, this was the closest his face came to smiling.

"What's so funny?" the other wanted to know.

Jonah was thinking of what he'd seen in the can at Cellblock just a few hours ago—the guy kneeling between two urinals with his mouth open. Men wandering in to relieve themselves sent a near-steady stream of piss down his throat. The more enthusiastic ones made a point of splashing his face and neck.

"You call that stuff fantasy?" Jonah asked. "That's as close to real as those guys are ever gonna get."

He shouldn't have said that. This trick was never going to know what he was talking about. Sure enough:

"Those antics can hardly be called reality," the older man said. "By day, hard as it may be to believe, most of those men are respectable professionals."

"Yeah," Jonah said, "but that's the fantasy."

The trick seemed taken by surprise. He looked at Jonah for a long time before answering. "That's—well, that's an interesting perspective," he said at last. "I suppose you can see it either way—and I suppose it depends on what your fantasy is."

"What's yours?" Jonah asked. It was, after all, his business to know. The john's fantasy was the most important weapon in a hustler's arsenal.

The other smiled faintly. He held out both hands. "It's you."

I t wasn't a line. Wes had no lines. Jonah embodied every ache Wes woke up with in the morning and went to sleep with every night, and all he wanted was to take the boy home. After their fourth round, he put in his bid.

"You know, I have plenty of tequila at my place," he told Jonah. "And plenty of room too, if you'd like to stay."

The boy hesitated. "I don't—you know—do anything," he said at last.

"I won't ask you to."

It was a vow of sorts, one from which Wes would never waver. He took Jonah home, mixed him several more drinks, let him soak in the Jacuzzi while his clothes were in the wash and turned down the bed for him.

"I'm going to stay up for a while," Wes told him. In fact, he was to stay up until morning, not daring that first night to even get into his own bed. Instead, he lingered in the doorway like a watchdog, hour upon hour, watching Jonah sleep. When the sun came up, he fed the boy breakfast, gave him money, and asked him to come back that night.

From that day on, there was never another boy for him. Wes took Jonah under his soft, manicured wing and tried to give him anything he wanted; brought him to Broadway shows and SoHo galleries and five-star restaurants; taught him which fork to pick up first and how to use a pepper mill.

More than anything, Wes loved teaching the boy about art. He took pride in the fact that an afternoon with him was as educational as any guided tour. He could hold forth on nearly any painting: the quirks of the painter, the trends of its period, what phase it represented in the artist's career. He imparted all of this information to Jonah who, surprisingly, absorbed it without resistance, sometimes even with interest.

They were in the Museum of Modern Art when Jonah stopped in front of that masterpiece as familiar to Wes as his driver's license photo, an immense canvas that commanded its own wall. The painting rendered five naked women in a semicircle. From left to right, their faces were increasingly distorted, until the last one crouched behind what appeared to be a mask.

"What about this one, Wes?" Jonah asked. Apparently the boy had never seen or even heard of it before. He was innocence itself—precious, priceless.

"You are looking at what is likely the most important painting of the twentieth century," Wes told him.

"*This?*"

"This is it."

"Well, what is it?"

"This is Picasso's *Les Demoiselles d'Avignon*," Wes told him. "The setting is a turn-of-the-century brothel in Barcelona."

"Brothel?"

"A bordello."

When Jonah's look of confusion didn't change, Wes tried again. "A whorehouse."

"Oh," Jonah said. He turned back to the painting. "Those are some scary-lookin' whores."

Wes suppressed a smile.

"Why is this one painting so important?" the boy wanted to know.

"Well, because it's generally considered to have marked the birth of Cubism."

"Oh," Jonah said again. And then: "Who's that?"

Jonah's own preferences emerged over time, reliable in their otherworldly darkness. He was drawn to the madness of Van Gogh and the delirium of Chagall, the bleak landscapes of Edvard Munch and the blue period of Picasso. He liked the theater too and even liked the opera. It was a startling pleasure to experience art with someone who never put on airs, who didn't struggle to seem erudite, but just looked and listened and spoke without guile. Wes took him all around the city, to permanent exhibits and visiting shows and private collections. Whenever Jonah expressed a special interest, Wes bought him the relevant books or postcards or prints.

Despite all the time they spent together, Jonah would never belong to Wes. He came and went as he pleased. And often he was wild, out late, head spinning with cocaine or mescaline or any other substance available to him—all generously mixed with alcohol—consorting, too, with all kinds of promiscuous women and other marginal characters. But he knew he could always stagger uptown to Wes's—at any ungodly hour, in any condition—and be taken in, no questions asked. Wes was provider and protector, father and mother, benefactor, patron. And so Jonah returned to him, maybe even cared about him. Wes understood that the boy also despised him in a way—on some level, Jonah would despise anyone who loved him—but he kept coming back.

Their relationship barely ventured into the physical realm. If Jonah harbored any sexual desire for men, he never revealed it, and he preferred not to even receive bodily ministrations, let alone reciprocate. This was not only acceptable to Wes, it was virtually essential—Wes whose devout Catholicism made other gay men abhorrent to him, and sex all but impossible anyway. In the beginning, though, they did share a bed: Jonah tolerating Wes's arm around him, or the older man's shoulder beneath his head. It was enough; more than enough. It was a male presence next to him, the epitome of male; fresh from war, the terrible war that had been the epicenter of such high drama for so long. He was a *boy*, a tough little boy with cold blue eyes; a *prize*, hard and compact and impenetrable. But look—here they were, together. For long hours at a stretch, whole nights, there was a room with no one in it but Wes and Jonah.

These hours did not always go unbroken. One black Connecticut night, maybe two hours before dawn, Wes woke to find the other side of the bed empty. Reaching out, he touched only cold sheets. The bathroom was dark and the door ajar—he wasn't in there. Instinctively, Wes knew he wasn't in the house at all and hadn't been for some time.

Later—years, decades later—Jonah would describe to Wes how he knew, always, where to go in a fire. How there might be a dozen other men covering several floors of a burning building, searching every inch for a baby reported inside. And how then he would enter the building himself, crawling in the dark, unable to see or hear, and go straight to the baby as if guided by radar.

In his own life Wes had only a single experience with which to compare this phenomenon, and that was descending his own stairs in the dark and going out onto the front lawn of his house, where unaided by streetlight or porch light or flashlight he would cross the dew-soaked grass in his bare feet to find Jonah curled beneath some shrubbery.

Asleep. The kid would do that. Post-traumatic stress disorder, as it came to be called: he actually felt safer, more acclimated or something, out there. Wes would rouse him gently, clumsily.

"C'mon, son. Let's go back inside."

And Jonah would stumble—somnolent, somewhat shame-faced—back into the house. Back to bed.

After some time Wes noted that a certain combination of factors worked to avert this nocturnal sojourn. In fact, if the older man was especially careful, Jonah would not only sleep through the night, but even rest easy. Left to his own devices, Jonah was fitful, agitated and sweating; he had nightmares. But if Wes took certain measures that had proven effective over time, it seemed that the boy's demons might be kept at bay. It was important that he eat well but not too late at night. A stretch of several quiet hours afterward was desirable, in which Jonah could drink a moderate amount of wine while listening to one of Wes's recordings—something calm, like Brahms, or maybe Debussy. Then a long soak in the Jacuzzi, with the water as hot as he could stand and the massage jets on high. After all this, wrapped in the older man's velvet bathrobe with the drawstring hood, Jonah might fall into a rare peaceful sleep, his troubled face reassuming a sweet boyishness, his breathing deep and regular. And Wes would experience an infrequent feeling of real accomplishment, of having brought about a priceless circumstance.

Jonah found that the more time he spent with Wes, the less necessary the rest of the racket became, and after a while he stopped hustling altogether. It got to where Wes was the one fixed point on his blurred terrain: the point of return. The rest of the time was drift and delirium: hammered in the ring by day, medicated by night in what he thought of as the netherlands, that underground realm where everything seemed to move in slow motion, in a haze of sweat and heat.

Wes didn't keep him from these places, nor from the females he went with. The after-hours clubs were as much a fix as the alcohol. Going there was like climbing back through a window into the territory he had so recently come from.

The nights in these clubs had a rhythm of their own. He'd come in with a woman after several hours of drinking, strike up easy conversation with some like-minded couple. Soon the women would be on their knees, while the men passed a bong back and forth.

After a while the women would trade places.

Before long, even the tighter couples tended to drift apart, surrender to the fray, until everything melted into the same dizzy dream: bodies to be taken, mouths to swallow him. Painted lips and knowing hands. It was one long rush, a headlong nightly flight into the wild.

Wes was a place to land.

Jonah remembered reading something about what to do for newborn kittens that had been separated from their mother. A heating pad and ticking clock wrapped in a blanket, a baby bottle filled with milk, and the blind orphaned animals wouldn't know the difference.

Sometimes in that place between sleep and waking—with the warmth of an older, softer body beside his own, the heartbeat against his ear—Jonah too could almost be deceived. It settled in softly, spoke directly to the body—the faint shadow, lost promise, of something like home.

═══

The call came in February of 1973, to report to the Fire Academy on Welfare Island—The Rock, as it was called—for twelve weeks of basic training. The idea was familiar: boot camp, but this time the point was saving lives instead of taking them.

There were a couple of other vets at the Academy. They liked to joke that after Parris Island, the Rock was not a hard place. It was true; the training was easy for him and afterward he was assigned to Ladder 119, by the Brooklyn Navy Yard. Jerry Fitzgerald was in the housewatch when he arrived on his first day. He was smoking a pipe and, except for a hint of gray amidst the red, his whiskers were just like Garth's.

"Probationary firefighter Jonah Malone reporting as ordered, sir," Jonah said.

"Malone!" the man said. "I've got your file right here. How ya doin'—I'm one of the senior guys in the company. Jerry's the name."

"Good to meet you, sir."

"Sir. Ha. I like that. I don't have to guess where you've been, I got it right in my hands. Malone, it says here that you completed a nine-month tour in Vietnam and then volunteered to go back for another one."

"That's right, sir."

"And now you want to be one of New York's Bravest."

"Yes, sir."

"Well, son, I'd say you're overqualified."

He hadn't expected a kind word so soon. The seasoned firefighters were supposed to be hard-assed bastards and probationary firemen knew to expect some months of hazing. The FNGs—fuckin' new guys—came in ready to suck it up and bust their balls till they proved their worth. But here was one of the senior members of the company, treating him like he already had.

He took care not to cringe, then, at the other man's next words.

"And it also says you were a Golden Gloves contender last year. I been waiting my whole career for a kid like you. Boxing is the only sport where the cops can ever whup us. Next Friday night I'm gonna put you up against their boy, this big dago bastard they've been parading around all winter. Sammy Santangelo. He's gone undefeated since Christmas and it's getting on my nerves."

This did not seem like the time to explain that he'd wanted his start on the job to mark the end of boxing—that he meant to lay the gloves down forever and let his fight be with fire.

Still, he had only boxed in the middleweight division. This big dago bastard sounded like a heavyweight. What if he went down, or even got knocked out in front of everyone? Jerry might dust him off as fast as he'd taken him in. But wouldn't that happen anyway, and sooner, if he didn't at least give it a shot?

"All right," he finally answered, then realized there had never been a question.

"Next Friday night, now. Don't line up any early evening dates. I'll take you down there after work. New York's Finest'll never know what hit 'em."

That was how he found himself in crimson trunks in one corner of a Brooklyn boxing ring. His trunks were printed with the letters FDNY and he felt those letters through the material like they were branded into his flank. They were worth whatever he had to do.

This Santangelo had several inches on Jonah, not to mention about forty pounds. He was well over six feet tall, with eyes so heavy-lidded they seemed half-closed. He looked puffed up as if by steroids and hot air, and he bobbed in his corner of the ring like a giant blow-up doll. Cops and firemen were filling the bleachers, placing their bets.

Jonah leaned back against the ropes. Jerry was behind him, squeezing his shoulders and rattling into his ear.

"Now look son, you're the great Irish hope tonight, you're the ace up the fire department's sleeve. You're goin' out there for the sisters of Erin. For the brotherhood. For the motherland! I know you can take this guinea son of a bitch, I seen it in your eyes day one. Every underdog has his day and this is gonna be your night. All right? Make us proud—"

Santangelo was lit from behind, featureless, a grotesque silhouette with bulbous hands. His elongated shadow crept across the floor, lapping at Jonah's feet. And Jonah, in the ring for father love—again—was sweating already, almost sick by the time the referee's whistle split the air.

Then Santangelo took the first swing and Jonah knew everything was going to be all right. His opponent didn't know how to move; he hit like a dying wind-up toy. You could see everything—even his jabs—coming from a mile away, and in Jonah's heightened state, the other seemed to be moving in slow motion. *Bap-bap-bap-bap-bap:* it was like knocking at one of those inflated clowns that kept bouncing back.

Relief made him generous. He played with Santangelo, held him at bay without finishing him off, pulled his punches so as not to do real damage. He drew out the match, let it go a full nine rounds.

Afterward, at Paddy Reilly's, he was surrounded by firemen vying to buy him drinks. Jerry was nearly bursting with pride.

"The minute I laid eyes on this kid, I was knowin' he could whip that wop. Tell me I ain't got an eye for 'em, now!"

Shots of tequila lined the bar. He was surrounded by smiling faces, acceptance and admiration. Too good, it was almost too good. Like flying on smack with no built-in crash just ahead.

"Malone!" Jerry was jostling his arm. Jonah looked up to see another man standing with the lieutenant. "This is someone you want to know. He's an officer from Ladder 154, the coach of the fire department football team, and as fine a man as they come: Lieutenant Seamus O'Day. Seamus, this is our new boy, Jonah Malone. He just come on the job last week."

Seamus O'Day towered above most of the other men in the bar, a strapping square-jawed man, but the paw he extended was surprisingly gentle. "Do you play football?" he asked as they shook.

"No, sir," Jonah admitted.

"Listen to him!" Jerry crowed. "Did you ever hear such a polite, well-mannered kid? He calls everybody 'sir'! He thinks he's still in the Marines."

"He's a hell of a fine kid," this Seamus O'Day agreed. "And I'm gonna buy him a drink." He turned to the bartender. "Give us a couple more shots over here."

He eased himself onto the seat beside Jonah's. "I like the way you handled yourself in that ring," he said.

"Sir?"

"You pulled your punches for one thing. That was a class act on your part."

Jonah was too surprised to say anything.

Seamus laughed. "You were afraid at first. That's all right. In the right measure, fear is your friend. Guy didn't know the first thing, did he? But you couldn't know that till he came at you."

"How . . . " Jonah trailed off.

"I'm a coach, son. I can read an athlete's attitude from a mile down the sidelines. The body has a language, and it never lies."

The two shots of tequila came and Seamus knocked his glass against Jonah's. "Hell, anyone would've been scared," the lieutenant went on. "The other guy was a lot bigger than you. But that just made you the crowd favorite." He smiled with one side of his mouth. "On the football field, the little guys used to surprise me," he told Jonah. "Not anymore."

Jonah felt a pang of regret. "I guess I'm too old to start, huh? At football."

"Well, most guys your age what never touched the ball, I'd tell yes."

"What about me?"

"Son, I'd suit you up in a Brooklyn minute if I thought that's where your heart was. I can look at you and see you could do anything you wanted. But that ain't where you're at anymore. See, you don't want to hurt anyone," he explained. "And most of the time that's a real good thing. But it ain't a good thing on the football field."

"What about boxing?" Jonah wanted to know.

"In the end, boxing ain't about hurting the other guy," Seamus said. "It's about gettin' hurt."

Jonah wondered if the lieutenant knew everything.

"But I'm gonna have my eye on you," Seamus told him. "And I don't mind sayin' I think Jerry's got a real good break here. Because son, you're gonna keep making the fire department proud. And he's one of the lucky dogs what's gonna get to show you the way."

———

The first person Jonah pulled from a fire never recovered consciousness.

It was his sixth month on the job and his first four-alarm fire. The second story of a Clinton Hill tenement was burning, and a woman who lived alone in apartment 2A was by all accounts still inside. Flames were blowing so hard out of the second-floor window that the men couldn't get within five feet of it. They had the ladder positioned at the third floor, with the red devil—as they called it—raging just below. Jonah ran up the rungs and as he neared the window he got his first taste of the fire, a heat no one could stand up against.

There on the ladder a sudden memory came to him, a memory of his mother testing the iron. He saw her licking a finger and touching it to the metal; he heard the sizzling hiss. And just as suddenly he knew how to go about it: in and out and in. He ran up and broke the third-story window like touching the iron, a sucker punch to the pane, then backed down several rungs and got ready to dive in. It was like boxing, that dance around the opponent: in with a jab, dancing out of reach, then in again with the knockout punch. He was nothing now but his breath and adrenaline and the picture in his head, a clear and curiously fearless picture of himself diving through the window, and he got a running start back up the ladder when he heard his name through the roar.

"Malone!"

The authority in that voice stopped him in his tracks. He peered over his shoulder. The chief was standing at the foot of the ladder, screaming like a drill sergeant from the street.

"Back off, Malone! Back the fuck off!"

He didn't think he could be hearing right. There was supposed to be a woman inside. Jonah stood frozen on the rungs, unable to process the command.

"Malone, goddammit, get the fuck down from there! I'm telling you to get the fuck down!"

It was an order from a superior officer. Jonah clambered back down and stood on the sidewalk while they moved the ladder to the fourth-story window. He had to run up the extra distance and enter apartment 2A from the interior of the building. Four stories up and two back down, several precious minutes fucked away in the meantime.

The woman's bedroom was black with smoke. No air to breathe except what was in his mask, and no visibility, but Jonah found her right away, almost tripped over her body. She was facedown on the floor. Jonah dragged her out and across the hall to the opposite apart-ment, which wasn't burning yet. She seemed heavy for her size; it was his first encounter with what they all called deadweight. He radioed for backup and started giving her CPR.

It wasn't until he was in the back of the ambulance—he insisted on staying with her on the way to the hospital—that Jonah got a real look at her. She was a sweet little thing with dark hair and pale skin, long eyelashes. He had managed to get her breathing again but her eyes never opened. After forty-five minutes in the waiting room, where he realized for the first time that his own ears were burnt, an orderly came over to him.

One look at the guy's face told him what he already knew.

"She's gone," Jonah said.

The orderly nodded. He said very quietly, "The doctor pronounced her at 9:17."

Jonah didn't move. The orderly put a gentle hand on his shoulder. "You need to let someone take care of those ears."

"What was her name?" Jonah asked him.

The other consulted his clipboard. "Jo Malone," he said after a moment.

"What? No, *I'm* Joe Malone. What was *her* name?"

"Talk about fate," he would say later at Ryan McFadden's Pub, where he would stay until the barmaid was mopping the floor around his feet. His first loss on the job, a woman with the same name as him. It was eerie, brushing up against odds like that. It rattled him so much he asked if he could see her again.

If the doctors thought it was a strange request, they didn't say anything. The orderly brought him to the room where she lay and left him alone with her. He stood beside the door a moment holding his helmet, then went up to her bed. The prayer that came to him was nothing he remembered from any Mass, but a fragment of a poem: "Do not go gentle into that good night . . . " he whispered.

It was a long time before he could lift the sheet from her face. Though her color was going, she did not seem lifeless yet, just asleep. Jo—(Josie? Joanna?)—Malone. He touched the lips he had pressed his own against, just two hours—a lifetime—ago. They were cold.

Why had he listened to that fucking chief? How many minutes had he wasted? If he'd been there two minutes earlier, she would be alive. He would have got burned but Christ, he got burned anyway, his ears were all blistered. He would be hurting worse, maybe even bad enough to take him out of the action for a little while but he would have got her and she would have been all right.

"Why'd I listen to that guy?" he said to Jerry, who'd joined him at the bar for the first couple of rounds.

"I'll tell you why," Jerry said. "Because he's the fuckin' *battalion chief*. Now look here, Malone. You just started, for cryin' out loud. It's too early to be a fuckin' vigilante. I know you seen a lot of action before comin' on the job and that makes you a little different from other probies. But this ain't a cowboy operation here. You got to listen to your superiors and take direction, right or wrong."

"Two minutes earlier and I would have got her. All that fuckin' around with the ladder was nothin' but a waste of time."

"Malone, that ain't up to you to decide. The chief called it like he saw it—you listenin' to me?—and he saw an untenable situation. He can't send his men into an untenable situation; he's got his own conscience to contend with."

"I ain't blamin' him. I blame myself for listenin' to him."

"Look, Malone. I know you're hurtin'. It hurts every time you lose someone. This was the first time for you, but I can tell you right now, you're gonna lose more of 'em and it's gonna keep hurtin'. It's one thing to feel bad. That's all right—you can't do nothin' about that. But what you're doin' now ain't no good to nobody."

"Two minutes earlier," Jonah said again. "And she'd be makin' eyes at that orderly right now."

Jerry gave up halfway through the third round.

"Listen, son. Try to get some sleep," he said. He let his hand rest a moment on Jonah's arm before walking out the door.

Jonah stayed at the bar by himself.

Do not go gentle into that good night . . .

How long had he stood whispering at her bedside, before he realized he was talking to himself?

The second person Jonah took from fire was a five-year-old girl who not only lived, but got out unscarred and scot-free. It was his first successful rescue and everything about it seemed blessed, graced. For one thing, it happened on a holiday, St. Patrick's Day, 1974. An important day for many firemen: an army of them had marched in uniform in that afternoon's parade and by now were staggering cross-eyed from bar to bar. Jonah was working; he had volunteered. He found that he liked to work holidays, to stay on watch while everyone else went to parties.

The firehouse dinner that night was a fancy affair. There was one other Irishman working the night tour and he made Jonah baste the lamb and slice potatoes for the soup. There was soda bread and blancmange pudding and sugar cookies cut into shamrocks. They got through the supper without a call and were loading the sink when at 21:42 hours, Box 52 transmitted a 10-75—an "all hands" fire, calling for three engines and two trucks.

Jonah felt a thrill whenever the alarm sounded, a thrill that never went away. It was the moment the men became a platoon. The handball match in the backyard would be dropped at game point, talk cut off mid-sentence, dinner left to get cold as the men moved as one toward strangers in need. If it was the middle of the night, they all jumped out of bed and hit the ground running. They came when they were called, unwavering as a military response, *no excuse, sir, there is no excuse.*

Now as Ladder 119 approached 154 Lorimer Street, he could see that fire lit the top two floors and the usual crowd had formed in the front yard. Jonah scanned the front of the building for trapped occupants and saw just two: a young woman clutching a baby at a fourth-story window. She had three minutes, maybe four, before the heat would make her desperate. She would probably try to throw the baby to someone below, then she would probably jump. Jonah had already seen people jump from much higher places; fire made checking out that way an easy choice.

The street was beyond fucked, every inch of the curb blocked by double-parked cars. There was no space for the rig to pull up close to the burning building, so the chauffeur of the truck did the only thing he could do: he started raising the aerial ladder to the window from several buildings away. This was a safety hazard in itself: a severely extended position would threaten an aerial ladder's hydraulic seals, create the danger of a collapse. This was all Jonah had time to see before being ordered to assist the roofman in searching the premises from the rear.

The next few minutes were a blur. He took the adjoining tenement's interior stairway to the roof, then crossed over the parapet to the burning building. Jerry was the roofman and Jonah could see at a glance that most of the ventilation was under way. The bulkhead door was open. The skylight and draft-stop were shattered. The other man had the partner-saw fired up and was starting his coffin cut. Jerry never passed up the chance to instruct him, and he started in the minute Jonah joined him.

"I'm sure I don't have to tell you this, Malone, but when you're making your cut, always stand with the wind at your back. That way, when the flames come up, they're blowing away from you. Sounds like common sense but you wouldn't believe how many assholes don't think about it. Okay now, get behind me, it's gonna blow." Two seconds later, a column of flame shot straight into the sky. Jerry tugged him toward the rear fire escape. They went down the gooseneck ladder to the top-floor balcony. Jerry took out the window with his six-foot hook, smashing the glass and mullions in one motion. "Always turn your window into a door, Malone. Got that? Knock the whole thing out clean. You want to leave yourself an easy exit."

Next he went to work on the window gate, using the fork end of his Halligan tool to pop the hinges. "And look here, always go for the hinges, Malone. Don't waste time with the locks."

As the gate gave way and Jerry kicked it in, an urgent message came over the radio. The woman and her infant had been removed, but her five-year-old daughter was still trapped on the fourth floor.

"All right, look, Malone, I'm gonna search this flat," Jerry said. "You drop down and grab the kid."

Jonah took the fire escape to the fourth story, where he knocked out the window and gate just as Jerry had done above.

Luckily the child's bedroom was at the rear of the building and had just begun to burn. She was sitting up in bed and when he saw her, time slowed the way it did with the help of his late-night narcotics. He was able to take in every detail of the picture before him: the tears on her face, the quilted pattern on the bedspread. Her whole body seemed to blaze with light. In her white nightgown, she was like a vision. Real this time instead of chemical: a vision of his redemption.

Adrenaline was pulsing in his muscles and the little girl seemed almost weightless when he picked her up. "It's okay, honey," he said. He pressed her to his side and pulled his coat around her. "It's okay, don't be scared. I've got you."

Remembering the compromised aerial, he radioed for a portable ladder. Even as he did, he realized it would not reach the fourth floor, so he took the rear stairwell to the third. Here the smoke was much lighter and as he made his way to the front of the apartment, Jonah could see Pete McTigue through the jagged remains of a window, knocking at the last stubborn shards with his ax. The other man was on the portable ladder, waiting to carry the child down to the ground.

Jonah approached with the girl.

"Any others?" McTigue asked. He laid the ax on the windowsill and reached out with both arms.

"Last one," Jonah said. And then, to the little girl, "Okay, honey, Pete's gonna take you now." Over McTigue's shoulder he could see the woman who had been in the fourth-story window just minutes before.

Now that the baby was safe, three or four cops were trying to keep her from running back into the fire for her other child.

"My little girl!" she was screaming. Animal screams. She was fighting like an animal too. "My little girl's in there!"

"We've got her, ma'am!" McTigue called from the ladder.

And in the wake of this announcement, everything seemed to go still, suspended in the moment like a breath caught and held. Then a whoop went up from the lawn. Everyone below—the whole crowd of neighbors, firefighters, paramedics and cops—broke into cheers.

Jonah felt a rush as powerful as a hit of acid. This time, everything was going to be all right. They'd made it in time; luck had been on their side; what was irreplaceable had been saved.

Jonah moved to lift the child from his hip. She held on a moment, looking into his face.

"C'mon, honey, Pete's gonna take you now. I have to stay here and help put out the fire."

She released him wordlessly but continued to hold him with her gaze as McTigue locked her inside his right arm. They started down the ladder.

"C'mon, smile," begged the photographer from the *Daily News*.

"I am," Jonah told him.

I rescued a little girl.

Jonah tried out the phrase in the privacy of his apartment afterward. He had his own place now, a fifth-floor walk-up on Chrystie Street, just off Delancey on the Lower East Side of Manhattan. It was a tiny railroad flat, badly insulated and cold in the winter, but it was his. He could still stay at Wes's whenever he was feeling high maintenance. And when he wasn't, he could be alone.

I saved a child.

When he came back from Vietnam, they called him *baby killer*. The ones who had stayed behind, secure on the shores of home, safe from the land mines and the jungle and themselves. What would they call him now?

He had not killed any children. The only child he had killed was the one he had been. But he had spilled a lot of blood; no way around that. At close range and from afar. He had even killed an American soldier, a kid who panicked and fucked up, bolted into Jonah's peripheral vision when he was supposed to stay down. Shit like that happened all the time, nothing anyone could do about it.

But what did this rescue make him? And if he spent the rest of his life saving people, what would he be?

A beautiful little girl is alive right now because of me.

───

"**Y**ou're a hero!" Wes said, raising his glass. "But I already knew that."

"Come on, Wes," Jonah mumbled, uncomfortable and pleased. They were at Peter Luger's to celebrate the rescue. A bottle of Dom Perignon was off to one side, nestled in a silver pail of ice. Steak was on the way, a T-bone for Jonah and filet mignon for Wes.

They clinked glasses and Jonah took only a taste before setting his own back down. Ever since the rescue, a little bit of drink went a long way.

"This is only the beginning." Wes spoke with conviction.

"How do you know?" Jonah asked.

"I have a feeling," the older man said simply.

Jonah looked at Wes and saw what he always saw. It was plain and unmistakable and he drank it in not caring where it came from. It was love. Not kindness or pity or charity; not ownership or expectation. Just love.

Love that said: *You are so beautiful to me.* Love that said: *My home is your home.* And: *How was your day? You must be tired. Sit down and let me bring you a drink.*

The girls he went out with weren't like that. They were wildcats, brazen and clawing and thoughtless. Their one-room apartments were always small and shabby, with overflowing ashtrays and clothes all over the floor.

But Wes held out peace and comfort and quiet. His penthouse was high above the dark streets. The place was clean and there was plenty of room. Wes always had a stocked refrigerator and, all right, no hard stuff, but rack upon rack of very good wine. Jonah even had his own set of keys, with each one marked according to its lock.

Most important of all, there was that look in Wes's eyes. It was like sunlight on his face and he was ashamed of how he needed it; how he would take it, apparently, wherever it was offered.

"Tell me again. Every detail," Wes coaxed. "She was the last one left in the apartment."

"Right. Her mother and the baby were trapped at the front of the building. We took them down the aerial ladder even though it was overextended and dangerous."

"And the little girl's room was toward the back."

"Right. That's how come she wasn't unconscious from the smoke already."

"She was wide awake?"

"Sittin' straight up in bed. Sweetest thing you ever saw. She was scared though. She didn't know what was goin' on but she knew it wasn't nothing good."

"And Jerry Fitzgerald, the senior man in the company, shook your hand afterward and said, 'Good job.'"

"Yeah, he did."

"Can you imagine what it must be like," the older man sighed. "To be rescued by a fireman. It must be heaven."

"You're fucked in the head, Wes. You know that? Nuts."

"Just about you."

W es was to see his prediction borne out sooner than even he would have believed. Jonah saved two more people the following year, four the next. By the end of his first decade of firefighting, he had been cited for heroism on twenty-two occasions and accumulated a stunning array of medals. Five of them were for valor, the highest award the fire department had. Wes's file of newspaper clippings, each one meticulously cut out and mounted, was more than two inches thick. On nights when he felt especially low, he could get out his scrapbook of Jonah's rescues. This always buoyed his spirits when all else failed: the knowledge that he played a part in the life of such a man.

No one else had been as longtime a companion to Jonah. Wes watched the younger man through the seasons and over the years—watched and served and placated and provided. Even after Wes retired and Jonah was a lieutenant, making a very decent salary for a single man with no family to support—whenever they had dinner out, Wes took the check. It was the way they were.

When Jonah stopped by Wes's apartment for any reason, he was yielded the best chair while Wes fetched all of Jonah's favorite things from the kitchen: tequila, rice pudding, fresh fruit. The television was switched to whatever channel Jonah felt like watching: usually CNN, occasionally a boxing match. If Wes happened to have any special delicacy on hand, a gift from someone perhaps—Godiva chocolates, imported caviar—this was opened and laid out on the spot.

Jonah could always, of course, spend the night there if he wished, although he was no longer willing to sleep beside Wes. When he did stay over, Wes insisted that Jonah take the bed while he himself adopted the couch. And whenever Jonah was sick, Wes made chicken soup from scratch, went out for medicine, brought him orange juice and ginger ale. Doting on Jonah continued to bring him the greatest pleasure life had ever offered. It was better than the sex he remembered having in his twenties; better than opera, better than art.

But did Jonah love him?

Wes never really knew. Maybe love was too much to hope for. There were times when Jonah even seemed to hate him. And this was understandable, really. Nothing was more frightening than the unknown, and to the best of Wes's knowledge, Jonah had not experienced love before. Sometimes he went weeks without calling; sometimes he looked at Wes with open scorn. Once in a rare while, he would take up with some woman steadily. These affairs were always intense and, thank God, short-lived, but while they were going on, he could barely be bothered with Wes, would brush him off like a mosquito.

Far less important but occasionally worth pondering were his own feelings. It went without saying that he loved Jonah. But it would seem that Wes, too, was guilty of hatred. This had come out, reared its ugly but fascinating head on a handful—only a handful—of occasions in the past ten years. And whenever it did, Wes was helpless beside the stranger that was himself. Like that time Jonah had eye surgery, for instance. That was the worst, most unreal time.

Wes had accompanied Jonah to the eye doctor for some corrective surgery. Afterward, a nurse handed them a prescription for Tylenol with codeine, for the pain that would soon set in. One capsule had to be taken every four hours for the next twenty-four and Jonah was supposed to rest during that time—to sleep, if possible, until the next morning.

Jonah came home with Wes, and within about forty-five minutes, the pain set in as predicted. And Jonah—Jonah who could endure pain like no one Wes had ever known—Jonah was whimpering. "Wes, where's my codeine?"

Wes handed him a plain Tylenol from the bottle in his own medicine cabinet. "Here. The nurse said to give you one Tylenol every four hours."

It was a refrain he would repeat over and over like a doll that talked when you pulled its string, except his tone was different each time, by turns reasonable, gentle, pained, smug. Then nettled, impatient because Jonah seemed not to understand, and finally adamant, righteous, downright despotic. "Here's your Tylenol. I'm giving you what the nurse said to give you."

"Tylenol with *codeine*," Jonah bellowed, helpless and furious, frightened and blind. He could not open his eyes; the light made the pain even worse. And oh, how it hurt Wes to see his baby like this, but how delicious at the same time, how satisfying.

For the first time ever he could torture Jonah, make him suffer, listen to him beg. The city's great hero was sightless, reduced to utter helplessness, and Wes was presiding over it. He could take the pain away but he was choosing not to. He was finally punishing the man who never stopped punishing him. Perhaps when Jonah was able, he would retrieve his power to punish with a special vengeance. Perhaps he would beat Wes senseless—an idea not without some appeal. Certainly he would take some kind of revenge—the anticipation of which was skin-tingling.

But meanwhile he was howling. Baying. And finally, crying like a pup.

"For Christ's sake, Wes!"

The nurse said.
"Help me, goddamn you!"
To give you one Tylenol.
"I'll kill you motherfucker!"
Every four hours. I'm just following the nurse's orders.
"What do you want me to do, Wes? Tell me. Anything!"
The nurse said to give . . .
"You sick fuck!"

And on it went, Wes in a trance of horror and disbelief and unspeakable, vicious pleasure. Finally, well into the night, the pain seemed to lessen. Wes was riveted to Jonah by now, almost nerve for nerve; he could *feel* when the pain eased its white-hot grip—like oil in a pan, as the heat ebbed it was sizzling with less violence, popping only sporadically. It dulled; and limp with exhaustion from fighting so many hours, Jonah slept on sheets soaked and pungent with sweat. And Wes crumpled in relief onto the living room sofa. Out like a blown fuse.

In the morning, Wes knew even in that place before waking that Jonah was on the threshold between bedroom and living room, staring at him. He feigned sleep, not daring to move for eternal minutes. Had he really done what he had done? It was impossible. And yet the knowledge of it was taking on the weight of certainty as he woke.

Finally he opened his eyes. Jonah was standing there looking at him. Wes suddenly thought of the myth of Demophoon—the infant son of Demeter who was placed within fire, a rite that was to render him immortal. Jonah on the living room threshold was no less mythical. His eyes were open, the pain was gone, and looking into that fathomless gaze, Wes felt his soul shrivel inside him.

"Why'd you do that to me, Wes."

Jonah's voice was hushed.

Wes waited a long moment before speaking weakly, uttering the one sentence available to him, the words spilling by rote into the empty air. "The nurse said to give you one Tylenol every four hours."

Jonah moved to the edge of the sofa. Wes cringed down into the pillows. Jonah brandished the prescription at Wes: "This is for Tylenol with *codeine*, you sick fucking bastard."

Jonah's hand came closer, holding the square of paper an inch from

Wes's eyes, then against his face, palming it, plastering the prescription against the older man's skin. Then suddenly the hand was gone. Jonah crumpled the paper into a ball.

"Eat this, motherfucker."

And Wes's lips parted of their own accord; he took the paper in his mouth and held it like the communion wafer.

"Chew it, scumbag!"

Obediently he ground it between his teeth, feeling it form a sickening lump.

"You're gonna fuckin' swallow that, I'm gonna *make* you swallow it—"

But he was afraid to try, afraid he'd choke.

"C'mon, get it down, you're eatin' that fuckin' prescription—"

The paper would not come apart into manageable pieces. Wes panicked, worked it frantically, but it stayed whole, stubborn, thick and chalky. Jonah slapped him and the wad flew out onto the floor. Instantly Jonah's hand was on the nape of his neck, dragging him off the sofa, mashing his face into the carpet.

"Pick it up, you scummy mutt!"

On all fours, held by the neck, Wes hastily retrieved it with his teeth and tried, tried to chew it once again. It was vile, bitter. He felt his erection, full and painfully rigid, against his belly. Tears were coming, tears of shame and hot, agonizing pleasure.

"You better have it down in ten seconds or I'm gonna break every bone in your body."

Wes chewed desperately.

"*Ten . . . nine . . . eight . . .* "

—chewing for his life

"*seven . . . six . . . five . . .* "

—it wouldn't dissolve, wouldn't budge

"*four . . . three . . . two . . .* "

—and he *made* himself swallow

" *. . . one,*" Jonah finished.

Wes began to gag and retch. Paper and bile pooled on the floor. Jonah pushed his face into the mess and held it there for a long moment before delivering a vicious kick that sent him sprawling. Then he walked out the door without looking back.

———

D awn. Sunrise dazing the streets.

The stars had faded and with them the long, terrible negotiations of the night.

Jonah put one foot in front of the other. Left, right, left . . . the plain absence of pain was a sensation all its own, a hymn ringing in his ears.

He was everything at once. Blank and cold with denial: *It's okay. Nothing happened.* Beneath that, battered and crushed. And deeper still, at his core, purged and pure. He was hollow as the plastic angel that used to top his mother's Christmas tree, and similarly lit from within. Ablaze with martyred glory.

Wes had finally shown himself. The savage stranger inside that suit and tie, the one inside everyone. And who was he, Jonah, to judge a man on that score?

Or maybe Wes had finally seen him for what he was—someone deserving not worship but torture—and found the balls to deal it out.

Or maybe they were both sick men, riveted to one another by need and perversity.

Layer upon layer: denial and disbelief, outrage and shame. Flashes of clarity. Even something resembling relief.

Home again. He paused in his own doorway a minute, looking at his Salvation Army furniture: the bed with its stained comforter, a second-hand dresser, two chairs. A TV that switched back and forth from color to black-and-white. A refrigerator that didn't light up when he opened it, and nothing in there but a single beer.

Jonah stood there at nine in the morning and drank it straight from the bottle. His aimless gaze found the single Chinese take-out menu pinned to the fridge with a Burn Center magnet. The dishes under Chef's Specialties needled him with their promising names: *Happy Family, Lucky Phoenix Rising, Lovers In The Stars.*

The first hint about how things were going to be came within two weeks, when Jonah's monthly car payment was returned. Bewildered, he called Pontiac's customer service number, only to be told that the balance on his automobile had been paid in full.

"The whole amount—paid off? How? I mean, when?"

"Yes sir. Full balance paid last week, let's see now, by way of American Express Gold. Cardholder a Mr. Hansen?"

So Wes was still there. He was paying for what happened, trying to pay anyway. Squaring away the Pontiac on the sly. It was an eight-thousand-dollar bribe, the first of many.

Not much later the bill for the eye operation was paid up too. Another thirty-five hundred bucks. A risky move on Wes's part, to let his amends be mixed up with the crime. But it saved Jonah almost two months' pay.

Still later a new TV, twice the size of the old one, was delivered to his door. The sender had withheld his name, but there was no mystery.

Jonah did not acknowledge these gifts. Week after week he stayed away from Wes, savoring his righteous hatred and holding his silence. He avoided all their usual haunts and did his drinking in different bars.

A local alternative to The Whiskey Bar was Babylon, a soul food place on Ninth Avenue with good house champagne and a piano. Following the eye incident, Jonah took to drinking there alone. His third evening at the bar, he met Sherry, who was working the last shift. Sherry was a dancer with shining black hair and, according to the taxi driver seated next to Jonah, the way she moved around behind the bar kept many a man coming back night after night.

"Are you a fireman?" she asked as she filled his glass for the third or fourth time.

"Yeah," he said. "How'd you know?"

"Sometimes I get a feeling," she told him. "You have kind of an aura."

"No kiddin'," he said, impressed. By the time he remembered he was wearing a baseball cap with the letters "FDNY" he was too far gone to care. In the meantime, she had taken to calling him Hero.

"Hey, Hero. Ready for another?"

"Oh—uh, yeah. I guess so. Thanks."

"It's on me, this time."

"It is? Well, uh—thanks. That's very nice. Thanks again."

He was miserably inept at flirting. It always took him far too long to realize that someone was flirting with him. He could never believe women liked him. But as the night wore on and the bar crowd thinned, Sherry began to give him almost undivided attention.

"Do you live around here?" she asked.

He shook his head. "I'm down on the Lower East Side. But I was detailed this morning to the firehouse on 48th Street. Why, do you?"

"Just around the corner. But I'm moving the minute I get enough money."

"Oh yeah? Where you goin'?"

"Somewhere not so sleazy and dangerous."

"You think it's so bad?"

"Well, it doesn't help that I usually get off work at around three in the morning."

Jonah glanced at the clock above the bar. It was nearing that hour now.

"Speaking of which . . . " she continued. "If you're gonna be here until closing time, would you mind walking me home?"

Sherry lived in a fifth-story walk-up just off Tenth Avenue and slept on a mattress on the floor, which they reached without even turning on a light.

When he woke, he didn't know where he was. The small room with its single window felt like a cell. Then he became aware of the slender girl sleeping beside him. He didn't have to look at her clock to know there was no time to lose.

"Jonah?"

"Hey. Sherry. I got to go, all right?" He was already tugging on his clothes.

She struggled awake, sitting up on the mattress. "Do you want some breakfast? I can—"

"I got to go to work," he said. "I'll eat there."

"Or just some coffee then? I'll be making it anyway."

"Look, I'm sorry—I ain't got time. I'll see you around, okay?"

"Listen . . . whatever."

When Jonah pulled up to the firehouse, there was no place to park.

Rows and rows of cars—the familiar cars of the other firemen—were double- and triple-parked in front of the building.

The firehouse flag was flying at half-mast.

He left his car across the street and walked through the garage to the kitchen. Everyone from the company was already there. Some of the men were in uniform, some in street clothes; almost all were in tears. And suddenly, for no real reason—there hadn't been time to see who was missing—he knew Jerry was dead.

He stood looking around at all the other firemen. They stared back at him, pain in every pair of eyes. He wet his lips with effort. "What—" he said.

Captain Reilly came over and put a hand on his shoulder. "I guess you ain't heard," he said.

It was a midtown fire, on the eighth floor of a high-rise. Jerry was trying a roof-rope rescue, looking to save a trapped firefighter from another company. The rope snapped and both men were killed by the eight-story drop.

"The funeral's on Wednesday, out in Queens," the captain told him. His voice was very quiet and Jonah could see that even he was close to tears. "You're covered for the day tour today if you want to go. We'll get detailed guys in here for anyone who feels like taking the day off." He paused. "The city offers free counseling to the Fire Department. Sometimes guys feel the need for it in situations like this. Do you think you might want that number?"

Jonah shook his head, trying to clear it of the picture of Jerry falling all that way.

"Are you all right?" Captain Reilly asked.

He didn't answer, just stood there shivering.

The captain studied him a moment. "Go home," he said softly.

Jonah walked back outside to his car. He didn't have to wonder what to do with himself. The captain had said to go home, so Jonah drove straight to his apartment and, once inside, looked around as if for the first time. The place seemed dazed. Dust motes hovered in the rays of light; they made him dizzy. What was it like to dangle eight stories above the street and feel your lifeline breaking? Did it make any sound as it snapped? Or did it just weaken and let itself come apart? He turned on the radio, wanting only a deejay's steady voice, but almost immediately heard the report about Jerry. He turned it off again.

Afterward, he wouldn't be able to say how he passed the day. He must have slept, off and on, or else a full twelve hours went by while he lay on his back in bed, hands laced beneath his head, staring at the ceiling. The world darkening outside his window, day turning into evening.

When night had finally fallen, he knew where to go. Everyone would be at Suspenders, drinking one stiff one after another, telling stories about Jerry and crying without shame. A couple of bagpipe players would be there, kilted and diligent, shrilling their mournful rendition of "Amazing Grace." But in the end, everybody but him would go home to someone, to their wives and kids; and some would even go to their mothers.

Onward to one of his clubs, where all kinds of powders and pills could be had, to blot out devastation—as well as the nightly parade of players who would go to work on him. Under circumstances like these, he might not even get it up. Or maybe he'd get hard and stay hard, his body withholding release. There was even a chance that someone very good would get him off—after which, spent and empty, he would be no closer to relief than before.

To Babylon, then, in desperation. Sherry at the bar like a vision— an angel. He would lunge up to her, eyes wild, hair in disarray. Declaring his love, pleading to be saved. Her sweet face would register alarm, and how could he blame her? A one-night stand had its own code, and no one knew the rules better than him. Wasn't he the one to enforce them that very morning? She would freeze him out, her cold politeness making conversation impossible. If he were feeling stubborn, he might persist in drinking there: one shot of whiskey after another until she refused to serve him anymore. Bouncers in pressed suits, discreet and implacable, would be stationed in the wings to back her up.

By this time the sky would just be lightening. The early morning a stillborn blue. Crazed and brokenhearted, defeated and exhausted, he would hit the street again. Always the street again. Knowing the one place left to go.

The doorman would recognize him and let him in. The elevator man, too, would take one look and press the button for the penthouse without having to ask. Jonah's bloodshot eyes and agitated demeanor would discourage all small talk during the ride up.

He had thrown away his keys and would have to knock. Pound on the door with his fist, as if to wake the dead. Hurried footsteps from within, then the door easing open a crack, the chain still in place. Wes's fearful expression breaking into joy as all the tortured waiting of the last several months—the candles lit in church, the prayers to Saint Jude—took the shape of the maniacal, beloved form before him.

The chain dashed from the lock, the door flung open. Wes in his bathrobe, arms outstretched.

Jonah! My darling! Come in, oh, come in . . . ! For God's sweet sake, come in.

Before the Blaze

"Captain."

Seamus O'Day looked up. It was Jake, with a pair of binoculars in his hands.

"Captain, you got a minute? You gotta come see this."

Seamus stood and followed the other fireman up the stairs to the roof. It was just getting dark outside. Jake pointed to the building across the street.

"Third floor, second window from the left." Jake passed him the binoculars.

Pink curtains were pinned to either side of the window, yielding a full view of a young woman's room. There was her vanity table, lined with the little bottles and jars that held her mysteries. There too was her half-open closet, and the generous organdy-covered bed.

"She's in the shower," Jake said. "Don't worry, she never takes long. And she never lowers the blind."

Even as he spoke, she was emerging rosy and naked, a towel wrapped around her hair. Sweet Mother of God, she was lovely—the young breasts full and way up high; her hips tapering smoothly into long slender legs.

"How 'bout that, Captain?"

"Sweet Jesus."

The two of them watched in silence as she rubbed lotion all over herself, Jake from his real distance and Seamus as if from the windowsill. Next she took a powder puff from its round box and disappeared in a talcum cloud. This whole display was causing Seamus, in spite of himself, to remember Lorena.

Now, delightfully, the towel came off, and a swath of water-darkened hair spilled nearly to her waist. A pause full of silent appreciation, then: "She's a real blonde," Jake put in. "You can't tell 'til it's dry." Still naked, she seated herself at the vanity and began combing it out in slow, hypnotic strokes. She was like a mermaid in a painting.

Leave it to Jake to know about this. Seamus lowered the binoculars to shake his head at the younger man. Jake shrugged, grinning. "Hey man, you know me. The nature lover."

"You can only watch birds for so long, I guess?"

"Look again, Captain. She's getting dressed."

Sure enough, she was at the closet, pulling out all kinds of clothing. This was better than a video, better than a peep show—it was a real girl in a private moment. She was holding different outfits up against her body, deciding who she was going to be tonight: the Ivory-soap virgin in a long gauzy dress or backseat Betty in a leather skirt. She finally decided on The Girl Next Door, with tight jeans molded to her butt in a way that made him a little short of breath.

Her hair was drying, lightening to gold as promised. She moved to the window and Seamus could tell she was looking at her own reflection in the pane. Then she stopped short, staring straight at the two of them before jerking at the curtains. Seamus lowered the binoculars.

"She sees us," he said. "Let's go."

"This way," Jake said, moving to the other side of the roof. "Down the fire escape. Or she'll know we're from the firehouse."

He was right. They went down on the other side of the building, sneaking back in through a window, like kids. This was what he liked about Jake, the eternal youth he offered to everyone around him. Firemen stayed young longer than most men as a rule—necessarily in good shape, inured to constant pranks and practical jokes—but Jake even more so than the others.

"Captain, do you see why it's so hard to walk down the aisle?" he was saying. "When girls like that are everywhere?"

Jake was thirty-seven and had never been married. God in heaven, imagine that! Seamus himself had been hitched by the age of twenty-one, to his high school sweetheart, Matilda. This meant that by now Jake had—what was it?—*sixteen years* of freedom on him. He was engaged to his girlfriend Caryn, a sweet little thing, but now he had cold feet.

"What am I gonna do, Captain?"

"How long ago did you propose to her now?"

"Christmas. You know how it is. If I'd given her anything but a ring it would've been the silent treatment at least through New Year's. I didn't want to go through that again. Man, I just didn't have the balls."

"Caryn's a good girl," Seamus said.

"She is a good girl. That's the problem," Jake said. "We have nothing in common. So how am I gonna wake up next to her every morning for the rest of my life?"

"That's how it is. 'Till death do you part.'"

"Tell me what to do, Captain. Should I go through with it if I already feel this way?"

"That's where I'm no good," he had to tell the kid. "I can't advise about whether or not to stay with a fiancée. If she was your wife already, I'd know what to tell you."

Lorena floated into his thoughts again, like the ghost she was.

"Listen," he said to Jake, partly to push her memory from his mind. "While I've got you here, there's something I want to run by you. I was talking to Jonah Malone last week, and he's thinking of offering you a spot in Rescue 2."

"Captain Malone said that?" It was easy to see Jake was pleased.

"Sure enough he did. Now, I'd hate to lose you, but how many firemen get a chance to learn under a guy like that? I told him I'd let you know."

"But Captain O'Day," Jake said sincerely. "It's always been the best working under you. I don't know if I'd want to leave Ladder 104."

"Hell, son, look here. I'm good at what I do and I'm proud to think I'm running a real tight ship. But I don't mind saying that, in terms of firefighting, very few men can hold a stick to Joe Malone. You get a chance like this, you ought to think hard about it before letting it slip."

"Well, I'll do that, Captain. And thank you," Jake said.

Seamus glanced now at the clock. It was just about six, almost time to leave. Jake nudged him suddenly. "Hey, Cap, look what's comin'."

It was the girl from the opposite building, crossing the street with the gait of some regal cat. Her blonde hair hung in careful ringlets and her face was made up. She looked good, although some of her magic was lost at close range.

"Evenin', ma'am," Jake said with a straight face. Seamus respectfully touched the brim of his baseball cap.

"Hey guys," she said. She smiled at them. "How are you?"

"Better all the time," Jake assured her. "What can we do for you?"

"I just thought I should let you know," she said. "I live across the street . . . ? In that building there? And about half an hour ago, while I was getting dressed, I saw two guys watching me from your roof."

This report was met by a shocked silence.

"The firehouse roof?" Jake said finally. "No way."

"I swear."

Jake turned to Seamus. "Captain. Could anyone be sneaking up our fire escape from the backyard?"

"You got me," Seamus answered. "Unless maybe it's those guys who use our basketball court."

"That's right, Captain. I wouldn't've thought of that." Jake turned back to the girl. "We have a few residential buildings behind the firehouse. Sometimes people hang out in the backyard, shoot some hoops. And we've always been pretty laid back about it, never gave anyone a hard time. But sneaking up to our roof to peep in people's windows . . . that ain't right."

"No sir," Seamus agreed. "What did they look like?" he asked the girl.

"I couldn't really tell. It was already dark out."

Seamus rubbed his chin. "I'll let the rest of my men know," he said. "Tell them to keep an eye out for trespassers."

"And I'll have a word with our neighbors," Jake put in.

"I really appreciate it," said the girl.

"Thanks for telling us," Seamus and Jake said at the same time.

"Sure thing. And you know, you guys are great. I should mention that too. I feel lucky to live across the street from a firehouse."

"You got a fire alarm?" Seamus asked.

The girl nodded.

"It works? You check it out regular? Check it out. Make sure the batteries are fresh."

"And what floor are you on?" Jake asked.

"Third floor," she said.

"Third floor. Perfect. Our ladders'll reach you easy."

"Now remember," Seamus said on his way out. It was six o'clock. All the firemen staying for the night shift had gathered in the kitchen for dinner. "The first football practice of the season is Sunday afternoon." He scanned the table for his players. Four of them were here. "Danny-boy. Jake. Mulligan. And Shively. I want to see all of you at Marine Park at one o'clock sharp."

"Aye, aye, coach."

"See you Sunday."

"All right, then." Seamus went out to his car.

Ah, football. Seamus had a passion for football, for the very idea and invention of it. Regular men turned gargantuan—helmeted and padded, grease-painted and grass-stained—lunging on cue, clashing and crashing, with the understanding that the most important thing in the world was to put the ball into the other team's end zone. That this was worth everything—getting tackled, pummeled, bruised and crushed. Worth the possibility of broken bones or a concussion, worth the money you put down betting on your side.

It was an extraordinary concept that everyone bought into. Whenever the Giants were nearing the Super Bowl, for instance, men throughout the city laughed easier, cut each other a little more slack. It made everyone happy, almost like Christmas.

Not quite as wonderful, but almost, was baseball, with all the heroes of his youth: Scooter, DiMaggio, Yogi, and of course, the Mick. How he loved to initiate boys into this tribe. Whenever a woman in the neighborhood gave birth to a son, Seamus would flash forward, five or six years down the line, to the new Little Leaguer he would be outfitting. Every boy within two miles of the O'Day household would come into his hands to learn discipline and perseverance, stamina and endurance. He watched their bodies change, their confidence develop, their aim come closer and closer to true. He saw the reverence in their young eyes, heard it in their childish voices when they addressed him. Once in a while, they would slip and call him Dad. And the fact was, he was the closest thing to a father that some of them had.

There was no one he couldn't do something with. "No job is too small," was his joking motto. Something about these boys was altered when they put on a uniform, climbed into the logo-imprinted jerseys and caps as if into a new and promising skin. Right away they stood a little taller, a little tougher. Squared their shoulders and composed their small faces into stoic expressions. It did something for fathers too, when fathers could be found. He was used to grateful paternal gazes and hopeful eyes. He was sculpting their progeny into little men worth a damn, and it did wonders for morale across the board.

Coaching within the fire department brought him no less joy. Seamus had started the firehouse football and baseball teams and they took at least one trophy a season. That kind of teamwork on the field carried over into firefighting and the firefighting drills supplemented the teams. It was circular and beautiful and he was engineer and overseer. They put out for him, all of them; they changed into something else. It was an amazing thing to witness, a thrill every time.

A coach held a sacred place in society, and surrogate fatherhood came with the territory. His players came to him for all kinds of counsel. Like Jake tonight, looking for advice about his love life, not knowing whether he should stay or go. Well, that had brought back some memories. It wasn't so long ago—was it?—that Seamus himself was asking his elders that same question. Seven years, could it be? Since Lorena had spun his head and made him waver.

They had just moved to Jackson Heights. She didn't look like any of the other women on their new block. Probably because she had no children, wasn't lost in a world of bottles and diapers, encumbered with a carriage.

She was slim with shoulder-length dark hair, in which red highlights gleamed like the odd threads on a complicated skein. Her skin was cop-per-colored and smooth, her eyes a startling shade of hazel. Unlike the other neighborhood wives, she did not bring a coffee cake or cobbler, but invited him and Matilda over that evening for a nightcap. After unloading furniture and boxes all day, it was just what they needed.

Her husband was out of town on business. Whatever he did, it was clear that he made money. Their house was the largest and most hand-some on the block. As he and Matilda crossed the toy-strewn street, its warmly lit windows were like an invitation in the twilight. It was an image Seamus would hold in his mind and associate with her memory forever—that big house lit up against the dusk, and Lorena like a caged cat within, restless and pacing.

He and Matilda had changed into clean clothing—jeans. Lorena answered the door in a gray angora sweater and tight black leggings. She smiled warmly, first at Matilda, then at him. "I'm so glad you could come," she said. "It's lonely when Steve's on the road."

She showed them into the dining room, where they sat at the table and drank the blackberry brandy she served in deep red shot glasses. Seamus was jittery, off guard. He would have preferred a beer, some-thing that would fill his fist, that he could gulp at length. The brandy in its shot glass was something else entirely—delicate, potent, surprising. It wasn't like anything he had ever tasted before.

Lorena told them that her husband was in sales.

"That's why he travels so much," she explained. "He sells to corpo-rations all over the Northeast. He does well but he's gone all the time. Sometimes I wonder whether it's worth it; I mean, what's all the money for if he doesn't have time to enjoy it?" She paused to pour them all a second round. "I get stir crazy, being alone so much."

"Do you work at all?" Matilda asked. "Outside the home, I mean," she added tactfully.

Lorena shook her head. "Steve doesn't want me to. He's old-fash-ioned that way, I guess. He says he doesn't want his wife working, and that he'll always make sure I never have to. And you?"

"I'm a foster care caseworker," Matilda said. "And wild horses couldn't drag me away from it."

Seamus felt a rush of love for his wife, mixed with a more compli-cated, less comfortable emotion he couldn't name. Matilda did love her job, but he sensed that she was also protecting his feelings. After all, their household would hardly get by on his income alone.

"Do you mean you find homes for children? How gratifying that must be. I know Steve would be shocked to hear this, but I'm jealous of women with careers—especially meaningful careers."

Matilda flushed with pleasure, as well she might. This rich young woman who looked like a movie star—jealous of *her*?

"And Seamus?" Lorena asked.

"Seamus is a fireman," Matilda said.

Lorena met his eyes for a moment longer than she had allowed herself all evening. The information affected her, as it did most women. Seamus was used to this. What he wasn't used to was it cutting ice with someone of her status.

"How exciting," she said again, turning back to Matilda. "And how wonderful. Both of you serving the community in such important ways—and working for something besides just money. You must feel so good about that."

And sitting in that dining room, letting the brandy penetrate, they did feel good. It was easy to feel good around Lorena. Forget the overtime and the side work it took to make ends meet; forget how much overhead they had now with a new house, a second car, three kids and the likelihood of more to come. This elegant woman admired them, even envied them. Their lives were full, and interesting, and *meaningful*.

"Tell me about your caseload," Lorena was asking of Matilda. "How many children are you responsible for? Are they orphans, or mostly from abusive homes?" For the rest of the evening, she plied Matilda with questions and paid attention to the answers. She paid far more attention to Matilda than she did to Seamus, as she would whenever they were all together, but even as early as that first night, he sensed that there was something careful and deliberate about this.

Later that week he saw her husband, Steve, parking his Camry in their driveway and carrying his attaché case into the house: pale, softbodied, and apparently the owner of the beautiful female who had entertained them a few evenings ago. Seamus was stricken and elated at once. It was all wrong and yet at least he wouldn't torture himself with the idea that the other man had anything on him.

The first time he was alone with her was in late November during a heavy snowfall. Her husband was out of town again and Matilda was at work. It was mid-morning and he saw Lorena struggling to unearth her car from the heavy snowdrifts. Seamus crossed the street and took the shovel from her. It was the kind of task he loved to barrel through, hard and fast with his formidable arms. In minutes he'd cleared all the snow within five feet of her wheels and there was an easy path to the street.

"This is so kind of you," she murmured. "You have to at least let me feed you some lunch."

"I wouldn't want you to go to the trouble," he said, reciting a line he'd picked up from somewhere, knowing he would accept no matter what else he had to do, it was too valuable an opportunity to pass up. And perfectly aboveboard, like helping her shovel the snow.

"No trouble at all," she recited in her turn. "Come at one o'clock."

Lunch turned out to be a complicated affair, which flattered him. Later he would learn that Lorena loved to cook, to entertain on every level, and in fact had little else to do with her time. For now, he was delighted, appreciative in a way that was unusual for him. There was cold Chardonnay, lobster bisque and a dozen soft-shell crabs—ten for him, two for her—eaten while she listened with unflagging attention to his stories of firefighting, coaching and his raucous boyhood. Her gaze was dark and fixed, penetrating him with the same heat and flush as the wine. Her hands, whisking things from the table, were deft and slender, her wedding ring flashing a warning from the left, the nails polished a light shell pink. As he helped her clear, something he never did at home—she protesting, he insisting—they accidentally touched hands once or twice. She kissed his cheek in a neighborly way when he left.

The next time they saw each other, of course, Matilda was there too. His wife liked Lorena—how could she help it?—the other woman went out of her way to be nice to her. The four of them—he and Matilda, Lorena and Steve—often got together in the evening for cards. (He and Lorena, Matilda and Steve.) Lorena was careful, always hovering over her husband—refilling his glass of beer, brushing a stray lock of hair back behind his ear—and almost overly attentive to Matilda as well.

But once, Lorena had gone upstairs in search of a second deck of cards and passed him in the corridor as he was coming back from the john. As she passed, she touched him right in the center of his chest. Not a word was spoken, but downstairs again, in the same room as Steve, Seamus could feel himself taking on mythical proportions. He could picture how it would be, with Lorena. He would have to hover a few inches above her, support himself with his arms so as not to crush her. He'd make every time she'd ever been with her husband seem like two or three jabs with a junior Tampax. One hour with him, and she would know for the first time what it was like to be a woman beneath a man.

It wasn't until February that something finally gave. Steve was on one of his many trips; Matilda was at work and the kids at school. It was around ten o'clock in the morning. Seamus had just come in from a twenty-four-hour tour at the firehouse. The lieutenant's test was coming up and all the guys were studying for it. Seamus needed the promotion as much as anyone, but it wasn't easy to find uninterrupted time to focus on the books. Now came the rare chance to put in some of those hours. He was at the kitchen table with *The Fire Officer's Handbook of Tactics* open in front of him when the phone rang.

"Hello?"

"Seamus?"

The low honeyed voice was unmistakable. It sent a little ripple of disbelief through him. Whenever Lorena phoned, it was to speak with his wife. She never called while Matilda was at work.

"Yes?" he managed after a few seconds' delay.

"It's Lorena," she said, as if he didn't know. "I was hoping you might be able to help me. I was doing the breakfast dishes and I washed my wedding ring down the drain." She sounded ready to cry. "Do you think there's a chance of recovering it?"

"It's down the kitchen sink?" he said. "Well, I could give it a shot."

"Could you? It doesn't have to be this minute. I mean, if you're busy right now . . . "

"No, no, it's okay. Nothing that can't wait. I'll be right over."

He crossed the street with his toolbox and a plumber's snake. She answered the door in a pink silk kimono, as if too distraught to care what she was wearing.

"Thank you for coming," she said. "Thank you so much. I was just starting to panic."

"Well, we'll see what we can do. Your floor might get a little dirty though."

"Oh, please. Don't worry about that," she said.

He went to work beneath the sink. It was a wet and grimy job and soon it seemed only sensible to remove his uniform shirt, which he hadn't bothered to change since coming home. Lorena took it out of his hands and arranged it carefully over the back of a kitchen chair. Seamus concentrated on the task at hand, taking the pipe apart bit by bit, but it was hard not to be aware of Lorena pacing around the room. From his position, he could see the lower part of her legs, her firm calves and the delicate gold chain around one ankle. "Firefighting keeps you in good shape," he heard her say.

He was glad his head was obscured beneath the sink so she couldn't see the color rushing to his face. "Yeah, well. You got to be, when lives are at stake," he said. "If you're gonna run up those stairs and carry people out." He paused to wipe his hands on his work pants.

"Wait, I'll get you a towel," Lorena said. She left the room and Seamus heard her climbing the stairs.

He had taken apart as much of the pipe as he could and now he reached up inside the part of it that was still fixed in place. There where it curved into a shallow basin, his fingertips found the ring. Without calling out, he rose and rinsed it under the tap.

Her diamond was twice the size of Matilda's. It had been goading him for months. He could pocket it and hock it at some pawnshop outside town. No one would ever know and it would take the sting right out of those post–Christmas blues. Even if it weren't insured—and it had to be—Steve could afford to buy her ten more just like it.

But when Lorena came back with the towel, he took her left hand and wordlessly slid the ring onto her third finger.

"Seamus," she gasped, "you got it!"

"I got it."

He hadn't let go. She looked up at him, then down at the ring, and after a long moment up at him again. Her offer came then, so soft and shy he had to lean down to hear it.

You may kiss the bride.

After this afternoon, they were together at least once every week. This was easy to arrange: Seamus worked two days out of each week and the other five were his own. Lorena had no schedule to observe, other than attending to her husband when he was home. But he traveled all the time and Matilda worked every weekday. Their opportunities came often and were seldom wasted.

Lorena loved his size, reveled in his strength, exulted in the way he could lock both her wrists together in one casual fist. And Seamus was no less enraptured. The affair awakened feelings he hadn't had since his honeymoon.

Her body was a joy and a torment to him. She was lithe and lean and, once summer came, tanned from lying in the sun all day. From his upstairs window, Seamus could see her in her lawn chair, basting herself with Coppertone and reading dime-store paperbacks. She called them bodice-rippers, and they all featured heroic, muscle-bound men whom she claimed reminded her of him. They were ridiculous, she admitted, but got her hot and bothered nonetheless, drove her upstairs to the bathtub where she relieved herself with the detachable showerhead. The picture she painted came to Seamus at odd times of the day: at work, especially during the slow afternoons; in the backyard while he was trimming the hedges; even at the dinner table.

The reality of their hours together matched the fantasies he had the rest of the time. The best days were the ones where he came to her straight from work, still in his uniform, arriving at around ten in the morning after twenty-four hours of thinking about it. "Don't change your clothes," Lorena always begged him. "Please keep your uniform on." Lorena loved to beg, and he loved to hear it.

"Little rich girl," was something he crooned into her ear, poised on top of her, penetrating her just a little.

"Please," she would pant, eyes wide and wild.

"Poor little rich girl."

"Please."

"Please what?"

"Oh please . . . " Drawing back to watch her bite her lower lip.

"What's this, is the little rich girl begging?"

"Please, Seamus." She grasped at his hips with both hands, tried to pull him into her. She might as well have been trying to budge a statue. He laughed down at her.

"What's the matter, little girl, don't the rich man give it to you every night?"

"Not like this."

"Like this?" A single, slow thrust, in and out, leaving only an inch of him within her, as before.

A moan torn from the deep: "Ahh, Seamus, please!"

"You been a little rich girl so long, you don't even know how to beg right."

"Teach me then."

"Oh, I'll teach you."

Another hard and deliberate thrust; another low moan. Real tears came into her eyes. "Seamus, please, I need it, please give it to me."

"Get on your hands and knees when you beg me."

Withdrawing altogether then, so she could assume this position. Taking her from behind, his face buried in her fragrant hair.

No matter how often they had it, their sex retained a sense of desperate urgency. Lorena liked having the clothes torn from her body, her blouses ripped in half like in the trashy books, and since it was Steve's money, everything was replaceable. She caterwauled beneath him, bucked and arched, dug her fingernails into his back, all those things you only saw in the movies. The two of them were like a movie of their own: better than porn, brighter than technicolor. It was romance and action and thriller twisted into one, and he was the star.

When he came home to Matilda, then, something was askew. The hero of the movie was suddenly expected to help unload the dishwasher, walk the floor with an infant, submit to a game of Candyland. It was a return to the dailiness of bills and budgets, toothpaste and Preparation H. Everything was a little smaller, a little shabbier. Bedclothes were made of flannel and Matilda nudged him every few hours all night, whenever his snoring became too loud for her to sleep.

With Lorena, there was nothing but coupling and conspiracy. There were afternoons registered at cheap motels under made-up names. They were illicit, explicit, full of their own daring and subterfuge. Even on regular evenings, when the adults on the block gathered on one lawn or another, to survey their children's games and trade gossip, there were quick, meaningful glances: hastily averted, shared. At these times, Matilda seemed to take on a whole new persona: almost sisterly, almost childlike, an innocent who had to be protected from what she couldn't fathom. Lorena was as solicitous as ever—gentle, mild, paying homage to her as an errant nun to a preoccupied Mother Superior.

One evening the phone rang and Matilda picked it up in the kitchen.

"Hello?" she said. "Oh, hi, Lorena, how are you?"

In the next room, Seamus froze in his seat and held his newspaper still.

"Of course we're still on for cards tomorrow night," his wife was saying. There was a pause, then: "Well, how nice. I'll tell Seamus. Can we bring anything? Nothing at all?"

"They want us to come for dinner before we play cards," Matilda reported after hanging up. "Lorena has some new recipe she wants to try and she says she needs an excuse. Can you pick up a bottle of wine on your way home from the firehouse tomorrow? She said not to bring anything but I'd hate to come empty-handed."

When they arrived the following night, the feast that awaited them was unlike anything they'd ever had, even in a fancy restaurant. There was a salad strewn with flowers you could eat, some seafood concoction served in scallop shells, and a white praline mousse accompanied by dessert wine. The evening went later than usual; the abundance of dinner let them drink a little more than usual too, and the card game took on the atmosphere of a party. "Wasn't that just lovely," Matilda kept repeating after they'd gone home. "Can you imagine the trouble she must have gone to?"

After this, their card games were always preceded by a home-cooked dinner and each one seemed more lavish than the last. They had roasted ducklings, racks of lamb, whole lobsters with melted sweet butter, prime rib so tender it fell off the bone.

"I look forward to the poker game all week," Steve said once, "because I know that's one night I'm going to eat like a king."

"I do it for you," Lorena told Seamus after the second or third such banquet, as if her husband's remark hadn't already given this away. They were in her bed. She looked more beautiful than ever, and he tried to fix every detail of her image in his mind so he could pull it back out like a photograph later. The rose-colored chemise and shiny dark hair. Her burnished shoulders and the pale swell of her breasts. Seamus wished that just once he could go somewhere with Lorena on his arm. "I do it all for you and it makes me so happy. Sometimes it takes all day, and those are the best days. I go out early to shop and I pick out the very best of everything. And I don't care how expensive it is, because it's for you. And then later, all those little tasks that used to drive me crazy . . . the washing, trimming, peeling, slicing . . . sautéing and arranging . . . it's all different now. It's not tiresome anymore."

She was lying beside him with her head on his shoulder but now she raised herself up on one elbow. "Try to picture it," she said. "I've got the radio on and I'm singing along with all the love songs. I stand there in my bare feet with my hair pinned up, I'm wearing some old apron, and I feel beautiful. I feel peaceful. Because you're coming home to me after a hard day of fighting fires and saving lives. I pretend you're my husband and it's Matilda who's married to Steve."

This was before sex, or maybe after. In its way it was as exciting as the physical part: Lorena dreamily talking on and on, relating these details, her voice hypnotic in its devotion, casting a kind of spell that let Seamus see these scenes exactly as she painted them. Lorena at the sink, or bending into the oven. Never mind the fact that it was rare, if ever, that individual firemen really got to save lives. Never mind that whole afternoons went by without a run. Let her have her fantasy, let it get her through her own afternoons. Happy in her kitchen. He thought of the phrase *labor of love*. That's what it was, and it was all for him.

Another time she told him, "I dropped my wedding ring down that drain on purpose."

As the months went on, Seamus began to feel as if he had two wives. And if ever a man had a better arrangement, he had never heard of it. There was Matilda: sturdy, matter-of-fact, competent, as familiar to him as his own reflection. She even looked like him—a feminine version, that is, with a similar kind of rough good looks and Irish coloring. She had the same Bronx accent and manner of speaking, although being a teacher, she made a more intelligent impression. (She corrected his grammar sometimes, absently, as if he were one of the kids.)

What he had in Matilda's bed was different from what he had in Lorena's, but he needed it just as much. It was in this bed that Matilda took care of him whenever he had a fever or flu. It was here that his children brought him breakfast in bed on Father's Day; here that they occasionally crept after a nightmare. When he and Matilda lay together at the end of the day, it was a place to rest, a space where they could talk together without interruption, trade observations about the children.

"Guess what Namath said to little Bernard today?" Matilda related once. Namath was one of their twin boys; he and his brother Montana would be five in a few months. Bernard was their friend from down the street. "They were talking about what they want to be when they grow up. Bernie said he's going to be a millionaire like his uncle, and Namath said, 'I'm going to be a fireman like my dad.'"

Seamus chuckled, then spoke gruffly to cover his pleasure. "Well, if that's the case, this family won't be seeing any millions for at least another generation."

Sex in this bed was satisfying, and there was no pressure. With Matilda he could skip the measures he felt compelled to take with Lorena: the thorough shower and second shave, a mouthful of Listerine and a comb through his unruly hair. Lorena did the same for him, he knew. Seamus had never seen her anything but lotioned and perfumed, carefully made up, hair freshly washed.

Lorena: glinting, burning. Holding nothing back.

Matilda: maternal, gentle, practical, with a reserve he didn't quite understand. He had known her since she was a girl, and it hadn't always been there. Sometimes during sex, her eyes had a certain glazed and inward look, as if concentrating on a private vision, and he knew that whatever it was in him that led him astray, it was in her too, although she seemed to have no name for it yet and nowhere to put it.

Lorena's passion left no space for any such reserve. Sometimes she looked up at him with a helplessness that bordered on reproach, as if bewildered by her own captivity. Her beauty was nothing like his wife's or his. It was more dramatic: the fine-boned planes of her face, the wide hazel eyes and silken skin. She was polished and sleek and she spent a good deal of time keeping herself this way. She had seaweed wraps and facials, manicures and pedicures, and occasionally what women called makeovers. (Matilda hadn't the time, energy or money for such vanities and Seamus didn't think she particularly cared.) Lorena would never think of correcting his speech, even though she herself was high-class and spoke like it. Maybe it was because of their class difference that Lorena would always seem exotic and somewhat mysterious to him.

How long had this perfect situation gone on? It couldn't have been more than six months before all hell broke loose. Seamus came home after work one July evening to find the house as still as a tomb. No childish excitement greeted him at the door, no wifely kiss either. At first he thought no one was home. Then he saw Matilda through the kitchen door.

She was by herself at the table, smoking a cigarette. This was an immediate tip-off that something was wrong; she'd given them up with her first pregnancy.

"Matilda?" he said.

She looked up at him with an expression he had never seen. It was almost as if she didn't recognize him.

"Did something happen?" he asked. "Where are the kids?"

"I took them to my mother's. I thought they should stay there for the night," she said.

"Matilda," he said, afraid to approach her. "What is it? Tell me."

She returned her gaze to the space in front of her, stabbing the cigarette out with a single, vehement gesture. "I got a phone call today," she said. "A call from Steve Sopher."

"Yeah?" Seamus said. "What did he say?" He wasn't playing dumb.

His first thought was that something had happened to the baby or one of the twins. Terror had confused him, so that even with this information he hadn't yet comprehended what was going on.

Suddenly his wife was on her feet and lunging at him. "Oh, you cheating son of a bitch—how long? How long have you been screwing that slut?"

The hysterics lasted all night. Thank God Matilda had the foresight to get the kids out of the house. Neither of them got any sleep, even after they retreated to separate quarters (she to the bedroom, he to the sofa) and he could only imagine what was going on in the house across the street.

"How could you," Matilda asked him over and over. "How could you let me think she was my friend? All these months? How could you sit at Steve's table playing cards, drinking his gin—don't you have any shame at all?"

When she put it like that, he too had to be horrified. Seamus didn't want to ask, and yet he needed to hear: "How did Steve find out?"

Lorena's husband had found a love letter she had written Seamus, of all things. How could she have been so careless? Lorena had been fantasizing for a while about the two of them running away together. Was she trying, in some way, to force his hand?

The next morning, incredibly, Matilda went to work as usual. As soon as her car pulled away, Lorena appeared on the front porch, no less distraught than his wife. She started crying as soon as he opened the door.

"Oh, Seamus. Seamus, I'm so sorry!" She flung herself against him. He held her without speaking.

"I thought she'd never leave," Lorena said, the words muffled against his chest. "Steve was gone by six. He went crazy yesterday, Seamus. I never saw him like that. Screaming, calling me names, breaking things . . . it was the most miserable night of my life."

"It was bad," Seamus said tonelessly. He was bleary-eyed with fatigue and unprepared for another round of hysteria.

"I tried to stop him from calling Matilda. I begged him not to tell her, Seamus. There was nothing I could do."

"He called her, all right."

"What's going to happen now?" she sobbed.

"I don't know," he answered dully. "I suppose we'll have to move."

She raised her face to his. "Who's 'we'? You and me? Or you and *her?*"

"Lorena," he said with an effort. "I have a family."

"And I have a husband! That doesn't change the fact that I'm in love with you, and you're in love with me! We belong together, Seamus. You've said so yourself. And I could make you happy—happier than she ever did or ever could!"

"Lorena," he pleaded. "What do you want me to do?"

"I want you to leave her," she said. "And come away with me."

This plea marked the beginning of what Seamus would later think of as his Gethsemane. He endured three or four days of wrenching indecision: Lorena plying him with her pipe dreams by day while Matilda's mounting terror filled her eyes each night. His wife was soon past ranting at him. She must have realized she could not afford her own rage. She had three little ones under five years old and a beautiful woman after her husband.

"Seamus, listen to me," Lorena entreated him. They were together for the first time since being found out. Everything was different now; even her bed seemed like a different place. There was no way to relax, even for an hour. "I can't give you up. Don't ask me to give you up, you're the best part of my life." Tears were running down her face. Even when she cried she was beautiful. "You know what we have. Do you have it with Matilda? Can you really say that?"

"It's different," he said. "You know that. It's a whole different thing. It ain't right for you to ask something like that."

"Well, is it right to stay married to the wrong person?" she demanded. "How old were you on your wedding day? Twenty-one? I was eighteen. Think about it—that's barely out of high school. We were too young to write the ticket to the rest of our lives."

Seamus thought about this. It had never really occurred to him before. "Yeah, we were young—just kids, really. But then, we've done pretty good so far. You know? Me and Matilda—we've been all right."

"I'm not talking about all right," Lorena said. "I'm talking about something better than that. You've made me happier in six months than I've been in my entire married life. I wake up wanting you and I go to sleep wanting you. I feel alive when I'm with you and like I'm just waiting the rest of the time." She took his face in her hands. "Try and tell me you don't feel the same way. You've said you think about me all day long."

"I do think about you."

"You've told me you want me all the time."

"I do want you all the time." Even this minute, he wanted her.

"Then really think about never seeing me again. Never having me again. Is that what you want?"

The idea was more than he could stand. He didn't answer. Lorena pressed her advantage. "Listen, Seamus, we didn't plan for this to happen, but here it is. I was looking into your eyes when you put that ring on my finger and I know what I saw. You were imagining that I was your wife—can you deny that? And I want to be! I want to cook your dinner and hear about your day and make love to you every night without having to sneak around. Imagine that, Seamus. You know what we have together. Imagine having it all the time!"

The funny thing, he thought even in the midst of the crisis, was that as different as the two women were, the factors that would hold him in place were the same ones that were tempting him to go. It all came back to the weight of his responsibilities, and how they seemed to bring a lid down on his life.

Thirty-two years old, he was, and his adventures would seem to be at an end. Reason said he was in too deep ever to leave: the mortgage payments, car payments, children and pets. But what if it was really possible that all those ties could snap like a rubber band? Leaving him free? Lorena was a reminder that he was still a young man.

"I'll remind you, Seamus," Matilda said, "that even if you've decided your wedding vows count for nothing, we have three young children who think the sun rises and sets with you. Haven't you done enough damage? Do you want them to grow up without a father?" Her voice cracked whenever she spoke to him and she lost the fight against tears many times a day.

Both women, since the affair had been discovered, were not able to stop weeping. What was it in women that made them leak at the eyes whenever they were upset? Everyone came into this world crying, as if even from birth they could guess what lay ahead. And all kids did it too, but then the males had to stop. They had to just dry up. It would probably be a relief if he could break down that way, but this wasn't the kind of thing that could bring Seamus to tears, and he would bet the same held true for Steve. But then again, who knew? Who knew what white collars did?

Thank God for the firehouse, a refuge from anything female. He could escape to it before he lost his mind, and put this thing on the table. His brothers and elders would keep his dilemma within the firehouse walls and give him good advice if anyone could.

"It's like this," Seamus said to the group of firemen assembled in the kitchen. He stared down at the scratched surface of the table and then around at all of them. "All of you know my wife, Matilda. We've been married eleven years now and we got three kids. Matilda's a good girl and the kids are the best. I ain't got a bad thing to say about a one of 'em."

Seamus paused. The kitchen was quiet.

"Anyway, it's like this," he continued after a moment. "I kind of fell in love with another woman from the neighborhood." Lorena's words came back to him and he repeated them in the telling. "We didn't plan for this to happen but . . . it did happen and . . . I never felt anything like it before. And she feels the same way. She says I'm the best thing that ever happened to her. She wants me to leave Matilda and be with her. She's working on me night and day."

Seamus searched the faces of the other firemen. So far no one had interrupted him or even cracked a grin. He drew a deep breath and went on. "I love Matilda. But it's different from what I feel for Lorena—that's the other one's name. She says we both got married too young to know what we wanted, and I understand what she's saying. Because I never wanted anyone like this. It would just about kill me never to see her again . . . but that's what it's coming to, because her husband found out about us and told my wife. So now I either got to be with her like she wants, or let her go for good. And I don't know what to do."

Seamus sat back in his seat and looked around the table. He had a sudden surge of feeling for these men. He knew they weren't judging him. They were all tomcats themselves, married or not; a rowdier bunch of skirt-chasers would be hard to find. They would understand what it meant to have a dream girl, a fantasy come to life and there for the taking. They would see how impossible it was to walk away from that. He could almost hear what they were about to say to him: *Man, you got to follow your heart. You only live once, and life's too short to stay in one place. Do what you gotta do and the rest'll work itself out somehow.* They would absolve and release him, and when he went with his pleasure, he would in some way be doing it for all of them.

Captain Gallagher was the first to speak. "Go home, son," he said. His tone was gentle but uncompromising. "Go on home, that's all there is to it."

Around the table all the men were nodding, and their voices were a chorus of agreement.

Go home. You took the vows; Matilda's your wife.

Go home. You got three kids, as fine a brood as God ever made.

Go home. You got a family. Your family needs you and you need them.

On this issue they were unanimous. Yes, he'd had some fun on the side, and maybe he had some feelings for the lady. That was all right. But what, after all, did any of that have to do with family? You have a *family*, they explained patiently. And gradually as they spoke he understood there was nothing to decide. He saw the sweet faces of his children—the twin boys and his baby girl. And his cheerful and competent wife—too good for him, she was, without a doubt. How could he have considered abandoning his family, even for a minute? It was madness. Looking down at the table, his eyes found the *TV Guide*. On the cover was a still from a sit-com: *Bewitched*. The word lodged itself in his head. Was that what had happened to him? That must have been it; he had been bewitched.

Seamus did as they instructed. He went home. Home to Matilda that very hour, where he begged her forgiveness on his knees.

His first instinct was correct. They'd had to move.

To this day, whenever Seamus imagined where a different decision might have led, the sweat of relief would bathe his temples. Without the counsel he'd gotten at the firehouse, he might well have jumped ship—so besotted was he with his mistress at the time. Where would Matilda and the kids be without him? He would have been a fool to leave them, abandon the warm gold for the lonely glitter. And where would he be, without them? More than five years had passed before Seamus got the answer to that one.

It was more than half a decade after the move when, on his way back from a fire expo upstate, he had driven through their old neighborhood in Jackson Heights. This was mostly with the idea of visiting the firehouse but he couldn't conjure any part of that place without seeing Lorena in the picture.

Though it was a long shot, he hoped to run into her on the street. At the same time, he didn't want to be seen by Steve, who had threatened, way back when, to kill him. Of course this threat was hard to take seriously, unless the other guy planned to buy a gun and shoot him. But the truth was, Seamus was ashamed of what he'd done, bedding his neighbor's wife, sometimes within twenty-four hours of their card games.

He couldn't think of the affair now without cringing. It was all unforgivable: Matilda's devastation, the betrayal of his poker buddy, even Lorena's heartbreak in the end, when it was clear that he couldn't really be her hero for more than a few hours a week—and then not even that anymore.

He didn't know what he hoped to gain by seeing her. Maybe some spark after all these years—some recognition of what they'd shared. Maybe they could take each other's hands for a moment, look into one another's eyes, and even laugh.

He went to the firehouse, was slapped on the back, clapped on the shoulders, even enveloped in a bear hug by one of the officers, a guy he went through the Fire Academy with. But it was Brian Flanagan, his former lieutenant and a captain himself now, who told him later in the privacy of his office.

"Seamus, I have bad news if you ain't already heard," he said. "Remember—ah—that lady friend of yours? Lorena Sopher?"

A painful quickening of his pulse. "Yeah? What about her?"

"She passed away just before Thanksgiving. It was bone cancer. I wasn't sure if you'd have any way to know."

And all he could do was stare back at Flanagan. So here it was: the absolute end. There would be no postscript, no redemption. She was gone and he'd never even known she was going. He tried to imagine Lorena on her deathbed, in pain—lonely and abandoned, forsaken by him. He pictured the skin pulled taut over her delicate features, her slim body wasted and gaunt, the dark eyes hollowed out. More fragile than ever.

For days afterward, he tortured himself with these images. There was no one he could go to, even secretly, for the details. He knew no one close to her except Steve, and he even entertained the thought of going with the other man into a bar to mourn her together: the woman they had both loved. In the end, what did their old enmity matter? They were together in their grief and it would feel good to drown some of it side by side in a dark Irish pub with sawdust on the floor. Some sad-eyed bartender brooding in sympathy as he filled their mugs with some strong amber tonic. Seamus lived by a code of brotherhood so strong that the idea seemed almost reasonable.

But no. He didn't think it was in Steve to acknowledge their bond, and so Seamus did his mourning alone and undetected. Matilda mentioned that he seemed quiet lately—preoccupied. Was everything all right at work? That was the closest anyone came to reading a difference in him.

He could not, of course, mention a word of it to his wife. Matilda had given him so much to be grateful for. She never brought up his indiscretion, never threw it in his face or used it against him, so nothing could make him speak Lorena's name to her now. The sharp part of his sorrow lasted about two weeks, before he let her go once again.

She remained his one infidelity. He never strayed outside his marriage again. And their life together had grown over it, like scar tissue over a wound that had been left alone.

He pulled into his driveway and cut the ignition. He was home.

"Mom!" Matilda heard the back door slam and the sound of her eleven-year-old sons.

"Don't slam the door, boys. Yes?" Namath burst into the kitchen, clutching a bristling orange cat. "Montana found a Maine coon in the vacant lot behind Gino's." Gino's was the local pizzeria. "Can we keep him?"

"Oh, Namath. You shouldn't have taken him."

"We didn't take him. He followed us."

The animal appeared to be nearly half the size of her son. Matilda came over and rested a hand on its back. It started to purr the moment she touched it.

"How do you know it doesn't belong to anyone?"

"He doesn't have a collar."

"That doesn't necessarily mean there's no owner."

"He followed us all the way back here, Mom! If he does have a home, he must not like it very much."

She found the cat's knobby spine and began kneading it. It arched against her hand, then suddenly it was in her arms, and she was cradling it as if it had been hers from a kitten. Holding its animal warmth against her.

"Mom?"

"Why don't you open a can of tuna fish for him and we'll let him eat it on the deck."

"Does that mean we can keep him?" Namath persisted.

"Let's see what your father says."

Matilda often pretended someone was watching. It was the only way to manage everything the way she did. She ran a very full house: six kids of their own, and the occasional children from the Catholic Foster Care Bureau they would shelter in an emergency. A beagle, two hamsters, the rabbit her youngest daughter had been given for Easter, a garden in the backyard and flower boxes in every window. At this very moment, she had soda bread in the oven, soup on the stove, and a bottle of wine chilling in the fridge. All this and her full workweek, as well.

She was a good wife, had been a good wife for almost twenty years, and she was a good mother too. She cooked traditional Irish dinners at least once a week, kept the pantry stocked with Seamus's favorite liquors and rubbed liniment into his back whenever he complained of an ache. She washed the uniforms of the Little League teams her husband coached, two or three loads of the filthiest striped shirts and pants each week, always with fabric softener and color-safe bleach. She was even known to go to the games, a petite blonde in a baseball cap cheering on the sidelines, a reassuring figure on the bleachers. Matilda always had exactly the right amount of money ready when the paperboy came collecting, and hot chocolate for him in the winter.

She could never have made it this far unless someone were watching. And since no one was, she'd made him up. This had begun many years ago and it was some time before the idea was in full flower, but by now his presence was palpable, could work miracles. It modulated her voice, stretched her patience, brought out all her gentleness, competence and stamina.

He was always there, just beyond her peripheral vision. Nothing was lost on him, and his constant audience let her rise above the endlessness, the tedium. He saw her stitch the cornflower blue curtains for the kitchen window. He watched her grade papers, clip coupons, wax the floor. He admired her cleverness and diligence; he made it all possible.

Once in a while she had an interlude to herself, maybe an hour or so a week, when the kids were all in bed and Seamus working overnight. She might stretch out on the sofa then, shoes kicked off, eyes closed, and sinking into this lovely luxury was like lying down in his arms.

She imagined that certain religious people communed with a similar presence. Why else have a crucifix casting its shadow over the kitchen sink? What better witness than Christ?

The most important tribute to *him* was a certain melting tenderness she poured onto everyone and everything around her. Her kids at home and the ones they occasionally took in. The family pets—even this cat, for instance. She scattered sunflower seeds for the wild birds and squirrels in the yard and had to restrain herself from feeding the mouse that sometimes turned up in the kitchen at night.

And her husband. More than most of the long-married wives she knew, Matilda had a special tenderness for her husband as well. She couldn't have asked for more of a man: he was six-foot-four, broad-shouldered and square-jawed, strong and handsome and devoted to sports. Other women had always loved him too. Sometimes too much.

Matilda had married at nineteen. That was what you did back then, and it wasn't so long ago either. If you were steady with someone who had a decent job, you just settled down. She knew Seamus was hard-working and would take pride in keeping the wolf well away from the door. He had rugged good looks and considerable charm. He knew the words to many old Irish songs, and he sang in a baritone that made every woman in the room want that voice beside her ear in the dark. Often when they were walking down the street or riding in the car, he would begin to croon sweetly at her:

Waltzing Matilda,
Waltzing Matilda,
You'll come a-waltzing Matilda with me . . .

They married for love and not because of family pressure or accidental pregnancy. And now, nearly two decades and six children later, they were still together. By that alone, they had done better than most.

Seamus was an attentive father who delighted especially in sharing sports with his sons. He spent countless hours in the park with them, working on their passes, catches and tackles. She envied them those afternoons, their tight-knit trio steeped in the thaw of March, cleats splashing in the rain-scented mud. He took them to games and coached their junior league teams. In a more distant way, he loved the girls too.

Distance: maybe that was the right word. To describe what was between them. Not absence. He came home at night, the nights he wasn't working, that is. He was affectionate but preoccupied. Being a captain brought a lot of responsibility, and he coached the fire department teams as well. Then there were all the occasions to drink: holidays, promotion and retirement parties, commemoration ceremonies, funerals. Memorial Day and Medal Day. And each of her pregnancies. Every time Matilda had conceived, Seamus got drunk upon hearing the news and frequently during much of the next nine months. He did fine once each child arrived; it was their anticipation that gave him trouble. More responsibility, more expenses . . . she could understand his anxiety. But she had hardly made each baby by herself.

Other than that, it was difficult to pinpoint what was missing in their marriage. She and Seamus talked about important things, still occasionally went out in the evenings, and had sex as often as any other long-married couple. Their lovemaking was sweet if somewhat matter-of-fact. To her friends, Matilda joked that Irish foreplay was: "Ya ready?" Often when looking up at his clenched jaw, the cords straining in his neck, Matilda couldn't help thinking of a bull or steer. Especially since he bellowed when he came, as if a lariat had suddenly pulled him up short.

Afterward she slept in the crook of that mighty arm, nestled into one broad shoulder. Or Seamus curled spoonlike around her, overlapping her body with his own, surrounding and containing her. They fit together well in sleep, despite or maybe because of the dramatic disparity in their sizes. Usually he kept one heavy leg flung over her two slender ones, pinning her in place. His heartbeat against her back. It was at these times that she felt closest to him. He was all hers, then: he engulfed her. Sometimes she deliberately stayed awake to savor it.

"Dad!"

Seamus was home. There was the sound of his car in the driveway. The kids were storming the front door, clamoring about the cat before he'd even made it up the front steps.

"That's all we need," she heard her husband say. "Another free-loader."

"Please, Dad! Just wait till you see him . . . see how cool he is . . . "

"Where is he? Not inside, I hope."

"On the deck. Mom let us feed him."

Seamus came into the kitchen, followed by Namath and Montana. His entrances always charged the air. He hurtled in and out of the house with a bristling energy, bringing into her kitchen the same enthusiasm that would draw his boys into a huddle, stalk the sidelines, punch the air in triumph. Now as he glanced through the sliding glass door, Matilda could almost hear his assessment: *Not a bad-looking animal, at that. Big, solid guy. Probably eats a lot.*

Matilda left the stove to kiss his cheek and caught the familiar fragrance of smoke coming from his pores. He'd have showered at the firehouse, would perhaps shower again, but the smoke went deep and left in its own sweet time. She liked it.

"Hi, sweetie," she said. "How was work?"

"Full day," he said. "Building inspection all morning, then two bad-ass jobs back-to-back. What you got cookin'?"

"I have bairneac chowder on the stove and a soda bread in the oven."

"What's this about the cat?"

"Well of course, I'm in no hurry to take in another pet. But I must say I like this cat. Must be that he reminds me of you."

"Of me?"

"Well, he looks so big and strong." She winked at the kids before going to the liquor cabinet. A martini for Seamus, just the way he liked it—extra dry, with three green olives nestled at the bottom—wouldn't hurt the campaign. She saw him studying the cat while she measured out gin and vermouth. When Seamus's drink had been set before him, she filled a saucer with the bits of fish that hadn't made it into the chowder.

"Paddy!" she called, sliding open the door to the deck. "Still hungry?"

"Paddy?" Seamus echoed.

"He looks like a Paddy. Don't you think?"

This was a giveaway that Matilda, too, was set on keeping the cat. A fine Irish name like Paddy was a direct appeal to her husband's heart—a fact that wasn't lost on him.

"It's seven against one, is it? What on earth is a cat good for?"

"Well, they're not much trouble. They take care of themselves. They don't need to be walked or bathed. All you have to do is feed them."

"That one looks like he could eat us out of house and home," Seamus grumbled. But even the kids could sense something theatrical in his objections, for they resumed their wheedling.

"So can we have him, Dad? Please, Dad?"

"We'll see. I don't make any important decisions before dinner."

Montana crouched beside the sliding glass door and tapped on the glass. "Dad's thinking about it, Paddy."

"It's getting to be a petting zoo around here. Maybe we should start charging admission," Seamus said. Then, to his wife, "He really reminds you of me?"

It was easy to see he was pleased by the comparison. She came over and snuggled against him. "Sure he does, darling. Because underneath all your huffing and puffing . . . "

Seamus eyed her suspiciously. "Yeah?"

She looked up at him, smiling, and put her arms around his neck. "You're nothing but a pussycat."

Sometime after dinner, the children summoned Seamus to the den. "Dad! Come here!"

"What is it?" he called, reluctant to leave his chair in front of the fireplace.

"Come see the news on TV! It's about a fire!"

This information pulled him to his feet. He went into the den to see what it was about. A woman reporter was on Atlantic Avenue in Brooklyn, a ring of firemen clustered behind her. Seamus could immediately identify them as Rescue Two.

" . . . possibly the most spectacular rescue in the history of New York City. Here we have firefighters Henry Dugan and Dennis Lynn as well as Captain Jonah Malone of Brooklyn's Rescue Two. Without these three members of New York's Bravest, there is no question that two citizens of Fort Greene would have perished this afternoon in a four-alarm inferno . . . "

"Turn it up," Seamus said. One of the kids adjusted the volume.

"Toldja you'd want to see this," Caitlin said. The cat was curled on her lap.

"You were right," he said. "Quiet, now."

Someone, a civilian, had captured the rescue on video camera, and they were airing the footage. The candid clip showed a Hispanic man crouching on a windowsill twelve stories above the street. He was barely visible, nearly engulfed by smoke. Christ, the guy was in trouble. Poor bastard had another minute up there, at most.

Now, as if from nowhere, a fireman appeared in mid-air. Dangling at the end of a rope. He was lowered until he hovered in front of the man on the ledge, then he reached out with his arms and the man went into them. They spun, the two of them, entwined in the black air, two scared men hovering twelve stories above rush-hour traffic and the shouting throng below. Then they were lowered, inch by careful inch from overhead, to the expanse of windows on the floor below.

The fireman swung out with one arm and knocked out a window-pane. Seamus understood that he was signaling their location to the rest of the team. Sure enough, within seconds, a host of helmets appeared at the broken window. A six-foot hook was extended to pull the two men to safety on the eleventh floor.

Beautiful. Un-fucking-believable. The camera was back at street level now with the woman reporter and the whole grinning rescue crew behind her. He leaned forward to catch the rest of the details. Apparently after that rescue, they had gone to the other side of the building where a second victim was trapped, and repeated the procedure. Yes, it was a four-alarm fire, but no lives had been lost.

It seemed that Jonah Malone directed the rescue. He and his men had run all the way to the roof, only to find that there was nothing up there to anchor the rope. Fire Department procedure demanded that there be some fixed object on the roof to tie the line around. But Malone had swiftly determined that official procedure, in this case, would save no one.

Malone himself held the rope in his bare hands, backed up by three other men in the company. They had all but gone over the edge themselves. Henry Dugan was lowered in the rope harness to the first trapped occupant, Dennis Lynn to the second. All of them had taken a very serious chance. It was how Jerry Fitzgerald, his old buddy, had been killed . . . and Malone had come on the department under Jerry—how about that. Just a scrappy, glancing-eyed punk in oversized boxing trunks . . .

But look at him now. He was Jerry's living legacy and so were all the rest of them. It was teamwork at its best: six pairs of brass balls laid on the line. It was the Bravest in top form; it was brotherhood, beauty.

"Daddy's crying," he heard Caitlin say.

Seamus thought about the rescue for days. It seemed to invade his every waking moment. The hardest part to get past was the idea of the civilian on the ledge—crouched on the outer ledge of a window while inside, the room where he had lived and worked was already gone. What was fire, exactly? In all these years, Seamus never felt he had the answer. But in its grip, things disappeared, crumbled. Evaporated or melted.

Since he was a boy, he had liked to sit by the fireplace. There was a threshold in the air that you couldn't cross, a place where the hot pleasurable glow would bite. It was the same bite that came when he slit a bag of microwave popcorn open too soon—a stab of steam.

While the trapped man crouched on his windowsill, that threshold had moved behind him, breathing at his back like some mythical dragon, wilting his clothes against his body. That terrible wall of heat would soon push him from the ledge and twelve stories of cool gangster air would hustle him to the concrete. Eight inches was all he had; eight inches had become the width of his life, and he hung there like a lobster over a pot, with about thirty seconds to go before he would let himself fall.

Then he had heard something overhead. He heard, *Stay there.* The words so faint and yet distinct; lost in the roar yet apart from it. He must have thought it was God. *Just stay there, hang in there, I'm coming.*

Looking up then, he saw a boot. A boot just over his head, draped over the parapet above. Looking up brought on a rush of vertigo. He returned his gaze to the wavering air in front of him when, surreally, a man appeared in that air. It must have seemed vaguely ludicrous, like a cartoon or something from a slapstick comedy.

First boots, then legs, waist, torso and head—lowered foot by foot from overhead. He was gesturing: *Come. Come on.* He loomed closer and the trapped man stepped off the ledge into the firefighter's embrace.

During the endless seconds that they hung there, he was no longer alone. Another life was locked to his. They would die together or they would survive. A man he'd never met had joined him in this limbo.

What was it like then, in the next moment, to feel his feet touch solid stone? To have so many strong arms pulling him in, supporting him? And to know that his life—which could have been estimated in seconds just a minute ago—had been restored to him in its entirety: the weeks, months, years opening before him like a new road.

Seamus wondered if it amazed him that these white men would do this for him—risk their American lives for his foreign one. And what about the frenzy of the crowd below, when he stepped into the arms of his rescuer? The same careless, cutthroat hordes who stepped over people every day, stopping for nothing and no one, had stopped in their tracks. Strangers all, to him and to each other, yet they were exultant, in an uproar; they were cheering themselves hoarse. The business of the hour had been suspended, everything was on hold, as they came together in the street below to celebrate the saving of his life.

The next time Seamus saw Jonah Malone was Medal Day. Malone no longer received two or three medals at each ceremony because he was a captain now. If a fireman deserved a medal, it was up to the captain to write him up for it. Malone, of course, did not write himself up, and so his rescues were rarely commemorated with decorations anymore. Still, Seamus knew what he had done this past year, and he wanted to show it hadn't gone unnoticed.

"Malone, you got to let me buy you a drink after this," he said at the ceremony.

A flash of the still-shy smile. "I guess you could buy me a Coke."

"You quit drinkin', Malone?"

"Five years now."

"You mean . . . are you one of them A.A. guys?"

"That's right."

Seamus was flustered. He didn't know what was in order—congratulations or condolences. He fussed with his tie.

"And you just come to it on your own?" he asked finally. "I mean, you ain't married, so it ain't like your wife made you do it or nothin'."

Malone laughed. "No. I figured out I was an alcoholic all by myself."

"Jesus." Seamus shook his head. "Five years. Has it been that long since you and I had a drink? I don't know where the time goes, Malone. It seems like just yesterday that Fitzgerald was entering you in that fight."

Malone grinned. "You remember that?"

"Everyone remembers it. Who could forget? A little probie punk, still wet behind the ears, doing more for department morale than a raise." Seamus shook his head. Awkwardly, he reached out and kind of patted Malone's shoulder. "You done good by his name, Malone. You made him proud last month."

Malone dropped his gaze, but not before Seamus saw the water standing in his eyes. It was a moment before he spoke, and when he did his voice was gruff. "Aw, that. I didn't do much. Henry and Dennis were the real heroes in that one."

"You called the shots," Seamus said. "You held the rope." He looked at the man Malone had become: the lines at the corners of his eyes, the hint of gray in his hair. He was momentarily overcome by these details, left almost speechless. Always so much of what he had to say was left unsaid; the brotherhood that bound them was subject to a code which relied on hearing between the lines. So it was now, with his next words. "That's worth a Coke in my book."

The point was, of course, that it could have been anyone on that ledge. This came to Seamus later, in the bar, with the intense and special perception that drinking stirred into being. It could have been him on that narrow threshold between the known and unknown, with only seconds to go before the heat would make him leap. It could have been him at the end of his rope, swaying back and forth in the wind, hanging and shaking, dangling and unknowing, before his brothers reached out with their hook and brought him home.

Vigil

"**O**h, Jonah. Listen to this one. It'll restore your faith in humanity."

Matilda took a card from the stack of mail in her lap and began to read to him.

Dear Captain O'Day,

I have been praying for your recovery ever since I read about your tragic accident in the papers. I've even put in a special request about you to Saint Jude. Always remember the power of prayer. If you have faith, Christ will heal you quicker than any hotshot doctors. Now, to help you along, I'm sending you the most powerful source of protection I have. Enclosed within is an actual tooth from the mouth of Saint Paul, a holy artifact on its way to becoming a Relic. Now, the Church won't let just anything be a Relic. No sir. First it has to prove itself by performing three miracles. Well, the tooth has already performed two so far. I gave it to my neighbor when his dog got hit by a car and the dog made a complete recovery. Then I let my nephew have it for his high school basketball playoffs. I gave it to his mother the night before and she sewed it into the lining of his shirt. Well, they won the big game and our boy made the winning basket. Now I'm sending it to you. Keep it at your bedside at all times, and if you recover, it will be miracle number three.

God be with you, Captain. I'm praying for you.

Sincerely,
John Malley

P.S. Could you please send the Relic back to me when you no longer need it.

Matilda slid the card back into its envelope. "Where would we be without the kindness of strangers?"

"Let me see that," Jonah said. "I ain't believin' that came from anywhere but Bellevue."

"Clifton, New Jersey," Matilda said. She handed him the card and sure enough, at the bottom of the envelope was a grayish, half-eroded molar.

Jonah read the letter himself. Unbelievable; it was fuckin' unbelievable. The balls of this crazy fuckin' scumbag. Then he caught Matilda's eye. She was laughing at him.

"You think that's funny, huh?" he muttered.

"I think it's a scream."

They were sitting in plastic hospital chairs at the bedside of Matilda's husband, who was at this moment sleeping his drugged sleep. They had spent most of the last three weeks in these chairs. There was no telling how much longer it might be, and it was hard to know what to wish for.

Captain O'Day was burned beyond relief or repair. Every minute of every day he was enduring unendurable pain, the kind of pain there should have been another word for. He lay stranded in bandages and gauze like an insect in a spider's web, IVs and tubes hanging like loose threads. There was a feeding tube in his nose, a ventilator tube down his throat, and a catheter in his bladder. His already massive body had swollen to twice its original size, and beneath the bandages it was a ghastly patchwork: raw and purplish, blistered and peeling, overlaid with mesh and pieced together with staples.

Jonah couldn't look at him without remembering another incident from early in his firefighting career. It was a roadside fire. A hunter on his way out of the city was tinkering with his engine when the gas tank exploded in his face. When Jonah and the other firemen reached him, the man was crawling in circles in the dirt. His clothes had melted into his body and his face was eaten away. He was screaming in a way Jonah hadn't heard since the war. Blind and out of his mind from pain, he dragged himself toward them and groped for their boots.

Every day for the next few weeks, Jonah put in twice his usual time at the gym. He made his workouts as hard as he could stand, then went straight to the corner bar and stayed there half the night. Nothing helped him to forget the guy begging them to take his rifle from the front seat and shoot him.

Jonah himself had been burned on the job many times. Nothing too bad, but enough to know that no other kind of pain came near it. Death would be a blessing for Captain O'Day; he was on the threshold and Jonah was with him, hanging with him in that limbo.

Limbo, the street game he'd played as a kid, was where you bent over backward to pass under a sawed-off broomstick that two people were holding a few feet off the ground. Every time you made it under, the stick was lowered, while the other kids stood around chanting, *How low can you go?* You couldn't touch the stick and, except with your feet or skate wheels, you couldn't touch the pavement. This was kind of like that. He was bending over backward, contorting to hang between two boundaries, life and death. They were closer than most people knew, close enough to blur, but there was a space between them and Seamus was in it and so was he. Once you were there, that space widened around you, became a world of its own. It contained a thousand shades of light and darkness; it was filled with shadow and radiance.

He had been there once before. It was in a jungle. It was like a long delirious fever. Life and death all around, each day bearing the real chance of being his last, side by side with strangers who had become his closest kin. They were getting mutilated, blown into pieces, picked off one at a time. Some would make it though. Some would go back to what they persisted, out of habit or wishful thinking, in still calling home.

Jonah would never be at home here again. Not just because they spat at him and screamed at him when he got off the plane and on many occasions afterward, but because none of them knew the first fucking thing, they were all walking around with the same impossible innocence. They had never gone down that dark road into themselves, never gone anywhere, and there were certain things they would never have to know. America was so sheltered, sugarcoated, smug. With her insulation and wallpaper, her little picket fences. Seamus was out of it now, though; Seamus had met Jonah inside the walls with the roaches, beneath the floorboards with the rats, in the dark without a nightlight, and they were here together. Beyond rescue or consolation, where only death would bring relief. Together they could look at the others with their faces pressed against the glass. Watch their well-meaning mouths move, and listen to the loaded silence.

Sometimes it was hard to remember that he and O'Day were two separate people. When Seamus was admitted to the hospital, he had spoken from the gurney. He looked up at Jonah and said, "I want Malone to take my place."

He meant at the firehouse, of course.

Jonah was on his way to an A.A. meeting the night Seamus got burned. Even after five years of sobriety, he still went to a meeting every day, unless he was working a twenty-four-hour tour. The meetings were an exercise in humility—lining up at the coffee machine with his styrofoam cup, filling it with that bitter black brew, *my name is Jonah and I'm an alcoholic*. The serenity prayer and the strangers' hard-luck stories were his ritual and his maintenance. From the very first meeting, his life had been one long dry season: no backsliding, no slip-ups, no exceptions. He had a talent, it seemed, for giving things up.

His meeting that night was in a church basement on Driggs Avenue. It was near Ladder 104 and he figured he'd park in their lot. The garage door was just going up when he pulled in; the rig was on its way out. Jonah reached for his fire radio but before he could get it to his ear, Jake Schiller leaned out the cab window and hollered to him.

"Around the corner!" he yelled. "Bedford Avenue and South Third!"

He had to grin at the way Jake had read his mind. A good kid, Jake. And a good fireman too. For some time now, he'd been thinking of offering Jake a spot in Rescue 2. The guy had what it took to hold his own in a rescue company. He wasn't a good Samaritan type but he'd wade into anything. Jonah knew from their conversations over the years that all of Jake's extracurricular pastimes were as dangerous as firefighting. He spent his off-days on the ocean or in the mountains and he seemed to look at fire as just another element to be conquered. You could count on him to respect the fire but not to fear it, and that made for an asset to any company . . .

When he turned the corner and saw the building they were running toward, something touched the back of his neck and crawled down his spine. From Day One on the job, it had been with him, this ability to sense a bad fire before it happened the way dogs could sense a storm. Inside him, now, the intuition uncoiled like a cobra and rose into his throat. But this time it was useless. *He* was useless—out here on the sidelines without turnout coat, mask and ax.

Rigs were coming from every direction as he neared the building. He stood trembling as the men leapt down and ran inside. The stairwell swallowed a whole file of them and Jonah was left on the sidewalk, a surge of wasted adrenaline scattering stars across his line of sight.

There were no flames yet, just dark smoke coming from every pore and seam of the building, even the mortar between the bricks. For a few minutes there wasn't much to look at and then came the sight that stopped his breath. The smoke was being drawn back in.

Fuckin' son of a bitch, he breathed. *Oh Jesus Christ no.*

Two battalion chiefs were a few feet away. He watched their faces contort with the same understanding. A moment later there was an explosion of shingles and glass. Flaming shards showered down like hail as the backdraft burst every window on its way through the roof.

The first firefighter carried out of that oven was dead, his body burnt so black they'd need his dental X rays for a positive I.D. The coffin at that funeral would be closed, and if the guy had a mother, they wouldn't let her see him. The second was also blackened all over but still moving. The paramedics around the stretcher prevented Jonah from getting more than a glimpse. At these times it was still a surprise to see medics arriving by ambulance instead of helicopter.

The third man was fucked up too, maybe just as bad, but he was wide awake. His teeth were bared and he was bucking on the stretcher.

Jonah came closer and sudden recognition took him by the throat. It was Seamus O'Day.

There was no room for Jonah in the ambulance but a couple of police cars were lining up to trail it to the hospital. Jonah went over to the nearest one.

"Officer, can I come along with you?"

The cop riding shotgun looked up at him.

"I'm a firefighter over in Rescue 2," Jonah added, since he was in civilian clothing, but the man was already out of the car, yielding him the front seat. "I know who you are," the officer said, before easing himself through the back door. "And I just wish we were meeting for any other reason, Captain Malone."

The burn unit of the New York–Cornell Medical Center was the same as it ever was. It was a place he kept coming back to, a place he couldn't help taking personally. It was waiting here for him whenever he was burned, whenever he lost a victim or reached one late, whenever another fireman was hurt bad. Sterile and overheated, echoing with unheeded screams. The temperature was set and held at sweltering: the comfort zone for those stripped even of their skin.

They were just starting to cut Seamus's clothes away when Jonah reached his side. The captain's face was drawn but no longer twisted with pain; shock had set in.

"Hey, Seamus," Jonah said.

O'Day was staring at the ceiling, unable to turn his head, but he rolled his eyes in Jonah's direction. "Malone," he rasped. "Hey, Malone. How ya doin'."

"I'm all right, Seamus. How about you?"

"Where's Danny?"

Daniel Flanagan, as Jonah had learned on the way to the hospital, was the other fireman who was hurt. Joe Moore was the one already dead.

"He's here, Captain. He's alive."

Seamus's face relaxed.

"Malone," he said next. "How bad off am I?"

"Well, it's a little hard to tell right now. We'll see in a few minutes."

O'Day's clothing was a long time in coming off. Much of it clung like tar and threatened to take his skin along with it. As the medical team gently cut and lifted and peeled it away, a cold sweat broke out across Jonah's back. O'Day was fucked. Beyond fucked. He was crazy fucked all over, the kind of injury there was no coming back from. It was the worst he had seen anyone look and still be breathing: ravaged from neck to ankle, the damage worsening below the waist. Dark purple burns everywhere; deep tissue erosion up and down the legs. In some places the captain had what they called fourth-degree burns, going past the muscle to bone.

Turning away, he saw Matilda O'Day for the first time. She stood in the doorway, a girlish figure no more than five-foot-two, slim and pale-haired in faded blue jeans. As she moved to her husband's side, Jonah saw that she was shivering beneath the heat shields. But to his surprise and admiration, her face never changed.

"Matilda," Seamus said. He was hoarse from the smoke.

"Oh Seamus," she murmured, with no more than the slightest tremor in her voice. She looked straight into his eyes and tried to smile.

"Mrs. O'Day?" Jonah asked.

It was a moment before she turned to him. "Yes?"

She had the warmest blue eyes he had ever seen. For a moment he forgot what he was going to say.

Then: "I'm Jonah Malone," he said. "I'm a friend of your husband's."

"How do you do?" she asked blankly.

"And I'm Kevin Delorey." Jonah turned to see the battalion chief coming toward them, and for some reason the sight of him was a relief. Delorey was another ex-Marine. He knew everything that Jonah knew and then some. As he joined them beside Seamus, it was all Jonah could do not to snap to attention.

"Hey, O'Day," Delorey said gently. "Looks like you're gonna have some time off for a while."

"Chief," Seamus managed. It was getting harder for him to talk. "I want Malone to take my place."

"We can arrange that," Delorey said. "Don't worry about anything." He turned to Jonah. "How do you happen to be here, Malone?"

"I was in the neighborhood," Jonah said. "I mean, where the fire was."

"Well, you might be back there real soon. Ladder 104 will need a covering captain for the day tour tomorrow."

"Yes, sir," Jonah said.

The chief then turned to Matilda and put a hand on her shoulder. "Mrs. O'Day, I'll be brief. I'm sure you'd like to be alone with your husband as soon as possible and I won't be keeping you. I just want to take a minute to say a few things."

Matilda nodded. Delorey ran a hand through his gray hair. "Mrs. O'Day," he began again. "It's a very noble thing to be a firefighter's wife. It means living every day with the kind of risk that most wives never have to think about. We can't fix it so none of our men get hurt, but we can uphold the brotherhood code when it does happen. The fire department is your family now. We will do anything in our power to sustain and support you through whatever lies ahead. The department has already appointed someone to assist you during your husband's stay in the hospital. His name is John Callahan and he'll be by in the morning. But beyond that, if you need anything at all, don't be afraid to let us know right away."

"Thank you," Matilda said. She looked a little bewildered.

The chief turned to Jonah. "So. Malone. Can you fill in at Ladder 104 at oh-nine hundred hours?"

"Yes sir."

"Well, good. Why don't you get some sleep in the meantime, then."

"Yes sir," Jonah repeated. He turned to Seamus. "I'll be back to visit tomorrow. After work. Anything you want me to tell the guys?"

The other man's words were hardly more than a wheeze. Jonah leaned down to hear. "Tell them," he began, and stopped.

"What'll I tell them?"

"Tell them not to let this fuck up football season."

It turned out that this John Callahan could not handle the assignment and Jonah didn't blame him. A few minutes beside that bed was a lifetime in itself. And besides, Callahan had a family of his own.

When Jonah learned that the guy was begging off, he went down to department headquarters on Livingston Street to speak with Chief Delorey.

Delorey was a veteran of the Korean War and in his firefighting days had racked up quite a few medals himself. Crossing paths with him was like happening across someone from one of his old platoons, and he had the feeling Delorey saw it that way too.

"Malone!" the chief said when he caught sight of Jonah, captain's hat in his hand, standing in the open doorway. "Come on in and sit down."

Jonah took a seat on the other side of Delorey's desk and looked around at the office. As in his own bedroom, framed medals and rescue clippings took up most of the wall space. There was Delorey in his younger years, soot-blackened and grinning in the faded photographs, something broken about his grin though, that same something.

"What can I do for you, Malone?"

"I heard Callahan's looking to get out of the O'Day assignment," he told the chief.

"Yeah, well, he was bugging from day one. He's got balls enough for ten men in a fire but he ain't got the balls for this."

"Look, sir," said Jonah, "with no disrespect, he ain't right for the job anyway. He's got a wife and kids at home, for cryin' out loud. It ain't fair to put him in that kind of spot."

"All right, well, no one's gonna sue him. It's a tough situation." The chief shrugged. "What are you driving at, Malone?"

"Just that I'll fill in for him. If you're amenable to that."

"You, Malone? Come on. You got your own firehouse to worry about."

"Someone can cover for me."

"All right, but why you of all people?"

"Well, look at it this way," Jonah said. "For one thing, I got no family, no side jobs, nothing to keep me from puttin' in long days. But the main thing is, I know I can handle it."

There was an uncomfortable silence. "Listen, Malone," the chief said finally. "We don't ask someone in your position to do this kind of service."

"I ain't above doing a service for Captain O'Day," Jonah said.

"You're a captain yourself," Delorey pointed out.

"Yeah, well, I'd do the same even if I was commissioner," Jonah said. "Seamus is a real good guy. The best. I'd shine his shoes."

The chief held Jonah another moment with his hard stare. Then he passed one hand over his face, pressing thumb and forefinger into the corners of his eyes. "If I consider you for this, Malone, you got to know what you're up against. O'Day's fighting a losing battle here; there's no happy ending to this thing. But we don't want another man jumping ship; it's not good for the morale. Have you slept on this one a couple of nights? Because it ain't an easy thing you're tryin' to sign on for."

"Look, Chief," Jonah said. "I'll swear this to you and God and anyone else right now. I'm dedicating my life to Seamus O'Day until the day he dies or walks out of there. I ain't gonna change my mind about it."

Delorey took his hand away from his face. "All right, then," he said finally. "You got an open-ended leave of absence from Rescue 2 for the duration of Captain O'Day's stay in the hospital. I'll authorize it right now. The paperwork should be ready by this afternoon." He reached for the phone.

Jonah's arm came halfway up in an impulse to salute the chief. He caught himself and, as he rose to go, turned the motion into a handshake instead. The back of his shirt was damp with the sweat of relief. "Thank you, sir," he said, replacing his hat. "Thank you very much."

"So," Matilda said now, putting the mail aside. "What do you want first, the bad news or the bad news?"

"What—you know something I don't?" Jonah asked.

"Dr. Dresden came by while you were downstairs getting the paper."

"Oh yeah? What'd he say?"

"Helene's asking to be relieved of Seamus's care," Matilda told him.

"*Helene?*"

Helene was one of Seamus's full-time nurses. She'd been with them from the beginning—nearly every day for three straight weeks—a quiet girl as competent as she was lovely. She reminded Jonah of the girl from his high school dances—she had the same honey-colored hair, the same soft hint of a smile. And no one was more gentle with Seamus.

"I know. I know you liked her," Matilda said. "I liked her too."

"What's the matter with her?"

"Well, I don't know. But she says she just can't do it anymore," Matilda told him. "Of course Dr. Dresden didn't really give me details, but I overheard two other nurses talking about it. Apparently she's having nightmares, crying jags, I don't know what all . . . she said something about . . . his eyes following her around the room. It unnerves her."

"Oh," Jonah said. "Well."

For a moment, Matilda seemed to hover on the edge of tears. Then she bit her lip and rallied back. "Maybe we should fix her up with John Callahan," she cracked. "They seem to have plenty in common."

"That's right," Jonah said. "A match made in heaven."

The fact was, though this wasn't the time to say it, that Jonah knew what Helene was talking about. It was an eerie thing: that ravaged body, immobile, mummified, and within it, those living eyes. Those eyes went back and forth, sometimes clouded over, sometimes clear as ice. It was a relief when they were milky: it meant he was out of it, in a morphine fog. It was terrible when they were lucid, blazing *No Vacancy* like a neon sign. He didn't really blame the girl for needing to get away, any more than he blamed Callahan. And if they couldn't stand the heat, then for Christ's sake get 'em the hell out the kitchen. Not everyone, after all, could be like him.

Jonah spent sixteen hours a day at Seamus's bedside, wiping the sweat from the captain's forehead, holding his hand. Crooning to him in syllables that weren't always intelligible and didn't need to be. Steadying and holding him: Seamus with his face of an animal mangled in a trap, weighted to the earth, all shining terrified eyes and quivering nostrils. A hint of something womanly now in this most masculine of faces—the bones slackened beneath the skin, softened with morphine—a face otherwise spared by the fire. Seamus was beyond speaking now, and even if he weren't, the tracheotomy would have prevented it. It was hard to keep up a one-sided conversation, but in spite of the awkwardness, the inadequacy he felt all the time, he managed to press on and on.

"I know you're hurtin', Seamus. But you're hangin' in there real good," he would say. "And the whole city's behind you, man. Not just the city, either. I mean, this has made national news. You wouldn't believe the amount of mail you've got. With more comin' in every day. You're everyone's hero, believe me. And you're my hero."

He said other things too.

"I know how bad you want to make it through this, Seamus. I seen how hard you been fightin' and ain't nobody tougher than you. But if it gets too hard, and you need to go, you got my word that we'll take care of Matilda and the kids. Me and all the guys. I promise you that."

In some ways, of course, he was already taking care of Matilda. If nothing else, she could depend on him to see this thing through with her, and know she wasn't alone with it.

"Look, Matilda," he told her now. "I'm real sorry about Helene. But look, for whatever it's worth, you still got me. I promised Chief Delorey and I'll promise you: I ain't goin' nowhere till this is over, one way or another. All right? Just so's you know."

"Jonah, if you weren't here . . . " Matilda said. She left the sentence unfinished.

M atilda O'Day didn't mean to fall in love with Jonah. And not now, at the worst time imaginable, as her husband lay dying, ossifying into sainthood. But here he was, he was here all the time, strong and whole, serious, kind, and devoted to their cause with the most startling single-minded intensity. He was guiding her through the nightmare, taking on the worst of it, protective as the father she never had.

In the earliest days of the ordeal, before she was offered sleeping quarters at the hospital, he picked her up at the Waterway Ferry each morning and drove her into the city. When she got off the boat he was waiting there like a long lost lover, like a brother, like home. He always stood against the wall, in his captain's uniform, narrowed eyes trained on the flood of passengers descending the gangplank. (Waiting for *her*—looking for *her*.) Without a word, he relieved her of whatever she was carrying, and with the briefest touches on her shoulder or the small of her back, he guided her to the chief's car. He unlocked the passenger side first and opened the door for her.

"Sleep all right?" he usually asked first.

"Well. Better than last night, anyway."

"Eat yet?"

"I had a cup of coffee."

"That's all? Just coffee? Then let's get some real breakfast into you first."

It was always like this. She willingly put herself into his hands to steer. She ate when he told her to eat and drank when he said to drink. Otherwise she might not even remember.

It was on one of these mornings that he helped her resolve the issue of the children wanting to visit Seamus. They were having breakfast in the hospital cafeteria when Matilda decided to bring it up with him.

"Jonah?" she said. "I need to ask you about something."

"Well, ask me."

"I just don't know what to do about the kids," Matilda confessed. "All I've wanted is to protect them from the worst of this, but they're not babies anymore and they have ways of finding things out. There are certain details I've tried to keep from them, but they read the papers and they watch the news." Carefully she set her coffee cup down on the saucer. "All of them want to see their father. And the truth is they might never have another chance, so I don't know how to tell them no. But at the same time I can't, I just can't let them see him like this. They might never get over it." She hesitated, then added, "And if he doesn't make it, I don't want them remembering him this way."

"I hear you, honey." Jonah spoke quietly. "That's a tough call. But you got to go with your intuition. Personally? I think you're doing the right thing by protecting them."

"You do? You think I'm right?"

"It ain't my call. But yeah, I think you're right. What would be the point in bringing them here? He can't talk to 'em. If adults like Helene and Callahan can't handle it—and they're supposed to be professionals used to tragedy—what's it gonna do to young kids? I mean, it's horrible, honey. It don't get much worse than this."

"All right, then," Matilda decided. "I'll stick to my intuition, like you said. Oh, I'm glad I asked you, Jonah. I know some of the other firemen from the company think I'm wrong."

"What?" Jonah stopped eating to stare at her. "What other firemen?"

"Well, a lot of them have been out to the house to see the kids, which is nice," Matilda said. "But Tom Donovan, I think it was, apparently told the boys that he agreed with them. He said they should have the right to make that decision for themselves. It made me wonder if maybe I was making a mistake."

She was unprepared for Jonah's reaction. He slammed his fist down on the table, making the cups and saucers jump.

"To hell with Donovan," he exploded. "Where the hell does he get off sayin' anything to them? He ain't their mother. He ain't even family. He's fuckin' nobody. It's none of his fuckin' business and I'm gonna tell him so to his face."

"No, no, Jonah. I don't want—"

"Don't take up for him, Matilda, he's way out of line. Look, I'm gonna talk to the whole firehouse. Don't forget, Seamus named me as his covering captain back at the beginning of all this, so I think I got the right. Anyone else there got anything to say about you, they got to come through me first. You hear me? Or I ain't doin' my job. No two ways about it."

"Well," she said. "All right, then." His outburst had left an excited little flutter in her pulse.

"Don't even think about it anymore," he said. "Just leave it to me."

"Thank you, Jonah. You do so much for me. For all of us."

"And listen, while we're on the kids," he said. "We should talk to them together about why it's not a good idea for them to come here. I'll help you explain things."

And that was what he did. They'd all gone to dinner the very next night and he helped her dissuade the children from wanting to visit the hospital, putting it in terms of Seamus's protection instead of theirs. He explained how emotionally taxing such a visit would be for everyone involved. *They* could take it, he said, but it would be dangerously stressful for their father, who needed every ounce of energy for the war he was waging. They accepted this judgment coming from him; it was possible that they were even relieved.

Then at Seamus's bedside he was something to see: a four-star major general playing nurse. She wouldn't know what Jonah was whispering to Seamus; she stood at these moments as a child stands at the edge of the dinner table while the adults have their coffee, uncomprehending but secure. They were conferring on another plane, in another world—a man's world of combat and war. In another place and time, Jonah would probably be putting Seamus's last cigarette between his lips, and promising to inform his family.

Seamus couldn't even answer, yet Matilda knew there was a transaction taking place, a dialogue and a resolution that did not involve her. Other firemen were stationed just outside the room, guarding the door, keeping the public at bay. They were a voluntary brigade, trading shifts; they had worked it out among themselves without needing to bother her. Somehow she was in the inner circle of this very male regiment, protected as a queen bee at the center of a hive. The uniformed men had arrived at her door to deliver the bad news, the helicopter had alit for her. The helicopter with its great chopping blades, the very sound of which disturbed Jonah to this day—she saw the shadow fall across his face whenever one clacked by overhead. They were ill omens, nothing good could come of them.

In the meantime, she no longer knew whether she wanted her husband to live or die. If he survived, he would be a shadow of his former self, disfigured and crippled, probably confined to a wheelchair. Certainly he would never fight fire again.

It was impossible to imagine Seamus with a compromised body. All his life it had been his special pleasure to perform feats of strength. Once, all by himself, he had shifted a double-parked Volkswagen into one of the spaces it was straddling. This was in a lot outside Giants Stadium where there were no other parking places available. The family stood by, thrilled, as he lifted the front fender, moved it a few feet to the left, then went to the back of the car to repeat the feat.

It pleased him if you needed him to open a jar, loosen a lid. He loved to show off how easy such tasks were for him. He could hoist several kids into the air at one time and still, after twenty years, sweep Matilda off her feet with no effort. At the annual local fair, his favorite booth was the one that tested your strength—where you brought a hammer down with all your might, tried to ring the bell at the top of a scale. Every year as far back as she could remember, Seamus made that bell ring until each child in the family had a stuffed pet to take home.

He could bench-press three hundred and fifty pounds. Where would this man be, who would he be, stripped of his might?

The other two firemen trapped with Seamus had died already, and Matilda was starting to think they were the lucky ones. Joe Moore was dead on arrival. Daniel Flanagan never recovered consciousness and was gone before the next morning. Matilda would never forget that heaving chest, the comatose body burst open from the heat. They hadn't informed Seamus of Daniel's death—there was no need for that; it only would have broken his heart along with his body. The younger fireman had been his main concern as they bore him into the hospital. One of his last conscious questions was: "Where's Danny?"

"He's here, Captain. He's alive." It had been the truth and there was no reason to amend it later. Over the next several days, when the boy's death made every headline in the city, no one was allowed to bring a newspaper into Seamus's room, or turn on the television set.

The death of Daniel Flanagan would have unhinged Matilda had she not needed to focus on her husband. Daniel had been from their own neighborhood, the toddler turned Boy Scout turned junior varsity linebacker—a boy she and Seamus considered a nephew. Seamus had helped him get into the fire department and ultimately assigned to his own firehouse. *Danny-Boy*, that was what Seamus had called him all his life.

"Did he call you Danny-Boy at the firehouse, too?" Matilda once asked him, when they were talking about his probie days.

"Yes he did, and it was a long time before I heard the end of it," he told her with a rueful grin.

"And what about you, did you call him Uncle Seamus?" she asked next.

"No I didn't. Not there, I didn't. Not even the first day," the boy said. "I called him Captain."

"So," Jonah was asking now. "Is that it for the mail?"

"That's it for the good stuff," she told him, and smiled. She was sure he knew what she wasn't saying out loud: that letters like the one from this Malley secretly inspired as much fury in her as they did in him. How long did Christ suffer, after all? Three days?

So far Seamus had hung on for twenty days and nights, and the ordeal seemed slated to stretch into infinity. The hospital had even arranged in-house living quarters for her. For the first eight or nine days after Seamus was admitted, Jonah had picked her up at the boat every morning and dropped her off again every night. But in the middle of the second week, Dr. Dresden came up to her in the hall while she was taking a cigarette break, and let her know that one of the residential rooms had opened up in the east wing.

"The hospital likes to offer sleeping accommodations to the families of our intensive-care patients whenever possible," he told her. "If you can spare yourself that commute from Queens every morning and night, it's just as well you don't wear yourself out that way. Housekeeping is in there now, but it should be ready by this afternoon. I'll take you over there in a couple of hours if you'd like."

And later that day, when she went to look at it, Jonah came along. It was at the other end of the building and Dr. Dresden gave them an update on the way.

"We had a renal consultation this morning," he said, "and Seamus's kidneys haven't rallied in the way we'd hoped. As we've discussed before, the kidneys are usually the first organs to be overwhelmed in a severe burn situation, so this is hardly unexpected. But we'd like to put him on dialysis starting tomorrow."

They arrived at the little residential alcove and Dr. Dresden unlocked a door stenciled with the number 2. "Here it is," he said. "What do you think, Mrs. O'Day?"

As Matilda stepped into the room, a jolt of terror sent her neck cords into a spasm. What was so frightening? She didn't know. It was a clean, spare room, nothing wrong with it. The bed was neatly made and the pale blue carpet still bore vacuum tracks. There was a sofa and closet, a desk in one corner and a chest of drawers. The watercolor paintings on the walls were carefully serene: pastel tulips and pale daffodils, tranquil springtime scenes. But desperation hung in the air. The tragedies of a thousand families before her seemed to hover in the space. It was a room for people waiting for the worst and she knew she could never spend these nights within its walls all by herself.

She was aware then of Jonah looking at her; he took one glance at her face and she felt his swift appraisal.

"I'll stay here too," he said. "I'll sleep on the couch." Unlocking her voice so a grateful rush of words could come at last.

"It's perfect, doctor," she answered.

"Well, I guess I'll go get dinner," Jonah said now. "What do you think about pizza?"

"Sounds fine."

"Anything on it?"

"Whatever you want."

"All right then. Be right back."

Matilda watched him leave, held his departing back with her gaze until he disappeared. He was such a strong, handsome, good man. It was amazing no woman had snatched him up by now.

And while she was counting her lucky stars, there was no overlooking Dr. Dresden. They were so fortunate to have Seamus under his supervision. He was a great surgeon, the best, undivided in his devotion to his patients and tireless in the care he gave them. According to the nurses, who all seemed to worship him, he sometimes did surgery for ten or eleven hours straight, in an operating room kept at 101 degrees Fahrenheit. He had operated on her husband four times already.

Beside her, Seamus was opening his eyes. She turned to him and tried, as always, to smile. Here was the hardest challenge of the day, finding an endless stream of soft, comforting words to pour over this man who had no way to answer.

Oh, Seamus. She laid her hand against his cheek. *Do you know how much I've loved living with a big man? I don't just mean your size and strength, although it was a fine thing to always feel safe when you were near. But you were big in so many other ways too: the kind of captain you were, the kind of coach, and how many kids you fit into the corners of your life. You made them think their size wasn't what was important either. If they had the heart to play, you had the heart to coach them.*

Then there were all the strays we took in over the years. Children from the Catholic Foster Bureau, staying with us between homes. Friends of our own kids, who weren't getting what they needed from their real families. So many of them were always sleeping over at our house, eating at our table. And even all the animals that found their way to our doorstep—you made room for them too. We were a good team that way.

As far as I can remember, you were never afraid of anything. You were always as brave and tough as they come and yet you were always so gentle at the same time. Never raised a hand to me or any of the kids, not once in twenty years. And though you were always one for drinking, you never got into brawls. No, you were the one who could break them up all by yourself, and that's what you did. You saved your aggression for football and fire.

They limited your visitors here, Seamus, you know that. Dr. Dresden thought it best for you to save your strength, and not have unnecessary exposure to germs. But the people come anyway. They come and they talk to me. Sometimes when you're asleep I go have a cigarette in the hall, and there's always a small crowd waiting for a word about you. They tell me stories about you, things I never knew about. I had no idea how many lives you've touched. People I've never heard you mention, and yet you're so important to them. They give me letters and gifts for you. When you're a little better, we'll go over every single one. I've got it all written down; I'm keeping track.

And I don't need to tell you what a wonderful father you've been, or how much those kids love you. All six of them—they always have and they always will. And even now, those two boys both want to be firemen. I hope you're proud of that, Seamus. I hope you have the peace of mind that you deserve.

Even as she spoke to him, it took all of Matilda's resolve to hold his gaze. His eyes were like a promise that he was being spared nothing, that he was suffering as much as a person could suffer. How was it possible for someone to hurt so much and still live? How long could it go on?

Mercifully soon, he was under again. She knew they had the morphine to thank for that, though Dr. Dresden had warned her of the necessity of weaning him off it before long. And then what?

She sat back in the plastic chair and looked out the window. Since the accident, she had passed hour upon hour beside this window, gazing outside at the world as she used to know it. Morning into noon into late afternoon. Then evening settling like an afterthought, the yellow-purple of a bruise, casting her tired reflection upon the pane. When Seamus was asleep and Jonah wasn't around, there was nothing to take her out of her own head. Nowhere to turn for distraction or relief. These interludes seemed like a prelude to the future stretching before her, as blank a slate as the opposite wall.

If Jonah weren't here, she was sure she would have lost her mind by now. It used to be that if she wanted a little time to herself, she had to carve it out—by walking the dog, maybe, or taking a bath. There was always far too much to do. A little breathing space, just to hear herself think, was a rare luxury in her regular life. It had never occurred to her that not having that time was a kind of luxury too.

Certainly, it had kept her out of trouble. She had never strayed outside her marriage before, even in her thoughts. Seamus could not have said the same. He'd had at least one affair that she knew of, many years ago, with a woman—Lorena—who lived across the street. She recalled the many nights they had all gotten together for cards—she and Seamus, Lorena and her husband. Week after week, they all met in the same room and Matilda never had an inkling of what was between them. The other woman wanted Seamus for herself and did her best to convince him to leave his family.

Matilda would never forget how she felt then. She had never before understood how terror and grief translated into physical pain. Terrible pain: her body hurt for days. She could barely move or breathe. Going through the motions of the day, she was slowed to a near crawl. Her stomach clenched; her heart was a throbbing wound in her chest; her throat ached morning till night with the childish howl it held: *I thought she was my friend!* She could not even swear that what she felt now was worse. This, after all, was nothing personal.

It was the fire department that had returned him to her. He went to the firehouse in his indecision and the men he worked with pointed him straight back home. They moved away soon afterward and some years later Lorena died of bone cancer. It would probably surprise Seamus to learn that she knew this. She had her sources, old girlfriends from the neighborhood. Long-suffering wives who even seemed to take some vicarious pleasure in relating the news.

Matilda was to outlive both of them, it would seem. Was this her revenge? It seemed more theirs than hers. They had done it again, left her out, left her behind. They had gone together into that land outside the living and she would be left in her house with the porcelain and the china and the kitchen that needed painting. Monthly mortgage payments and taxes she didn't know how to file.

After all these years, she was astonished to find that the thought of them together still stuck like a scream in her throat. What had the two of them exchanged in those hours? What whispers, what secrets? In some ways it didn't seem all that different from the intimacy between Seamus and Jonah now. Weren't they in another world as well, one beyond her reach? Seamus was *her* husband. She wondered what, after all, that counted for in the end. She got to witness his liaisons. Was that all?

The pizza that Jonah brought back was strewn with peppers and onions.

"That's exactly what I like," Matilda said in surprise. "How funny."

"Well, not really," Jonah said. "That's what you asked for last week, when we got a couple of slices across the street."

"You *noticed* that? You *remembered*?"

"I notice a lot of things. I'm pretty observant, I guess," he said. "Something I picked up from my old man. He was a detective."

Matilda shook her head and, with one of the plastic knives, began cutting a piece of pizza away from the pie. Without looking at him, she asked, "So what else have you noticed about me?"

The question was so brazen she couldn't quite believe the words were hers, and she wouldn't have been surprised if he hadn't answered.

He did answer, though. He answered right away. "I'll tell you," he said. "I'll tell you what struck me about you right from the start."

Matilda looked up at him.

"When I first seen you come into the burn unit," he said. "When you came up to Seamus, I was watching your face. I remember you seen how bad he was burnt but you didn't let on. You didn't let it show. You stayed strong for him. I admired that."

His words, and the knowledge that even then he had been *paying attention,* was enough to leave her breathless with amazement.

"And all this time," Jonah continued, his eyes holding hers. "You been strong for him and strong for the kids. I know how bad you been feelin'. I know you cry over him every day. But you ain't cried in front of him. And that's good, Matilda. You're doin' real good."

She was crying now. His recognition had undone her. After all these years, someone was finally telling her she was doing a good job. She pushed the box of pizza out of the way, put her head down on the table and wept. After a minute she felt his hand stroking her hair.

"That's right, go on," he said. "It's only me now, so go ahead and cry."

Later that night, as she was falling asleep, a revelation came to her. It came with such sudden force that her eyes flew open and she lay staring into the darkness.

Her witness. That male presence who was always there, the one who saw everything, who was keeping an account. The man in the shadows, just beyond sight, her guardian and angel, overseer and lover.

She sat up and searched the shadows for his prone form. She could just make out his outline on the couch. He was no more than ten feet from her, his breathing barely audible, so different from her husband's. They had been sleeping in the same room for some time now: a comfort and torment to her. She got out of bed and walked over to where he lay, then knelt to stare into his sleeping face.

"It's you," she whispered.

At the newsstand out in front of the hospital, Jonah ran into Helene. Seamus was on the cover of the *Daily News* and he wanted a copy for himself. Helene was buying some women's magazine. He came up behind her and touched her on the shoulder. When she turned and saw him, a stricken expression crossed her face and she hesitated before speaking. "Captain Malone."

"Hey Helene. How you doin'."

She hugged her magazine to her chest. "I'm glad you're still speaking to me," she said. "I'm glad you don't hate me."

"Come on. Of course not."

"I hate myself. For being so weak. Maybe I shouldn't have been a nurse."

"You're a great nurse."

"I've taken care of so many suffering people," she told him. "Dying people—children, even, with cancer or AIDS—but I never had to face an ordeal like the one Captain O'Day is going through. I was so afraid I was going to break down in front of him. And when I got home afterwards, those evenings, I couldn't eat, couldn't sleep . . . sometimes I even felt like I couldn't breathe . . . I'm sorry. I know you don't need to hear this."

"It's all right," he said.

"I wish I had your strength," she said. "I know you volunteered to be here with him. But can I ask . . . can I ask why you're doing it?"

He stood looking at her.

"Forgive me," she said, after a moment. "That was a very personal question. And you certainly don't owe me any explanations." She turned and walked away. Jonah watched her go through the front entrance of the hospital.

Delorey had asked him the same thing. And he hadn't really answered the chief either. There was no one he could imagine telling his reasons to. He thought Seamus understood them, and maybe Matilda did too. No one else mattered, and neither of them would ever ask him to explain.

His motives were selfish; he knew that. No matter how it looked or what everyone thought. His grief, which changed shape but never gave up its grip on him, was heroic for the time being. It had a noble focus; it was something he could share. And it was giving him the chance to be part of a family.

What else? There was his jealousy. How could he ever talk about that? It was worse than crazy, the fact that in some way he coveted the other captain's situation. *I want Malone to take my place.* Well, why couldn't he? *Why couldn't he?* Seamus wanted to live. That much was clear. In spite of everything, Seamus wanted to live. And Jonah wanted to die. That old longing never left, and it would be well worth the torture to know the end was in sight. Given the chance, he would take

Seamus's suffering upon himself, lay himself down on that bed of flames and let Seamus rise up, healed.

  Or, if they couldn't switch, Jonah wanted to merge with the other man completely. Where was the communion wafer that would let him share Seamus's bones and blood? Where was the sacred wine? There was nothing to do but what he was doing: rubbing up against it, getting as close as he could.

There were times when the almost other-worldly connection between them seemed ordained. Take Seamus's new tattoo, for one thing, acquired during a skin-graft operation.

"Burned tissue is dead," Dr. Dresden had explained. "It doesn't heal. It won't regenerate. If left in place, it will only breed infection and resist antibiotics. So we need to cut it away, as soon and as thoroughly as Seamus can tolerate, and graft new skin over the remaining healthy tissue."

"Where does the new skin come from?" Matilda wanted to know.

"Well, the best skin, of course, would be his own. Ideally we could harvest it from the few unburned areas left on his body. But he's far too unstable for that right now. So we'll be using a temporary skin until he's ready." The doctor paused before adding carefully, "Most likely that will be cadaver skin."

And so now Seamus had a tattoo on his forearm, taken from the shoulder of another man. A tattoo that Jonah wouldn't have believed if he hadn't seen it with his own eyes; an unfurling scroll that read, "Semper Fi." What was that if not a sign?

Of course, this connection was sure to be cut sometime soon. And in the meantime, there was another long day ahead of him. Back upstairs, he found Matilda still asleep. That was good; she needed any time out she could get.

Jonah went to Seamus's bed and took his usual chair. The other man was awake but still. Above the feeding tube, his eyes met Jonah's. *Malone,* he could hear, as plain as if Seamus had been able to speak. *Malone, help me. Help me.*

Seamus. As gently as he could, Jonah brushed the other man's hair back from his forehead. It was damp with sweat. *Seamus, do you remember the first time you met me? Jerry Fitzgerald brought you over to me after I won that boxing match for him. Do you know how bad I wanted Jerry to be my father? My old man wasn't much good to me;*

drinking ruined him. Do you remember that night? You asked me if I played football. I had to say no but I wished to hell I could of said yes. I knew right then why they all wanted to play for you, Seamus. The biggest man in the bar, and the one with the least to prove. Your voice was real quiet and when you shook hands it wasn't like you needed to crush the other guy's paw, you know?

And all those teams you started. You were saving lives with those teams, man. Young guys, they need combat, they need someplace to put all that aggression. Me, I got sent overseas with it, I was a pawn. You know? A pawn in a game I didn't even understand. I did damage there's no walkin' away from. And at the end of the day over there, no one got up and shook hands and walked off the field. I never had a good place to put that energy, not till later. The fire department gave me a reason to get up in the morning, but it's too late to undo all what I done. That's part of why I've always been ready to die in a fire. Or at least get hurt real bad.

Seamus, I always expected to be in the spot you're in now, and if I could take it off you, lift all the pain off of you and take it onto me, you got to believe I would. I swear I would. I wish to hell I could. Bein' around you has been one of the greatest honors of my career. I seen what real courage is all about, you know? I seen what real endurance is all about. You're an inspiration to everyone. You're like everyone's father and everyone loves you. I'm a better man for knowin' you.

So like I said, we all love you and need you here and if you want to keep fighting I'm with you every step of the way but if you need to let go, your family's in good hands, and you tell Jerry it won't be long before I see you guys again.

Jonah secretly dreaded the time Seamus would leave him. He could gaze into the other man's eyes with all his might, like gazing at his own reflection in a pool of rain until the earth drank it back in. The earth was drinking Seamus back in; he was draining away by the hour. Soon he would be gone, there wasn't much doubt about that, and then where would Jonah be?

Free-floating once again, without an anchor. Waiting for the next catastrophe to hit. He was worth something in a crisis, adrift without one. Tragedy freed him to feel and to connect. Regular life left him cold; he just wasn't good at it. It was pain, or nothing. Nothing or pain. As far back as he could remember, it was only one or the other for him.

His father used to have a mean temper. As a kid, Jonah had tried to avoid coming within ten feet of him when he was drinking. At those times his old man would knock him across the room as soon as look at him. Still this was better than his mother's total abstinence. In his whole life, she had never hugged him, never held him or kissed him or told him she loved him.

This schism persisted even after he was out of their house: streaks of pain and numbness running in tandem. He could shut like a shell on the ocean floor, tossed harmlessly by the waves, indifferent and protected. Or he could emerge and the currents, torrents, would threaten to drown him. Once in a while, he might break the surface and see the stars; by lucky chance, he could find himself riding a wave. But always as he neared the shore, the undertow would pull him out again, take him back to the dark depths.

When he shut, there was no telling when and if he would open again. That was deep freeze, and no living creature could survive with him in its climate.

He was in deep freeze, for instance, the time he let the cat go. This came up in a conversation with Matilda, in a coffee shop near the hospital. Seamus had been scheduled for debriding, the most dreaded hour of the day where they sloughed away the dead skin that could become infected if left in place, scrubbing where it was agony just to be touched. Anything was better than dwelling on that.

"You know, something like this forces you to take stock of your life," Matilda remarked, tracing invisible patterns on the table with her stirring straw. "It gives you plenty of time to go over every regret you've ever had. You know what I mean? Do you know what you regret the most?"

Only Matilda could ever pull him into such a discussion—right now, her stakes were as high as his—and even with her he played it safe. For one thing, he made her go first.

"The night before Seamus went to work for the last time," she said, "he came home drunk and I wouldn't make love to him. I didn't mind him having his boys night out, but why did he always have to come home so late and so drunk? Most men in that condition wouldn't even be able to get it up but oh, Seamus . . . ! He never had a problem. People talk about drinkers having a wooden leg. I say my husband had a wooden you-know-what. Anyway, he was raring to go and I wouldn't. I was angry." She kept her eyes fixed on the table as they filled and spilled over. "Sometimes I felt that was the only power I had. To say, No way, not if you're coming to bed like this. He frustrated me in a lot of different ways, and there were times I used any kind of leverage I could find. But what wouldn't I give now, for the chance to do it over again? It's something I'll have to live with the rest of my life."

"Oh, but honey," Jonah said. "You couldn't have known. It ain't worth beating yourself up over that, it was just bad timing, bad luck. You gave it to him for twenty years, didn't you? You gave him six beautiful children. You were a good wife for twenty years. You got to focus on that."

"I *was* a good wife," Matilda conceded. "I tried to be, anyway. It wasn't always easy."

"You stayed together," Jonah said. "That's more than most anyone else can manage these days."

"All right, so now what about you?" she asked. "What do you regret the most?"

She didn't know what she was asking. He searched for a light answer. "You got time for my whole life story?" he joked.

"Just pick one thing. Anything. Something small, even."

So he found what seemed like something small. He told her about the cat. His own cat, a cat that loved him. This was many years ago but the memory still brought him agony. A neighbor's calico had given birth. He agreed to take two kittens as soon as they were old enough to leave their mother. One was a tawny male that was pretty much indifferent to him; the other was a gray female that loved him.

It was a mistake to accept them in the first place. They were nothing but aggravation. He would come in late at night, drunk and fucked up, and curse them for being there, weaving around his clumsy feet. In the morning it was worse, their cries adding to the hammers already splitting open his head. If they jumped up on his bed, he would knock them across the room, and the tawny one didn't care. It recovered itself and stayed away, and if a cat could talk, it would've said, *Well fuck you, then.* But the other one loved him. She tried to cuddle with him, curl into him, huddle near his warmth and console him. More than once, he sent her flying with one thrust of his arm in his drunkenness, meanness, fear.

For a long time she wouldn't heed these warnings. She was forgiving, she was affectionate. Always trying to lick his face. He knew he'd have to get rid of her, of her always asking for what he'd never be able to give. Why couldn't she be like the other one; why couldn't she *learn*?

It started out as a plan to give her to a friend of his. Bailey ran one of the horse-and-carriage stables in Central Park, and the stalls had rats. The rest of the litter had gone to him, and he'd issued a standing offer to take these two as well. Without knowing why, Jonah brought the male to Bailey and held on to the other.

It was lonelier for her after her brother was gone. Needy and forlorn, she turned to Jonah even more, imploring his attention, rubbing against his legs. He was always tripping over her when he walked, which drew muttered threats and more than occasionally an irritated kick. She never retaliated, never even hissed. She'd find a corner of the room and curl into a little ball. He felt shame then, and regret, but restrained himself from going over to her and trying to make it up. He didn't want her to come to expect it.

But even after she went away from him and didn't try anymore, he could still feel her gray presence. It filled the room, made it overly warm, made his eyes water and itch. He knew it couldn't go on.

It was late autumn, verging on winter, when he finally got rid of her. Just a touch of frost on the ground and on the branches. The colors in the park were muted; life had retreated indoors for the most part. The trees were bare and everything was strangely desolate, primed for the cold to come. In his mind, though he had never spoken it aloud, the little cat had a name, and its name was Dotty. This was because her eyes were so round; even the pupils were rounder than the narrow diamonds cats usually had. When she blinked, he could almost hear her eyes clicking in her head, like two billiard balls knocking together.

Dotty was in the box he was carrying, her body tense with alarm. He could feel her fear through the cardboard, register the fact of it without it arousing any answering emotion within him. He was cold through and through. He was shut down. He was also a little confused: he thought he knew where Bailey's stable was, and yet it was nowhere in sight. Had it moved? Not likely. Had he come in the wrong entrance? Where was he, anyway? He looked around. This was a deserted area of the park, where the trees were dark and dense. It seemed to be haunted by the homeless:

every few feet he'd see them, slinking in and out of the trees like gooks, exactly that silent and slick. He was sweating, desperate to be gone already. But he was on a mission and he had to carry it out. He could not afford to falter; he could not take this cat back home with him.

Bailey was nowhere. Jonah couldn't begin to imagine where he was or how to get there. What did it matter? Cats could fend for themselves. Everyone knew that. They weren't like dogs; they knew how to hunt and kill.

He set the box on the ground and lifted the lid. The cat jumped out immediately, then slunk in swift afterthought near Jonah's feet, nearly flattening herself out in an instinctive effort to stay low. Jonah picked up the empty box, pried it loose where it had been glued together, and crushed it flat. He would no longer need it. Dotty was scared, he could see that. Her gray tail puffed up and the short fur on her back stood straight up. She growled low in her throat.

"Good-bye," Jonah said to her. A raw knot was where his throat should have been but the rest of him was numb. She'd be better off without him. Someone else would probably find her and take her in, someone who liked cats. He began walking away. When she tried to follow him, he kicked some leaves at her.

"Go on now," he said.

She sat down, looking confused. He turned away and resumed his departure. This time he didn't look back. After about ten minutes, he ventured a glance around. She wasn't there. Good. He found his way out of the park, walking east, the hot heart of the sun bleeding to death behind his back.

When he got home the apartment was strangely still. Nothing ran to greet him, nothing begged for attention. It was a relief. He turned on the television to stir the silence and stretched out on the couch. Nothing leapt up beside him to snuggle. Better this way. No responsibility to any living creature. The TV would never ask anything of him, never reproach him. His throat was hurting; it had taken on a fierce, insistent tightness. He wondered whether he was coming down with something. When he went to the kitchen to rummage for something to eat, he saw that there were still a few cans of cat food on the shelf. What the hell was he going to do with that? And the kitty litter left beneath the sink. He supposed he could just throw it away.

————

At the end of this story, Matilda looked relieved.

"Is that all?" she asked. "I thought you were going to say you killed it."

"Yeah. Well. I've done plenty of that," he said. "Not cats, though. Just people."

To his amazement, she laughed. "Just people," she echoed, as if it had been a punch line. "Well, that was war. In war you're supposed to kill people. And as far as the cat's concerned, you were right. Cats take very good care of themselves. We've taken in a number of strays over the years, cats that apparently belonged to no one. And you know, not one of them seemed at all undernourished. Especially not Paddy— that's the one we have now. That cat must weigh twenty pounds if he weighs an ounce, and he was just as big when we found him, believe me. In fact, he might even have lost some weight since then."

B *ring on the night . . .*
    It was the fragment of a pop song, a male voice crooning. Matilda caught it while setting the alarm on her clock radio.

Bring on the night . . . I couldn't stand another hour of daylight . . .

It was the way she felt all the time. Each evening was like a light at the end of the day's tunnel. She longed for the hour she could drop into oblivion, and the sweet interval before, where she and Jonah spoke most intimately.

These conversations were different than the ones they had beneath the harsh fluorescent hospital light or the sun coming through the day-room windows. Before going to sleep, they always talked in the dark— closer then, in their separate beds, than when they were face-to-face the rest of the time. Sometimes after Jonah fell asleep, she crept to the couch and looked into his sleeping face, as she had the night of her revelation. He looked so vulnerable when he was sleeping, and years younger than he did awake.

"You know what the hardest part of all this is?" she said one night into the blackness. "It makes you realize how alone you are in this life.

It's one thing to *say* we're all alone. It's another to know it—know it in your bones. I mean, look at Seamus and me. We've been married twenty years. We've brought six children into the world. We've lain together night after night for—I realized this today—more than seven thousand nights. But even with all that, I still can't take on any of his suffering. I can't absorb any part of his pain. He's there and I'm here."

"I hear you, honey."

"And then the idea of losing him. That takes it to a whole different level. I mean, there's alone and there's alone. You know? The thought of sleeping by myself in that king-sized bed—and oh God, of seeing those kids through adolescence without their father there—I tell you, it terrifies me."

"You wouldn't be alone," Jonah said. "There's no one like Seamus, that's for sure. But it's like Delorey said. The department is your family now. It's a brotherhood, and we take care of our own. The guys from the company, they're out at your house all the time, right? Mowin' the grass, patching the roof . . . I even heard that Jake wants to trim your trees. None of them would ever take a dime from you and that's the way it'll stay. Anything you need, any time of day or night, you got a team of men there to get it done for you." In the pause that followed, she could hear the alarm clock ticking. Then he added, "And you got me."

"That means so much, Jonah. You have no idea how much. The kids are crazy about you already, and it's not just anyone that could win them over. You're enough like Seamus to be a comfort to them."

"They're great kids. You should be proud of 'em."

"I am proud."

"The boys look just like their dad. Spittin' image."

"Yes. And they want to be firemen too."

"Well, they got an open invitation to come over to Rescue 2 anytime they feel like it. They can come along with us on the runs, stay for dinner—even sleep over if they want."

"Isn't that against the rules?"

"Sure it is. That's why it helps to know the captain."

Matilda laughed for the first time in days. "I'm sure they'd be thrilled. They spent time at their dad's firehouse, but I don't think they ever stayed overnight."

"When I was a kid," Jonah told her, "the firehouse was my favorite place to sleep. I was always runnin' away from home. At least at the firehouse, I knew I'd get a square dinner and a roof over my head."

"Oh Jonah, that sounds so bleak. I mean, if that was as good as it got."

"Yeah," he said. "That was about it. A good night's sleep, no knock-down drag-out fights to listen to, no screamin' and cryin', no broken bottles or plates." He was quiet for a moment. Then: "Talk about alone," he said. "I been alone my whole life."

"I don't understand that," she said. "You have so much to offer. You'd make some lucky woman such a wonderful husband."

"I guess I never met the right one."

Thank God for that. "I'm sure you have very high standards," she said. "And of course you should."

"Well, and Matilda, you know, I was an alcoholic for a long time. The girls I ran around with were as crazy as me. Not what you'd call marriage material, take my word for it. We'd get our cheap thrills at places like Plato's Retreat—"

"What's that? A club?"

"You never heard of Plato's Retreat? It's one of those swingers clubs. Yeah, see, there's no reason for a respectable woman to even know what it is. But I was a wild one. I was wild even before I went to war, so you can imagine what I was like when I come back. I was one crazy cockeyed kid. And it took me a long time to grow up."

"Well, no wonder," Matilda said. "It sounds like you never had a childhood. It's hard to outgrow what you didn't have."

There was silence for a little while. Then: "I guess that makes sense," Jonah said. "I never thought about it that way. You're a real smart lady, Matilda, you know?"

The pleasure she felt at this was like a wrench turning her heart and it was a moment before she was able to answer. "Not really," she said. "It's just that, working in foster care all these years and raising six kids of my own, I've picked up a thing or two about child development."

"Yeah, I'm sure you have," he said. "And I bet you're a great case-worker, but you're a smart cookie on top of that. Believe me."

"Oh, Jonah. Well, thank you. It's nice of you to say that."

"Nice got nothin' to do with it."

What would he do if one night he were to wake and find her beside him? When their conversation finally tapered off and she was drifting into sleep, she pretended that the pillow beneath her cheek was his chest. I love you, she mouthed into the hospital linen. *Oh how I love you.*

"Listen, Matilda," Jonah said.

It was almost a full four weeks already since the beginning of this crisis, and there was no way he could go on without saying something to her. This situation was so unusual and so extreme that all kinds of boundaries were blurring.

He and Matilda were together every day, for hours on end, enduring something terrible side by side. He was as bonded to her already as he'd been to anyone in his platoons. She cried in his arms, often, cried tears for both of them. They talked for hours every day, exchanged confidences and confessions, even developed a certain black humor. And ever since the O'Day family had been granted quarters at the hospital, Jonah slept there too, on the couch. Matilda needed him there; he knew that. His presence was enough to keep her panic at bay. He was sharing the worst of the horror with her, and he was acting as a surrogate father to the kids. But there was something else too, something he didn't like to notice or consider, and that was the way she looked at him. Mixed in with the gratitude and dependence and nameless grief was something more. It was the way a woman looked at a man. This heated him through, quickened his pulse, and tightened his gut with regret all at the same time. But in the end it didn't matter how he felt. And in this respect he even had to overlook how Matilda felt. Seamus was still the most important part of his job.

"Listen, Matilda," he repeated. "I know there has to be some transference going on here." *Transference* was a word he'd picked up during a brief stint in therapy—free therapy for Vietnam vets that he tried for a couple of months once—and he liked the way it came to him now, as if all that talk about feelings had really given him something he could use.

"And that's only natural," Jonah went on, pleased with the sound of his own voice, his understanding and sensitivity. "In an intense situation like this, all kinds of crazy emotions get stirred up. You feel alone and afraid and you need someone to lean on. Ain't nothing wrong with that. That's the reason I'm here in the first place. And of course there's the fact that your husband and I have a lot in common."

Sympathy and acceptance. The voice of reason. The way he was going, he had half a shot at passing as a shrink himself.

"And you're a very attractive woman," he added, the soul of gentleness and tact. "But nothing—you know—could ever happen between you and me," he concluded. "Even if I wanted it to. My own code of ethics wouldn't allow it."

After he wound up this little speech, which he'd practiced in the shower for a few mornings running, Matilda was quiet for a long time, staring out the dayroom window. When at last she spoke to him, her voice sounded strained but at least she wasn't crying. She understood, she assured him. And he was right. He was so wise, she said. And so good.

Her tone unnerved him. Beneath its reasonable calm he could sense a certain hell-bent tenacity. There was no way this discussion would convince her to leave alone what was between them. He might as well ask a drowning woman to let go of a life raft. And if she went so far as to reach for him some night, what would he do? He couldn't answer that question even to himself.

"Captain Malone?"

He turned. It was Gina, one of the nurses.

"A man just called for you, a Mr. Hansen? He said he was in the area and he wants to come by with your mail. I hope that's all right."

Wes. Why the hell hadn't he thought of Wes before? "Oh yeah," he said, in a rush of relief. "That's just fine. Thanks, Gina."

"Wes, this is Matilda O'Day."

Wes actually made a slight, formal bow. "It's an honor, Mrs. O' Day. I only wish we were meeting under different circumstances. Please accept my heartfelt sympathy at this very difficult time."

"Thank you," she answered. "And the honor is mine, Mr.—?"

"Wes," he said. "Please call me Wes."

"All right, Wes. Then I'm Matilda."

"Thanks for bringing the mail, Wes," Jonah said. "I never even thought about it piling up like this." He was still shuffling through it. "I wouldn't've even remembered to pay rent this month. It's like something from another life."

"I know just what you mean," Matilda said. "All of that seems so distant and trivial now."

"Yes, well, unfortunately it's still important to Nynex and Con Edison," Wes put in.

"No question about that," Matilda said with a faint smile.

"Has someone been bringing your own mail, Mrs. O'Day?"

"Matilda," she reminded him.

"Forgive me. Matilda."

"Not so far. It's been just as Jonah said—it never occurred to me either. The only mail I've seen is what's been sent here to the hospital—the letters people have sent to my husband."

"If you'd like, I'd be more than glad to pick yours up as well."

"That's very nice of you, but my house isn't as accessible as Jonah's. I live out in Woodside, Queens."

"There's a bridge which goes there, if I'm not mistaken?"

"Oh, I couldn't let you do that. It's an hour each way with any traffic, and—"

Jonah interrupted her. "Wes, that's a good idea. Matilda, let him go and get it. You won't be able to do it yourself anytime soon and it's dangerous to let it go like that." He turned to the other man. "Come on, I'll see you down to your car and tell you how to get there."

He moved off toward the elevators. Wes made another slight bow, then followed without a backward glance. Matilda did not protest again and even if she had, it wouldn't have done any good. Jonah had spoken.

"Listen," Jonah said to Wes when they reached the older man's car. "This is good; I'm glad you came. I want you around."

He had never seen Wes look happier than he did then.

"I'm all she has to lean on right now," Jonah continued. "All day long, it's just me and her in the trenches, in a very isolated kind of position, you know what I mean? It's a little too intense between us. I want you to be around, running errands and all that, and kind of making friends with her. I want you to do for her the way you would for me. You understand what I'm saying?"

"I understand precisely."

"Good. I'll see you later."

After this, Jonah found something for Wes to do every day. The older man brought special meals into the hospital for Matilda, returned phone calls for her, took her thank-you notes to the post office and hunted down football magazines for them to read to Seamus. He picked up clothing and other items from her home and brought back anything the kids wanted to send their father. There was always something to do and when there wasn't, he was good at finding reasons to drop by anyway. Once in a while, Jonah had an errand of his own that he had to do in person—pay his phone bill, for instance, before they cut off his service. At these times Wes would stay at the hospital with Matilda. When Jonah returned, the two of them were always deep in conversation, like they'd known each other for years.

With Wes there to pick up the slack, he could take an hour out every couple of days and find an A.A. meeting. This was a real relief because, in the five years since he got sober, Jonah never wanted a drink more than now. This situation was bringing on that old thirst with a vengeance.

For so many years he'd managed to swallow his life with nothing to wash it down. It was like one long parched road and he was running on empty: plunging into fire, risking it all again and again for whatever was within its clutches, stretched out on the rack of his days. He'd taken away everything that could make it easier, slowly but surely, vice by vice. All of life's pleasures had fallen away; he would allow himself none of them. No alcohol. No drugs. No sex. No love. At night he tossed and turned and whined and cried to the empty black air. Lonely. Sad. That was all right. It was only life, and he had to make his balance out.

It was as if his life had turned on a hinge. He didn't know how many he'd killed and didn't really know how many he'd saved. What did partial rescues count as, for instance, things like CPR or mouth-to-mouth? How did this service to the O'Day family fit in? Did they make it all balance out? In his heart, he knew it didn't work like that, that the blood wasn't coming off his hands no matter what he did. Right beside that conviction, however, was another one: that he could do what he could do, that he *had* to do what he could do. And that was all he could do.

And so he did, without complaint. He went as far as he could go in every situation, no matter how untenable; there was no risk he wouldn't take. If he could never make up for all that had come before, it was still his intention to die trying. And so, of fire at least, he had no fear.

He remembered an incident when he was breaking in a probie. They were fighting a bitch of a fire. The new kid was inching forward on his belly, Jonah half-crouched above him.

"It's too hot for me, Cap'n, it hurts!" the probie cried out.

Jonah leaned close to him to be heard, pulled his face mask aside to shout above the roar. *"Take the pain!"* he bellowed. If he could brave the heat standing on his feet, then the kid had to be able to take it prone upon the floor. He didn't ask his men to do anything he wouldn't do himself. The two of them fought it out until their oxygen was almost gone and the flames under control. Only then did he allow them to be replaced by fresh men.

Afterward the probie had a couple of first-degree burns and Jonah sent him to the hospital. The kid was grinning ear to ear all the way there; he was proud of his burns and Jonah was proud of him. About a week later, he overheard the guy on the firehouse phone, telling the story to someone. He listened as the kid's voice rose in a very fair imitation of him: *"Take the pain!"*

He was famous for such one-liners. Another one was: *This is war!*—uttered with equal passion in the aftermath of a different fire. The captain of another company had yelled at him to evacuate a burning building where the roof was about to collapse. Ceiling beams were coming down around them but he still didn't know for sure that no one was trapped inside.

"Get the fuck out of here, asshole!" the guy shouted at him. "It's all gonna come down; get the fuck out now!"

But not since losing Jo Malone had he deferred to another's instinct if it went against his own. "Just one more minute," he yelled back.

Later, on the street, the other captain came over to him. "Hey, man, I'm sorry for cursing at you like that, but it was crazy in there," he said.

Jonah, wild-eyed, the fire not yet fully behind him, turned on the other man in a near-fever. "That's all right, man . . . *this is war!*"

The phrase had since become a firehouse joke. His men punctuated many remarks with *this is war.*

"Sorry to burn the potatoes, guys, but this is war."

"Santoro, are you gonna be able to pitch Saturday, in the game against the cops? You gotta be there, man; this is war."

He always smiled with them, but to him it was no joke. These were the phrases he lived by. *Take the pain.* That was his mantra. *This is war.* His manifesto. He pictured them etched like the commandments into the stony remains of his heart. It was what he delivered and what he demanded; it was what it was all about.

This is war. Take the pain. Pay your dues. Do your time. No one said it would be easy. No one promised you a fuckin' rose garden.

His penance took many different forms. He gave all the money from his medals and awards to charity. He crossed the street in front of the firehouse whenever he was working, to the vacant lot the ghetto kids used as a playground. He knew most of these kids by name and Garth was never far from his thoughts as he asked them gently and sincerely about school and how things were at home.

There was one special boy, Diego, a deaf eight-year-old who approached him on the street after the roof-rope rescue. Just came right up to him and handed him a note:

I seen you on TV

A thin, scrappy little kid, black eyes liquid with worship. Jonah brought him into the garage, gave him a tour, and let him climb on the engine. Before leaving that day, he'd given the boy an FDNY T-shirt and the kid never took it off. Now the boy was like a fixture in the firehouse. Most of their communication had been on paper until Jonah started taking a sign-language class just for him.

These were his efforts on the sidelines. They were the least he could do. Even if they didn't amount to anything and never would.

The real thing—the only real thing—was the fire. It all came down to that, the need to immerse himself in it. As if it were a burning lake with the power to purify him, he took every chance to be baptized anew. He worked overtime whenever he could. He worked every holiday too: Christmas Eve and Christmas Day, New Year's Eve and New

Year's Day. Thanksgiving, Easter, any and all of them. Why should it be any other way? Let the guys who had wives and kids be with their families. Most of the time Jonah had no one to celebrate with anyway, and it was better to be at the firehouse than alone.

What if this year was different? He was starting to think it might be. The O'Days were like family now, and he had a feeling they would invite him to their home on these occasions. And what if they did? What if they continued to need him? Would he be doing the right thing if he went?

"It does not look good," Dr. Dresden told them on the thirty-eighth day, after Seamus's seventh operation. "Seamus's blood pressure is dangerously low. He isn't responding to the fluids. His white blood cell count is way up and his heart is wearing out. If this doesn't turn around, we'll be forced to resort to vasopressors."

Dr. Dresden himself did not look good. He looked exhausted. And while any man who'd just spent ten or eleven hours on his feet in the operating room would look shot, the doctor's exhaustion seemed deeper than that. Somehow, for reasons Jonah couldn't guess at, everything was at stake here for him too.

"Vasopressors?" Matilda repeated.

"By that I mean the administration of epinephrine, dopamine . . . medications that increase blood pressure, give the flagging system a temporary boost."

"Are vasopressors bad?"

"They're not bad," Dr. Dresden said quietly. "It's just that they're the last resort."

"Oh."

Matilda asked nothing more, but after a moment the doctor went on.

"Mrs. O'Day," he said. "Your husband is one of the most courageous and resilient men I've encountered in my medical career. He's fought the good fight longer than any of us would have initially believed possible. And none of us are giving up on him, not for one minute. But at the same time, it's important to be aware . . . "

The doctor's voice faltered. Jonah flashed on a thought he'd had many times before: that Dr. Dresden was of the same nameless tribe as himself and Chief Delorey. He was, in his way, a soldier. If he wasn't likely to die on the battlefield, his life was still laid down on it hour upon hour, day in and day out.

After a moment the surgeon was able to finish his sentence. "It's important to be aware of the serious adversity we're facing at this point."

So they had been warned, and none too soon. On Seamus's fortieth day in the hospital, Jonah came back from the corner deli to find the captain's room in an uproar. A throng of orderlies were around the bed and Dr. Dresden was shouting commands. Seamus's chest was open— they had to be trying to jump-start his heart. An IV crash truck came hurtling toward the door.

He stepped aside to let it through and then made himself keep moving down the corridor. On the right was a door marked MEN'S ROOM, the stenciled letters like an injunction. Hadn't his whole life been pointing him toward this door? He went through it—he had the right—past the row of confessional stalls, all the way to the back. On the wall above the sinks, a speckled mirror: that daily reproach. He put water on his face, then went to his knees on the black-and-white tile and begged.

Please. Please.

Behind his back, he heard someone enter, stop in his tracks, then leave again. He would never know who it was.

Please, he whispered out loud. A sheen of sweat came out on his forehead and the blades of his back were bunched together with tension. *Give me strength. To take the pain.*

Back in the hallway, Dr. Dresden was coming out of Seamus's room. Jonah went over to the man who had done surgery on the captain seven times, who had worked around the clock to save O'Day, putting in sixteen-hour shifts back-to-back for almost six straight weeks. Looking into his drawn and defeated face was like confronting a twin.

"We lost him," the doctor said. His shoulders slackened beneath his white coat and suddenly he was weeping. Jonah embraced him and felt his own tears coming at last.

Within minutes, the entire floor had crowded into the captain's room. All the nurses were crying; all the doctors and firemen too. Jonah stood slightly apart from it all and watched everyone bending, bowing, over the bed. It was shimmering, beautiful like a dance with everyone in their different costumes. Whites and aquas and blues. The orderlies in their sea-green scrubs, the doctors in their jackets and the nurses in smocks. Matilda in a dress the color of the sky. Hovering like angels, bending like swans, and the great man in the center of it all dead on his back, glazed eyes half-open still, the pain vanished.

Jonah imagined there was music only Seamus could hear, the music Monet had tried to paint: something pale, floating and ethereal. That was Wes's word, ethereal, and that's what the music of deliverance would be like—but it wasn't for him, had never been for him, and he didn't know how much longer he could wait.

The funeral was two days later.

It was at St. Patrick's Cathedral and every fireman, cop, and local politician turned out to mourn the tragedy that had racked the city. Jonah sat up front with the family and tried to listen to the speeches but found he could only focus on the different kinds of light: the shafts streaming in from the small windows near the ceiling; the stained-glass mandala above the apse; the white altar candles shuddering in their jars. The cathedral was packed to bursting, everyone bathing one last time in the communal light before departing with their separate shadows. He wondered what he would do and who he would be now that this was almost over.

At the close of the ceremony he stepped through the church doors and paused at the top of the stone steps. Mourners lined Fifth Avenue as far as he could see in both directions; there must have been ten thousand people there. There was something unreal about the scene and it took a moment for him to identify it as the quietness: every man, woman and child observing a silence so immaculate they might have been figures in a photograph. The birds overhead were the only audible presence in the street.

The pallbearers stepped through the cathedral doors, holding the flag-draped coffin on their shoulders. Seamus was sealed away in that dark box. As it passed him, Jonah's arm went up in final tribute, hand stiffened in fervent salute. Later on the news he would see himself captured in this act: his face a crumpled caricature of grief, mouth turned down at the corners like a tragic mask, one white glove poised at his brow.

Ladder 104's truck was waiting at the bottom of the steps and the men used the hydraulic lift to hoist the coffin onto the rig. Jonah followed in its wake with Matilda and the kids to the limousine behind it. No one spoke as the car pulled away from the curb.

A two-mile stretch of Fifth Avenue had been shut down for the funeral, and as the procession made its way east, Jonah could see the same was true of the F.D.R. Drive. Cars that had been pulled over were parked all along either shoulder of the road, the drivers seated on the hoods or leaning up against them. They looked irritated and angry but as the funeral approached, Jonah could see their faces change. Seamus's stay in the hospital had been a media circus from beginning to end and his death had made the cover of every paper in the city. As the sidelined drivers realized whose funeral was passing, resentful expressions gave way to a stricken awe. One by one, the people left their cars to come near the hearse and make some gesture.

Hats were removed, heads were lowered, respects were paid with every turn of the wheels. Dozens of people made the sign of the cross, and Jonah even saw one of those Old-World Jews rip a hole in his shirt. Viewed through the tinted windows of the passing limousine, the spectacle was like a silent movie. It was like watching an old-fashioned newsreel unfold, with the strange, slow-motion delirium of a dream.

Within their own velvet quiet they pressed on. The promised land would soon be in sight, its white stones like a vision in the afternoon sun. They were going to it, down the long aisle of highway, carrying their beloved across some final threshold to his eternal bed.

Cars continued to line both sides of the road like the parted waters of the Red Sea, the crowds rushing forward and pulling back again like sorrowing waves. After forty days—each one well worth a year—in the scorched and forsaken desert, Captain Seamus O'Day was coming through.

Asway

Inside the Brooklyn Brewery, beer and sentiment were flowing together. The sawdust on the floor had become a grainy paste. Music from the jukebox was drowned out by the bagpipes, which were well into a slow rendition of "Fiddler's Green." The stranger whom Jake had just introduced to Alicia leaned closer.

"What did you say?" he asked her.

"I said, it's you." A tremor came over her and she clasped her own arms to hold herself still. "I know you."

"You know me?"

"You saved me from a fire when I was five years old."

Both men stared at her.

"*I* did?" Jake's friend—Jonah—*Jonah Malone*—said. "How do you know?"

"I remember you."

"Where was this?"

"It was our place on Lorimer Street. You came into my room and got me out of bed."

There was a long pause. Then: "Yes," he said. "Yes, I did."

They stood looking at each other for another moment and then she went into his arms. Her ear pressed against his heart as it had so long ago. It was still beating.

"Amazing," Jake said. None of them could get over it, but Jake was the one to articulate it over and over. "Fuckin' amazing, man! What are the odds? Malone! How does it feel to see a beautiful woman and know you're the reason she's on the earth?"

Jonah shook his head. He seemed bewildered, almost in a daze. "This is a first," he said. "I've gotten to meet people I've rescued afterwards, but never so far after the fact."

"So tell me, man, how does it feel?"

"It feels good."

"We got to drink to this. What are you drinking, Malone?"

Jonah held his near-empty glass to the light for Jake's inspection. "It's only seltzer," he answered. "I'm a recovered alcoholic."

"I can buy you some more bubbles then. I got no problem with that," Jake said. He swaggered off to the bar.

Alicia looked down. Her beer was between them. She didn't usually drink beer; she had accepted it mostly to please Jake but now she didn't want it. In her hand or on her breath. She set it on a nearby table and did not pick it up again, despite the awkwardness of being empty-handed. Already her alliances were shifting. Let a full glass of beer grow warm on the tabletop; let Jake notice it. What did it matter, now?

The gesture wasn't lost on Jonah. "It's all right for you to drink in front of me," he said. "If it wasn't, I wouldn't be in a bar."

"I don't want it."

Jonah nodded toward Jake, who was across the room vying for their second round. "Is he your boyfriend?" he asked.

"No," Alicia said. She looked straight into his eyes, saying this. "No, he isn't."

"Just a friend, then?"

"Just . . . just someone I know."

Jake was shouldering his way back to them now, a sweating amber bottle in one fist, a glass of soda in the other. At his approach they spoke in lowered tones, the beginning of complicity between them already.

"Do you want to go for a walk?" Jonah asked. "In a little while, I mean."

"I'd love to," she said. "Whenever you're ready."

"Is Schiller gonna mind? I mean, you did come with him, didn't you?"

"It doesn't matter," she said. "Trust me, it doesn't matter at all."

The night was warm. They pushed through the throng in front of the Brewery, crossed Wythe Avenue, and kept walking west.

"That's a nice dress," Jonah said.

"You like it?"

"It's beautiful."

It was in fact her favorite dress: a white vintage slip, form-fitting yet demure, intended tonight to make Jake change his mind about leaving or at least entertain some serious doubts. Everything was different now.

The way Jonah was looking at her made her think of a man behind bars. And she was no less overwhelmed by his presence. After years of looking for him, it was hard now to look away.

"Let's walk over to the water," he said.

When Jonah had lifted her out of bed all those years ago, Alicia had experienced a sensation of floating above herself, looking down—at the flames, the burning furniture, her own small body in the fireman's arms. Within the deafening crackle and roar of the fire, there was a nimbus of quiet and calm and she was in it, unblinking and tranquil, as if drugged. Now on the nearly deserted piers with Jonah, at the railing overlooking the river, she was experiencing something similar. Over the pounding of her heart, she heard herself holding up her end of a coherent conversation. Jonah was speaking to her and she was answering and her voice was somehow steady and clear.

"I pulled a guy out of here last year," Jonah remarked. "In the dead of winter. Took me about a day to get warm again."

"What was it, a boating accident?"

"No. An attempted suicide. What happened was, the firemen dragged his ass out of the water and the cops slapped him with a five-hundred-dollar fine. Can you beat that?" He turned to her. One corner of his mouth went up. "That's the difference between firemen and cops."

"That's one difference."

"What's the matter? You don't like cops?"

"I just don't like the way people always put them together with firemen."

"Well, you know. It's because we both work for the city. And both jobs are dangerous."

"Okay, but firemen are better people."

He was amused. "You might have reason to be a little biased, honey."

"Maybe so, but still. If it wasn't for the chance to save people, why would anyone become a fireman? The money's not what it should be. The everyday conditions are terrible for your health. Even if a fire doesn't get you, you're breathing in smoke and carbon monoxide all the time . . . "

"Yeah," Jonah said. "You got that right."

"But it's different for cops," Alicia went on. "They get to run around with guns and pull rank on the rest of the world. You know, the worst . . . " she hesitated, wondering whether she should go on, then took the plunge. "The worst experiences I've had at work have all been with cops."

"What kind of work do you do?"

"Well, I want to be a writer. That is, I *am* a writer." A pause. "But to get by, I also work as a stripper." She searched his face as she spoke. It didn't change.

"Cops come in a lot?" he asked, as if she hadn't said anything out of the ordinary.

"All the time. They're in plain clothes but they're still packing. They get out of control right away and take it further than anyone else. They think they're above the law and of course to an extent they are. The managers don't want to throw them out—they could always invent some reason to fine or close down the club. The bouncers aren't going to hit them. So they steal our clothes, put their paws all over us . . . "

"They must be all over you," is all he said. "You're so pretty."

"And you're beautiful."

"Aw, c'mon. I'm an old mutt."

"No, don't say that. How old are you?"

"Forty-three," he said. "In dog years."

She smiled. "That's young."

"For some people maybe."

After a while they sat down by the railing, where the concrete was slightly elevated. As easily and naturally as she had gone into his arms an hour ago, she took his hand.

"I've looked for you for years," she said. "With almost nothing to go on. I've stared at every fire truck going by and any fireman to pass me on the street. I never even learned your name. Pete was the name of the one who carried me down the ladder."

"Pete McTigue," Jonah confirmed. "Sure was. Good memory, honey."

"How could I forget something like that?"

"No, you're right," he said. "And we never forget either. For every major job I've been to, I can name the neighborhood, draw a layout of the building, say how many injuries there were and how many casualties. And I can remember, clear as day, every person I ever saved."

"Even me?"

"Especially you." He reached over and moved a strand of hair that had fallen in front of her eyes. "You were my first."

"No," she said. "No . . . ! *Really?*"

"It's God's truth, honey."

"Well, I must have been the first of many, then," she said. "Jake said you're the most decorated fireman in New York."

"Well, I ain't keepin' track. But I've been lucky enough to save a lot of people."

"Lucky," Alicia repeated. "I'm sure luck is only part of it."

He began to talk to her then and did not stop. She had the sense of a dam breaking. He told her about rescue after rescue: the kids he pulled from a burning opium den, the famous roof-rope rescue in downtown Brooklyn, the unconscious man he carried down nine flights of stairs, and at least a dozen others. It was as if he had needed to find her—his beginning—in order to begin.

When he ran out of fire stories, he told her about his service to the O'Day family. "That was the hardest thing I ever done, honey," he said. "Harder than the war, even—harder than anything. It was putting my whole heart and soul into a lost cause. 'Cause even if he made it out of the hospital, survived all the surgery and whatnot, he never would've been the same. He never would've fought fire again. It was better for him not to hold on. I just don't know why he had to suffer so long."

After a while, they left the piers and wandered along Kent Avenue. Not far below Tenth Street was a twenty-four-hour diner where they shared a stack of pancakes. He told her about the neighborhood kids he tried to look after, as the firemen on his block had once looked after him. He told her about his young deaf friend, Diego. He pulled out his wallet to show her photos of the three Asian children he'd "adopted"—the small, dark-eyed faces of two girls and a boy.

"Is that like a Sally Struthers thing?"

"It's one of those. Not the same agency she pushes, but one like it. I wanted one that would let me pick the country the kids were from."

"Oh. So those kids . . . are they from China?"

"Vietnam."

The waitress returned to pour more coffee. They were quiet until she went away.

"Jonah," Alicia said then. "You're like an angel. I mean, you've done so much. You *do* so much. What drives you?"

The question seemed to bring him up short. He took a while to answer and when he did, his voice was quieter.

"A lot of people think I'm driven by guilt," he said. "Guilt about the war. But that's too simple a way to think about it. It's a lot more complex and I don't know if I can show you how I see it."

"Try," she urged.

"Well . . . " he said slowly. He picked up his fork and raked patterns in the syrup left on his plate. "It's more accurate to say that Vietnam tapped a certain energy in me and channeled it in a very destructive way. I was seventeen and I believed in what I was being called to do and I gave myself over to the Marines and let them harness that energy in whatever way they would. And honey, I'll be honest with you—it was ugly over there. Real, real ugly."

Alicia nodded. She held him with her eyes, inviting him to continue.

"Firefighting," he went on, "see, firefighting taps that same energy, but takes it in a whole different direction. You been to Jake's firehouse, right? You seen that goldfish they got there? Maybe he told you and maybe he didn't, but that fish survived the fire that killed those three men."

"He told me."

"All right. Good. Well, I'll tell you a story that will maybe show you what I'm sayin'. I remember a guy from my platoon. Joey Veseglio. He and his best friend Frank come over together and for eight and a half months, they both managed to stay alive and whole. Two weeks left until their tour was up, Frank trips a land mine and gets blown into bits."

"Oh God," Alicia murmured.

"Right? Okay, well, later that same day, Joe tortured a stray dog to death and we all watched him do it. It was horrible, honey. I won't tell you the details. But he was just broken up over the idea that this dog—this fuckin' *dog*—was alive, and his best friend was dead. We felt sorry for the mutt but we understood how Joe felt. No one stopped him, or even said anything.

"All right. Now think about that, and then think about the fire department. Look at fire department mentality in the same situation. Here this firehouse lost three of their men in a fire, good men who died the worst kind of death you could think of, and a fuckin' *goldfish* survived. If those guys had gone a little nuts, put a pencil through its eyes, say, or nailed it to the fuckin' *wall*—well, that would be a horrible thing to do but you'd understand. Right, honey?"

Alicia nodded.

"But here's the point," he concluded. "The point is, firefighting takes that same energy—believe me, it's the same energy—but somehow harnesses it in the opposite direction. A fish survived the fire that killed their brothers, but they've taken it in, they're taking care of it." He released the fork and leaned forward. "Can you understand all this, honey? I don't know how else to show you, but that's why I'm a fireman now."

It was all Alicia could do to stay on her side of the table. She pushed away her empty coffee cup and reached for his hand.

"I understand that. I do understand. But now let me ask you something else."

"Ask me whatever you want."

"You take such tireless care of so many people," she said. She sought his eyes. "Who takes care of you?"

He sat back and exhaled sharply. The sudden vulnerability in his face made him look years younger. "Nobody," he answered.

A fantasy was taking shape there in the vinyl booth; it was assuming the form of a mission. She held his hand between both of hers and spoke softly.

"You need someone to take care of you," she said.

"I know. I know I do."

The waitress came back and left their check. Jonah laid some bills on the table and then they sat there and looked at each other. It was four in the morning. What to do now? She was afraid to leave him, afraid of breaking the spell, but it was also too soon to sleep with him. Too soon to brave the morning after; the stakes were too high.

"Look," Jonah said finally, addressing the unspoken. "If you want, you can come home with me. I don't need for nothin' to happen, so please don't take it wrong—that can come later, if it's meant to be. I just want you with me. If that's all right with you. If it ain't, I can get you back to your own place too. What do you want to do?"

"I want . . . to go home," she said. The disappointment in his face made her hear her own words and realize she hadn't been clear.

"What I mean is," she explained in a rush, "I want to go home with you."

True to his word, that first night he held her. Nothing else. It was nearing five A.M. by the time they got into bed. She lay with her head on his shoulder, her cheek resting against his chest.

"Listen, honey," Jonah told her. "I've got to go to work in a few hours."

"Oh God," she said. "I had no idea. I've kept you up all night!"

"I'll be all right. I can sleep at the firehouse if there ain't a run. Sunday mornings are usually pretty slow."

"I love Sundays," Alicia said drowsily. "The Catwalk's closed. It's the one day of the week I never have it hanging over my head."

"You sleep late, then."

"What? Oh no, that's all right. I can get up with you."

"You got anything to do in the morning?" he asked.

"Not really . . . but I wouldn't feel right staying in bed when you have to get up and out."

"I want you to," he said. "I like the idea of it."

"You do?"

"Yeah. You sleep as late as you want. The front door'll lock by itself when you leave. And look, I'm gonna leave you a spare set of keys so you can get back in too."

Startled, she raised her head and stared at him. He looked back at her steadily through the near-dark.

"When do you get off work?" she asked after a minute. "Are you working twenty-four hours?"

"No, not tomorrow," he said. "I get off at six."

"I could make dinner for you here, if you want," she offered.

"You like to cook? 'Cause we could go out, too."

"I love to cook. I'd love to cook for you."

"That sounds real nice," he said. "If you're sure you feel like it."

She brought her head back down to his shoulder. "What do you like to eat?"

"I eat anything. I'm real easy, honey."

"All right. Then I'll surprise you."

The next afternoon Alicia went to the Farmers Market at Union Square. She got fresh mesclun and cherry tomatoes and balsamic vinegar and a loaf of sourdough bread. From the flower stand she picked out different-colored roses for the table. She went to a regular supermarket for steak.

The afternoon was sun-dappled, dazzling, shot through with a sense of unreality. The ordinary tasks of shopping and cooking would absorb her for long minutes and then the shock of memory would pull her up short, rob her of breath. She had found the man she'd been looking for all her life, and his apartment keys were in the pocket of her jeans.

So miracles happened. Jake bringing her over to Jonah was nothing less. And how startling it was now to remember Jake. For the first time since June, he'd been displaced from her thoughts and the idea of not seeing him anymore had lost its sting. She could see him clearly now for what he had been: a conduit; a means to an end.

"All day at work," Jonah told her that evening, "the guys were breaking my balls. They knew something was up, because on a day-to-day basis, I'm not exactly Mr. Happy. You know? And it got worse when Seamus died. But today was a different story. What's he smilin' about, they all wanted to know. He musta got laid last night, they said. But all I'd tell 'em was: it's better than that."

"All day I felt the same way."

"Do you believe in fate, honey? Because even if I didn't before, I would now."

"I know what you mean."

"It's like what Jake was sayin'. What are the odds?"

"Odder still is the idea that it was Jake who brought us together."

They had finished dinner and were still at the table, hands clasped across the wooden surface.

"So honey," Jonah said. "I know there was something between you and Jake. You don't have to tell me about it if you don't want to. But I just want you to know that you can. I mean, the bottom line is, you can tell me anything."

Anything. Could he possibly mean that? Could anyone ever really mean that? And if he did, what would she tell? There was a pause while she sifted through confessions no one had ever heard. *I've been so lonely. Sometimes I feel like I can't go on. I'm scared that moving so much has left me unable to form real relationships. I'm more vulnerable than anyone would ever guess, but it's so hard for me to let it show.*

"I slept with him all summer," she said after a while. "That was about the extent of it. And that kind of thing is pretty unusual for me. I think in a way it was an antidote to stripping. It was a chance to feel genuinely sexual again."

Jonah nodded. She searched his face and could find no censure there.

"Anyway, all I can say for sure is that it's over," she went on. "It was over by the time I met you. We were at the benefit only as friends."

"Did he tell you he's engaged?" Jonah asked.

"Yeah, he told me. Not right away, but he did tell me eventually. For some reason it didn't bother me. I mean, I never thought we were going to ride into the sunset together. And he never misled me—that's one thing I can say for him. If the two of you are friends, I hope this hasn't made you . . . I don't know, hate him or anything."

"Hate him?" Jonah repeated. "Hate him? Honey, I'd like to send that kid a case of champagne." He started to laugh.

After a moment, Alicia began laughing with him. He pulled her from her chair and onto his knee. She clung to him and shakily buried her face in his neck. They sat there together for long minutes, holding each other and laughing like two fools.

For the next two months they were together all the time. Some nights they stayed at her apartment, but most were spent at his. Sometimes Alicia slept at Jonah's even when he was working overnight at the firehouse.

Jonah's sleep was restless, even after sex. Each night he resumed his side of an ongoing nocturnal dialogue: whimpers and pleas, an occasional shout. It was as if sleep were a station where he switched trains, rode deep into the heart of all that haunted him. Alicia could pull him from this terrain but never penetrate it, and her reassurances were like so much rain running off the roof: *Shh. Shh. It's okay. It's just a dream, and I'm here.*

He dreamed about Seamus all the time. And Jerry Fitzgerald, and Vietnam, and people he hadn't managed to save. When she woke him, he would tell her the dreams, and his tone was always confessional:

I was detailed to Ladder 145. We were at a three-alarm; it was in a brownstone. People were jumping out the back windows. Seven or eight people had already died, either from getting cooked in the house or from jumping onto the concrete. I was on the second floor, talking to the chief on the radio. I'd already called down to him the first time, primary negative. *That means I did the preliminary search and found no victims on the premises. I called the same thing after the second search:* secondary negative. *There was a crib but no baby in it, nothing under the blankets, nothing on the floor underneath.*

*No one in the closets—sometimes kids hide in the closets. I figure
everyone got out okay. Then I hear on the radio,* Ladder one-four-five
O.V. to Ladder one-four-five. *That means the outside vent man is calling up to me. He says,* We got a jumper in the rear, a young woman,
she broke her leg but she's still conscious. She's screaming about her
niño—her baby. *From that it sounds like the baby's still in the apartment. I tell him to find out where it is. First they have to find someone
who can translate, someone who speaks Spanish, and that takes forever. Then they call me back and tell me the baby's in the bottom
dresser drawer. Inside my mind I'm crying no. No, it can't be. I rush
over begging God, please no, but there he is, he's in there under a little
blanket. Stone still with his eyes closed. No breath, no pulse. I take
him out to the hall and start CPR but it's way too late for the poor little guy. If I'd only known during the primary search, or even during
the secondary, he might've made it. He's dead from smoke so he's not
burnt up, he looks like he's asleep, and when I carry him outside the
mother thinks I got him in time. She's holding out her arms for him, so
grateful she's crying, thanking me for saving his life, and I can't look
her in the eyes.*

Alicia responded, always, as if to a true story. If it wasn't always
clear whether the dream had been lifted straight from life, she knew at
least how real his sense of inadequacy was. "There was nothing different you could have done. There was no way for you to know about him.
You're not God, you can't know everything. Think of all the ones you
did save: the dozens of people who are alive today because of you."

At this point, fully awake and somewhat recovered, he liked to tell
her that *she* had saved *him.* "For real, honey," he would say. "You know
the story of the lion and the mouse? A lion saves this little mouse and
the mouse promises to return the favor someday. The lion laughs
because he can't see how a little mouse will ever be able to help him.
But some hunters catch him in a net and they're going to take him to
the zoo or some fucking thing, lock him up for life, right? And the
mouse finds out and rounds up his buddies and they gnaw through the
net and the lion gets sprung."

This fable and the way he told it always made her laugh, but he
never meant it to be funny. "You don't know, honey. You don't know

how sad I was. Just walkin' around whipped, barely draggin' my ass through the drill. If you hadn't come along when you did, I don't know what I would of done."

Because he needed her, because he seemed to need her so much, an amazing breakthrough was taking place. For the first time in her life, she was letting her love go, holding nothing back. With Jake she had been closed tight, curled into hiding, but with Jonah she was opening like a flower to the sun. No restraint or camouflage seemed to be called for, and even her job was no special concern. She didn't have to apologize for it and she didn't have to wear it like a flag. Jonah regarded strippers with neither the fascination nor contempt that most other men seemed to harbor for them.

When she mentioned this to him, he said, "Well, I was kind of a hustler once myself, honey."

Hustler.

The word sent her reeling for a moment. There were different kinds of hustlers, but it wasn't hard to figure out which Jonah was talking about. So did he mean . . . had he ever . . . and if he had? Within seconds, one fierce thought weighed in like an anchor, displacing all the others: *if Jonah did it, it has to be all right.*

She heard herself asking calmly, "When was this?"

"It was right after I come home from overseas. I was nineteen years old and just like some kind of wild stray animal looking for someone to take me home every night. That's how I met Wes."

"Did you have sex with men?" she asked, then added, "Like you said to me the other night, you can tell me anything."

"I know that, honey. And I would never lie to you. The truth is, I never had to have sex with those men. Believe it or not, a lot of those guys weren't really lookin' for that. They just had some little game they wanted to play, and that game was like sex to them. Do you know what I mean?"

Relief drew the breath back into her body. "Well, sure. Of course. It's like at The Catwalk. Men drop hundreds, even thousands, a night in there, and all they're getting is teased."

"That's what I'm talking about," Jonah said. "It's like that special back room you been telling me about. You told me what it goes for, a couple hundred bucks, right?"

"The Champagne Lounge starts at $300 an hour. And I've had men stay there half the night just to talk."

"That's what I'm sayin'. If they really wanted sex they could find a hooker—even a real high-class call girl—and pay less than that."

"It's true."

"Well, that's how it was with me. Look at Wes. He never tried to do anything heavy with me. He doesn't want to be gay, you know? Not that there's anything bad about it, but he's a devout Catholic and he thinks of it as a sin. So it's like I could satisfy something in him enough so that he didn't have to go any further with it. You know what I'm sayin', honey?"

"I understand that. It sounds like you two were lucky to find each other."

"It's nice of you to say that, honey. It's real nice the way you look at things. You got a special way about you, honey, you're a real special lady. A lot of women would be bothered by something like that."

"Well, I'm not a lot of women. But it seems you got something redemptive, maybe even something beautiful, out of it."

"That's what I think. See, you understand that, honey. No matter what I been through in my life, no matter how dark it was, I always kept my eyes open and I got to see the hidden beauty. There were beautiful things, beautiful moments, even in the middle of the war. Even at Seamus's deathbed."

"And while the redemptive aspects don't justify the terrible things, they do give you a reason to keep breathing."

"That's right, honey."

"Take Seamus's death," she went on. "Nothing in the world could ever compensate for it. But still—the deaths of those firemen led to the department holding that benefit. And if it weren't for the benefit—well, you and I might never have met."

"How about that, honey," he said. "How about that."

"Come here and lie down with me, honey."

Jonah was calling to her from the sofa. It was six in the evening and in another hour she would have to leave for work.

She went over to Jonah and lay down beside him. He put both arms around her and she drifted off to that space between sleep and waking: floating with the muted sounds of traffic outside the window, anchored by the comfort of his body. Awareness at bay but not altogether gone.

Pressing down on this silken languor was the knowledge that very soon she would have to get up, dress in the dark chill and go downtown. Eight hours of gyrating under the neon glare were in store, along with the eyes and hands of strangers. The prospect seemed terrible in a way it never had before.

Meanwhile Jonah was sleeping soundly for once: no nightmares, no struggles. She hated to wake him, hated to move at all.

"Jonah," she whispered finally.

He stirred but didn't answer.

"Sweetheart," she murmured. "I have to get up. I've got to be at work in half an hour."

He opened his eyes. "That's right," he said. "I almost forgot."

"I wish I didn't have to go," she said. "It feels so good, just lying here with you."

"Stay put just another minute," he said. He added: "I'll drive you down there."

They were quiet in the car. A light rain beaded the windshield. Alicia was still sleepy. The thought of dancing until four in the morning was almost unbearable. When they got to Church Street, Jonah pulled the car over across from the club and parked.

"C'mere," he said.

She moved across the front seat and let him pull her close.

"Listen," he said. "I want to tell you something."

He wasn't looking at her, but at the entrance of The Catwalk, where two bouncers flanked the front door.

"You know I ain't got a problem with you working here," he said finally. "I don't want you to get the wrong idea. I respect you and trust you and all the rest. But at the same time . . . "

He trailed off. She sat up and waited for him to go on. When he stayed silent, she said, "Yes?"

"At the same time, I just want you to know you ain't got to do it. If you feel like stopping, I want you to know you can stop."

"Do you want me to stop?"

"I just want you to do whatever you want to do."

"I want to be a writer," she said. "I mean, you know that. But I can't support myself with writing yet."

"I'll support you."

The sudden threat of tears made her stop and swallow hard. There was a long pause while she waited to be able to speak.

At last she said, "Jonah, it's beautiful that you would offer something like that. But even if I could accept it, I don't see how it's possible. I mean, the main reason I feel trapped in this job is that my apartment's so expensive. You can't pay two rents—that would be crazy."

"So let your place go," he said. "Give it up and live with me."

Alicia turned away and looked out the window. Her eyes were stinging and filling again and her throat was an aching knot. She waited until she trusted herself not to cry before turning back to Jonah. When she spoke again, her tone was hushed and careful. "Jonah. Really. Isn't it a little too soon for this?"

"It ain't too soon for me."

And just like that, a chapter of her life closed behind her. The club with its aquamarine "*TOPLESS!*" signs was still across the street. The man she'd thought of as her boss, someone she had lived in fear of angering, remained somewhere within its walls. The dreaded door was still standing open, but suddenly she no longer had to walk through it.

She sat there, choked up and overcome, looking at Jonah. He was holding out something that had never occurred to her. It was shelter within a wilderness she had gotten too used to. Lifted out of it suddenly, safe on the other side, she wondered for the first time how she'd survived.

———

Mid-January.

Almost too cold for snow: no more than a few stingy flakes from the still-black sky.

Five o'clock in the morning and Wes was picking up Jonah and his girlfriend, to take them to LaGuardia Airport.

It was Jonah's vacation and they were going to Puerto Rico for a week. Wes didn't exactly know when it had started, this ritual of chauffering Jonah to LaGuardia or Kennedy or Newark and saving him the cost of several days' parking in airport lots. Of course Jonah could always take a cab or a car service, but this was something they always did. Whenever Jonah had a trip, business or pleasure, with or without a female companion, Wes would drive him to the airport at any ungodly hour, in whatever weather, and be waiting for him at the gate when he returned home. It was the way they were.

He stood before Jonah's building and savored the moment. There was a certain satisfaction in rising in the dark while most of the city slept, getting out here in the biting chill to warm up the car for Jonah and provide door-to-door service. For a minute, it felt like old times— before *she* came along.

He pressed the button for Jonah's apartment—10C. The intercom crackled. "Wes?"

"It's me."

The buzzer sounded and he went in. It had been a while. The lobby had been painted since he'd last come over, a fresh coat of white and a new teal trim. Ever since Jonah had hooked up with this new one, Alicia, their contact had been minimal. Jonah could hardly be bothered to return his phone calls and their dinners out—which used to happen on a weekly basis—had dwindled to once a month at best. And even when he did find a little time for Wes (usually the evenings *she* was working—if you could call exhibitionism work) he had to drop her name into every other sentence. Alicia this, Alicia that. Alicia was a brilliant writer. (How would *you* know? Wes thought nastily.) Alicia's cooking was better than anything he'd had in a restaurant. Alicia could play the piano.

Riding up in the elevator, Wes steeled himself for all the irritation the next hour would hold.

Jonah's apartment door was slightly ajar. Still, Wes tapped at it before walking in. There they were, suitcases in tow, bright-eyed and happy, wearing matching Rescue 2 sweatshirts. It was unbearable.

"Hey, Wes," Jonah said from across the room. He made no move to come over, but Alicia sidled up and kissed his cheek.

"Wes, it's so nice of you to drive us," she simpered.

"Not at all," he demurred. "It's my pleasure." Most of the time, anyway.

Against her protests, Wes took Alicia's bags down to the parking garage and, once at the car, insisted that she sit in the front seat—that is, beside Jonah, who on this occasion would take the wheel—while he himself took the back. As was his place. He always paid elaborate homage to the females in Jonah's life, speaking to them with the utmost civility and graciousness even as his heart smoldered in his chest. This morning would be no different, no matter how vexing the situation, despite the sight of her hand resting possessively against the back of Jonah's neck. He stared at the slender female hand, marveled at it. How was this possible? Some young brat, some kid in her *twenties,* claiming easily and carelessly and comfortably what he had worshiped more than half his life, not daring for the last fifteen years more than the proprietary handshake. How could he swallow, digest the monstrous fact of it?

This girl, Alicia, she was a dangerous bitch, penetrating Jonah more fully and immediately than anyone else Wes could remember, ever. She was beautiful, there was no way around it, wide-eyed and tangle-haired with a lithe young body. The most compelling thing about her was her direct gaze, unspeakable recognition and at times even insolence in it. *I know you,* she seemed to be saying to him sometimes. *I know who and what you are, but I can do it better, consummate it in a way you can only dream about. He puts me to nightly as well as daily use—he puts me on a pedestal, and over his knee. He loves me.*

It made him want to kill her slowly.

There was only one woman in Jonah's life whom Wes truly loved and honored and that was Matilda. Devastated, grief-stricken, middle-aged Matilda, whose husband had suffered so much. Seamus O'Day could have claimed Jonah for his own slave, if he'd been conscious enough to notice. Even in death he commanded more loyalty from Jonah than Matilda ever would or could. She was cute and feisty but she could never make Jonah violate the brotherhood code, and therefore Wes was free to love her without reservation. He did whatever he could for her during the crisis and afterward, chauffered her around wherever she needed to go, took her to restaurants and museums as he had done with Jonah so long ago. At first she was intimidated by his background. She thought of him as *high-class*. Which of course he was. And she was afraid of pronouncing something wrong in front of him, of seeming ignorant or provincial. But he soon put her at ease as he was skilled at doing, and now he was her closest confidant.

Matilda adored Jonah, ached for him; Wes could see that. He could also see how frustrated she was and would always be in this endeavor. He could imagine her after an evening out with Jonah: driving home alone, tears blurring her vision until everything was a colored wash of traffic and streetlights, her pain so sharp that she wouldn't even pull over but tempt disaster instead.

As much as he loved Matilda, that was how much he hated Alicia. She was nothing but an arrogant whelp. She'd escaped all the torture, the whole ordeal of the hospital. She hadn't even been around for it. The nurse Jonah dated briefly, she was galling in her way, but if Jonah were going to be with someone in the wake of that vigil, it should at least be someone who had endured it with them. What had happened with that nurse, again? Oh yes, on their second date, she'd made dinner reservations under his name. When they got to Carmine's, the hostess smiled at him and said, "Right this way, doctor."

"Doctor?" Jonah repeated once they'd been seated. "Where'd she get that?"

"Oh," the nurse—Tanya?—said. "It's an old trick. If you make a reservation under a doctor's name, you almost always get a better table."

Jonah had stared at her—this was according to Matilda, who'd gotten the story from the horse's mouth—in a way that made her shrink back in her chair. And finally he'd said, very quietly but with a frightening intensity, "Don't you ever—*ever*— put me down anywhere as a doctor again. Do you understand? I," he told her, pausing after each word for emphasis, "am . . . a . . . *fireman*."

That had been their last date.

Still, he could have picked another nurse, any one of the single nurses. What about Helene? Couldn't he tell she liked him? A nurse and a fireman—that was acceptable, it happened all the time. A fireman—*his* fireman—and a stripper . . . well, that was infinitely less palatable. As Matilda would say, it had no class.

And Jonah was so taken with her. Nowadays, she was all he talked about with anyone, apparently. Couldn't he see how he was hurting Matilda? Did he have to rub salt into her wounds? That's what he was doing with this flighty little thing. You would think, after all Matilda had been through already, that he would have a little more sensitivity.

And the way she—Alicia—looked at Jonah. Fawned on him. It was truly sickening. Reportedly she had told him—and this Jonah found so deeply moving—that he had served humanity all his life, and now *she* wanted to serve *him*. What on earth did that brazen little bitch know about service? *Real* service? Not just playing slave for a night or two, dressing up in a French maid's outfit maybe, playing O at the god-damned chateau, or whatever the hell they did together—but *real* service, the service of a dog? She would never know anything about that: the menial, unglamorous, constant caretaking that made no demands, brooked no reciprocation.

Meanwhile, Jonah talked as if no one had ever expressed such a desire to him before, acted like this was a brand-new and earth-shattering idea. What do you think *I've* been doing all these years? Wes wanted to scream. He could take being used, could even revel in it, as long as there was no one else in the picture usurping his place. But Alicia was. That was clear. For now, anyway. She was in tight, frighteningly so, in possession of his apartment keys, coming and going as she pleased. More than once, Wes had called early in the morning and she'd answered, sounding sleepy. It was like an ice pick in his heart each time it happened, and yet he couldn't stop himself from taking the chance.

"Hello," she would murmur drowsily, luxuriously, basking in her status.

"Oh, hello, I'm sorry to wake you," Wes would say, unfailingly courteous and respectful. "I was looking for Jonah."

"He's not here, may I take a message?" was her next line, just as courteous, but with a sly and silky undertone. Or even worse: "Just a minute." And then, muffled, "Honey? Are you awake? The phone's for you, I think it's Wes, do you want to take it?"

The worst was when he could hear Jonah mutter in the background, "Nah, tell 'im I'll call 'im back later."

And Wes's day would turn black, just like that. The hours would stretch out relentlessly, the phone not ringing, the pictures in his head dancing. She was nestled like a lamb in the blankets of his bed. She was in his arms. Eventually *he* would get up and go out while she stayed in bed, regal and indolent—Jonah rose first, Wes knew this—and he'd go to the corner and get coffees and the *Daily News*. And maybe even a pastry to share, which *he* would feed to *her*. Rousing her gently. Or maybe letting her sleep.

Worst of all, Jonah was happy, happier than Wes had ever seen him; he was flying, he was high. This girl *was* taking care of him, in all kinds of ways Wes had no access to. She was a girl. She was what nature had intended for him. Wes went to services every Sunday and she was practically a whore, yet Wes knew which union the Catholic Church would sanction first. She was little and cute, she could sit on his lap, dance in his arms, give him children. All this and more she had on Wes. But what did Wes have that Alicia didn't? He couldn't think of anything. Anything except history, which was as much a liability as a boon. And Jonah loved her. There it was: *he loved her.*

Once, just over two decades ago, he and Jonah had gone to dinner to celebrate the saving of her life. Now Wes wondered if maybe it wouldn't have been better if she'd burned to death.

Once at LaGuardia, Wes accompanied them to the gate, as he always did. He stood off to one side as they checked in at the little desk. He saw the airline attendant glance at Jonah and then do a double take. "Are you a fireman?" he asked.

"That's right," Jonah said.

Wes realized it was more than the insignia on Jonah's sweatshirt that the attendant was recognizing. Jonah had been on television earlier in the week, on a rerun of the program *Rescue 911*. No doubt this man had seen him in the footage of his famous roof-rope rescue in Brooklyn.

"Why don't you just step to the side for a moment," the flight clerk suggested. He added: "We'll put you in first class."

The gesture made Wes swell with pride even as his heart threatened to crack in two. As Jonah and Alicia moved to the left of the desk, smiling delightedly, Wes saw him wink at her. Within a few minutes they were holding upgraded tickets, their vacation charmed before they'd even left the city. Meanwhile, Wes couldn't help considering the fact that although he had been close to Jonah for more than twenty years, they had never taken a real trip together and it was highly doubtful that they ever would.

Their flight would be boarding momentarily. First-class passengers, as Wes knew from his own experience, did not have to wait to be called like everyone else. He went over to bid them *bon voyage*.

"Thanks again, Wes. See you on the nineteenth," Jonah said.

"Yes, thank you so much, Wes!" And he had to endure her lips against his cheek once again. Soft, they were so soft . . .

And then the two of them were gone, walking up the ramp without looking back.

After they disappeared, Wes stood for some time by the great Plexiglas windows, looking out. He would stand there until the plane pulled away from the gate and made its inexorable progress down the runway and out of sight. Always it struck him as a cause for wonder: the idea that something so heavy, so apparently weighted to the earth, could defy everything you thought you knew about gravity and its merciless pull. That it could just turn its back, gather an unforeseen momentum, lift itself into the air . . . and then before your very eyes, fly up and away and away.

———

Matilda scanned the menu for familiar dishes. She was hungry. Wes had taken her to another fine European place where the cuisine would be almost too beautiful to eat but her appetite would never be satisfied. She saw only a few items she could actually identify: formaggio and sausage quiche. Pâté de foie gras. Brie on cracked wheat thins. She sighed. Was a plain old pizza too much to ask for?

"So," she said, pushing the menu away, trusting Wes to order whatever was best, "you've seen her."

"Too many times now."

"Is she pretty?"

"She has a certain coarse charm." He added gallantly: "She's no Matilda O'Day."

"Jonah's really fallen hard," Matilda said, staring into her empty wineglass.

"She's not the first and won't be the last."

"But he says he's never felt this way before."

"That's what he always says."

"Really?" Matilda looked up.

"Yes," Wes said. "I've seen it all unfold at least half a dozen times before. That's not a lot of relationships if you consider that I've known him over twenty years. But he's remarkably consistent. He goes head over heels. She's the sun, the moon and the stars. He's been waiting for her all his life. But then . . . "

"Then?"

"Then he pulls back," Wes said. "Trust me, Til. A man like him doesn't reach the age of forty-three without ever having married unless there's a very good reason. Waiter? Could we start with the hearts-of-palm-salad? Make that two, actually. And we'd like the St. Lucie Sancerre, please."

"The girl's so young," Matilda said, once the waiter had moved away. "How can she possibly understand where he's been?"

"Well, of course she can't. She simply can't. That's why it will never last."

"And if she were a woman of substance, I could understand. But a topless dancer . . . "

"The whole idea offends my sensibilities as well," Wes said. "I like to think I raised him better than that."

They laughed together as their salads arrived. Matilda ignored hers for the moment, which irked Wes, as he always waited for the other to begin eating before he would even touch a utensil.

"Wes, maybe you think I'm an old fool," Matilda said. "But I couldn't have imagined a match that would make better sense than Jonah and myself. I mean, given the circumstances. He needs a family. My family needs a man. The kids already love him."

The waiter returned and brandished a wooden mill in the air.

"Pepper, Matilda?" Wes asked.

She declined; Wes accepted. An offer of Parmesan drew the same reception. Still Matilda made no move to eat. Wes gritted his teeth and sat on his hands.

"I think even Seamus would have given it his blessing," she went on. "Do you know what he said when they were bringing him into the hospital on the gurney? He said, 'I want Malone to take my place.'"

"Well, but Matilda. He meant as covering captain of Ladder 104."

"I know that!" she said. "But sometimes things have more than one meaning. Don't you think he could have meant both?"

"I think your husband wanted to live."

There was an awkward pause. Matilda looked down at her plate. Eat, Wes thought. Eat.

"Wes, you might not believe this. But I know Jonah felt something for me. I know that in some way he was in love with me. Women know things like that."

"I don't doubt that," Wes said generously. "The two of you went through a very intense experience together. It would make sense that a lot of extreme feelings were stirred up. But I know Jonah couldn't have been comfortable with those feelings, especially an attraction to you, the wife of the man he was trying to assist. His mission, as he saw it, was first and foremost to attend Seamus."

"Okay," Matilda said. "And no one could have done it better. But like you said, he and I became close during that time. Very close. And we stayed close for months afterward—right up until this little twit came along. We talked every day, Wes. Sometimes for hours. He visited me and the kids at least twice a week. He was the only one who really understood what I went through." Tears came into her eyes. "I miss him. I feel like he's lost to me."

"I'm telling you, he'll be back."

"He hasn't been out to the house once since he started seeing this girl. And he almost never calls anymore."

"He hasn't been calling me much either," Wes said. This was a considerable understatement, but pride kept him from sharing his own angst. "I know how you feel. But I've been through this with Jonah before."

She said nothing, just pressed her fingertips against her closed eyes.

"Look, Matilda." Wes sighed. "There are a few things you have to understand about Jonah. I know you've gotten close to him in the last six months, but I've known him for over two decades, and I have a perspective you couldn't possibly have."

"All right, then. Enlighten me."

"The first thing you have to realize is," Wes began, "Jonah's one man in a crisis and another out of it. When the chips are down—when something dramatic and terrible happens—no one keeps his head better, or instinctively knows what's called for, the way Jonah does. That's part of what makes him the fireman that he is. He'll go to just about any lengths when disaster strikes; in that context, he's utterly selfless. But once the worst has blown over and you're out of the woods . . . well, he's never there in quite the same way. Everyday life is not his forté."

Matilda was listening with the same polite air she adopted whenever he was lecturing about music or art.

"Something else you should be aware of," Wes continued, "is that Jonah has never been able to sustain a romantic connection with a woman. He's been in love before, yes. Or thought he has. But the sad reality is that Jonah has a serious problem with women. I'm sure it has to do with his mother. She was a chronic alcoholic who apparently never gave him any love or affection. At the same time, she was terribly sexually possessive of him—she would fly into a rage, for instance, if he were planning to take a girl to the school dance or some such thing. Even when he was well into adolescence. So, no wonder he has these problems."

"That's awful," Matilda said. "He never told me that. But she's been gone a long time, hasn't she? When did she die?"

"That's another piece of the puzzle," Wes said. "She died while he was in Vietnam. It was an alcohol-related death, cancer of the pancreas, I believe. His sister was the one who took care of her. He wasn't able to be at that deathbed. And you want to know something else about our crazy friend? After nine months of combat in Vietnam, after he'd completed his tour and they were ready to send him home, Jonah *volunteered* to stick around for another nine months. Maybe it was easier for him to endure that nightmare in the jungle than to come home and face his mother's death. So you see? You see how those primal relationships affect everything? I mean, don't you think that has something to do with the way he took care of Seamus?"

Matilda looked troubled. "I didn't know any of that," she said slowly.

"You know, many people who have been traumatized try to go back to the scene of the crime, so to speak," Wes said. "They re-create the traumatic event, but they try to make it come out differently. By taking such diligent care of Seamus, Jonah was really trying to make something up to his mother. That's my theory. He superimposes the same pattern upon everything he does, looking for redemption. By risking his life to save others every day, he's trying to make up for the people he killed in the war. By reaching out to the kids in his neighborhood, he's paying back all the firemen who took care of him. So sometimes this crusade of his manifests itself in wonderful, selfless acts. But other times it just results in pure self-destruction. He's carrying this guilt toward his mother, he has a sense of having abandoned her, so he's internalized all her pathology. In other words, he's still playing by her rules. She wanted to possess him absolutely, wanted him to have nothing to do with girls, even if she was unable to give him anything herself. So for forty-some years, he's never let himself sustain intimacy with women. I mean, he allows himself a taste every once in a while. That's what he's doing right now. Just enough to provide him with another loss to mourn. And then he finds some reason why it can't work, or he goes a little crazy and sabotages it. The upshot being he has something else to suffer over."

Wes sat back in his chair, spent. He had never quite spelled it all out before, not even to himself. It was terrible and reassuring at the same time. As long as Jonah remained crippled in this way, he would always be back. Meanwhile, Matilda was staring at him.

"You've really seen all this played out before?" she asked.

"Again and again and again."

"It's so sad," she whispered.

"Yes it is."

"And you feel certain that his new relationship with this girl—with this Alicia—is headed for the same end?"

Wes looked into her eyes and saw himself mirrored there. It was the same mingled emotions—sorrow over this deal Jonah had struck with his demons, and guilty gratitude for it just the same. He would light a candle in church and pray to be purged of this un-Christian attitude, but like everything else he hated about himself, it would burn on long after the wax had melted away.

"I'd stake some serious assets on it," is all he said. "My stocks in Microsoft maybe." When she looked unconvinced, he added, "My house in Connecticut."

"That's nothing," Matilda said. A hint of a smile showed on her face, the first he'd seen in weeks. "What about your Chagall?"

"I'd stake the Chagall on it, yes."

"No! Your *Picasso*. Would you put up your precious little sketch?"

"I'd even put up the Picasso sketch."

"Well, all right then," Matilda said, and finally picked up her fork.

Driving home alone, Matilda lit a cigarette and smoked out the car window. No matter how many years she managed to go without, the most stressful times of her life always brought the craving back. But now, comforted by Wes's prediction, she could take a few drags and snuff the rest of it out.

This new romance of Jonah's was bringing up so many unmanageable emotions. It went beyond his absence, which was bad enough. It was turning her into someone she couldn't stand: possessive, jealous, grudging. She recalled a phone conversation she and Jonah had during the week.

"I know you're very involved with your topless dancer," she said. "But it would be nice if you managed to see the kids some time this month. They miss you."

"Do you mind not referring to her as 'your topless dancer'?" Jonah asked.

"Isn't that what she is?"

"She has a name, all right?"

"It's just hard to believe that you'd be so serious about someone like that. I thought you had a little more character."

"Have you ever met her, Matilda? Do you know anything about her? She's a writer, all right? She's supporting herself with the dancing temporarily, that's all. And believe me, no matter what she does, she's a good girl. The best."

"Well, the girl part I'd agree with. What is she, half your age?"

"C'mon, Matilda," Jonah pleaded, in a tone she found vaguely familiar somehow. "I deserve a little happiness in my life."

"Oh, no doubt. At that, I suppose we *would* be a little depressing to be around. The poster-widow and her six half-orphans."

She heard him exhale sharply and knew she'd gotten to him. "Look," he said, after a long pause. "You know how much I care about you and those kids. And maybe in the whirlwind of the last couple of weeks I haven't been over there as often. But I've got my own life, Matilda. I put it on hold when the worst of this thing went down, and for months afterward. But there comes a time when I have to think about myself too." He paused again and sighed under his breath. "All right, listen," he said finally. "What about Saturday afternoon? Will you guys be around then?"

Matilda hesitated, torn between telling him not to do them any favors and the stronger desire to see him. "Looks all right so far," she said at last.

"Well, how's about I drop by, spend part of the day, maybe early evening with you guys."

"That would be very nice. If it doesn't put you out too much," she couldn't resist adding.

So, today was Wednesday. That made only two more days she'd have to live without him. The thought almost made her reach for another cigarette. *He'll be back,* she repeated to herself over the bridge and through the traffic and sitting still at the lights. *He'll be back. Wes said he would and Wes knows him better than anyone.* Amazing, what Wes knew. The two of them had such a history. Matilda had to wonder about it. Clearly Wes was gay, clearly he had always been in love with Jonah. Did they have a past that went beyond friendship? As close as she was to both of them, she could never bring herself to ask either one.

Whatever the case, his perspective was so reassuring right now that she didn't even care. What was it he'd said just before they'd went their separate ways this evening? Something half-comical, yet meant to be taken seriously.

"These brazen hussies come and go, spin his head, make him dizzy, take him away for a while. But he always comes back. Just remember that," were his parting words.

Just remember that, she told herself as she pulled into her driveway and parked the car. She looked critically at the flowers lining the walk as she approached the front door. The pansies were looking tired; the ones in the window box were too. She'd been letting them go. Maybe this evening she would give them a little attention.

Just remember that. She went into the house and saw that the light on the answering machine was blinking.

Remember that and everything will be fine. She pressed play and Jonah's voice filled the room. See that? Here he is . . . he called and it's not even a return phone call . . .

She listened to his message and then played it again. And again. She played it half a dozen times and then walked around in a few dazed little circles before she picked up the phone. Her hand was trembling and she kept hitting the wrong buttons. Twice she had to hang up and start again before she managed to complete Wes's number.

"Wes? It's Matilda . . . what? I sound strange . . . ? Well . . . yes. I suppose I do, it's . . . Jonah called. He's getting married."

———

A perfect afternoon in late June to be at the ocean and Jake was stuck in the hot city. Not that he would have missed this, but . . . it was exactly that combination of sun and wind that made for optimum surf. Instead he was in church, in the stiff dark suit he hadn't worn since his father's funeral. And beside him was Caryn, with that look on her face: wistful, dreamy, tinged with sadness. The tension between them these days was out of control, and he couldn't imagine what would be more likely to aggravate it than another—and younger—girl's wedding.

Caryn, of course, thought he was here as a friend of the groom. In a million years she would never suspect that he had also had a torrid affair with the bride. And he was sure that Malone would just as soon forget that fact as well. What had Alicia told him about it? Did he know about the strap-on? That would not be cool.

"Why don't you take off your jacket," Caryn suggested. "You're sweating."

She was right. He removed it and draped it over the back of the pew. As he did so, he caught sight of Matilda O'Day a few rows back. Malone's friend Wes was right beside her. They didn't look too happy to be here either.

Fuckin' weddings. He hated them. The obligation to bring a date. The smarmy music. The fuckin' *electric slide,* for Christ's sake. The whole thing was just another way society had of making everyone miserable.

Meanwhile. *Malone,* his hero, that die-hard bachelor of forty-three, was actually getting hitched. And to *Alicia,* his—Jake's—girl on the side, the spare wild card up his sleeve. He didn't know what to think of it.

Obviously Malone took her seriously. What did that mean? Should he, Jake, have taken her seriously? Even if he were the marrying type, a girl like that didn't seem like marriage material.

From the organ came the opening strains of the *Pachabel Canon,* which he recognized from commercials. And here she came in her wedding dress. This, Jake knew, was why girls wanted to get married. It all came down to the chance to wear that cascade of white lace and walk down the aisle real slow, cradling the bridal bouquet, dragging the material on the floor. The center of everyone's attention. All the girls wondering when and if their own chance would come. All the guys thinking that's one more broad they won't be banging.

It seemed to Jake that he could barely recall ever seeing Alicia fully clothed, let alone covered head to toe. There was something surprisingly exciting about it. It made her more of a mystery, swathed in all that white as if insisting on her own purity. She was beautiful, more beautiful than he'd even realized now that she was forever out of reach. She was smiling and her eyes glistened with tears. She was smiling at Malone, up there on the dais already. Jake couldn't believe the way she was looking at him. It was a full, radiant smile with no hurt in it, no smirk. Nothing resigned or bitter, nothing held back. Was this smile something only Malone could bring forth? Or had it been there all along, in reserve, waiting for an invitation? Was it something that might have been directed at him, if he had only allowed it? He hadn't allowed it, had been dimly aware of not allowing it the whole time he was with her. He never gave her that chance; he cut that possibility off at the root. Suddenly he recalled a fragment of a conversation they once had, one that must have been hurtful for her:

"Do you love me?" she asked.

After months of hearing Caryn ask the same thing day after day, the question was starting to annoy him.

"No," he said. It was a relief to just be able to say it flat out. "I won't lie to you. I don't."

He heard the sharp breath she drew before she could stop herself. He had once heard her make that same sound after ripping a Band-Aid from her skin. She was quiet for a moment and then tried to laugh it off. "Well, then . . . am I allowed to love you anyway?" What was it with girls, why were they always nailing themselves to some fucking cross?

He raised an eyebrow, as if he didn't quite get the question. "You're *allowed*," he said, shrugging.

Now as she joined Malone at the altar, her expression never wavered. It was all for him now, that outpouring, those natural resources. Jake knew well enough what she had in her. He knew she longed to care for, shower tenderness upon, a man. None of her efforts to disguise this had ever fooled him. Well, now she apparently had someone who could appreciate it. Who *needed* it.

He studied the girl he had given up. He thought she was doing the right thing. And hell, Malone was getting a good deal. Underneath that long length of dress, there was a garter around her thigh like the promise of a pearl within the oyster. *Bad girl makes good,* he thought, and the romance of that expression struck him with a special resonance. It was the idea of a commercially sexual woman making a decision in midstream to redirect all her skills, beauty, services, to a single man— and the idea that this redeemed her. She had decided to *settle down, leave her wild ways behind.* She was tamed and no longer dangerous. Someone had *made a respectable woman of her.* But underneath that snowy veil, inside the sugar-white bride in her floor-length gown, there still remained her thrilling know-how, the tricks of her former trade. Stripper tricks, whore tricks. All for Malone.

They were exchanging vows now; they were exchanging rings. The look on Malone's face as he put the band on her finger took Jake's breath away. It was ardent, tender, and utterly possessive. He was *claiming* her; he was taking her away from every other man on earth. At that moment, crazily, Jake was jealous of Alicia instead of Malone. No: he was jealous of both of them. Jealous of the amazing aura around them, jealous that they were sure.

The priest was pronouncing them man and wife. Malone lifted the veil like a man uncovering a treasure. They kissed, up there in front of everyone, kissed deeply and beautifully. Beside him, though he refused to turn to her or touch her, he heard Caryn sobbing. And she didn't even *know* them, for Christ's sake; she didn't know either one of them.

Amazing. He had to admit it. Weddings were kind of amazing, in the end. A moment ago they hadn't been husband and wife. Now they were. It was hard to get his mind around it.

I fucked your wife, he thought at Malone. *I had her first.* But it didn't bring the satisfaction he'd anticipated. It didn't really help at all.

In the truck the afternoon before, coming into the city from Montauk, he said to Caryn, "What time is the wake again . . . ? I mean, the wedding?"

She shot him a furious glance. It was an honest slip of the tongue but he could tell Caryn thought he'd made a deliberate joke at her expense. Not that she was unreasonable to think so. He'd been picking fights with her night and day. He knew he was being an asshole but he couldn't stop himself.

This put Caryn in a no-win situation. Whenever she tried to adjust and accommodate to keep the peace, a wild contempt took root inside him, flourished like a weed. On the other hand, when she fought back, she was just proving his point that they didn't get along, so what was the use in spending the rest of their lives together? He drove her to tears of frustration nearly every day, but her tears had long since ceased to make him feel anything but guilt.

Meanwhile. How long had Alicia been with Malone? Less than a year. He'd introduced them last August and now it was June. They were barely together five months before getting engaged, and today was roughly five more months after that.

Okay. Now, how long had he been with Caryn? Nearly five *years*. He still didn't know whether or not he was actually going to marry her, but he was beginning to strongly suspect that he wasn't. He didn't enjoy her company. She didn't really love or respect him for who he was. She was high society and she wanted to teach him to pass as upper class himself. She was always correcting his grammar and buying him clothes he couldn't stand.

What had he liked about her in the first place? He tried to remember. They liked to do a lot of the same things. She was a natural athlete: an excellent skier, and her form on a surfboard was probably better than his. She didn't have his balls though. Very few people had his balls. She wasn't ready and willing to die on the slopes or the crest of a killer wave and so she could not do the things he did. He remembered explaining this to Alicia once: "I don't want to die," he told her. "I don't know anyone who enjoys life the way I do, and if I could be a vampire and live forever, I'd do it in a heartbeat. But I'm willing to risk my life if I have to, in order not to compromise the way I play. If I can't do it on the edge, always on the edge, there's no point in doing it at all. I risk my life almost every damn day: on the mountain, in the ocean, running into fire. I risk dying to be as good as I can be. That's why, that's how, I'm able to live the way I do and why my life is as amazing as it is."

Caryn, of course, did not share this attitude, and so she held him back. When she skied or surfed with him, he always felt he had to kind of stay with her, watch her back, and it kept him from going all the way into something the way he needed to. They appeared to be sharing a sport, enjoying an activity together, but they weren't really together at all. She was content and he was frustrated. It would almost be better if he had a girlfriend who wanted nothing to do with sports.

He knew his outlook on life was all right for a certain kind of man: the reckless playboy type, the daredevil, the stallion. It was not all right for a husband and it especially wasn't right for a father. He didn't even have to think about which he wanted to be more. So how could he even consider going through with a wedding of his own?

After the ceremony, in the receiving line, Alicia put her arms around him and hugged him tightly. Her body pressed against his, probably for the last time. "Thank you," she whispered in his ear. "Thank you for bringing Jonah back to me. I'd been looking for him for so long."

"Aw, girl!" Jake said. He fought to sound kicked back and cool with this whole thing. "You got to know how amazing it's been for me. What an honor it's been. It's a killer story, I've told it a hundred times already." Then, gallantly: "You look beautiful, girl. Malone's a lucky man." Beside him he sensed Caryn stiffening in bewilderment. To buy time, he went on to shake Malone's hand, clap him on the back, finally lock him in a bear hug.

As they broke away from the bride and groom, Caryn turned to him with a puzzled look. "Jake, how do you know that girl?"

The thing to do was get to the bar as fast as possible. Liquor had a tendency to smooth the way for his stories. "I'll tell you all about it," he said. "Let's just get something to drink."

He asked the tuxedo-clad server for a double Absolut with a shot of Cuervo floated on the top. That would take the immediate edge off his tension. He got a glass of white wine for Caryn and let her take a long swallow before he began to explain his acquaintance to the bride.

"She's a neighborhood girl," he told his fiancée. "Lives on Bedford Avenue, right near the firehouse. When she was a little kid, a fireman saved her life and she'd been looking for him ever since. She came by one afternoon and described what she could remember about him and I said, 'Sounds like Malone.' Now, to tell you the truth, Malone was just a shot in the dark. I figured it had a good chance of being him just because he's saved more people than anyone I can think of. Plus he's been on the job long enough to have been the one. So I mentioned this firemen's benefit to her, said she should stop by. I figured even if it *wasn't* Malone, there'd be dozens of other firemen all in one place for her to check out. So she shows up and I point him out, take her over to him, not seriously thinking for a minute that it would really be him. But fuck me if it wasn't. Fuck me if it wasn't!"

"That's very uncanny," Caryn said. "That's some intuition you had."

Jake went on, embellishing the story. "And Caryn, man, when she saw Malone . . . when he saw her . . . when they *realized* . . . love at first sight, girl. Love at first *sight!*" This at least was close to the truth, from what he understood.

Tears welled in her eyes for probably the tenth time that day, and he had no doubt that she would stay at this emotional pitch throughout the rest of the afternoon and evening. There was a time when he kind of liked that about her. It was always easy for him to make her cry. Hit her with any halfway impassioned declaration of love, any well-planned romantic gesture, and she was gone. The poor chick. She deserved better than him. She needed the kind of guy who would bring her flowers for no reason and take her to nice places where they would eat by candlelight. He wondered if Malone and Alicia did stuff like that. Malone was kind of worldly in his way, and captains made good money.

The whole thing was still so hard to believe, though it had helped to tell that story to Caryn. Malone was so much older than Alicia. He had to have seventeen or eighteen years on her. Why did girls dig older men so much? And what was he doing getting engaged when he could keep getting young girls like her up through retirement?

When it was time for Alicia to throw the bouquet, he could see Caryn's struggle on her face. She was still unmarried, and so eligible to try to catch it. Of course, she was supposedly engaged already. But the engagement was so uncertain that she knew it needed any help it could get. They'd had a fight last week, such a terrible and bitter exchange that she took off her ring and put it on the table between them.

"Take your ring," she said. "Obviously you shouldn't have given it to me in the first place."

Truer words were never spoken, he thought. "Look," he said out loud. "I'm not taking anything back. No matter what happens, that ring is yours."

"I don't want it," she said. "I really don't. I don't want anything from you."

"Then leave it for the waitress," he said coldly. "It can be our tip."

She hurled it at him. He caught it easily, one-handed, and in a single fluid motion meant to infuriate, set it calmly back down on the table. Finally she dropped it into her purse, holding it between two fingertips like it was a used Kleenex she'd keep with her until she could find a trash can.

Two nights ago he called her to make up, primarily because he didn't want to come to this fucking wedding alone and he thought not showing up at all would make him look bad. People might think he was upset about it, maybe, as ridiculous as that idea was. Now the ring was back on her finger.

At last Caryn took her place among the other girls. Alicia stood with her bouquet. She had an air of importance that made her seem almost childlike. He thought he saw her notice Caryn; he thought a twinge of something—jealousy? pity?—crossed her face. And when she tossed the bundle of flowers, he imagined that she subtly aimed them at Caryn. He watched his girlfriend reach up—she would show no sign of strain, not his refined woman—and with the ease of the athlete she was, pluck it gracefully out of the air. Everyone applauded. Next Malone would throw the garter. Alicia was already seated with her hem lifted; Jake caught a flash of that taut, slender leg. Malone knelt before her and eased the garter down to her ankle and into his hand. Now all the young guys clustered behind him. Jake was out of his seat and standing with them before he knew it. Two factors had motivated him: one, he'd be damned if any of these other bastards were going to slide that band of lace up Caryn's leg. Second, he wanted that garter. Caryn would stash it somewhere and forget about it and eventually he could snag it.

Malone turned his back and tossed it over his shoulder. It was a few feet wide of Jake and he lunged, nearly knocking some skinny guy over to get it. He then stood holding it and feeling sheepish, resisting the urge to sniff it, not wanting to surrender it even temporarily. At last he turned to face Caryn. Her face was lit with a dazzling smile. It had been so long since he had seen her looking genuinely happy that for a moment she was unrecognizable. As a stranger she was briefly desirable once again and he was able to kneel before her as Malone had a minute ago knelt before his bride. Run his palm up the silken length of her leg. Let his hand come to rest on the lean muscle of her thigh.

Amen

Every time Jonah went to work, his young wife sent him off with the same words. "Be careful," she pleaded each time he left. "Promise me?"

It was always the last thing she said to him before he went and it made his every exit dramatic. Sometimes it was 7:00 A.M. and she was standing on the threshold of the apartment door, clad in one of his fire shirts and holding out his coffee in the thermal mug.

Or, if it were a rainy morning, she might murmur these words from bed, still half-asleep. The red satin sheets—a wedding present from one of her stripper friends—lent her the glamour of an old-fashioned centerfold, but reaching out to him with both arms she looked like the child he had saved so long ago.

Or again, if he were leaving for a night tour, she might be leaning into the car to kiss his cheek, before whispering this entreaty in his ear.

And he would drive down the F.D.R. Drive and over the Williamsburg Bridge with its echo in his ears.

Be careful. Promise me. Take good care of my baby.

"I'll take care of you the rest of the time," she said. "But when you're at work, I can't do anything but trust you."

She did take care of him the rest of the time. There were so many little things she did that made his life different. She made his coffee every morning and, because he liked it very light, even heated the milk so it wouldn't be lukewarm. Freshly squeezed orange juice was something else she liked to put in front of him. When he got home at night she had dinner ready, flowers on the table—a record playing, maybe. Girl stuff, though the fact was that not too many girls even did that kind of stuff anymore. ("I'm a throwback, Jonah," she once said to him wonderingly. "Yeah, well," he'd answered. "I ain't throwin' you back.") His apartment was always clean now, the bed made and the laundry all done. She often picked things up for him during the day: books she thought he might like to read, his favorite kind of ice cream, sometimes a bottle of massage oil that she would use to rub him down.

Ah, to have this pretty girl who took such pretty pains! Sometimes he still couldn't believe it and he knew that there were plenty of other people who couldn't believe it either. All the guys at the firehouse for instance. None of them could get over how young and lovely she was. Garvey, his lieutenant for the last ten years—the senior man in the firehouse and another Vietnam vet—was the only one who could get away with saying it to his face.

"Malone! What's that little doll doin' wit' an old dog like you?"

And Wes. Wes couldn't refer to her in conversation without much ironic rhapsodizing. *Dewy nymph,* was something the older man called her. *Silken sylph. Your tender, wide-eyed child bride.* He was mocking, of course, in his mild way. But that didn't mean his words weren't apt, and Jonah secretly took these phrases to heart, whispering them to himself in the car alone.

Be careful. Promise me?

I promise, was something he could say easily for the first time in his career. Somehow, these days, he was able to be as good as his word. He was aware of easing up somewhat, of guarding his life a little more closely. *He had a wife at home, after all.* He had what other men had. "I've got a family," was something guys in the movies said, whenever they were staring down the barrel of someone's gun. As if there were a code all men acknowledged, in which the welfare of women and children outweighed their own.

And so he stayed in formation when searching a building instead of breaking out on his own. He wasn't as quick to abandon the protection of a charged hose line. In the firehouse one evening after a run, he was moved to write something about his newfound caution.

I used to pray that a child's smile was worth dying for, he wrote on a yellow legal tablet that was lying on the housewatch desk. *Now I pray that a child's smile is worth living for.* He was enthralled by the sound of it and couldn't wait to show it to Alicia—couldn't wait to get home to his wife.

It was a strange sensation, this impatience to get home. Work had once been his greatest solace. Arriving at the firehouse for a twenty-four-hour tour meant his loneliness would be suspended for a full day and night. The captain's quarters were like a phone booth where he changed into an action hero. Alicia liked to tease him: "All you need is a cape. Or wait, I know—I'm going to sew a huge red *F* on the front of one of your shirts. It's a bird . . . ! It's a plane . . . ! It's—*Fireman!*" But it was true: even buttoning the white work shirt with the captain's bars—to say nothing about the turnout coat and helmet—he was transformed into someone he could stand to be. And usually this reprieve lasted only as long as his working hours.

Now these hours were many and slow, and driving back home again filled him with delicious anticipation. The only other time he could recall feeling this way was in the very early days of his adopted kittens. Before they were agile and loud enough to irritate him, they slept in a little box by the radiator. He didn't have a heating pad but he figured that was a warm enough spot. He did have an alarm clock, and he wrapped it in a towel just as the article instructed, to serve as the pretend mother cat. Then when he got home, he held them in his arms against his own heart, their bodies so soft and warm he couldn't put them down. He went straight to them the moment he walked in, even before his coat was off or the television on.

These days, when he came home, Alicia was sometimes playing the piano. This was still a miracle to him, that the piano he polished but could not play had come to life in his own living room. Until now the piano had been a silent stranger inhabiting so much space.

It was another firefighter, John Shaughnessy, who'd sold him that piano. He was buying a new apartment and didn't want the trouble of moving it. "You know anyone who wants a piano, Malone?"

"I want it," he said immediately, surprising even himself.

"You? You play the piano, Malone?"

"Well, I don't really. But I always wanted to try it."

"Sure you don't want to try it *before* you make that investment?"

"How much you askin' for it?"

Shaughnessy hesitated. "I don't know. It's a pain in my ass at this point. You really want it, you can have it for a thousand, I guess."

"I'll take it." It was worth more for sure—much more. He scribbled out the check before Shaughnessy could change his mind. "What if Juliet wants it back one day?"

Juliet was Shaughnessy's ex-wife, and the piano had been hers.

"The bitch can eat her heart out."

It was a steal, there was no doubt about it. Moving it was another story, and Jonah came to see why his friend hadn't wanted to deal with it. The price of getting it from the other man's apartment to his own was nearly what he paid for it. Once there, it took up most of his small living room, but he didn't mind. In fact he felt a little less lonely.

Isaias Casares, the man he had rescued from the window ledge, gave him his first lesson. Isaias played the keyboards in a salsa band and taught music at a high school in Spanish Harlem. It thrilled Jonah that he'd saved a musician; that because of him, there was a little more music in the world. He went a few times to hear the band and Isaias offered to teach him to play.

Jonah didn't want to make it a regular thing, knowing that Isaias felt indebted to all the firemen and would never charge him, but he couldn't resist an introductory lesson from the man he'd saved. He couldn't learn much in an hour. They covered the difference between treble and bass clef, the location of middle C, how to play the simplest scale. And the opening of *Joy To The World,* which was nothing more than the C scale played backward, with the appropriate pauses between notes. It was enough. He felt sufficiently enriched, pleased. Those notes in the beginner's books, climbing up and down the bars of their cages, were like a code and Isaias had initiated him into their mysteries.

He resolved to take real lessons but never got around to it. Instead he used a bottle of lemon seed oil that Isaias gave him to shine it regularly and lovingly, like a rare good memory of his mother. And sometimes he sat just touching the keys, those remnants of elephants from another continent.

In the two years since he'd taken it in, the piano had been all but mute. Now when he got home, the delicate music reached him even before he was out of the elevator. Sometimes when he walked in the door, Alicia didn't even hear him. At these moments he stood there with a sense of peering into a warmly lit room from the street, looking at her slim back, the spill of dark hair and her moving hands. A little spotlight cast its glow on the sheet music. There was usually some fragrant cooking aroma in the air. Bread might be baking in the oven, or soup simmering on the stove. Was this the dark and lonely apartment he'd lived in for eleven years? He would stand there listening to the piano, gazing at his cozy living room, at his wife, his life—until the moment she would somehow sense his presence, look over her shoulder. And then she was upon him.

Asunder

"Jonah, at the football game yesterday?"

"Yeah?"

The day before they had gone to see Seamus's firehouse—Jonah still thought of those guys as Seamus's—play a company from Queens. He knew that when Ladder 104 played, it was still for their lost coach. And so he went to watch the games.

Alicia liked to go too. At the beginning of the season she understood nothing about football, but now she could follow what was happening on the field and she even got excited about it.

"I saw Garvey at the hot dog stand," she was saying now. "He told me the chief's test is next year and he wanted to know if you were studying for it. I said I didn't know." She paused. "Why didn't he just ask you himself, I wonder?"

Jonah grinned. "Probably doesn't want to put the idea in my head."

"Why wouldn't he want you to take the test?"

"Well. If I became a battalion chief, I'd be leaving Rescue Two," Jonah said. "And I been workin' with Garvey, oh, must be over ten years by now. He likes having me around. I'm the only other vet in the firehouse."

"That makes sense," Alicia said. She smiled. "But are you?"

"Am I what?"

"Studying for the chief's test."

"I don't know," Jonah said. "It's still about nine months away."

"But you told me that guys study for those tests for years."

She was right. Guys did study for those tests for years, and he had put in the same kind of time for the lieutenants and captains tests.

"I glance at the books now and then," he told her.

"Well," she said. "Are you planning to get more aggressive about it?"

"I don't know," he repeated. "Why do you ask?"

"It made me wonder, that's all. I know how much work you put into becoming a lieutenant and then a captain. So if you were putting in the same kind of effort now, I would think I'd know about it," she said. "I guess it surprised me to learn that the test is so soon and apparently it hasn't been a priority to you."

They were at the kitchen table, the remains of breakfast littering the surface. Jonah stood and brought several items to the sink. Then he took his time getting a refill of coffee. "Want some more coffee, honey?" he called to his wife.

"I'm fine, thanks," she said. The slight edge in her tone let him know she was waiting him out.

He returned to the table. "Look, honey," he said. "I don't know if I want to be chief."

"So I've gathered. I'm just not sure why not. Certainly no one's more qualified."

"Well, what's it to you? Is it the extra money?"

"Jonah, come on. Do you think I care about the money?"

"What is it, then?"

"I want to understand your decision, that's all."

He stared into his coffee mug for several moments before answering. "Look, honey. When you're a chief, you mostly just stand out on the sidewalk and direct the action. You don't really go into the fires anymore."

"All right," she said. "Is that a bad thing? It sounds like a good thing to me."

"Good for some people, maybe," he said. "But not good for me."

"No?"

"Honey, my whole life has been about fighting fire."

"That's true," Alicia said. "You've put in twenty hard years and done some extraordinary things. Your career has probably been the envy of the entire department. Can't you ease up a little now?"

"I ain't washed up yet. I got some good years left in me."

"Do all of your good years have to be spent on this one thing?"

"My heart's still in it, honey. What do you want me to do?"

She stared at the grain of the wooden table, frustrated. "Jake used to tell me he couldn't wait to retire," she said finally. "As soon as he has twenty years on the job, he's taking his pension and taking off."

There was a tense moment of silence before Jonah spoke. "I ain't Jake."

Alicia stood and began clearing the rest of the table. Jonah saw that she was trying not to cry. He went over, took the plates from her and set them back down on the table. "Honey, come on," he said, pulling her to him. "What's this all about?"

"I worry about you, all right?" she said. "That's what this is about. I can't believe you have to ask."

"I been all right so far," he said.

"Well, thank God for that. It's a miracle that you have. Why tempt fate now?"

He said nothing.

"We talk about having a baby," she continued. "What about that? Don't you want to be alive for that?"

After this conversation, *be careful* sounded different to him. It sounded less like a caress and more like a threat. As time went on, answering to it got harder. What did a promise like that mean, anyway, and how was a fireman supposed to be careful? Maybe a regular fireman could do it, but him?

Since his honeymoon, he hadn't been to a fire where anyone was really in trouble. But what about the next time lives were at stake? Rescues involved risk; it was that simple. Was he supposed to stop being the fireman he had always been?

Apparently, Alicia would have it that way. Well, what if she was right? Maybe it was time. As she'd pointed out, some guys with twenty years on the job retired and got half pay for the rest of their lives. While *that* was out of the question, maybe it was okay to be a little less reckless. It wasn't so long ago that he'd told Matilda that he deserved some happiness. Now he tried telling himself. He'd done his job, done his time. What were the last couple of decades but time marked by a marked man?

But that was dangerous territory to enter. That was deadly. For as he allowed himself to entertain that idea, it was like a button marked *play* had been pressed inside his head, and the old tapes were set in motion once again.

He was a murderer, as marked and set apart as Cain. Condemned to wander the earth alone for the rest of his days. So how had he gone astray, fallen in with this innocent girl? How had that happened?

"Jonah?"

Alicia was calling him from the bedroom. It was a Sunday afternoon and he was watching the Jets lose on TV.

"Yeah, honey."

"My sister's birthday is Thursday so I have to go to Macy's." She emerged with her purse and took the apartment keys from the coffee table. "I shouldn't be too long. What's the score?"

"We're sunk, let's just leave it at that," he said. He looked up at her. The collar of her shirt was open to the third button. "Hey," he said, reaching over to close it. "You don't want to look like a slut." He was amazed at his own words the moment they were out, as if his mother had spoken from the grave instead of him.

"What?" Alicia said. She looked confused and pulled away. "What are you doing?" Her voice wavered between hurt and disbelief.

Immediately he was overcome. "I'm sorry," he said. "I'm sorry, I don't know why I said that. I didn't mean it like it sounded."

She said nothing. Her eyes were wide.

"I'm sorry, honey," he repeated. "I didn't mean nothin' by it." He groped for a way to explain. "It was kind of supposed to be a joke but it wasn't funny. Please, I'm real sorry."

"It's all right," she said.

He stared hard into her face. A sudden and nameless panic was swelling inside him. From the moment he met her, he'd been keeping a tight lid on himself. Airtight. And now for the first time his cover was slipping a little. What was she thinking? He couldn't tell. She looked more bewildered now than anything else.

"No, it ain't all right, but I'm sorry. I mean, I really, *really* apologize for saying that." He was unable to stop.

"Jonah, it's all right. Don't worry about it." She looked down and slowly fastened all but the very top button of her blouse. Watching her do this made him clench his jaw in shame; he had to look away.

She came over and touched his shoulder. "I'll be back in a few hours, okay?"

He nodded, then pulled her close and clutched her. "Honey, please forgive me. I'm so sorry."

She took his face in her hands. "Jonah, you don't have to keep apologizing. I was hurt for a second but it's okay now."

"I didn't mean nothin' by it. It was just kind of a joke."

"It's really all right." She put both arms around him and held him tightly, then ran one hand over his short, bristled hair like she was petting some pathetic mutt. "It's fine, okay? Please don't think about it anymore. I'll be back in a couple of hours."

"Can I come with you?" he blurted.

"Come with me? I'm just shopping for my sister. I'll be going to women's stores."

"It don't matter. I just want to be with you."

She wavered for a few seconds while his panic threatened to overwhelm him. Then: "Sure, of course," she said. "If you really want to. I'm just afraid you'll be bored."

"It don't matter," he said again. "I'm happy just bein' around you."

"Well, I'm glad to have you, then."

She didn't look glad though. She looked worried. I'm scaring her, he thought. It's showing.

The afternoon was excruciating. She was right; he never should have come along. Macy's was no place for him to spend even an hour of his life. He followed her up the escalators, through the crowded maze of displays, past women clutching shopping bags and fags trying to spray him with cologne. The whole thing was like a fuckin' anthill. His heart was beating erratically.

Alicia stopped at a jewelry counter. He stood off to one side while the saleslady showed her whatever she asked to see. Why had he come with her? It had frightened him when she was about to walk out the door. Like she might not ever come back. So like some mangy stray he had to follow her around, tag along where he had no purpose.

"Jonah?"

She was motioning him over. He moved to her side and she smiled up at him. "Jonah, you know, I'm really glad you came with me because I can't decide which pendant to get. Let me show you a couple on me, so you can tell me which one looks better."

She was trying to be nice. Trying to make him feel all right about being here. He felt a headache coming on strong and tried to relax his jaw.

Alicia tried on the first necklace, stepped back for his appraisal, then replaced it with another one. "What do you think?" she asked.

He chose the second without really looking and waited while she paid.

Soon she would realize. What a fuckin' nut job he was. This was still just a small crack in his cover. He would keep cracking; he would not be able to contain himself forever. How long would it be before she was running for her life?

Back in the car, he put the key into the ignition and just sat there without starting the engine. After a moment, Alicia leaned over and put a hand on his arm.

"Jonah?" she said gently. "Talk to me. Are you feeling okay? You seem so tense."

He turned to her. "Honey," he said. He tried to keep his tone light but it came out sounding abrupt. "I'm a little nuts, you know." He grinned crookedly but his eyes were begging.

"I know," she said softly.

It took him by surprise. "You know that, honey?"

"Yes. I do. I do know," she said, holding his eyes with hers. "I know you're a little crazy. I don't care. I love you."

Her words brought a rush of relief, but it was only a momentary reprieve. She didn't really know what she was saying. She had no idea what she was signing on for. She was too young. What was he doing with such a young girl? The year he went to Vietnam was the year she was born.

The second crack had to do with the hats. The night came when he couldn't hold out anymore, he had to cover his head when he went to sleep. It began with the hooded sweatjacket he wore to bed. After Alicia fell asleep, he pulled the hood over his head and tied the strings tight beneath his chin. He knew other vets who did this, who had to feel covered and concealed. The hood wasn't really as substantial as he liked but it was enough to tide him over for a while. Then finally after a week or so he took the plunge and got out the old ski hats, pulling them down over his eyebrows and ears. Even this wasn't ideal; he would have preferred the woolen winter masks with holes cut out for the eyes and nose. But that was too over the top. He couldn't ask Alicia to share a bed with that. The hats were hard enough to explain.

"I need to do this sometimes, honey," he told his wife. "I know it's left over from the war. Sometimes I don't need the extra cover at all. But then again sometimes I still do."

Soon afterward Alicia came home with a wrapped box.

"What's that?" he demanded.

"Something for you to wear in bed," she said, with a mischievous grin. "Open it."

He tore off the ribbon and paper, picturing silk boxers or satin bikini briefs, something like that, even though it wasn't his style. What he found was a suede pilot's hat, lined with sheepskin, with flaps on either side that came down over his ears. He looked at Alicia. She was grinning like the cat that swallowed the canary.

Maybe she really did know he was crazy. Maybe she really didn't care. Was it possible that everything would work out after all? He knew one thing for sure: at least she had a sense of humor.

"You think that's funny?" he bellowed, overcome with a sudden sense of well-being, optimism, euphoria. "Think that's funny, huh?" But he was laughing himself. She *was* going to save him. And he could accept that it was his turn. He had saved *her* once, long ago, when she was a child of five; but like in the story of the lion and the mouse, you just never knew.

Then came the flashback. He hadn't had one in years. There was a time when they happened almost every week, but that was right after the war. Anything could bring them on: a clap of thunder, flashing lights, a helicopter. The pop of a child's balloon could send him into a dive for the floor.

He knew this was part of what made him the fireman he was. The sight of flames, the sound of screams, sent him into automatic overdrive and set off his military instincts. On civilian time, though, the residual effects of the war had few redeeming features. They made people uncomfortable. His habit of checking behind each door, starting at every sudden noise, unnerved those around him. And certain staples of American life were just off-limits. He couldn't be outside on the Fourth of July, for instance. Forget about it. He couldn't be around kids with BB guns. He hated the sound of helicopters and certain music bothered him, like anything by the Doors or Jefferson Airplane.

All these reactions faded over the years until only twinges remained, and the full-blown flashbacks all but disappeared. He hadn't had one since meeting Alicia. But this one came on with a vengeance.

She was on the floor before him, sucking him as she loved to do, when suddenly he found himself staring down at Joey Bazura— Bazooka Joe, they called him—instead of his wife. Bazura was from Battalion R, a guy who thought he was fuckin' John Wayne or some shit. No one in the platoon could stand him. He picked a fight with Jonah on the wrong night, right after the youngest guy in their unit bought it from a land mine. They kicked the shit out of each other, rolling around in the mud outside the huts, but eventually Jonah had him down. And then Bazura was on his knees before him, with the barrel of Jonah's M-16 halfway down his throat.

What he remembered most clearly about this moment is that it seemed both indefinite and frozen. He didn't know what he would do. He could move his index finger a quarter-inch and spill his first deliberate American blood. It seemed at this moment that it would hardly make a difference; there was so much blood on his hands already. No one out here would miss old Joey, that was for sure. Quite a few of the guys were egging him on.

Waste him, Jo-Jo. Waste that maggot's ass. You got witnesses to say it was a suicide. Hell, you don't want to do it, step aside and let me at him.

His captive's neck cords were standing out in his terror. He was stiff and agonized, still as stone, frozen in this pose of supplication, performing fellatio on Jonah's gun.

Between you and me, was the phrase that went through his mind right then. *Well, now, pal, this is between you and me.* Nobody around them could intervene, even if they wanted to, without blowing the back of the guy's throat away. But the fact was that no one even seemed to want to. The ones who weren't downright enthused about blowin' ol' Bazooka into pieces were nonetheless watching the drama with the first flicker of interest they had shown in some time.

To this day, Jonah couldn't be sure how long they remained like that, how long he held the rifle there, before—thank God, thank God—he eased the gun back out of the guy's mouth and watched him puke in the tall grass before allowing him to crawl off.

But now, instead of his wife on the floor in front of him, it was that Marine, with his eyes of a horse in a thunderstorm, gagging as if at an oversized bit. (So that he became even harder, rigid and insistent, but there was no release. She could be down there for two days and there would be no release.)

That look. It dogged him his whole life long. Seamus's eyes above the tracheotomy had been the same: the irises like tiny islands inside so much white. The invaded mouth working in vain. More than once he tried to pull the trache out and they had to hold him down. *Hold him down* was something Jonah still muttered in his sleep, according to Alicia. An echo of the disembodied voices from the park bench, floating above his hooded head. *Hold him down!* Had it been rape? Had they raped Seamus, he and Matilda and the doctors, with the relentless surgeries and skin grafts and visits to the debriding tanks? Intensifying his torture, drawing it out, when he was just going to die anyway? "Y'know, I was raped," a girl once said to him accusingly on a date, like he'd been the one to do it to her. Like it was a good reason to hate all men forever. "Yeah, so was I," he said to her disbelieving stare. "It's fucked up, ain't it? I know how you feel."

Fuckin' women. Always making out like they were the only ones who had it tough. Meanwhile not a single one of them had been forced to go overseas. What the fuck did they have to complain about? It was unbelievable, the way they tried to manipulate you. Look at the way Matilda had been putting the screws to him. What a ball buster *she* had turned out to be. How in hell did Seamus get through twenty-some years of that shit? She was angry 'cause he wouldn't fuck her, that's what it all came down to. Here he'd just been trying to do the right thing by Seamus, and she was mad 'cause he wouldn't *fuck* her! That bitch! Digging in her fuckin' claws. Trying to drag Alicia through the dirt.

"Hi sweetie." This from Alicia. "How was your day?"

"Hey. It was all right."

It was early evening. He'd just come in from an A.A. meeting and she was writing at the kitchen table.

"Do you feel like going out tonight?" she asked. "There's something at the Film Forum that looks good."

"Not tonight. I'm tired," he said. The fact was that he was exhausted, even though he'd had the day off.

"What about just for dinner, then?"

"I ain't real hungry. Why don't you order something in if you want."

"All right," she said. There was a pause, then she asked, "Jonah, has anything been troubling you?"

"What do you mean?"

"You seem different lately."

"Different how?"

She put down her pen and took some time to answer the question.

"Just—you seem really preoccupied and anxious a lot of the time. Like you're somewhere else. I feel like we're not connecting the way we usually do. If something's worrying you, can you share it with me?"

"I'm all right," he said. "I've been tired lately, that's all."

She studied him a moment without speaking. Then: "Okay. Good," she said. "I just wanted to make sure."

It was true that he was tired. Winter was a hard season for firefighting. When the temperature dropped, everything got busier. More heaters were on, so there were more electrical fires. Plus the bursting of water pipes and boilers. There were frigid nights when the alarm went off every hour. Sometimes this was because of several fires back-to-back. Other times there were—still worse—twice as many false alarms. Punks pulling the call boxes for kicks.

When would he get to rest? He had a fantasy sometimes, an easy one: a deep dark hole. And like a gopher he was tunneling all the way into it, digging out a space just wide enough to hold him. Then dying— just curling up and dying. Was it so much to ask? Finally some peace— an endless, untroubled sleep. A silence not torn by alarm bells or steeped in jungle dreams.

He knew the other guys at the firehouse heard him whimpering and moaning all night, every night. Though this was one of the few things that these jocular, hard-assed, ball-breaking pranksters did not make light of. It was off-limits—they understood what it was about. The fire department itself bordered on a military organization. No long hair was allowed. And no beards. To compensate for this, many of the men grew their mustaches to ridiculous lengths—sticking straight out like cat's whiskers, or drooping like the tusks of a walrus. His own mustache, when he'd had one, was standard, no nonsense. Almost all the guys had 'em. Let him at least appear to blend in.

It was true that he was tired but not that he was all right. Alicia was on the money with that. Something savage was stalking him; it was at his heels again. It always came the same way: rolling in like thunder, breaking like a storm; and one by one, every single light went out. When it hit, food was tasteless, all conversation oppressive, the world as garish and warped as a funhouse mirror. It was all he could do to get through each day, and then there was always another lined up right behind it. Sometimes he slept until mid-afternoon. Often he cried for no reason.

Alicia would not stay when she saw how it was with him. And he wouldn't let her anyway, even if she thought she wanted to. It was all wrong. She was young and innocent and didn't belong anywhere near him. If only there were some way to get her away before it hit.

———————

After this inquiry, Alicia too began acting differently. She seemed quietly frightened, and her fear was infectious. But she wasn't trying to get away. No. Instead, she was clinging to him even tighter. It was nerve-racking. He didn't like anyone around when he was sick, and this was kind of like that.

She turned everything inside out, without even meaning to. Like his bed, for instance. At times like this, his bed had always been like a cave he could hide in. It was a place to rest, gather strength, check out for the better part of the day if he needed to. But having her there made it like another hoop he was supposed to jump through.

At this point, there was no way he could give her what she wanted. It was hard for him to get aroused, and even if he did, the sheer physical energy of the act was beyond anything he could manage right now. Three nights in a row, when Alicia reached for him, he abruptly put her off.

"Alicia. C'mon."

"What do you mean, come on?"

"I'm beat tonight."

"Well, lie back and let me do all the work. I'll get on top."

"Honey—please. I'm all wore out."

After the third such exchange, she suddenly started to cry.

"What's the matter," he asked, exasperated.

"Why are you always tired? How can you be tired every night? You haven't even worked since Monday."

"Look, it was a hard weekend. It carries over sometimes. You know how it is."

"All I know is you've never been like this before."

He was silent.

"There's something wrong," she said, almost to herself. "I know there is."

"Wrong how? Wrong with me?"

"Something's different. Admit it."

"What? What's different?"

"I don't know. Maybe you're not in love with me anymore," she said. She swiped at her eyes with the back of her hand.

"Honey, that ain't true. C'mon now. You just got to give me some space, all right? You can't put this pressure on me."

"How am I pressuring you?"

"You just got to let me be sometimes."

She sat up in bed and looked at him. He kept his eyes on the ceiling.

"I feel like you're pulling away from me," she said finally, "and I don't know how to reach you."

"Look," he told her. "I'm sorry. I don't know what you want me to say."

"I don't want you to say anything. I just want you to let me in."

"Well sometimes I can't do that," he said. "Sometimes you just got to let me be."

The guys at the firehouse had no trouble letting him be. They knew to stay out of his way at times like this. It had been a long time since anyone there had made the mistake of sneering, "Whatsa matta wit' *you?*" This was many years ago but the firehouse wall was still missing plaster where he'd rammed the guy's head. Now the men recognized the danger signs, and when necessary, kept exchanges to a respectful minimum. It was a fine arrangement, because if there was one thing he could still do as readily as before, it was fight the fire. His ability to make split-second decisions was unimpaired here as nowhere else. His energy kicked in the moment he needed it. And he had Garvey with him—Garvey who understood. Garvey the vet, who could say whatever he wanted to Jonah, not like the others.

"Malone," he said now. "You're about the sorriest sight I ever seen."

"I'm whipped, Garvey. Fuckin' beat."

"Yeah, I know how it is. Just ride it out."

"Sometimes I don't know, Garvey."

"Look," the other man said. "You know what they say at A.A. They say, One day at a time. And that's how you do."

"Yeah well. It don't get any easier."

"Just ride it out," the other man repeated. "All there is to it."

Jonah looked at his friend. Garvey was only forty-eight and his hair was already all white. His mustache was white. Deep crow's feet were cut at the corners of his eyes. He lived alone, had never been married.

"Garvey," he said. "You ever have days like this?"

"You don't need me to tell you that, Malone. Ain't a one of us got out of there free."

Being at work lifted the pall just enough for him to get through it. But taking off the uniform at the end of the day pulled him back into his invisible straitjacket. Driving home, his gaze kept turning to the concrete median in the middle of the F.D.R. Drive. It wouldn't be hard to just drive up and over it. Straight into opposing traffic, and let some truck finally take him out.

Home again, he went straight to bed. He and Alicia had reached a temporary truce; each of them was pretending that nothing was awry.

"Jonah? How was work?"

"Tough afternoon," he said. "I ain't feelin' so good."

"No? What's the matter?"

"I must be comin' down with something. My muscles are achin' something fierce. Or my joints. I don't know."

"I'm sorry, honey," his wife said. "Is there anything I can do? Do you want a back rub?"

"Nah, I'll be okay. I'm just gonna go lie down."

"Go ahead. Let me know if you need anything."

This was the most bittersweet part of the day: twilight, with its tender lilac sky. Its dusky perfume like a promise made to someone else. This was the hour that children's games were at their most heated— frenzied and almost desperate, as if beating something back. Their hoarse shouts floated up to him. Shards of street noise. Nostalgia like a message in a bottle sent across the years, washed up on his shipwrecked shore. A flash of what life had been like once, what it might have been again, if only—but no. Here he was on his back. Succumbing to the downward tug, all the little sinkers accumulated on his heart.

The phone rang. He didn't move. After two rings he heard Alicia pick it up in the kitchen. A moment later she was at the bedroom door.

"Jonah, do you feel like talking to Wes?"

He shook his head. She left and he imagined she was taking some pleasure in relaying his refusal to the other man. There was never any love lost between those two.

And fuck Wes, anyway. The sick bastard. Look what he'd done when Jonah was down, when he was *blind,* coming out of surgery as helpless as a kitten, a newborn kitten with its eyes sealed shut.

They fucked you. They bled you. They burnt you. It never ended; they never let up. At night was when they got you. In his sleep, they all came for him, flapping down from the same dark tree. The priests from school, their black robes like the wings of crows. The hands that pinned him to the park bench, the gooks from the jungle, the blackened victims he'd reached too late or not at all and their wild banshee mothers. Jerry came, and Jo Malone, and Seamus too. Reaching out for him, seizing, begging. And when he woke in a haunted sweat, Alicia's arms were just something else clutching at him, something else to shake off. And what was *she* cryin' about? What did she have to cry about? How, how had she gotten here? It was like he woke up one day and a girl was in his bed, calling herself his wife. And now there was no getting away from her. She *lived* here! Night and day, she was always here, across the table, underneath his covers. Reproaching him with her wounded silences. Whimpering the rest of the time. More dangerous than any cat could ever be. And how was he going to get rid of this one? Always leaking at the eyes. Obviously in some kind of distress. Caused by him? His fault? Of course it was his fault.

He had brought her here. Mistaken her for somebody, something else. Walked down that aisle to where she was waiting behind her veil, lifted that gauze away from her face and put his mouth on hers in front of God and everybody. A violation of the private pact he'd made long ago. How could anything good come of it? He had to take it back.

From where he lay he could hear the swish of cars. Below his window was a little park and just beyond that was the highway. All through the long night, a glowing snake of cars would twist on and on and on. Bearing freight, being careful not to touch. There was at least one waking person in each of them, cruising in his own sealed chamber. The whole world was like that.

Often he thought about just driving away. No good-bye and no explanation; no warning, no note. Just drive out of the city, out of the state, into the nowhere of the desert. Where it burned by day and froze by night. Where there was no water and every living thing knew how to make precious little go an endless way. That was a landscape he understood. Everything parched and gritty and dry, needled and spiked and self-contained. Snakes out there, but no vines. Nothing to fuck you up and play tricks on the eyes. A snake was a snake was a snake. What a relief that would be. No vines and no trees, no one to ambush you. Just buzzards waiting. He could see himself flat on his back, kind of like he was now but on glittering sand instead of sickbed sheets. The stinging particles blowing over his body, filling every crevice.

All night these pictures jangled in his brain. Feverish and crazy. Thoughts and nightmares all jumbled together.

Sometimes he woke to sunlight coming through the window and for a little while it was all right. There was an interlude of clarity and quiet, a brief breathing space. But even then there was the sense of something hovering overhead, something like a winged shadow. Rustling and overbearing, not descended yet.

Other mornings it was sitting on his chest, trying to choke him before he even opened his eyes. And what could he do then? It seemed dangerous to move even a muscle. Maybe if he lay very, very still . . .

If he couldn't die, what he wanted most was to lie in his room with the shades drawn and stay there. Not speak, not move, not face the endless and empty expanse of the day. Not answer to anyone or anything. Just play dead until it went away.

"Jonah."

It was a few weeks after the bedroom exchange. Alicia had given up on sex. Even conversation was an effort now. But if he didn't answer, she wouldn't leave him alone.

"Jonah," she repeated.

"What."

"I'd like you to do something for me. Would you do something for me?"

"What." Not looking at her. Gaze fixed on the blood red of the carpet.

"I would like you to see a doctor."

Rousing something in him, a flare. Enough to keep him talking.

"For what?"

"For this depression. I think you are dangerously depressed."

"Dangerous to who?"

"Well. To yourself," she said. A pause. "I don't think you'd hurt anyone else."

"That's right," he snapped. "I wouldn't. So you can quit worrying. And I ain't goin' nowhere."

"You're the one I'm worried about. Who else would I be worried about? This is a clinical, chemical condition, Jonah. It's not something you can conquer by yourself."

Clinical, chemical. Bitch thought she was so smart. "What's a doctor gonna do for me?"

"Well, to start with, maybe give you some medicine."

"Oh no," he said. "No way. I ain't been in A.A. ten years to start doin' drugs again now."

"Drugs?" she repeated. "*Drugs?* Are you putting antidepressants in the same category as, say, crack cocaine?"

"I ain't takin' any pills that fuck with your head. I don't care what you call 'em."

"Whoa . . . wait a minute," she said. She was careful to keep her voice down but she was starting to get pissed, he could tell. "Wait just a minute. Tell me this: if you were diabetic, would A.A. say it was okay to take insulin?"

"That's different," he snarled.

"How is it different?"

"Look, I ain't gonna argue wit' you. It's different."

When he refused to say anything more, she tried again, making an effort to recoup and stay cool. "Listen, Jonah. Insulin is actually a good comparison. People who are diabetic have a bodily imbalance, and when they take insulin, they're just supplementing what's missing. Antidepressants do the same thing. If you have a chemical imbalance, you're missing something everybody else has. And by taking medicine, you're just restoring a normal equilibrium. They're not happy pills, not uppers. You still have ups and downs like everyone else. You have good days and bad. The medicine just fixes it so they all don't have to be bad."

He was silent. Let her rattle on, why should he get pulled into it?

"Do you know what lithium is?" she was saying now. "It's only a salt. That's it—nothing more. But if it's missing from your system, you need to put it back in."

"I ain't doin' it," he told her. "This is the way I am. I been through this before. I just got to ride it out like I always do."

"What do you mean, you've been through this before?"

"It's like you been sayin'. You're right that I'm in trouble. But this ain't the first time it's hit. It's gotten me lots of times."

"You're saying you've been severely depressed before?"

"Depressed, whatever you want to call it. I been crazy fucked up before. Like I'm in a black hole. Or a pit. And it feels like I can't get out. But it always goes away if I wait long enough."

Alicia put a hand on his arm. "Okay. Then just explain this much to me, so I understand. Why is it so wrong to make it go away sooner?"

"I ain't doin' it," he said. "And that's it. It'll go away by itself, or it won't. It ain't up to me."

A sharp sigh of frustration. "Well, in the meantime, what am I supposed to do?"

"Who's askin' you to do anything?"

"I miss you," she said. Tears were filling her eyes as they did so often these days. "You're not the same person."

"Well, that's why I ain't been with anyone long term," he said. "I thought it would be different with you. I thought I had this thing kicked for good. But listen, Alicia, you got to know this—I might not be able to do it this time either."

"Do what?"

"I might not be able to be married."

The sentence hung in the air like a noose. It was almost a minute before she could answer and he could see how hard it was for her to keep from breaking down. "Don't you think you should have thought about that *before* proposing to me?"

"Like I said, I thought I was past it."

As she gave in to tears it was all he could do not to walk out of the room.

"Stop it," he growled. "I can't take your cryin' all the fuckin' time."

"So this is it?" she choked out. "This is all my problem now? I mean, having married me, don't you feel any responsibility for making this work?"

"It can't work," he said. "Look, Alicia, you got to stop cryin'. I can't talk to you when you cry."

"Why shouldn't I cry?" This was nearly a shriek. He fought the urge to cover his ears. "Don't I have a good reason to cry? My husband is losing his mind and won't do anything about it—and suddenly I'm supposed to just forget about my marriage? Well, fuck you, because I took the vows too and they meant something to me, even if they didn't mean anything to you! *In sickness and in health.* I said those words. Do you think I'm just going to drop everything and walk at the first sign of trouble?"

A tremor came over him. It took over his whole body. All thoughts fled his mind as he started to shake.

"Jonah?"

"I'm sorry," he whispered.

"Jonah, what—are you—"

"I'm sorry, I'm sorry."

His eyes widened, unseeing, and spilled over. His teeth began to chatter. He shivered and twitched as if in the grip of a seizure. Water ran out of his eyes and nose and mouth.

"Jonah!" Alicia tried to take his face in her hands. He shook her off. She knelt beside him on the floor. "Jonah, please look at me, talk to me."

"I'm sorry!" he screamed. "I'm sorry, I'm sorry, I'm sorry!"

In a frenzy, he began hitting himself in the face with both fists. Alicia started to scream too. "Jonah, stop it! Please Jonah, don't!" She tried to grab his hands and failing that, flung her arms around his neck and clung there, shielding him from himself, weighting him to the floor. He shook and cried in her arms. She held on, crying with him.

They lay like that on the floor for a long time, holding on.

——

"I want to know how the hell you got here."

These were Jonah's words, fired at Alicia across the table in his apartment. (It was back to being his apartment. Her clothes in the closet, all her little things scattered everywhere, no longer confused this issue.) As far as she could tell he hadn't slept or shaven in two days. His hair was disheveled, his eyes bloodshot, and gray-black stubble dotted his jaw. If she didn't know better, she would think he was drunk. (If only he were.)

He was disowning her. His stance seemed to go beyond renunciation to annulment. You'd think he woke one day to find a strange girl in his bed, calling herself his wife. If he were put to the same question—how did he get here?—he might plead amnesia, or temporary insanity.

For days Alicia had been struggling for breath. Sometimes alone in the apartment she stood gulping air like a landed fish. Her heartbeat was a constant throbbing ache above her ribs. Whenever she dared to truly consider her situation, something inside her spasmed and shuddered, gave off sparks like an electric eel.

All these symptoms were present right now: the pangs of adrenaline, the jagged chest pain and the breathlessness. But beneath her grief or alongside it, or maybe like an island within it—despite everything and despite herself—there was something else, something very much like interest. Alicia was interested in this stranger across the table—her accuser—and she was interested as well in the answers he was demanding.

I want to know how the hell you got here.

It was a good line. It could have come from a sailor finding a stowaway or an agent cracking a spy. It invited confession, a fluttering and voluptuous surrender. And she, discovered and caught—whom might she be? A tramp in a boxcar, cringing in the shadows; a kid in a casino. Cinderella the minute after midnight, back in her rags, unable to explain.

What if, by some trick of the light or her mind, while Jonah was pathetic and unstrung, he was also glinting with sensual danger? (Was *this* what got her here? Her tendency to steep every situation in her fantasies, to regard each twist of life as a story waiting to be written?)

As characters they had once been so straightforward and appealing. Jonah was the veteran turned hero fireman, Alicia the child saved from the flames. They'd met again many years later; the girl had become a woman and—as in some dime-store romance—they were wed. But now he was coming apart before her eyes; now he was demanding to know what she was doing in his life. And it would take considerable measures on her part—very desperate measures—to find something romantic about that.

A scant few months ago, everything was different. One day in particular came to mind, a day maybe six months back. On that morning she'd had a dream about The Catwalk. She was on a stranger's lap. Her top was off and his hands were all over her. She tried to stand and get away, but the quicksand of dreams kept her in place. Looking down, she saw that even her G-string was gone. She was caught and exposed and she'd brought this on herself and violation of some kind was seconds away.

She woke then to find herself naked and pressed into the shelter of Jonah's body. Her back was against his chest and his lips were somewhere in her hair. One of his arms lay outstretched beneath her neck; the other encircled her belly. His grip on her waist was emphatic, laying claim even in sleep. *I am here,* she thought. *I am loved. I am held. I am home.* She wasn't trapped, wasn't in trouble. She was *past all that.* It was a faint surprise each time, to find herself a wife, a full-time writer, and what people were now calling a homemaker.

She turned in his embrace and put her mouth on his. She could not touch him tenderly enough. Without opening his eyes he was kissing her back, maybe before he was even really awake. He grasped her hair in his fist while his other hand moved over her body, and then he was inside her without much delay. And without difficulty; she was ready. She always woke in a state of readiness after pressing against him throughout the night.

That they could depart for this place before a single word was spoken never failed to thrill her. And the act itself thrilled her, the way he gave himself to it, moving into and into her as if he needed something only she could provide. She moved with him, arms around him, arriving just as he did, and when they were spent they lay bathed in what seemed like the same sweat.

All was still then for some time. The window in the room was open just a crack and she watched the white curtain sway with the breeze.

They were breathing in synchrony and there was no reason to say anything. It was long minutes before Alicia broke the quiet.

"You know what we should do today?" she said. "Let's go on a picnic."

Jonah answered without moving, his voice muffled against her neck. "For real, honey? It's October."

"I know. I was thinking the Cloisters. It'll be beautiful this time of year. Have you ever been there?"

He hadn't. "I have my sign language class at eleven."

"That's all right, we'll go right after."

"What are we gonna bring? There ain't much in the house."

"I can get it together while you're at your class," she said. "It'll be a surprise."

The weather was on their side: mild for autumn, a pale sun overhead and the scent of charcoal in the air. The trees were aflame with color and full of birds. They spread their blanket on the lawn just behind the monastery and Alicia arranged the contents of the picnic. There were clusters of tiny champagne grapes, a pomegranate and a fire-colored pear. There was bottled spring water and some cranberry juice. Also a bakery assortment of cream puffs, petit fours and a few broken elephant ears.

Jonah seemed impressed. "This is real nice, honey," he told her. "You did a nice job."

She put her arms around him. "We have to always do these things, all right? Celebrate the seasons. Have ceremonies for no reason."

"I hear you, honey."

What she remembered of this day was not so much anything they said or did, but a certain impossible tranquility, the trees rustling and the quality of the light as it deepened from opal to gold and finally to soft slate. When their picnic had been exhausted and the trash thrown away, they stayed on the gently sloping lawn, on the blanket or wrapped in it, until it was almost evening.

It seemed to her that Jonah's gaze on her never wavered, whether she was talking or eating or working the Sunday *Times* crossword puzzle. It was concentrated and ardent, almost dazed: the gaze of a man who couldn't believe his luck.

"I love the way you look at me," she whispered to him once.

"I love lookin' at you."

How the hell had she gotten here? After years of resignation, of loveless sex, with only the thin compensation of stripping—its fix and its income—in the wake of her empty affairs. After years of being the kind of girl that men kept only on the side, she had found the hero of her childhood and he needed her as much as she needed him.

From the courtyard came fragments of a guided tour, a description of the Zen monks and their ascetic path. Thousand-mile pilgrimages were mentioned, in which the monks prostrated themselves on the ground after every step. Also their fanatic disciplinary rituals: eating dinners of plain rice one grain at a time, running barefoot up and down mountains before dawn. *All of life is suffering,* their credo went, and yet it seemed they were ecstatic.

Jonah had a limited repertoire of moods these days, none of them good. By turns he was withdrawn, hostile, or broken down. One advantage to his hostile periods was that she could engage him in conversation. The rest of the time he hardly spoke. He looked down or sideways, never meeting her eyes. It was clear that he was ill, but he wouldn't see a doctor. He wouldn't do much of anything in fact, besides go to work. (How he managed to function at the firehouse was a mystery. What did he do, go on autopilot?) He no longer went to his sign class, or ran, or read the paper. He picked at his food, scraped much of it into the garbage. Sometimes he didn't get out of bed.

How long had this been going on? Weeks, maybe months, its slow onset tempered by intervals where all seemed almost well again. If she had to pinpoint when the change began, she would say it was the discussion about the chiefs test. He was different after that—the alteration so subtle at first that if she weren't so attuned to him, she might not have noticed. He was tired a lot of the time, preoccupied and quieter. Not as affectionate. He reached for her less, and slept more.

If something dramatic had happened, maybe she could have

confronted it sooner. Instead, the symptoms just settled in and gathered weight. The silences deepened; the lethargy deepened. Irritability etched itself into his features and every day he seemed less accessible.

He would never admit that anything was wrong.

"Jonah, is everything all right?" Alicia asked from time to time. "I mean, has anything been troubling you?"

He always seemed surprised by these inquiries.

"I'm all right," he would tell her. "Why?"

"You seem different lately. I don't know."

"I'm just tired, honey. I ain't been sleeping that well lately."

And since his sleep was restless even in the best of times, she could not contest this.

He began to snap at her over little things: the cap left off the toothpaste, her papers strewn all over the table. He stopped wolfing down whatever she cooked and brooded at it instead. Sex dwindled from five times a week to once or twice at most. She worried that he was no longer in love with her.

For a couple of weeks, she spent a lot of time in front of the mirror, ate less and exercised more. She pored over new recipes and kept the apartment spotless. None of it made the slightest difference in Jonah's mood. He came home, pushed his dinner around on its plate, spoke in short syllables and was soon on the sofa watching CNN.

When did she realize how bad it was? Probably the night they had dinner at Chumley's. Their table was near the bar, where three or four young men were very involved in the football game. When the Giants pulled ahead in the final minutes, they erupted in raucous triumph. Jonah watched over his shoulder as the most vocal of the group, a dark-haired kid in a team sweatshirt, did a happy little dance in the sawdust. "Yeah, baby!" he crowed. "We won!"

Jonah turned around in his seat. "What do you mean, *we* won?" he said. "The *Giants* won. What the hell did you do? You watched them on TV."

The kid stopped in his tracks. He and his friends got very quiet.

"*We* won," Jonah repeated. He spat the words like they sickened him. "Glad you said something, pal, or I might have thought that we were sittin' here the whole time. *We* won. Well, all right!"

"Jonah," Alicia protested. She was as startled as the boys.

He glanced back at her. "Did you hear that shit?" he demanded. "*We* won? I can't stand that shit. These bozos tryin' to take some kind of credit when the Giants win."

As she looked from the boy to Jonah, it came to her suddenly, for the first time: *He is losing his mind.*

"Look, whatever, man," said the kid in the sweatshirt. He stood biting his lower lip. "No offense," he offered.

"Hey, come on, let's go," one of his friends said. "Victory party at Belinda's." They moved toward the door in a nervous herd.

"Jonah," Alicia said. She felt dizzy. "How could you be like that— so mean? That was ludicrous. They were just kids. And they didn't do anything!"

"Did you hear the way they were carryin' on? *We won?*"

"Everyone says stuff like that! Of all things to make into an *issue!*" She put her head in her hands. "How could you get up in arms about something so *harmless?*"

Jonah's expression changed so suddenly it was as if he had taken off a mask. He was swiftly and completely contrite. "You're right," he said. "You're right. It was harmless. I'm sorry."

In the car going home, she tried to press her advantage. "Jonah, listen. I'm worried about you."

"Worried how?"

"What happened at Chumley's seems like a symptom of something that's been building for a while now."

He stared ahead through the windshield and didn't answer.

"I think these are danger signs," she continued. "Signs of a mood disorder."

"What?" he said. "Are you fuckin' kidding me?"

"No, in fact, I'm very serious."

They pulled into the garage and the parking attendant started over to the car. "Look," Jonah said. "Let's not have the whole world in on this discussion, all right?" He took the keys from the ignition.

Once inside the apartment, she picked up where they had left off. "Jonah. Whatever your reservations, I'd like you to do something as a favor to me. Would you do something for me?"

"What."

"I would like you to see a doctor."

This request had led to a dramatic scene. Jonah admitted that he was "in trouble." He confessed, in fact, to a history of serious depression. But he didn't want to get any kind of help. All he wanted, it seemed, was out of their marriage. When the conversation became heated, he retreated into a near-catatonic state: shaking, crying, pounding his head with his fists. *I'm sorry*, was all he would say from that point on. *I'm sorry, I'm sorry, I'm sorry.*

The next morning, Alicia woke to find Jonah already awake beside her. He was lying on his back, staring at the ceiling, crying without making any sound. Tears slid silently out of both eyes and ran into his ears.

Alicia turned on her side and reached for him. Without speaking, she brushed her fingertips over his face, then touched them to her own lips.

His tears continued to come throughout the day, for no apparent reason. This was unsettling but also something of a relief. Whatever Jonah was suffering from, at least it was on the table now; at least he couldn't keep pretending nothing was wrong. She was sure that now he would have to do something about it.

She was mistaken.

He kept his head down and his eyes averted. He withdrew further into himself. Sometimes the tears came hard and fast. Sometimes his eyes stayed dry. He shuffled when he walked and mumbled when he spoke. He treated her like a roommate he was forced to tolerate but wanted nothing to do with.

I want to know how the hell you got here.

Jonah was looking straight at her now. He was talking to her now. As defendant in this cross-examination she had his full attention, and no matter where it led, she couldn't pass up the chance to have a real conversation.

"Well," she said slowly. Where to start? "We met at The Brooklyn

Brewery." Asking him to re-create this scene used to be a favorite request of hers. *Tell me about the night we met,* she would beg, as she used to coax her mother: *Tell me about the night I was born.*

"That night you found out angels really walk the earth," she said now, repeating something he had told her countless times. She laced these words with as much irony as she dared. "That night was something else."

His eyes narrowed into slits. "You were there with Schiller. You didn't even have the class to stay with your date. You were tryin' to use me against him, that's all. And I walked into your trap!"

She drew in her breath as sharply as if he'd struck her. "*Jonah,*" she protested. "You don't believe that, do you? Is that what you think?"

"The whole thing was a setup. You think I couldn't see it for what it was? You'd better fuckin' think again."

Was it true? The accusation hit her so hard that she had to wonder. Could it be that Jonah had been some kind of answer, some kind of antidote, to Jake? How much had his purpose been to *show* Jake? How much to show herself, that Jake wasn't the last word on whether she was worthy of love?

Despite her confusion, she rallied back, summoning the voice of reason. "How could it be a setup? Did I know you were going to be there?"

"You said you were lookin' for me."

"I was always looking for you. I went up to Jake's firehouse in the first place because I was looking so hard for you. The fact is I met Jake because I was trying to get to you, not the other way around." She paused to let that sink in. "And besides, I never truly cared about Jake."

"You loved Jake."

"That's not true."

"Don't try and tell me that."

Alicia chose her words carefully. "Jake and I had an intensely sexual but otherwise very superficial relationship."

"You loved him."

"It wasn't love. It was an exciting—"

"You loved him."

"—a very exciting arrangement, and it was good sex. I won't deny that. But it wasn't love."

"You loved him."

She held her hands out in frustration. "Don't you think I know what it was, or wasn't? I'm telling you the truth. It was not love. He didn't love me."

"I ain't said he loved you. I said you loved him."

There was a moment so quiet she could hear the clock ticking on the wall. Then: "Yes," she said. "Yes. I did. I loved him."

To her amazement, his face relaxed. "You see honey? I know how it is. That's just how women are—they hook into the guys they're sleepin' with. I know you cared about him, honey. It's all right with me."

"But Jonah," she said, speaking one of the only truths she still knew for sure, "I never even came close to loving him the way I love you."

She thought again about that morning six months ago, when she woke with Jonah clutching her. His body was strung tight with tension even in sleep. She turned in his embrace and put her mouth on his. Always she felt that in pulling him from that other country where he slept she was providing relief of some kind. Within seconds he was on top of her, inside her. Foreplay was not his strong point.

He moved inside her as if swimming upstream against a current and against all odds. It was the only thing she would have changed about the way they made love. Always this act had an edge of desperation; never once had he gone slow and taken his time. It was as if he needed something so badly that he would die trying to get it. Sometimes, lying beneath him, she thought of that Dylan song: *And I feel like I'm knockin' on Heaven's door . . .*

He thrust into her like he had to drill through her to get to some-thing else. A sheen of sweat came out on his body and his eyes glazed over with effort. *Knock knock knockin' on Heaven's door . . .*

Afterward she lay beneath him and tried to imagine where they could lie together, nothing more, the way they had on their first night together. Someplace easy and peaceful, and close to nature. Jonah wasn't big on nature. Once she had asked him if he'd ever like to go camping.

"No, not really, honey," he said. "That ain't really for me."

"No? Why not? Have you ever tried it?"

"Yeah, I have, actually," he said. "It was called Vietnam."

And that was the end of that.

But a picnic? Surely a picnic was a safe activity? When Alicia suggested it, he wasn't excited, exactly, but at least he had no real objection. His only misgiving was in not knowing how to get to the Cloisters.

"It can't be too hard," Alicia said. "I've always taken a bus. It's at the northern tip of Manhattan, I think it's a pretty straight shot."

"There's a firehouse in Harlem where I used to be a lieutenant," he said. "I'll stop in there on the way up and maybe one of the guys can tell me how to go."

That was what they did, and Jonah got directions. He talked to three different firemen and they all described the same easy drive. One of them rustled up a road map, and another sketched out a little line drawing of the route. Still Jonah seemed unsure of his ability to get there, and it wasn't clear where his anxiety was coming from.

"Honey, it'll be fine," she said at last. "It'll be easy. I'll hold the map and tell you where to make the turns, if you want."

In the car, it occurred to her for the first time that she didn't really know her own husband all that well. She said, "You must not travel very much."

"I hardly ever go anywhere. My whole life I never lived anywhere else. Except for the war. That was the only real time."

"Is that true? I can hardly imagine what that must be like. We never stopped moving."

"Well, that must've been hard," Jonah said. "Being an Army brat. Never staying anywhere long enough to make real friends."

"It was," she admitted. "It definitely was, and sometimes it still feels like such a luxury to be settled—to know I don't ever have to move again, if I don't want to. But Jonah, at the same time, this city's such a crazy place. Don't you need to get out once in a while?"

"Well," he said. "You can see how it is with me. I have trouble going new places, I guess."

"But if you did it more, it would become less intimidating."

"I ain't said I was *intimidated*," Jonah said, bristling a little. "I just don't like it, that's all."

But he seemed pleased when they arrived at the monastery without a hitch. And their day was so beautiful that Alicia thought, *It'll get easier. I can't push him too hard or fast. We can build on little trips like this and he'll gain confidence. Eventually we'll be able to go anywhere.*

But they hadn't gone anywhere for a long time now. For the past several months, the days had been pretty much the same. Jonah worked, or he didn't. If he was scheduled for a day tour, Alicia always got up with him. She would make his coffee and endure a silent breakfast, which Jonah would pick at while keeping his eyes averted. When the door shut behind him, she would pull the shades on the just-risen sun and fall into a few precious hours of unguarded rest. Deep sleep was impossible when Jonah was around. His morning departures always followed a long night of tossing and thrashing, putting on one of his hats and pulling it off again, getting up to prowl around the apartment.

Sometimes she woke in the night to find that Jonah wasn't in bed. She would lie there in the kind of terror that follows a vivid nightmare. She was afraid that if she got up she would find Jonah dead, the dreamed-of deed done. Any scenario was possible: wrists opened and soaking the carpet a darker red; hanging by the neck from a rope tied to the pull-up bar; or just icy night air blasting into the apartment from a window left wide open. When she worked up the courage to call out to him, he would grunt back from somewhere beyond the bedroom. At these times it amazed her that they could communicate at all; that despite everything, they still spoke some semblance of the same language.

When he left in the afternoon for a night tour, Alicia would shut off the incessant television and sink onto the couch, exhausted and spent, a tension headache tightening its screws at her temples. A few rote tears might escape, almost an afterthought. She usually fell asleep within seconds right there. Sleep was her only source of relief these days: a raft that held and lulled her.

She always emerged from these cat naps afraid and spent some minutes bracing herself for full consciousness. *It's okay,* she would whisper, coaching herself back from oblivion; *it's okay, it's okay, it's okay . . .* though her circumstances were anything but okay and it took all her resilience just to look at them. Jonah seemed to feel this way all the time; maybe it was contagious.

Once she was up, she usually went through the motions of cooking or cleaning, no satisfaction in it anymore, since it made no difference to anyone but her. Nothing she did would make a difference; she was starting to see that. She could cook all Jonah's favorite dinners, make perfect cups of coffee, shine his medals and bleach his work shirts and come to bed in a beautiful negligée. None of it would relax the grimace set into his face, an expression he probably didn't even know was there.

"And another thing," Jonah was saying now. He leaned forward, bringing all four legs of the chair back to the floor. "Another way you used me was to get me to support you."

"Get you to support me? You wanted me to stop dancing!"

"Yeah, well, I didn't exactly have to twist your arm to get you to quit that job, did I? And I don't see you gettin' another one, either. Is there a law that says you can only make a living as a slut? You think you have to pick between bein' a whore and sittin' on your ass twenty-four hours a day?"

"I was never a whore. And I was never a slut. If that's the way you—"

"Look, I know what you're all about. So don't think you can keep playing me like a record. Just because I ain't educated don't mean you can put anything over on me, all right? Always talkin' down to me. Like I'm stupid. Like I'm sick. Like I don't know no better. Who the fuck do you think you are, anyway. . . ?"

Well, all right. What of these accusations? She thought back to the night they had parked across the street from The Catwalk. She remembered the slashing rain and her own dull dread at the thought of getting out of the car. It was true that she'd been glad to give it up. And there was Jonah, offering to shelter and keep her, holding out that choice.

Maybe she should have understood that it was just a gesture. Maybe her mistake was abandoning herself to it, taking it at face value and swallowing it whole. She should have known it was just too easy. Rescue like that didn't come more than once in a lifetime and she had used hers up at the age of five.

But still, didn't he tell her she'd rescued him in turn? How many times had he told her that? *You saved me, honey. I was walkin' around whipped, just draggin' my ass through the fuckin' day. I don't know what I would of done, if I even would of made it, if you hadn't come along when you did.*

And yes, he took her out of the strip joint and gave her a home. But hadn't she given one back to him—hadn't she made his dreary, functional apartment a place of warmth and comfort and love?

None of these questions mattered anymore. The only one remaining was: what was she going to do now? Get her job back; pack and move out; return to the no-man's-land she'd lived in before?

And what about Jonah? Was she supposed to surrender him to his demons—give him back to the fire? She was starting to understand that he wasn't hers to give back. This was where her reciprocal powers ended. He had snatched her from the flames but that was one debt she couldn't repay—the issue of the chiefs test had proven that. He was gone already and she was pacing around the vanishing point, sleeping in a deserted and haunted house.

That morning of six months ago, when Alicia woke next to Jonah, he'd been having one of his nightmares. His whimpering was nowhere near its most tortured pitch; it was the muted whine of a puppy. It seemed his every moment of sleep was invaded by one enemy or another. When did he get to rest?

She couldn't tell him about her own nightmare involving The Catwalk. Not when his were of gang rape and Vietnam, four-alarm fires and human kindling. It was wearing her out—this endless tug-of-war between her and his dreams. She tugged him back to herself each morning and they dragged him away again every night.

She turned and put her mouth on his. He began kissing her back: a blind reflex, like a baby animal taking sustenance. Once in a while she thought that even the act of sex itself was just another blind reflex for him. There was no deliberation, no build-up or restraint. He just found her body and thrust into it, and it was fortunate that she never required much in the way of preliminaries. She was wired to receive him, it would seem.

Within seconds he was going at it full throttle, as if clearing a desperate path through some jungle. He went at her as she imagined Seamus O'Day battered the steel fire door with his body. Was she, too, ultimately closed to him? Was there some chamber inside her he would never reach, where flat-eyed, vacant goldfish circled coolly while he burned? He was burning. Almost feverish. His face was flushed with effort. Sweat came out on his forehead and before long was dripping in a steady tattoo onto her own, splashing occasionally into her eyes. He took a long time.

Later that afternoon, shopping for their picnic, she was suddenly overcome with a longing for wine. What was a picnic without a bottle of wine? But no. Never again.

"You can drink, you know," he always told her, usually when they were out for dinner. "You can drink right in front of me. It don't matter."

"I would never drink in front of you."

"Especially wine. Wine never did much for me. Now if you lined up a row of tequila shots and started knocking *that* back in front of me, I might start feelin' it. But wine? Wine's nothing."

"But I wouldn't *want* to drink without you," she said. "I almost don't want to drink at all anymore. If you can't have it, I don't want it. Like I wouldn't go to a party if you weren't invited."

It was true; at least it was true then. At that time, it seemed the point of drinking was to become intoxicated at the same rate as your partner; it was the mutual recklessness, confessions, audacity. Doing it alone, or with someone who was abstaining, only put you at a disadvantage.

She hadn't had a drop of alcohol since quitting her job at The Catwalk. In there, it was impossible not to drink. Men bought cocktails for the dancers all night long, and of course in the Champagne Lounge, the couple of the hour shared a bottle.

It was dangerous to drink too much at the club. To dance in four-inch spike heels, to even negotiate the stage steps, she had to know when to stop. And then too, everyone around her looked more appealing with each drink; that was dangerous too. But she always let herself have just enough. Enough to sand down the edges of the evening, bring things into soft focus, and make her good company no matter what mood she was in.

She hadn't made a deliberate decision to abstain when she'd joined her life with Jonah's, but there was no way to drink with him and she was unwilling to drink in front of him. She had never missed it before, but she wanted it now.

Jonah was living without it, and intended to forever. That had to be very hard. He still went to an A.A. meeting almost every day, and he often cited their credo: *One day at a time.* That was the way you were supposed to take it. The point was to not let yourself think about never drinking again. That was too much; that was impossible. The idea was just to think, *Not today.* Once he confessed to her that he used the same strategy to avert suicide. The option was always there, but he wouldn't do it today. Tomorrow, maybe, but not today, and in this way he rode out the most difficult phases of his life.

So outside the liquor store, gazing at the bottles of Chianti and Chardonnay, Alicia thought, *Not today.*

Later, driving to the Cloisters, their talk turned to films about Vietnam. How had this come up? They had seen some deer in the brush by the side of the road. "I'm so glad you don't hunt, Jonah," Alicia told him, thinking of Jake.

"I never have. I never wanted to," he said.

"I know for Jake it was just another macho, conquer-the-wild kind of thing. But I always secretly hated it."

"I never saw how hunting was supposed to be macho in the first place," Jonah remarked. "Give the deer some guns and I'll understand it."

Maybe that was how they had come to *The Deer Hunter* and other Vietnam movies. Jonah seemed to know them all. The most realistic ones, he said, were *Full Metal Jacket* and *Born on the Fourth of July.*

"There's a part in *Born on the Fourth* that's always stayed with me," Alicia told him. "Do you remember the scene where Tom Cruise is in a foxhole? All this commotion is happening around him, everything is confused and crazy, and suddenly this dark shadow is coming down on him from above. So he shoots at it—it's just a split-second reflex of self-defense—but when the smoke clears he realizes he killed an American, a kid in his platoon."

"Yeah, well. That shit happened all the time," Jonah said. He didn't look at her as he said this, but through the windshield instead.

"Really? Did you ever do anything like that?"

"Yeah," he said.

"You did?" Alicia was startled.

"Yeah."

"Did you—" she faltered. "Did you kill someone? An American, I mean?"

"Yep."

"You *did?*"

"How many times do you want me to say it?"

"I'm sorry, it's just—would you rather not talk about it?"

"I got no problem talkin' about it."

"Was it—did it happen like in the movie?"

"Same kind of thing. We were all down and we were supposed to stay down. But this kid panicked. He got up and bolted into my peripheral vision when we were all supposed to sit tight."

"So you shot him?"

"I didn't just *shoot* him," Jonah said, staring straight ahead at the road. His hands were white-knuckled on the wheel. "I blew him into about a hundred pieces." Then he laughed, a sound that made the hairs rise on her arms. It was a sound that made her think of the phrase, *laughed like a maniac.* Jonah laughed like a maniac, laughter without mirth that went on far too long.

The clues had all been there, after all, signs that something wasn't quite right. Oh, she knew he was crazy in certain ways, knew that from the beginning. But there was crazy and there was crazy. She had chosen not to notice certain things, or not to make much of them.

The temptation to be as selective in hindsight was powerful. The day they went to the Cloisters—the sex in the morning and subsequent picnic—had an infinity of facets, as did every moment they spent together. All her memories were like that, each one built layer upon layer, and it took considerable excavation to get to the parts she would rather not think about. So here, too, was another charge that might be brought against her in this hearing. Denial.

Not that her prosecutor needed ammunition. Jonah was raging at her still. "You gonna answer me sometime? I want to know who you think you are. What's the matter, ain't you got nothing to say now?"

His teeth were set and bared, exactly like some rabid dog's. Alicia wouldn't have been surprised to see him foaming at the mouth. "Come on, you got an answer for everything, so answer that! Who the fuck are you? Florence fuckin' Nightingale? The lady with the lamp? The lady is a fuckin' tramp, that's what I got to say. Don't you fuckin' cry!"

Even this struck a faint chord of truth. Alicia thought back to the hour she knew Jonah would never be the same again. They were in Tompkins Square Park; she was sitting beside him on a park bench. They had been sitting there for a good deal of the afternoon and in all that time Jonah had neither moved nor spoken. He stared at the pavement, rigid and unseeing. Spit hung from one corner of his mouth. He was like one of those relics on the porch of an old-age home, whom someone had wheeled out for an airing and would later wheel back in.

He seemed to have aged overnight. New lines creased his face and dandruff gathered in his lifeless hair. Sitting with him, Alicia was unsure, as she'd been so many times before, whether he would ever move again.

She was waiting him out, or trying to. She was going to lose again; she was going to speak first. If she didn't, what would happen? Would they sit there the rest of the day and through the night? She never had the stamina to find out.

Fifteen more minutes went by before she broke the silence.

"Jonah." It was her gentlest voice, the voice of a kindergarten teacher.

It was a moment before he answered as if from a trance, without lifting his eyes from the ground. "Huh."

She took his hand in hers and massaged it. "I love you."

There was no reply.

Several years before, Alicia had spent a summer's worth of Sundays with her aunt Ida, who was in her early sixties and dying. A terminal hypochondriac, she had gone to her doctor with imaginary ailments year in and year out until finally he gave it to her, the sentence she had been traveling toward all her life: *You have AIDS.* He even seemed to take a certain pleasure in it, Ida said afterward. As in: *You want it? You got it.* The bastard.

The circumstances of her infection were especially tragic. There had been an operation years before to remove a malignant ovarian cyst. The surgery was a success: the cancer cut cleanly away before it had a chance to spread. Afterward she was a little anemic, nothing she wouldn't have gotten over left to her own devices. Nonetheless, there was some debate about a blood transfusion. Ida didn't want the transfusion; the world hadn't yet heard of AIDS, but she was afraid of hepatitis. Her wishes were disregarded and now look.

Every Sunday that summer, Alicia took the subway to Midwood, bringing raisin bread or a pound cake, alighting at Avenue M. She did a little perfunctory straightening up in her aunt's apartment, then accompanied her on walks to the nearby park. What was this Samaritan mission about? It wouldn't be easy to say. Part of it was that when Alicia's mother had been diagnosed with terminal cancer, Ida had visited her regularly until she died. Part of it was a dreadful curiosity, the chance to safely rub up against the plague that was terrorizing the nation. But mostly it was a vision of herself too compelling to resist: Florence Nightingale moving softly about, skirts rustling, voice hushed. Tending to her afflicted aunt, the picture of compassion and tact.

Much of these afternoons would be passed on a park bench, and it was here that her role fell apart. For at this point her aunt always became quiet and withdrawn, retreating inward to a place Alicia couldn't reach.

A brilliant, sun-washed day made circumstances both more and less bearable. An overcast sky might threaten the spirits, but the hard, bright indifference of mid-summer had its own special sting. The elements refusing to empathize, the world turning as always.

And wasn't Alicia, in her youth and beauty, as merciless as the day? Six inches of space between herself and her aunt, and yet no two women could have had more unbridgeable distance between them. There was Ida—hunched in misery, swaddled in fur, her sparse gray hair carefully coiffed and stiff (she still went almost daily to what she called the beauty parlor), the childish middle-aged face quivering like a hunted rabbit's. Beside her was Alicia, nineteen years old and in perfect health, uncertainly and relentlessly chipper. Her own face rosy with the day's heat, her hair an extravagance of lustrous darkness, her days filled with sweet carelessness and petty troubles. And at this moment— leaning forward, anxiously solicitous—she was secretly counting the minutes until she could get away.

In a few hours she would go to Manhattan. The city was all hers, with its balmy evening air, its alleys and taverns and promising strangers. She was almost ashamed to be sharing this bench with her aunt, her gaudy good fortune and future an affront.

The very same feeling was upon her now. On the one hand, she could hardly imagine her life without Jonah, the return to her lonely days and neon nights. On the other hand, she was arguably living without him already. The Jonah she had fallen in love with was as gone as a stone over the side of a ship, and apparently as irretrievable.

And Alicia? In her secret survivor's heart, she had one eye on the shore. If he wouldn't let her keep him afloat, she wasn't going to let him take her under. Thank God she was only twenty-seven, young enough to cut her losses. Thank God they'd had no children and she wasn't pregnant.

"Jonah." That same soft tone of voice, summoned once again from some fantasy of herself.

A slight shift of his head, like a blind man turning toward a faint noise, was the only indication that he heard her.

"Jonah, we have the whole day to do anything we want. Is there anywhere special you'd like to go?"

He shook his head.

———

E leven days after their last conversation, Matilda broke down and called Jonah. Dialing his number had been such a careless practice once—the shelter she reached every evening, the lifeline. It had become, by turns, a source of some anxiety, and then a sickening risk, and by now it was undeniably a losing proposition. But at this point it was clear that if she didn't do the calling, they wouldn't talk at all.

"Hello?"

Sure enough it was Alicia. Matilda almost hung up but after a full three or four seconds spoke instead. "Is Jonah there?"

"Mrs. O'Day?"

At least the girl didn't have the audacity to call her Matilda. "Yes."

"Hi, Mrs. O'Day, how are you?"

It was hard to tell if this was meant as an overture or a reproach. Either way, it wasn't going to work. "I'm fine."

"Actually, Jonah's working tonight," Alicia told her. "Would you like his number there?"

"I have the number," Matilda all but snapped. I had it before you were born, she was tempted to say. It wouldn't have been much of an exaggeration.

"The thing is," Alicia said almost apologetically, "Jonah's not at his regular firehouse tonight. He was detailed to Ladder 44 in the Bronx."

"Oh," Matilda said after a moment. "Well then, I guess I need that number after all."

And the girl gave it to her.

"What I don't understand," Matilda told the doctor the next afternoon, "is why I can't be nicer to her. She's always pleasant to me. I mean, I don't like her, but I manage to be polite to lots of people I don't like."

This doctor was a young man, probably in his mid-thirties. He looked so soft compared to the men she had spent her life among, with his faintly bewildered eyes and rounded jaw and baby-fine light brown hair. Wes had dug him up for her and offered to pay. Even so, it had taken weeks for her to agree to come.

A grief-management counselor, Wes had called him, but please: a shrink was a shrink. Still, it did seem likely that grief was his specialty. All the books on his shelves had titles like: *Surviving: Coping With a Life Crisis; Accepting Bereavement; Death, Society, and the Human Experience; Reclaiming Life After Loss;* and *After the Funeral.*

For Christ's sake, lighten up, Matilda wanted to tell the kid. What kind of way is this to spend your youth?

Nonetheless she liked this doctor. He was nice. His office was nice too, and the quiet alone seemed worth the expense. A deep red oriental carpet covered most of the floor and swallowed the sound of her footsteps when she walked into the room. There was a couch against one wall, covered in gray suede. No family photographs on his desk, nothing on the walls except diplomas and a single print of an abstract painting that Matilda knew, from afternoons with Wes, was a Paul Klee: splashes of tan and crimson and teal, suggesting a biblical city.

"Let me ask you this," the doctor said. "When you think of this girl—of Alicia—what associations come to mind?"

"Associations?"

"In other words," he said, "does she remind you of anyone?"

"*Remind* me of anyone?" Matilda echoed. "No."

"No?"

"Who would she remind me of? She's young enough to be my daughter, but none of my daughters are anything like her. Thank God."

"How are they different?"

"My daughters will never dance naked for a living, I can tell you that much," Matilda told him. "They can get men to notice them with their clothes on."

"Ah," the doctor said. "Anyone else then?"

"Who else would there be? My girlfriends are my own age."

"Girlfriends?" the doctor murmured.

"Oh, you know what I mean. My friends. Of course they're women, not girls."

There was a silence.

"And none of them are anything like her either."

Still the doctor said nothing.

"I wouldn't have a friend like that," Matilda said, and when the doctor failed to respond yet again, she heard her own words and it came to her.

Once the association, as the doctor called it, had been spoken, Matilda couldn't understand how she hadn't seen it before. Alicia had the same dark hair and hazel eyes, the same free spirit and feminine wiles. The difference was that, in the end, Lorena hadn't succeeded in stealing her man and Alicia had.

Wes would appreciate this one. She'd never told him about Lorena, so there was no way he could have seen it himself. But he loved to pore over these kinds of puzzles; he loved to find connections everywhere. Sometimes Matilda thought that his paying for her to see this doctor was a way of enjoying it himself, secondhand. Wes seemed to make sure that all his important pleasures came to him in this manner.

Of course, Wes would also try to tell her, gently, that Jonah had never exactly been hers, and therefore couldn't have been stolen. But Matilda knew better. She knew how Jonah had felt about her. And maybe his sense of honor wouldn't have allowed him to act on those feelings this month or even this year. But if they'd kept up their intimate conversations, their phone calls and dinners, sooner or later a respectful interval would have passed and a different kind of relationship would no longer have qualified as a scandal. For a time, it had seemed as inevitable as the sun coming up after a long and terrible night.

The doctor, at least, had no trouble believing this. But he had other things to point out to her. Like where the whole equation fell apart; like all the differences between Alicia and Lorena. Alicia, for instance, had not been trying to take a married man away from his wife—had not even known, for that matter, who Matilda was. The irony of the situation was that in this instance Alicia *was* the wife. If anyone was the "other woman" in this picture, it was Matilda. And unlike Lorena, Alicia hadn't betrayed Matilda's friendship and trust.

"All right, all right," Matilda said at last. "Maybe I've been projecting my own issues onto her." Whenever she heard herself using the doctor's words, as she was now, she felt self-satisfied and somewhat demeaned at the same time, as if she were a pet who'd been taught a new trick. "Well, so now what? Is it enough that I figured that out? Or do you think I need to fix it up with her in some way?"

"What do *you* think?"

So they really did talk like this. Like the shrinks on sit-coms. Keeping a straight face the whole time, no less. But she'd be wasting Wes's money if she didn't try to swallow her cynicism.

"Well," she said out loud, "I have to admit, my motive for making any kind of peace with her wouldn't be very pure. I'd only be doing it because my relationship with Jonah is suffering."

The doctor swiveled in his chair. "Are you sure she's the reason it's suffering?"

"Well, I'm pretty sure. I mean, Jonah seems very angry at me."

"What makes you think he's angry?"

She thought back to a month or so ago, to something Jonah had said to her: "Like it or not, Matilda, she's my wife now. And if you can't be nice to my wife, you ain't respecting me."

"Well," she said slowly to the doctor, "he hasn't returned any of my calls for a long time. And I get the feeling that even when he's home, he avoids speaking to me. Sometimes when Alicia answers and I ask for him, she tells me to hold on, and then she comes back and says he's sleeping, or in the shower, or something."

Through the window behind the doctor's back, the sun was beginning to set. The fiery light was like a halo around his head and looking at it, she was reminded of her invisible angel, the one Jonah was supposed to have been. When she spoke again, she found herself close to tears.

"I suppose it's reasonable for him to want me to be good to his wife," she conceded, her voice ragged with the effort.

"I would think so too," the doctor said gently. "After all, he was very good to your husband."

The statement took her breath away, and with it, whatever resistance she had left.

"Yes," she said finally, feeling the tears come at last. That was another good thing—it was all right to cry here. This doctor was the first person since Jonah who was not alarmed by her tears. "Yes. He was."

Driving home from the city, over the 59th Street Bridge, Matilda had a sudden and unsettling inspiration. Maybe—just maybe—she would invite Jonah and his wife (the phrase was already less impossible) to dinner. One could get used to anything, she supposed. This whole last year, it was as if she'd been pushed down an endless set of stairs. Every time she thought she was finally on the dirt floor, it turned out that there were more steps to go. And here she was, barely breathing, but able to rise after all, able to invite Jonah and his wife to dinner. She would cook something complicated and special, and serve it on the good china.

This idea had actually come from the twins. They were always asking why Jonah never came to the house anymore.

"Jonah's married now," she told them, as if that were sufficient explanation.

Of course they weren't going to let her off that easy. "So?"

"So, newly wedded couples tend not to want to be apart if they can help it. Not even for one evening."

"Well, why can't he come over and bring her along?"

At the time that had seemed like a good joke. Now that she was steeling herself to extend just such an invitation, she wondered if she could really bear it. Just how painful would it be, to be in the same room with them all evening?

By the time she pulled into her driveway, she had the answer to that one: not as bad as having him drop out of her life altogether.

So: tonight was the night. It had turned out that Matilda was forced to issue the invitation to Alicia (Jonah being unwilling or unable to come to the phone—again). And it was Alicia who'd assured her that they would both love to come. They would be here at seven.

She was confident about the dinner waiting to be served: a cold sorrel soup (perfect for a summer evening), green salad and an herb-infused roast made from the venison Jake Schiller had brought her months ago (it had been in the freezer since May, waiting for a special occasion). By the time she heard their knock, everything was in place and she went to welcome them herself instead of having the twins let them in.

When she opened the door, her first shocked thought was: *they're not touching.* Jonah's arm was not around his wife; her hand wasn't on his arm. In fact, two people standing side by side could not have looked less like a couple.

Alicia was modestly dressed in a knee-length skirt and button-down blouse. Her hair was pulled back into a tidy ponytail. She held a sheaf of irises wrapped in heavy paper, which she immediately extended to Matilda. After being relieved of this offering, she stood awkwardly clasping her own shoulders as if holding herself together.

They were standing at exactly the same spot on the front porch as the firemen who had come to tell her that her life as she knew it was over. Jonah, too, looked like some grim messenger of death. His face was drawn and tired, the deep bone tired of many sleepless nights in a row. His hair was growing out of its crew cut and going gray; dark shadows were smudged beneath his eyes.

The effect was a schoolgirl and ghost-tramp. Or Hades from the underworld, with young Persephone in tow. Old Man Winter and Little Miss Springtime. Us, Matilda thought, and her.

"Welcome," she said after a moment, and found that it wasn't much of an effort, after all, to smile at both of them. "Please, come on in."

She gave them glasses of fresh-squeezed lemonade to drink on the deck while she put the finishing touches on the soup. After a minute or two, she heard one of her sons go out to join them.

"Hey, buddy," Jonah said to him. Where his tone with the twins had always been easy and relaxed, it now had a forced jocularity. "Good to see you." And then, a moment later: "Alicia, this is Montana."

"What a beautiful name," the girl said. "Were you born in Montana?"

"This kid? Are you kiddin' me?" Jonah put in before her son could answer. "This kid was made in the Bronx."

"I have a twin brother," she heard her son explain, "and my dad had two favorite football players of all time. Both were quarterbacks and both were named Joe. So he gave me and Namath their last names."

"Where's Namath at, anyway?" Jonah asked.

"He's finishing his homework. Mom said if we wanted to play football with you after dinner we had to have it all done first."

"What about the rest of the gang?"

Matilda stepped out onto the deck to answer that one. "The girls are at my mother's. It's quilting night at her house." She found herself directing this information at Alicia. "She taught every one of them to sew like a dream and it's a pastime they look forward to every week. Me, if I never thread another needle in my life, it'll be too soon."

"That sounds so nice," Alicia said. "I wish I knew how to quilt."

"I'm sure you'd be welcome to join them anytime," Matilda told her. She hoped the girl knew enough not to take this offer seriously, and she seemed to, for she only smiled and said, "Maybe sometime."

Would Jonah forgive her now that she was changing her ways? Could he see how hard she was trying? She'd been so sure that if only she could get him out to the house again, some of the distance between them would close. But now she didn't know what to think. For the first time she wondered whether her behavior was the main issue here after all. Jonah seemed as tightly wound as she'd ever seen him, and that tension was set into his wife's face as well.

"Can I help you with anything, Mrs. O'Day?" the girl offered.

"Not a thing. Everything's almost done anyway."

And so it was. When she ushered them into the dining room, there was no denying the table looked beautiful: covered in white lace, laid with the blue china, the irises a serene centerpiece in the antique silver vase. It was good that the twins were here, so it wasn't just the three of them. At the same time, she was glad the girls were away, or it would have been too much of a crowd. All in all, if this wasn't just the setup for breaking the ice, Matilda didn't know what would be.

But during dinner, Jonah said almost nothing. It was as if his thin banter on the deck had exhausted his resources for the evening. He spoke only when spoken to, and Matilda was gratified to notice that he maintained the same economy of words with his wife. He took just enough of the roast and salad to pass for politeness and ate without much comment.

Alicia on the other hand—probably to compensate—could not stop praising the cooking. Matilda and the girl kept up a steady, if somewhat self-conscious, stream of conversation, with the boys cutting in now and again. She was actually relieved when dinner was over and the twins dragged Jonah out back to toss a ball around. He was such a tense presence that Matilda felt a slight headache setting in.

He was different, no doubt about it. Different through and through, and only so much of this change could possibly be personal to her. He even moved differently, like it was an effort just to drag himself around. The fact that he was, at this moment, indulging the twins in a little football seemed like nothing less than a heroic feat. She hoped they would sense this and go easy on him.

Against her protests, Alicia helped her carry the dishes to the sink, and then, as Matilda was replacing the oil and vinegar in the cupboard, she heard the jet of the kitchen faucet. She turned to see Alicia struggling with the silver platter for the roast.

"Oh no," Matilda said. "Away from there. Don't even think about it."

"You cooked such a wonderful meal," Alicia pleaded. "Besides—"

"I mean it," Matilda interrupted. "You're my guest. Do dishes in your own home."

She walked over and took the platter from the girl's hands. "Out of my way," she said, in a stern tone that was only half a joke.

"Please," Alicia said. "At least let me do the drying. I miss doing this with my mother."

The vulnerability of this remark caught Matilda off guard. It was a reminder that this girl knew something about loss too.

"It's completely unnecessary," Matilda said doubtfully, but Alicia was already taking the dish towel from its rack on the oven door.

"I know that. But I want to."

"Well." What could she do but surrender? "That's very kind of you."

For a few minutes there was silence except for the clink of cutlery. Alicia did not try to force conversation. They washed and dried, and when the sink was empty—the plates replaced in the china cabinet—Matilda finally faced Alicia straight on. "There's something I want to say to you," she told the girl. "I haven't been very nice to you these last few months. And I apologize for that. I was very close to Jonah while my husband was in the hospital, and I guess I was threatened by anything that could take his time and attention away from me. I was afraid of losing him and I didn't want to like you. But the fact is you're lovely. You're a lovely young woman and you've given Jonah so much."

It felt good to be able to say these things. It felt like grace. They no longer felt forced or even less than genuine. "And there's one more thing. I want to thank you for bringing him by tonight. I've missed him and it feels like he hasn't really talked to me in weeks. So it was wonderful to have him here again, and I want you to know you're always welcome in my home."

When she finished this little speech, there was an odd silence. Alicia had gone so still that Matilda was a little unnerved. Then, to her utter astonishment, the girl began to cry. She took a step backward and brought the dish towel to her face. Matilda had no idea what to say or do.

"Alicia," she said. She took a step forward and faltered. "Alicia, what's the matter? Is it something I just said to you?"

She put a careful hand on the girl's shoulder. And then suddenly Alicia was in her arms, clutching her with a glaze-eyed desperation and crying as if her young heart had cracked in two. "He hasn't really talked to me in weeks either," the girl wept. "Oh, I'm so afraid, Mrs. O'Day. I'm so afraid all the time. I can't seem to do anything for him. I don't know what to do at all anymore."

Matilda stood holding her, breathless and amazed. A rush of something like elation washed over her, followed by a sorrow so sharp she felt tears of her own threatening to come. Wes had predicted all this. Matilda hadn't believed him. If only she'd been nicer to Alicia the whole time. What would it really have cost her, in the end?

Automatically, her hand had begun to smooth the girl's hair. It might have been one of her daughters she was holding, for all the tenderness she felt now—tenderness for this girl who was in for the heartbreak of her life. This motherless child clutching her because there was no one else to hold on to. This young and beautiful other woman who wasn't, after all, the enemy.

———

The blue-green *"TOPLESS!"* sign outside The Catwalk had been replaced by a neon red one. Other than that, nothing about the club had changed. The same bouncers still flanked the front entrance. One of them even greeted her.

"Hey, little Jezebel." George's face creased into a grin. "Where the hell you been?"

"Hi, George," she said, ignoring the question. "Is Randall still the manager?"

"Sure enough."

"Is he here tonight?"

"He's in there."

As she went through the front door, the music pulled her forward, its mindless undertow as strong as ever. Brandy and Candy, the blonde twins, were on the near stage. At a glance she could see that half the dancers were girls she knew, and even the patrons were mostly familiar.

Randall was standing by the register.

She went to his side and waited until he could focus on her. The glitter in his eyes meant he was flying on cocaine: all the better. The more fucked up he was, the less likely it would be that he'd remember the circumstances of her leaving: the fact that one night, she just hadn't showed up.

"Randall?"

He swung around to look at her. "Hey," he said.

Clearly he couldn't call even her stage name to mind.

"I'm Jezebel," she said. "Remember me?"

"Sure, sure. How you been."

"I don't know if you recall," she began. "I stopped working here to go to nursing school."

"Right. How's it going?" He wasn't even looking at her, but over her shoulder at the main stage.

"Well, I decided it really wasn't for me," she said to the side of his face. "So I was hoping to come back to work here."

"Days or nights?"

"Nights."

"I need girls tomorrow night. Can you start right away?"

"Yes. Anytime."

"Good. Come back at seven-thirty tomorrow. We'll work out the rest of your schedule later, I can't drag the book out right now, okay?"

"Sure," Alicia said. "Thanks, Randall."

"All right. See you tomorrow."

It was the day after the makeshift trial Jonah had conducted in his living room. Not twenty-four hours had passed and already she was reinstated in her old life. There was nothing to it—but why should that be a surprise? There had never been anything to it.

On her way back to the apartment, she got some clean cardboard cartons from the alley beside Woolworth's. Jonah would be working until six the next evening and it was as good a time as any to pack.

Maybe by the time he came home tomorrow, she could have all her possessions sealed into boxes. Would he be taken aback to see his home stripped of all that was hers? Her dresses and sweaters, papers and pens, bath oil, rose lotion, lipsticks and combs . . . the spices in their rack, the cutting board and rolling pin. Would he have to stop and swallow hard, even for a second?

By the time this was happening, she would be at the club. He'd walk in to find the cartons stacked against the wall. What if she didn't tell him where she was? Ten o'clock would arrive, then midnight, two A.M. and finally four. Would he worry? And would that fear and not knowing create any sense of loss? Might it make him realize he cared about her after all? It was a temptation.

Better yet, what if she could get even the boxes out of the apartment? Put them into storage or bring them to a friend's? That would truly be a trick, to vanish without a trace. These things happened, at least they happened in stories. Men arrived home to find their wives gone. But how did any real wife manage such a thing?

The theme of such stories seemed to be the power in disappearing, the leverage that came from withholding one's whereabouts. Runaways did it, calling home from phone booths across the country, rationing reassurance and stingy scraps of information. Always, the one who'd been left would snatch the phone up on the first ring, then stand clutching the receiver with both hands, frantic and begging. She tried to imagine Jonah in this position but it was impossible.

One of the boxes held her old go-go clothes, the skin-tight sheaths and feather boas and garters of every color. Her old persona was coming back, fashioned after some orphan in a Dickens plot: a girl about to hit the streets, not knowing where she would go. With nothing to hide and less to lose. Turning to that age-old barter: herself.

She did end up leaving a note.

Dear Jonah, I hope you had a good day and night at work. I decided to pack up my stuff since I'll be moving soon. I also thought it would be a good idea to get my old job back, so that's where I am tonight. I'll be home between 4:30 and 5:00 in the morning. Love, Alicia

So here she was, precarious in the stilettos that had once felt like part of her feet. Turning her beggar's smile upon every man in the room. Would she be able to pull this off again? Her body looked different in the mirror—too thin, breasts not as rounded or full, certainly not as firm and high. They no longer defied gravity. She herself no longer defied gravity. If she had managed to cheat some law of nature for a brief time, it had grounded her hard. Things had broken.

She went over to a man who looked clean and decent. He wore steel-rimmed glasses and his suit was pressed. A businessman, maybe a stockbroker.

"Hello," she said, widening her eyes, trying to appear as young and fresh and vulnerable as she could.

"Hey!" he greeted her. "How are you."

"May I join you?" It was a ventriloquist's skill and she'd almost lost it, this ability to speak through a smile. "What's your name?"

"I'm Bruce."

"Well, hi, Bruce. I'm Jezebel."

"What's your real name?"

This was a common question. Men wanted insider information. They seemed to believe that knowing a dancer's real name was evidence of their special status—proof that they were different from the usual losers in these places. And Alicia was ready.

"It's Rose," she said. "But please don't tell anyone."

"No problem, Rose. Your name is safe with me." He looked her up and down. "I haven't seen you here before. You new?"

"This is my first night," she told him, knowing it could only work in her favor. Few images were more compelling to the male imagination than a virgin on the auction block. Sure enough, Bruce brightened immediately.

"Is that so? Your first night?"

She nodded.

"Ever? Or just here?"

"Ever." She dropped her eyes as if reluctant to admit it. "But I've practiced at home. A lot."

"Is that so, Rose? Well—"

"Shh! Please, don't say my real name out loud." She put an entreat-

ing hand on his arm. "I don't want anyone else to know it. Call me
Jezebel for now, okay?"

"Okay, sorry, Jezebel. Anyway, you could probably use some practice here too, don't you think?"

"Does that mean I get to give you a private dance?"

A moment later, she was between his knees, her dress draped over a
nearby chair. This man was a good one to start with. He kept his hands
to himself, for one thing, and his smile was kind and faintly bemused.

In the dressing room, at the end of the night, she did a quick calcu-
lation. Landing her own place would require a broker's fee, a security
deposit, and the first month's rent. Three more nights here would do
the trick, and she would be able to move out by the end of the month.

At twenty minutes to five, Alicia let herself into Jonah's apartment
and waited for her eyes to adjust so she wouldn't need the overhead
light. If Jonah had managed to fall asleep, she didn't want to wake
him.

The first thing to do was take a shower. Showering transformed her
after a shift. She was still Jezebel when she went under the jet, with
smudged eyes and blackened nails and smoke in every pore. She could-
n't get into Jonah's bed like that.

The lights in the rest of the apartment were on when she emerged,
and Jonah was standing there in his undershirt and boxers.

"Hey," he said, after looking her up and down.

She gave him a tired smile, the first real one of the evening. "Hi,
honey. I hope I didn't wake you."

"Yeah, well. You know me. I wasn't sleepin' so good anyway." He
sounded subdued but lucid. "So. You went back to that racket."

"Yes."

"How was it?"

"Pretty much the same."

He was looking straight at her as he had the day before, but his eyes
no longer held any accusation. "Huh," he said after a moment. "Well, I
guess I ain't got the right to say nothing about it no more."

Say something anyway, she pleaded silently. But he only nodded at the wad of bills on the table, bound together by her garter. "You make a lot of money?"

"I haven't counted it yet. But I think so."

"Well. That's good, I guess." He passed a hand over his face, then glanced at the cartons lined against the wall. "You had a busy day, I see."

"I hope the boxes aren't in your way."

"You found a place yet?"

"Not yet."

"You didn't have to do all that before you had somewhere to go, you know," he told her.

"I thought maybe it would make me find a place sooner," she said truthfully.

He shrugged, turning away. "It's a wonder you had any energy left for your club," was all he said. Then: "You comin' to bed?"

It was a question she hadn't heard in months. "In about fifteen minutes. I just want to let my hair dry."

"All right then." He went into the bedroom.

Alicia sat down at the table and loosed the bills from the band of lace. It was a satisfying bulk. The sky outside the window was just lightening as she started to count it.

She wasn't mistaken about making a lot of money. The total came to just under seven hundred dollars. She folded it back up and put it in the pocket of her coat.

When she got into bed, Jonah was sleeping soundly.

<hr>

"Are you sure about this?" Matilda asked for the second or third time. "I mean really. The two of you took vows for a lifetime. Couldn't you just tough it out a few more months?"

It had been just over a week since Alicia and Jonah had come to dinner. That evening, after the two of them went home, Matilda sat alone in her kitchen with a strange sensation she couldn't name. It was similar to a feeling she experienced once or twice a year, at the end of a Broadway show, when the actors turned back into themselves. That abrupt metamorphosis had never failed to astonish her.

In her years of being a mother and foster care caseworker, she had watched many children become something else in a class play. Shy, reserved youngsters could turn raucous or amazingly comic, while the cutups—when entrusted with a serious role—could take on a grave and somber intensity you would never have thought possible. These were the ordinary miracles, the ones she was used to. It was something different altogether to come into the city for a professional performance and witness the reverse: to see Hamlet or Henry VIII or Don Quixote—a man of power and grandeur, ablaze in the hot spotlight—become an ordinary person about to go out the back door and dissolve into the dreary crowd.

They felt it, themselves. The actors. She was sure of it. Wasn't there always something ironic about their expressions during a curtain call? Beneath the triumph, beneath the pleasure, there was something else, something almost apologetic. As if they felt a little sheepish, in the end, about having fooled you.

It was like that with Jonah and Alicia now. They were different than they had been before. Jonah had lost his shining armor. Alicia was no longer a femme fatale off the set of *Dynasty*. And they weren't the only ones who had been transformed. The jealousy, the resentment, the hot acid splash around her own heart: all of it was gone, changed by some blessed alchemy into tenderness, sorrow, concern.

It was clear to her that Alicia needed a friend at this time and so today the girl was back in her kitchen. She'd taken the Waterway ferry from Manhattan and Matilda had picked her up at the dock.

Jonah was working this afternoon. They weren't concealing this little visit from him, exactly. But since there seemed to be no real reason to tell him about it either, it felt vaguely like a secret tryst. Matilda had woken with this sensation, and an hour later found herself dressing with care: a favorite pale yellow sundress—she was the only one she knew who could wear this shade—and the Indian-beaded drop-earrings she generally saved for special occasions.

"You can always walk away," she heard herself telling Alicia now. "Ending the marriage will always be an option. Saving it might not be." It was hard to believe it was she who was saying these words. If, just two weeks ago, someone had told her she would be coaxing Alicia to remain with Jonah, she would have laughed herself hoarse.

How had everything turned around? Somehow having the two of

them to the house had resulted in some essential revelations. One was that youth and beauty weren't enough to hold a man after all. Nor were the highest of hopes. At least, they weren't enough to hold Jonah, not for more than a little while. Jonah needed certain conditions to be anyone's hero. Without them he was a ghost.

And then along with this realization, it was as if the finality of Seamus's death were something she was understanding for the first time.

All the kids were going to their Aunt Catherine's in the country that Friday and staying for a week, so Matilda hung onto herself all the next endless day and night. But once they were on the train and she had the house to herself, she did all the things you heard about widows doing, things she hadn't done until now.

For the next three days, she didn't leave the house. In fact, she barely got out of bed. She wore her nightgown around the clock and didn't even bother to shower or brush her teeth. Instead she spent her waking hours on activities that could only be described as maudlin. Like hauling out every family photo album and looking at every single picture. Here they were, she and Seamus, before any of the kids had been born, wrapped in a blanket at a football game, sharing a flask of bourbon and a box of Crackerjack. Here they were with Heather and the twins at Rockaway Beach; at a Bear Mountain campsite; at a barbecue in their own backyard. (They'd had a fight that day—look at Seamus's hangdog expression and her own tight smile for the camera.) Here were the kids' confirmation ceremonies, their graduations, their Christmas morning frenzy and their Easter finery. Here they were with the Little League at Pizza Hut, and here at a fire department picnic.

After every album had been paged through and wept over, she started on the home movies. The early black-and-white ones first, then the later ones in color. She reread every card that Seamus had ever written her. And she kept up a near-steady stream of tears the whole time— a crying jag as cleansing as it was overdue.

On the fourth day, she got dressed and called what she'd always thought of as Jonah's apartment with the sole purpose of inviting Alicia back to the house. For the first time in months, dialing that number held no fear.

"Matilda," the girl was saying now—that was another thing, Matilda had been begging her to drop the "Mrs. O'Day" business—"if I thought it would do any good, believe me, nothing could tear me away. But I can't reach him, and I think that my being there is only making him crazier."

"Would you ever consider talking to Wes about it? Wes knows him better than anyone. In fact, in some way he seemed to see this whole thing coming."

"Wes hates me," Alicia said. And even though Wes was surely the least of the girl's problems, the sudden pain in her young face was almost more than Matilda could bear.

"No, no, he doesn't hate you," Matilda said in a rush, "please, you musn't think that. He's a little jealous, like I was, that's all."

The girl managed a smile. "Well, that's nice of you to say. But anyway, Jonah's the one who needs to talk to somebody, and he won't." She paused. "Even so, I would stay if I thought he wanted me to. But the fact is that he wants me to leave."

Matilda was quiet a moment. Could Alicia be right about this? Could Jonah be withdrawing from everyone, not because he was angry but because he needed to wage this struggle alone? She thought of all the times Wes had stepped back, given Jonah the space he needed, and waited for his return. Maybe the secret to Wes's longevity was that he'd never made the mistake of thinking Jonah was someone he could possess. And maybe it was Alicia's own wisdom that was bringing her to the same conclusion. The girl was young but as it turned out she was no one's fool. And in her own way, she was a tough little thing herself.

"If that's the case," Matilda said after a moment, "do you have anywhere to go?"

"Well," the girl answered, "not right this minute. But I got my job back earlier this week, and that'll make it easy to get another place."

"The . . . dancing job?" Matilda asked carefully.

"Yes. I could start apartment hunting by Friday if I worked every night till then."

"Friday? That's less than a week away."

"I know. But three or four nights should do the trick."

"Does it really bring in that much money?" Matilda couldn't help marveling at the idea.

"Yes."

And now the question Matilda was burning to ask seemed to escape of its own accord. "What's it like?"

"The dancing? There was a time when it was a lot of fun. When it actually seemed too good to be true—the idea that you could be admired for a living and make all that money. For a while, I thought it was the best setup in the world."

"And now?"

"Well—let's just say that over time you start to understand the drawbacks."

These girls, Matilda thought, and the choices they had today. She thought back to when she and Seamus were about to be married. The boys on the block had dragged him away for his last hurrah on the town. Good-natured guys in their circle of friends, neighborhood guys she'd known for years—suddenly, ever so subtly, they had become the enemy. She knew this idea was a little histrionic, but she couldn't help feeling that way. They were trying to show him all he'd be missing by marrying her. They were parading temptation before him. Of course, she never said a word about it. What went on during these bachelor parties, nice girls were not supposed to even wonder about.

Young brides-to-be didn't have "bachelorette" parties, as many of them did nowadays. There wasn't even such a thing as the Chippendales, back then. They did have bridal showers, where you received things like nightgowns, linens, kitchenware. Matilda had gotten, among other gifts, a very pretty silk chemise, a pair of pewter candlesticks, and a set of hammered copper pots and pans. The girls would help you decide on something old, something new, something borrowed, and something blue for the wedding. And the ones already married would dispense all kinds of wifely advice.

Oh, the innocence of that time! They'd actually imagined they possessed some womanly wisdom already.

"What *are* the drawbacks?" she asked, and felt herself coloring slightly. Well, but why try to hide it? She wanted details.

The girl appeared to give the question some thought. "A lot about the job starts to bother you," she answered after a while. "To most of the men in a strip joint, you're less a human being than a prize animal. And the management sees it that way too. No matter how hard you work or how reliable you are, you don't mean anything to them. There's always more girls where you came from, and they don't ever let you forget it. You're interchangeable with any other pretty face—interchangeable and dispensable. And then too, most people think being a stripper's the same as being a slut." It was all Matilda could do not to look away, hearing this.

"But for me, none of that's the worst part," the girl went on. "To me, the worst part of the job is all the people who tell you they love you every night."

"What's so bad about that?" Matilda asked.

"The fact that none of them ever mean it."

Not long after dropping Alicia off at the boat, Matilda had a sudden memory of Seamus, involving an incident she probably hadn't thought about since it happened. About a year ago, Matilda had taken Caitlin to a Saturday matinee for her fifth birthday, at the local theater where *Bambi* was playing. It was a choice she was to regret. Seamus was picking them up afterward—he'd managed to get off the day tour by four o'clock—and by the time they met him in the parking lot, the birthday girl was crying inconsolably.

"Oh no," her husband said, upon seeing his daughter's tear-stained face. "What's this?"

"Bambi's mother," Matilda explained in a murmur. "She dies at the end. I don't know why I didn't think about that."

Her husband's reaction surprised her then, and it surprised her to this day. Most of the time he was helpless in the face of female emotion, clumsy in his attempts to console. She thought she knew what he was about to say to Caitlin: "Aw, sweetie pie. C'mon. Don't be sad. It's just a story."

Instead he lifted the child and cradled her against his chest, right there in the middle of the parking lot, not caring who saw or heard. He rocked her and crooned into her hair. "Oh baby," he said. "I know. It's terrible, isn't it? Oh, I know, I know."

It was so out of character for him that Matilda had to wonder, later, what it was all about. Had Seamus had some kind of premonition? Some shadowy sense of his own imminent death?

She would never know. But his answer to the little girl's grief moved her so much that—though it was no easy feat—she got all the kids to bed almost an hour early that night, the sooner to be alone with him.

And *that* was what she wanted now, she realized. Spare her the Memorial Day speeches about death in the line of duty. Spare her the presentation of her husband's posthumous award, the blue-ribboned Medal of Supreme Sacrifice. Forget the newspaper eulogies and the well-meaning letters from strangers, forget the grief-management counselor and his earnest analysis. She wanted Seamus and no one else to rock her in his arms. That was the only consolation that could give her any ease. *Oh baby,* she wanted to hear him say. *I know. It's terrible, isn't it? Oh, I know, I know.*

What did it all come down to, she wondered, once the boat had pulled away, taking Alicia home again to her troubles and her choices, leaving Matilda to her memories. All the pictures in those albums, the breakfasts and the barbecues, the fire department occasions and family occasions, the arguments and the contentment? The lemonade stands, the tree house in the yard, the grass stains and scraped shins and fireflies trapped in jars?

Girls today—they could take all that, now or later, or they could leave it. They made their own money and didn't need a man for financial security. They could have sex with anyone they wanted, anytime they wanted it, without shame or a bad reputation or the terror of getting knocked up.

They could have careers, they could travel, they could conquer the world, they could dance naked.

But after two decades of marriage and widowhood at forty, what did Matilda have that a girl like Alicia could envy?

She could think of only one thing, but Alicia herself had made her see how much it meant.

She'd had a partner in her life for more than twenty years, someone she knew as well as she knew her own reflection. She'd had a husband who may have wavered, but always stayed. A man who'd told her he loved her, night after night, for more than seven thousand nights. A man who'd meant it every time.

"Jezebel, you all right, chica?"

It was Alicia's fourth night back at work, and she was in the locker room putting on fresh lipstick. Vixen, the dancer sharing the mirror with her, was applying false eyelashes and addressing her reflection.

"Me?" Alicia was startled. "I'm fine, why?"

"I remember last year you was the happiest girl in this place. Ever since you came back it's like, you been looking all sad."

"You think I look sad?"

"Like you ready to cry."

This wasn't good news. Happiness was a dancer's best asset. That was why, if you made a lot of money in the first hour of your shift, you were guaranteed a killing by the end of the night. A good mood went further than a D-cup's worth of cleavage.

"She's right, Jezebel," Brandy put in from the corner. "So what is it? Money trouble or man trouble?"

"It's a man." *But I don't think I can stand to have this conversation.*

"Didn't you get married last year? Jade and Keiko said they went to your wedding."

"I am married. But we're having some problems."

"I used to be married," Brandy said. "Before I knew the secret to dealing with men."

Alicia turned away from the mirror. "What secret?"

"You got to use 'em for what they're good for, and forget the rest," Brandy told her. "And you got to remember they're good for only two things." A dramatic pause.

"Well?"

"Laying . . . " she said, "and paying. That's all. Laying and paying."

Laughter broke over the room.

"Ain't *that* the motherfuckin' truth."

"A*men,* sister . . . "

Randall came into the dressing room. "All right, girls," he said. "There's too many of you in here. I want you circulating in the crowd."

He went out again.

"But then some men," Brandy concluded, slamming her locker shut, "some men ain't no good for nothing at all."

When Alicia stepped back onto the main floor, the music and strobe lights were like an assault and she was slow to adjust to the fact that the place was packed. Suits had taken over every table, and they were lined three deep at the bar. A lot of money could be made in the next few hours, if she could just get into character.

A man on one of the leather sofas reached out and touched her arm. "You. Are you available for a private dance?"

She made herself turn to him with her widest smile. "Yes I am. And I'd be delighted. My name is Jezebel. And you are?"

"John," he said. "Pleased to meet you."

"John, the pleasure's all mine."

A song was just ending, and across the room she saw the deejay wink at her. A moment later, the voice of Sade flooded the room.

"*Jezebel wasn't born with a silver spoon . . .*"

"Hey," John said. "He must be playing that for you."

"He is." She began a slow sway, stripping off her dress.

"I guess he must like you."

"He should. I tip him double what he gets from most of the other girls."

She shouldn't have told him that. It was bad form to remind a man that this was a business, especially in the middle of his private dance. To make up for it, she leaned in close to croon the song into his ear: "*She put on her stockings and shoes . . . had nothing to lose . . . she said it was worth it . . .*"

What time was it? It had to be at least midnight. Four more hours to go.

"Are you waiting for someone?" he asked. "Your boyfriend showing up here or something?"

"What?"

"You keep looking at the front entrance," he said.

"*What?* I do not."

"Okay—no offense. Maybe I have it wrong," he said. "Sometimes I get a feeling about people."

"And you feel like I'm looking at the front entrance."

"You're watching the door."

"If I was, I didn't mean to. I didn't realize." This wasn't good either. A dancer had to make a man think she had nothing on her mind but him. "You were doing it on stage, too," he said.

"Oh for Christ's sake. What is this?" All hope of doing the right thing by this one was out the window. The thing to do was move on as soon as possible. "When did you see me on stage, anyway?"

"Earlier in the evening. I was watching you. Look, I'm just trying to be helpful. You could probably make more money if you looked at the audience."

She didn't answer, but concentrated on the music instead. No one had to tell her how to do this job. She was a hands-down house favorite, always had been and would be again.

"Jezebel . . . Jezebel . . . the sun is gonna shine . . . every winter was a war, she said . . . I want to get what's mine."

The deejay cut into the end of the song to call the next set of dancers to the stage. "Darling Nikki . . . and sweet Caroline. Stand by for the main stage. Repeat: Nikki and Caroline, stand by for the main. Jezebel, stand by for the bar cage."

Not a moment too soon. "That's me!" she told John. She reached for her dress and pulled it back on. "I'm sorry to run off, but I have to go on stage."

He slid a twenty dollar bill into her garter. "That's okay, Jezebel. Take care. And remember: eye contact."

"Okay, thanks." Fuck him. More importantly, forget him. She couldn't afford to let someone piss her off right before her stage set. She crossed the room to the dancer's cage and eased herself between the bars. From here she had an even better view of the door. A group of men were coming in but . . . none of them . . . had a fire department jacket . . . or a dark blue T-shirt with a white Maltese cross.

That guy had been on to her. And he was right. She hadn't even been fully aware of it before, but she was waiting for Jonah to come in here. The old Jonah, the sane one, brought back from wherever he'd gone. She hadn't seen him in—what was his expression?—in a dog's age. And it felt like it had been years. Dog years.

What would Jonah—the Jonah she fell in love with—do if he did show up here? If she closed her eyes she could almost see it. He would come in looking like no one else in the place, with his graying crew cut and set mouth and the eyes that made people get out of his way.

He would walk past the cashier without paying the cover and even the bouncers would look the other way because no one wanted to fuck with Jonah when he was on a mission, it just wasn't a good idea. He'd spot her and start shouldering his way through the crowd, and no matter how packed the room might be, a path would appear for him—the way people managed to make space on a subway car, even during rush hour, if a maniac was coming through.

And suddenly she could hear him in her head. It was his voice in all its hoarse authority, low and plainspoken and resolute, and she heard it apart from the blaring music as she'd heard it once before beneath the roar of the fire.

Come on, honey, he said. *Let's go. I've got you. We're gettin' out of here.*

At the back of the dressing room was a window opening onto a fire escape. Alicia changed into her street clothes, then opened the window as far as it would go. Her bag of go-go clothes was still in her locker. Some other girl could have them.

She knew that escaping this way was melodramatic and unnecessary. She could walk right out the front door and no one could stop her. But she pulled herself through the window anyway and went down the metal stairs. From the bottom it was only a short drop to the pavement.

The last of her tainted pay was in her jeans. It was just past midnight, only halfway through her shift, so she couldn't have made more than three hundred dollars. It didn't matter anymore; she had what she needed.

If Jonah had given her nothing else that lasted, he had still made it impossible for her to dance at The Catwalk. She had thought he'd taken back everything he'd given her, but it turned out that something was left after all. What he couldn't take back, what no one could ever take away, was the distance his love had brought her. Too many steps to retrace, in the end; too much ground to lose.

If she had to—and it did look like she had to—she could go forward into the cold unknown, but it was no longer in her to go back. Not even if she was broke or brokenhearted or homeless. She couldn't strip for ordinary men after baring herself to Jonah. She couldn't go from *him* to them; not from love to that.

The apartment was dark when Alicia let herself in. She crossed quietly to the bedroom door and eased it open. Jonah was stretched on the bed, sleeping his recent peaceful sleep. His breathing was deep and regular.

She stood listening for long minutes before going to the shower, and when the last traces of the night's work were washed away, she wrapped herself in Jonah's worn blue bathrobe. She dried her hair as much as she could and then went back to the bedroom, not bothering to count her money. Jonah stirred as she lay down beside him. He turned to her and opened his eyes.

"Hey there, honey," he said, sounding sleepy. "Ain't it early for you to be here?"

"I quit," she told him, in just above a whisper. She felt peaceful and drowsy herself.

"Quit?"

"Yeah."

"Did somethin' happen?"

"Yeah, something did." She considered telling him about hearing his voice and escaping through the window. But after a moment she heard herself say only, "I realized I couldn't be there anymore, after all."

"Oh," he said. "Well, that's good."

"You think so?"

"Sure I do."

"But it means I might have to borrow some money. Just to set myself up somewhere else. I can pay you back later."

"You know I'll help you," he said. "I got no problem helping you. Did you think I wouldn't?"

"No," she said. "I just . . . I don't know. I thought I should get used to taking care of myself again."

There was an awkward pause.

"Look, honey," he said finally. "It ain't got to be all or nothing. I'm sad things ain't gonna work out with us, but it's got nothin' to do with you, not really. You're a good girl, all right? And I don't mind helping you out."

"That's nice of you, Jonah. I appreciate that."

He pulled her close and for a minute his lips rested against her forehead. "I'm glad you're out of there. I didn't think it was my place to say, anymore. But I didn't like the idea of you back at that job. Not at all."

Alicia felt her throat tighten and waited a moment to speak.

"Thank you, Jonah," she finally said. "I'm glad you care about me that way."

He brought her head down onto his chest and she closed her eyes. Her ear found its old resting place next to his heart. He laid his hand against her hair and she felt him stroking it as they drifted off. It wasn't like before and wouldn't be again, but it was something.

Epilogue

Alicia was in the checkout line at the grocery store when she saw the *Daily News* with Jonah on the cover. He wore a helmet and turn-out coat and held the prone body of a child in his arms. HERO FIREMAN SAVES BOY FROM DEADLY BROOKLYN BLAZE, read the headline. Forgetting her groceries, leaving her cart where it was, she paid for the paper without looking up, and walked out to the street.

An article on page six offered a detailed account:

An eight-year-old boy escaped certain death from the flashover that engulfed his Red Hook tenement yesterday, authorities said. The five-alarm fire at 14 Union Street broke out on the fourth floor of a six-story apartment building at about 10:20 A.M. Captain Jonah Malone, 44, of Rescue 2 was credited with the dramatic rescue of Brendan Bennett, who is listed in stable condition today at Downstate Medical Center.

A flashover. Oh dear God. From the year spent with Jonah, she knew what a flashover was. When the air in a burning room reached a certain temperature, everything in it would burst into flames at the same time. It was one of the most dangerous conditions a fireman could encounter.

The captain battled his way through the smoke-filled hallway on the fourth floor after getting a report that a child was trapped in apartment 4W. Direct entry to the burning apartment proved impossible, as the front door was already consumed by raging flames. Captain Malone forced the adjoining apartment door and crawled to the front of the railroad flat, where he began breaching the partition wall into the burning apartment.

"I was surprised when it turned out to be a brick-and-gypsum wall," Malone told the *Daily News* afterward in an exclusive interview. "Most partition walls are either made of Sheetrock or plaster and lathe." The unexpected resistance made the breach much costlier in time and effort than the captain had initially expected. "I had to give it about twenty whacks with my ax," he said. "For a minute there, I wasn't sure if I was going to have enough time."

Already Alicia was shaking, and she wasn't halfway through the article.

Once he had broken through the wall, Malone—who is believed by many of his peers to possess a "sixth sense" of where victims are to be found in a fire—located the unconscious Bennett in a matter of seconds. The boy was curled in a fetal position on the floor of the hall closet. No sooner had the captain dragged him back through the wall to the adjoining flat than the burning apartment succumbed to a flashover.

Alicia reached the door of her building and folded the paper. Once she was upstairs, she would finish reading the story. She'd been in her new place on the Lower East Side of Manhattan for about ten months now: a fifth-floor walk-up with access to the roof.

Her apartment was a single room that had once been part of a sweatshop. It had a row of windows overlooking the street and a wood-burning stove. Now that it was winter, she liked to warm her feet on this stove while she read manuscripts for *Glimmer Train,* the literary magazine where she was an assistant editor. This job paid less a week, after taxes, than she used to make in a single night at The Catwalk. Still, she was grateful to be able to read stories and poems for a living.

Besides the stove, there was a cherry-red futon, a round rag rug, and the wooden rocking chair she had found in a neighborhood thrift store. There were curtains she had made from rose-colored calico—the material carefully chosen from a fabric shop and sewn under the direction of Matilda's oldest daughter, Heather. There was the black-and-white cat, Domino, that she'd taken from the alley around the corner, and the little basket he slept in. All in all, it was about as cozy as a place for one person could be.

She pulled the rocking chair over to one of the windows and curled into it before resuming the article about Jonah.

"I don't know how he did it," said Deputy Assistant Fire Chief Silvio Cassavo. "Breaking through a wall like that, with the time bomb of a flashover waiting to explode . . . it was a superhuman effort."

Malone, who was hospitalized for exhaustion immediately following the morning's heroics, left Brooklyn Hospital this afternoon through the back parking lot, avoiding the reporters gathered outside the main entrance.

"He's a shy guy," said fellow firefighter Charles Cavanaugh, a lieutenant in Rescue 2. "He doesn't like anyone making a fuss over him."

Just how many seconds had there been to spare? And how violent had the flashover been?

In the year since they'd been separated, this was the third time she'd read an account like this, and the effect was always the same. Her emotions followed a trajectory that she could recognize by now. Fear always came first: an irrational panic after the fact, worry over yesterday's outcome. This terror for his life had been one of the thousand things about her—and love itself—that Jonah could not afford.

Almost certainly it was better this way, even where she was concerned. Fretting at the safe distance of a secondhand account in the next day's news. The happy ending already in print, nothing left to wonder about.

Then once fear had passed, a predictable desire would set in. This time was no different. Her trembling had barely subsided when she was suddenly racked with longing for Jonah, overwhelmed by the loss of him. Never mind the knowledge that life with him would not have been easy. Never mind the idea, even, that he was crazy. She wanted to be back at his side and beneath his roof, holding his face in her hands, listening to him breathe.

Not even writing about him could compensate for not being able to do that anymore. What consolation was there, then?

Night was coming on. Darkness fell early now. The moon was already in the dark blue sky, framed by the windowpane, just more than half full. Domino jumped up on her chair and she stroked the soft black fur on his back. After a while she would have to go back down to the street, retrieve the forgotten groceries, start thinking about dinner.

But before that, she would sit here just a little longer. Dwell on the idea of consolation, talk herself back from the edge of grief.

Jonah, she would remind herself, was someone she'd gotten on loan. Though she'd been looking for him for years, she had never really thought she would see him again. But fate had allowed her to find him. Fate had allowed her to be with him. If their time together had not been long, she still wouldn't trade it for anything in the world. So here it was then: what she had to remember. The consolation for having lost him was having had him.

All was well then for a little while. Stars appeared against the darkening sky. And as always, with this measure of serenity came the pictures.

She had to get to this place before they would come. But when this dreamy interlude of peace had set in, it was as if she could access her own sixth sense, an ability to see Jonah in action. This vision was like a fabled Gypsy gift, except it was the past she could see into instead of the future. She could see Jonah in the midst of the flames, and she could feel his emotions too.

At least she thought she could. Maybe it wasn't any sixth sense after all. Maybe it was a variation on memory, the memory of having really seen him in a fire when he'd come into her burning room to get her out. That image of him was seared into her mind forever; maybe she was just pulling up the old film and letting it play.

Or the whole thing could just be a wishful conceit. Perhaps her privileged vision came down to no more than a mix of newspaper facts and empathy. It was just that the pictures were so vivid, the exultation like a kind of grace.

There he was, on his knees, a two-fisted grip on his ax. Facing a wall made of harder stuff than he'd ever dreamed. Coming up against its resistance again and again, the shock of all those blows singing along the length of his arm. Nothing in his mind but the young life in the balance—the balance between that wall and his will to come through it.

Knowing that his own solace would be distilled to him from no other source but this. The consolation for all he'd left by the wayside would be in that first split second of breaking through. The gypsum crumbling, the bricks falling away. The flash of firelight through the opening, the flash and the rush, as the blade of his ax met the air.

Grateful acknowledgments are made to the following:

To my mother, father, and brother for their unconditional love and belief in me;

To Grandma Ruth, and the rest of my extended family, for liking this one;

To all the friends who have read my manuscript in its endless stages, and provided the responses that kept me going, especially Charles Ardai, Velma Bowen, Junot Diaz, Kim Epstein, Carolyn Farhie, Sandra Felt, Francesca Fragasso, Claudia Grazioso, Thomas Griesel, Joe Hurka, Sebastian Junger, Ben Lawsky, Julie Lynch, David Rody, Josie Schmidt, Claire Tisne, Terri Thomas, and Yoram Yovell. Most of all, special gratitude to Jennifer Alessi, who has been my writing check-in partner on a weekly basis for more than five years and who knows these pages almost as well as I do. Thank you, Jen;

To Pat Conroy, for sustenance at a very crucial point;

To the hundreds of firefighters who shared their stories, perspective, and wisdom with me; had me to their firehouses for dinner and took me along on jobs;

To Fireman Dave, who never wavered with his blessing;

To Amye Dyer at Lukeman Literary;

To Beau Friedlander, for letting the Context jar be big enough for the two scorpions we are, with sincere adoration. Thanks also to the other members of the Context family: Nick Einenkel, Lisa Chase, and sweet Mama Mel;

To Mike Heller, Steve Spak, Robert Mitts, Tsegaya Persons, Charles Kreloff, Tyler Huff, Jennifer McCabe, and Rudj Escobar for their generosity and effort on the graphic design front;

Very special thanks to Jeff Kleeman, for his invaluable insight, affirmation, and devotion to this book;

And finally, my most serious gratitude to Chief Mike for support on every conceivable front: material, moral, and emotional; for being my hero and my cherished friend.